# Hunter's
# Dance

By the same author
*Past Imperfect*

# Hunter's Dance

A Mystery by

Kathleen Hills

Poisoned Pen Press

*Hil*

Copyright © 2004 by Kathleen Hills

First Edition 2004

10 9 8 7 6 5 4 3 2 1

Library of Congress Catalog Card Number: 2003111698

ISBN: 1-59058-094-X

Poisoned Pen Press
6962 E. First Ave., Ste. 103
Scottsdale, AZ 85251
www.poisonedpenpress.com
info@poisonedpenpress.com

Printed in the United States of America

*for Chelsea Rae*

Chapter headings from *The Story of Gösta Berling*, by Selma Lagerlöf. Published in Sweden, 1894. English translation by Pauline Bancroft Flach, 1898.

*One can believe it or not, as it always is with hunting stories.*
—Selma Lagerlöf, 1894

# I

*Trust not the dance; many a foot slides lightly
across the polished floor while the heart is
heavy as lead.*

Constable John McIntire squinted through the brew of cigarette smoke and the dust brought forth by a couple of hundred
stamping feet to consult the clock above the door. Eleven-oh-
five. Past the halfway point at least. He yawned and lounged
back into the wall. Wall leaning was his job, after all, and,
being of lanky build, he flattered himself that he did it well. He
slid down another vertebra length. If he let his eyelids droop
a little, the murky tableau before him blurred even more.
Bodies swayed and gyrated, looming large as they came near,
diminishing as they were whisked away to obscurity in the pale
glowing haze. It gave the scene a surreal Dante's *Inferno* sort of
quality. But these whirling specters were accompanied by no
Paganini with a violin. They romped to the strictly metered
rhythms of Frankie King and his Polka Princes.

The music slowed and the dancers with it, strolling
sedately with measured tread, to erupt a half minute later
in another frenzy of flying skirts and stomping boots. The
Butterfly, a dry-land version of Crack the Whip set to music,
where entertainment value is measured in bruised toes and
dislocated shoulders. McIntire aimed what he hoped was a

encouraging smile in his wife's direction as she skipped past, clinging for life to the arm of the surprisingly nimble Doctor Mark Guibard. He fingered the empty glass in his hand and mused on what a bottle of Seagram's and an accordion could do for a bunch of phlegmatic Scandinavians and Finns. It was inconceivable that these whooping masters of Terpsichore were the same men who, if you met one of them in town tomorrow, would gaze intently toward the horizon, scratch, grunt out a few monosyllables about the weather and how it might affect the killing of deer or the felling of trees, and be on his stolid way.

*Terpsichore.* McIntire rolled the word around in his head and wished that he had the guts to speak it aloud.

Well, come to that, the cavortings of his lumberjack neighbors were no more remarkable than his own part in the festivities. If, a year ago, some seer had told him that tonight he'd be leaning against this wall with a badge on his chest keeping watch over the herd, it would likely have given him a mild chuckle. Had he gotten even the slightest glimmer that such a circumstance truly awaited him, he might have taken the easy way out with a leap off the Houghton bridge.

Frankie and the Princes bent their backs to a final downbeat and the thunder faded to a rumble. Dancers held their ground and fanned their faces, shifting from foot to foot in anticipation of the next round. Out of the corner of his eye McIntire spotted Arnie Johnson headed in his direction, threading his way through the crowd like a trout swimming upstream. It was evidence of his desperation that he felt no urge to flee at Johnson's approach. Even The World According to Arnie would be a welcome distraction tonight.

"Bump?" Johnson extended a hefty brown bottle, his hand strategically placed over the label. McIntire held out his glass to accept a measure of Arnie's generosity.

"Where in hell did all these people come from?" he asked.

"Ya, nice turnout." Johnson's sparsely thatched head bobbed in an emphatic nod. "Well, the weather's been so good, and we got all them uranium hunters hanging around. Out looking for a little excitement, don't you know?"

The band cranked to life again, a polka this time, only slightly less boisterous than the previous selection. The din in the hall was sufficient to defeat a lesser storyteller, but Arnie valiantly sucked in his breath and shouted out, "I remember back in, oh...I guess it musta been better'n ten years ago now, thirty-eight or thirty-nine, before the war, anyway, same kinda thing, good weather, big turnout. People came from over in Ishpeming, Houghton, even a bunch down from Marquette. Fishermen, miners, loggers on one last toot before heading out for the woods." He stretched up on his toes to give McIntire's shoulder a conspiratorial punch. "Maybe even a *hunter*, eh?"

Johnson was particularly animated in the telling of this tale. McIntire held his breath for the climax. A move prompted less by suspense than by his proximity to Arnie's firewater-laden exhalations.

"Well, like I say, same thing like this, that day started out piss-warm. Hell, it was like the middle of *Joo*-lie! But before the night was out, by golly if we didn't have three feet of snow! It was four days before the plows got through, and half that crew ended up stuck right here." He wrapped his lips around the neck of his bottle, flung back his head, swallowed, and smacked his tongue against the roof of his mouth. McIntire hastily lowered his glass.

"Sounds interesting."

"You bet." Johnson jerked back as a shoe from an energetic Cinderella flew past his chest and hit the wall. "And I tell you this for goldarn sure, you lock up a gang of miners and loggers for three-four days without much to eat, but plenty to drink by God, *and* plenty scared girls, and...well, let's just say the lawyers and parsons were kept busy *that* winter." Arnie paused for McIntire's dutifully appreciative chuckle and tipped up his bottle again, tilting back his head and swallowing like some kind of barnyard fowl. "Now there was a Deer Hunters' Dance to remember." He embarked on another vigorous round of head-bobbing, basking in the recollection, before asking, "Anybody giving you trouble tonight?"

"Not so far."

Johnson shrugged away his disappointment. "Ah well, the night's young yet. People're just starting to get oiled up."

His assessment of the situation was reinforced by a shrill scream that sliced through the cacophony and halted musicians and dancers alike in mid-polka. Within seconds the thuds, grunts, and curses issuing in through the open windows sent them all into action once more. McIntire barely made it out the door ahead of the stampede. He rounded the dark side of the hall and strode toward a cluster of pale-faced adolescents who fell silent and backed away like a flock of startled sheep at his approach. At the center of their circle a stick-thin youngster with lank black hair obscuring the upper half of his face, and blood pretty much covering the lower, struggled to rise from the frost-slicked grass.

McIntire stepped forward and seized the upraised arm of a sturdy youth lunging in for another blow. After a single brief attempt to free himself, the young man stood still. The injured boy slipped to the ground again, grabbing at his ankle with fumbling movements. McIntire grasped his bony shoulder and yanked him to his feet. He shuddered and swayed but remained erect. Blood spurted from his nose, and McIntire released his hold long enough to pull a handkerchief from his pocket and thrust it toward him. The boy glared and wiped his sleeve across his face. His gasp told McIntire that the nose was probably broken.

Damn. Now what? McIntire's first impulse was to give each of the combatants a healthy swat on the rear, send them packing, and get back to his wall leaning. He had absolutely no wish to know the details of this altercation. But, from what he'd seen, it was more than the usual hormone-driven shoving match. Not to mention that he had the entire community and then some standing at his back, probably even now taking bets on what action, or inaction, their constable would take. He tightened his grip on each antagonist's arm and leaned toward a group of shivering, wide-eyed girls. "Shoo!" They jumped and drew closer together, but held firmly to their ringside position. A muffled giggle came from somewhere in the dimness.

McIntire gave up and dragged the two into the cloakroom. He swept a collection of scarves and mittens off a wooden bench and shoved them down next to each other. They immediately moved to opposite ends of the seat, folded their arms, and sat staring straight ahead.

McIntire took a deep breath. "Okay, what's this all about?" His question was received with the silence he'd expected.

"You been drinking?" If they hadn't been they were likely the only non-imbibers over the age of twelve on the premises.

"You don't have to be drunk to show a goddamn redskin his place." The apparent assailant growled his response. He then abruptly swapped his belligerent pose for a more nonchalant attitude, stretching his stubby legs in front of him and speaking with a smirking confidence. "But if, in doing so, I've created a disturbance, I sincerely apologize. If there's been damage done, I'm sure my family will take care of it. It needn't concern you."

Would that it needn't. McIntire took his time dragging a chair from the corner and seated himself to face his prisoner. The boy reached to remove a pack of cigarettes from his shirt pocket but halted at McIntire's glare.

"What's your name, son?"

He sat up straighter and locked his eyes on McIntire's. In the light from the ceiling bulb he appeared older than McIntire had first guessed, eighteen or nineteen, maybe. He was stocky and muscular, with a glint of humor in his light brown eyes that almost served to soften the pretentious sneer. "Bambi

Morlen," he replied. "How unfortunate that we had to meet under these circumstances."

Bambi? Good lord, no wonder the kid had learned how to throw a right jab like that.

Bambi wiped his hand on his muddied shirt and extended it to McIntire. "And you are?"

McIntire ignored both the hand and the question. "Are your parents here?"

The response was an appropriately deerlike snort. Bambi abandoned his David Niven persona. "Are you nuts? My old man wouldn't be caught dead in a hick place like this."

"Do you live around here?"

His nose wrinkled as if McIntire had suggested that he occupied a basement apartment in the privy. "I *live* in Connecticut. My family summers here in Michigan, at the Club."

McIntire had no doubt as to the residence in question. "Club" meant only one thing in St. Adele, but he was perverse enough to ask, "And just what club would that be?"

Bambi smiled, showing dimples and perfect white teeth. "Oh, I'm sorry. How thoughtless of me. I was referring to the Shawanok Fishing Club, but of course you would have others. To which do you belong?"

McIntire could see that he was no more match for Bambi at not-so-thinly veiled derision than his other prisoner was at fisticuffs. He turned his attention to the "redskin." Lord, did people outside of the movies really use that word?

This particular redskin had picked up some unfortunate soul's scarf and wiped enough blood off his face for McIntire to recognize Marvin Wall, grandson of George Armstrong Wall, known to the masses as "Walleye" and to McIntire as the SOB who had so inconsiderately died and passed on to him this millstone job of township constable.

"Is your dad here, Marve?"

"Adam dropped me." Marvin spoke his brother's name with a note of pride that bordered on reverence and lifted his battered chin when he added, "I'm living at his place now. But he went home already."

"Well, as soon as you tell me what this was all about, you can both go, too." McIntire turned back to Bambi. "You might as well come out with it. I don't suppose your old man will be overjoyed if I have to call him out to a hick place like this…or to the county jail."

"Ask Karen Sorenson, she's the one that asshole's been bothering."

A girl. Hell, what else had he expected? So the fight was glandular-based after all.

McIntire heard the opening pulses of a lively schottische and wished fervently to be among those prancing around the room. Not that as constable it would be prudent to consume anywhere near an amount of alcohol sufficient to get him out on the floor for a schottische. Another penalty for being a civil servant.

He prayed for strength. The last thing he wanted to hear was a blow by blow report of the alleged bothering, particularly not from the defender of the young lady's honor. Did his position oblige him to ask the girl herself? He recoiled at the prospect of such a tawdry inquiry.

"Did Karen Sorenson tell you she was having a problem?"

"She didn't have to, I've got eyes in my head. And I can tell when somebody's not wanted." He turned an acid gaze on Marvin Wall. "Too bad I can't say the same for the goddamn redskin."

McIntire clenched his jaw. According to his watch, he'd been closeted with the two for close to fifteen minutes. Surely that fulfilled his civic duty. "You got a car?" he asked.

Young Master Morlen positively sniffed. "What do you think?"

McIntire motioned him to his feet. Bambi rose slowly, flexed his fingers and brushed a few flecks of dried grass from his sleeve. As he crossed to the door, Marvin Wall casually stretched a leg into his path. Bambi stumbled, righted himself, ignored Wall, and preceded McIntire out.

"Well, get in that car and get out of here," McIntire said. "Don't let me catch you in any trouble again. And," he added, "stay away from Marve. You just might find out he's not so defenseless as he seems."

What looked suspiciously like a complacent smile flitted briefly across Bambi Morlen's face before he said a formal "good evening" and disappeared around the corner of the building.

McIntire sucked in a few lungfuls of unsullied air before returning to the fusty cloakroom. Marvin Wall still sat on the corner of the bench, but his posture had gone from defiantly erect to a dejected slump. His arms remained folded, and he'd wedged himself back among the heavy overcoats that hung on the wall, no doubt to conceal himself from the bevy of revelers who had suddenly found some pressing need to visit their outerwear. McIntire herded the onlookers out and sat down next to him. It was time he addressed the reason he'd felt compelled to blow up this apparent molehill into, if not a mountain, at least a good-sized knoll.

"All right, Marve, hand it over."

"What?"

"Whatever it is you have in your sock."

Marvin pulled up the muddy cuff of his baggy twill pants, stretched back a wide rubber band, and extracted a leather-sheathed knife. He handed it to McIntire without argument. McIntire drew the knife from its sheath and felt his heart thump at the sight of the lethal five-inch blade protruding from the intricately carved bone handle. A *puukko* to his Finnish neighbors. He controlled his urge to shake the kid until his hair fell out, and regarded the swelling nose and crusted blood that decorated his impassive face. "Dr. Guibard's here. We'll get him to take a look at you before you go. Do you know somebody that can take you home?"

He already knew the answer to that. He'd warned Bambi Morlen to stay away from Marvin, but what could he say in a similar vein to Marvin himself? Steer clear of Bambi and his friends, and, while you're at it, stay away from all the other young people, too, and most of the older ones, for that matter? McIntire knew well what being...*different* was like, but also knew that the alienation he'd experienced at various times throughout his life, that still arose from time to time, was nothing compared to the ostracism suffered by the likes of Marvin Wall. Marvin's attempts to find friends among the white youngsters of St. Adele were unlikely to meet with anything but misery. He couldn't tell the kid that. Anyway he was no doubt finding it out for himself.

"We'll get you a ride back to your brother's." McIntire flipped the knife over in his hand. "This could have gotten you a whole lot worse than a sore nose, Marve." He put his hand on the boy's shoulder and dealt him one more blow, this time a little below the belt. "It's just as well that your brother's gone home. He wouldn't have been proud of you tonight."

Marvin stiffened and moved away. "Adam Wall never lets people push him around," he said, "and that's not the only knife in the world."

# II

*He was such a man as women create in their
dreams.*

Mia Thorsen poured a bucketful of water into the enameled
pot and swung it onto the wood range. Water slopped down
its sides, sizzling as it hit the hot stove top and sending up a
volcano of steam to add to the already sauna-like atmosphere.
She opened the stovepipe damper, lifted one of the cast iron
lids, and topped the glowing embers with a couple of chunks
of birch. The bark caught immediately, spewing out a plume
of black smoke in the seconds before she dropped the lid
back into place. She picked up a can of coffee and snapped
the key off its top.

A sudden breeze swept a cool, inviting breath in through
the open kitchen door. Mia hesitated for only a second, placed
the key back on the unopened can and surrendered to the siren
call, slipping out quickly before anyone could stop her.

It was like a dive into the lake on a sultry summer afternoon. She lifted the braid at the back of her neck and savored
the caress of chill fingers on her sticky skin.

Here on the dark side of the hall was an oasis of clear air
and blessed solitude. The audience that had collected for the
fist fight had gone on to other pursuits. Only a handful of
dark figures moved among the parked cars. High school age

kids seeking the privacy of back seats, Mia supposed, and people like herself, looking for a few minutes' respite from the noise, the heat, and the soup of odors: sweat, beer, ham, and tobacco—smoked and chewed.

Mia stepped off the porch and wedged herself into a niche between its railing and an overgrown lilac. The music and voices faded into a background rumble that sounded like the roar of the lake on a windy day. She pressed her back against the white clapboards and contemplated the frosty luminescence of the quarter moon floating in a thin layer of cloud.

She wouldn't have much longer before some busybody would come looking for her. It would be a simple thing to walk off through the trees and cut across the field. In ten minutes, maybe less, she could be under the covers of her own bed. No one would be surprised or concerned at her disappearance; it wouldn't be the first time she'd made an unannounced departure from one of St. Adele's social events.

She was in serious danger of giving way to the temptation, wondering if she could risk fetching her coat, when the crunch of footsteps on gravel sounded nearby, and an arrogant voice rang out, "Good evening, *Ma'am*. Arriving a little late, *Ma'am?*"

A surprised gasp and a whoop of laughter followed, and a man appeared around the corner of the building, heading toward the cars. His compact build and a cockiness in his walk were so like her husband that Mia started forward. If Nick was leaving, it wouldn't be without her! She stopped when he reached the glow of the yard light. It wasn't Nick. This man was considerably younger, more of a boy. She felt a clutch deep in her chest when she saw the dark blotch caked over his ear and the thin black trickle snaking to his collar. One of those mixed up in the fight, then. The kid didn't seem to be suffering much from his injuries. He whistled a tune through his teeth and strolled confidently across the grass toward a dark-colored sports car. It was the kind that Mia had seen in movies, only big enough for two people, and built so low that they'd be almost sitting on the ground.

When he bent to open the door Mia saw that once again she'd been mistaken. The apparent wound must have been a trick of the light or her mind; the young man's head was adorned only with chestnut waves, slightly mussed but unbloodied.

Two more shadows appeared from among the trees but stayed on the far side of the car. After a few minutes of mumbling and giggles, doubtless over how they'd all fit into the cartoonish vehicle, the three packed themselves in and drove off.

The brisk air that had been so welcome a few minutes before was beginning to feel decidedly frigid. Mia let her conscience, aided by her discomfort, be her guide and ducked back inside.

Eating had replaced dancing and brawling as the activity of choice, and a sizeable, if ragged line meandered along the wall toward the counter.

Mia nudged Sally Fergusen to claim a spoon. She'd spent the last hour and a half lugging water and tending the fire in the cookstove. She had no intention of now being shunted to the further drudgery of washing and drying the tin plates to keep ahead of the hungry throng, or, as Sally would have said, the "hogs bellied up to the trough." She inserted herself between Sally and Inge Lindstrom, added a blob of quivering red Jell-O to a plate, and slid it across the counter to a waiting Helmi Jarvinen.

Helmi rested her cane on the counter and shouted, "Now don't you worry, I'll be scooting right back to help soon as I'm done with my supper. Then you can get out of there and keep an eye on that husband of yours!"

Mia bent to the snowy head and spoke into Helmi's ear. "But that's why I took this spot, Mrs. Jarvinen. I can keep track of all Nick's shenanigans from here."

Helmi turned to look over her shoulder, nodded at Mia's wisdom, and shuffled off into the haze, managing the cane and full plate with impressive dexterity.

Mia's position, aided by her height, did give her as generous a view of the room as thick smoke and dim lighting allowed. She spotted Nick weaving among the tables, headed toward the dance floor in the wake of a blue-dressed matron she didn't recognize.

Before they left home Nick had announced his intention of dancing with every woman present, except, he asserted, Lucy Delaney. "I'm a brave man," he'd said, "but not fool-hardy!" He appeared to be well on his way to accomplishing his lofty goal.

As Mia watched, her husband gave a sudden lurch and grabbed for the back of a nearby chair. If the dear man wasn't careful he'd be jeopardizing his hard-won reputation for drinking more and showing it less than any man in Michigan.

"Beans!"

A grubby claw thrust the plate back across the counter. Mia looked down into a mottled face half concealed by a matted rug of iron gray hair. The abundant locks made a marked contrast to the sparse whiskers twitching on his pointy chin. "I like my beans! Toss on another scoop or two!"

She cleared a spot on the already overloaded plate and added a mountain of baked beans.

The bean-lover lifted his greasy hat and shoved a handful of hair under its brim. The sort of vermin that might have set up housekeeping in that cozy thatch did not bear speculation. The mere sight of the unwashed creature made Mia feel doubly the film of grit building up on her own skin. She concentrated her gaze on the wary, red-rimmed eyes.

"Thanks, Missy, I do like my beans." A stream of tobacco juice arced over the counter to land with a splat in the corner. If Inge had seen it, the guy would soon be little more than the pile of rags he resembled. Mia wouldn't mind throttling him herself. Let John McIntire break up another scuffle, earn the two and a half dollars they were paying him to be here. The man met her glare with a jack-o'-lantern grin, stuck a fork and knife into his shirt pocket, and picked up the plate.

Mia watched the skinny shoulders disappear into the crowd, which parted like the Red Sea for his passing. Obnoxious runt. And they'd probably never see that fork again. She wondered how he'd gotten here.

Her speculations were cut short by Sally's nudge to her elbow, and Mia looked up into the face of an angel. The next patron at the trough was definitely no hog. Here was a vision of thick silver-white hair, a gentle smile, and bottomless hazel eyes that said that smile was for her and her alone. The room suddenly became, once again, far too hot. Rivulets of sweat began to flow, sending chill tracks from Mia's armpit to her waist and gluing her blouse to her rib cage. She felt an overwhelming desire to scramble over the counter and nestle into the stranger's sweater-covered chest.

"No beans, thank you. Give my share to Yosemite Sam there." The man picked up his plate and bestowed his intimate smile on Evelyn Turner, who led him off, stuck to his side like a leech.

Sally poked her again. "Do you know that guy?"

"Never seen him before," Mia answered, without taking her eyes off the dampish curls at the back of his neck. No, they weren't long enough to be curls. Just endearing little wisps of silver lying on suntanned skin. The man found a seat and was descended upon by a group of middle-aged women who suddenly remembered that they had not yet paid their respects to Mrs. Turner. Mia had the feeling that, if the enchanting newcomer stuck around, they'd all be hearing plenty of him. Nick might have more than his reputation as chief imbiber to look out for.

# III

*Can anyone whose soul has been filled with*
*legends ever free himself of their dominion?*

Adam Wall lived in a twenty-five foot trailer house wedged among the stately beech trees that fringed the shore of Lake Superior. He'd hauled it over the ice the previous winter. This time of year his home was accessible either by water or a half-mile footpath that led from the grounds of his parents' only slightly more impressive dwelling.

McIntire chose to walk, even though it would mean a staring match, or worse, with Charlie and Eleanor Wall's two dogs, animals that Charlie proudly claimed to be "purebred Australian shepherds." McIntire might not be an expert on canine pedigrees, but even he could see that these two brindled brutes weren't pure anything except evil. This morning they occupied their usual positions on the faded boards of the Walls' front porch, chins on paws, eyes lazy yellow slits. He left the car at the end of the short driveway and set out, with feigned confidence, toward the yard.

On his first step, four bristled ears lifted almost impercepti-bly. On his second, the two sets of malevolent eyes opened and locked on his. On his third step, the pair rose as one, silent, languid, not a wasted movement, block-like front quarters slowly coming erect, then a momentary hesitation before the haunches followed in one sinuous movement. On his fifth step the blankets of hair on the shoulders rose up. McIntire decided against a sixth step.

The Walls' Plymouth was not in the yard. They'd likely gone to Mass in Aura; no hope of rescue from that quarter. But McIntire knew his part in this minor pageant, and he played it out as he had many times before.

Adam Wall's Ford pickup sat on low tires in its customary spot under a willow tree at the side of the drive. McIntire sidled up to it, and, without taking his eyes off the twin hounds of hell, felt for the door handle, pulled it open, and gave a short blast on the horn. The sound was met with a ferocious baying, not from the alleged Australian shepherds but from the beagle belonging to Sulo Touminen across the road. Without so much as a snarl in his direction, the sentinels abandoned their post and barreled down the driveway in gleeful pursuit of the canine interloper. McIntire, wishing he wasn't too dignified to sprint a little himself, walked very fast between the house and barn and headed for the sanctuary of the woods.

He might have elected to face off with devil dogs rather than taking the water route, even if he hadn't had a lifelong antipathy to all forms of water craft. This was the kind of day made for walking. The annual premature death of the Northern Michigan equivalent of summer was not without its compensations. Autumn could, at times, seem almost worth the pain of the winter that would follow. At least for now, he could luxuriate in the butterscotch light filtering through the flame colored canopy, temporarily forgetting that it presaged months when his life would be centered around little more than shuffling firewood and snow. Winter was something he seldom allowed himself to contemplate until he stood thigh deep in white. If he really thought about it, he feared he'd soon be packing up his fishing rods and his wife and boarding the first train south, or a plane heading back across the Atlantic.

He breathed deeply. Maybe if he sucked enough of the undefiled air into his lungs, he could clear out the residue of the semi-solid atmosphere that had filled the town hall the night before. Leonie had commented that she came home feeling like a chimney sweep. Just before falling asleep she had mumbled, in a voice conveying a mixture of dismay and awe, "When one bathes after an evening of dancing, one doesn't quite expect to see mud running down the plug hole."

McIntire strolled along the sandy path as the yipping of the thwarted dogs faded. Dogs, he thought, had to be among the most brainless creatures on earth. What did it say about Man that he had selected such mental deficients to be his best friend?

The trail ran gradually downhill, and almost too soon a sliver of water showed through the trees. He'd often envied Adam Wall his uncomplicated existence, a little fishing, a little hunting, waking up each morning to nothing but the sounds of the earth and the sight of the single biggest accumulation of fresh water she had to offer. McIntire had visited several times in the months that Adam Wall had lived here. Wall's little hunting and little fishing were frequently conducted with amazingly little regard for state game laws.

Adam Wall also played a little chess. The constable's official calls more often than not stretched into a few hours spent hunched over a board set up on a stump with McIntire agonizing over each move, while the younger man dozed, smoked, and in general paid scant attention to the game until he unfailingly administered the *coup de grâce*. McIntire had his suspicions about how much of the apparent unconcern was genuine. Adam Wall wasn't clairvoyant. He had to be putting a bit of thought into things. The guy should have taken up poker.

When the play got really slow, Wall whiled away the time by imparting to McIntire what he knew of the Chippewa language. Chippewa was the only tongue common to Flambeau

County in which McIntire could not claim fluency. It was a deficit he planned to attend to someday, but he would need to find a more knowledgeable teacher than Adam Wall.

The Good Life notwithstanding, Wall's lakeside estate looked anything but idyllic. The trailer, well-traveled long before Adam got hold of it, hadn't been improved by the trip over the ice. It sat propped on concrete blocks, listing to the west, shedding bits of its outer covering like a molting aluminum goose. An open lean-to stacked to the beams with firewood and a pretentiously large white-painted outdoor biffy, with a window overlooking the lake, completed the homestead.

McIntire found Wall standing with both feet in an over-sized wooden bucket, clutching a pole of peeled aspen in his hands. One end of this staff was planted on the ground, and he leaned onto it while energetically rotating his hips. He nodded in McIntire's direction but didn't slacken in his mysterious gyrations. McIntire walked to him and peered into the bucket. Adam Wall's booted feet, none too clean, trod several inches of wild rice.

"Thank God," McIntire said, "for a while there I thought you were trying to pole your way to town in that tub."

"Got to get the husks off," Wall panted. Using the pole for balance, he stepped out onto the grass. He squatted to sift the insubstantial looking grain through his fingers, gave a satisfied "humph," and dipped out a portion into a shallow birchbark basket. Shaking the basket lightly, he allowed the breeze to winnow away the loosened husks.

McIntire watched, fascinated. It was a procedure he hadn't seen before. Wall hadn't learned it from his parents. Charlie and Eleanor didn't bother much with the practices of their forebears, but their son had returned from his stint in the army, according to Charlie, "more Indian than Sitting Bull."

Only when he had dumped the stripped kernels into a dented pail and set the basket down on a rusty metal chair did he turn to his visitor. His eyes were bloodshot, and there were lines of fatigue on his face. "This about my brother?" he asked.

McIntire nodded and handed him the puukko. "So he told you about the fight?"

"Fight? Nah, I ain't heard about no fight." The upward lilt of Wall's voice made it sound like a question. "But I can't think of anything illegal I've done lately that would interest you. I got a feeling you didn't cut into your Sunday fishing just to pass the time of day. And," he added, "I do know that boy's having a hard time."

Maybe the man *was* clairvoyant. "He'd be having a hell of a lot worse time if he'd gotten the chance to use that thing," McIntire said.

"Thank you for returning it." The words sounded strangely formal. Wall snapped open the sheath and held the knife up to the light. "It was Grandpa's. The old man always said 'life circles around.' Looks like he was right about that. Grandpa got this the same way you did. Took it off a drunken Finlander when he was breaking up a fight. But he wouldn't even have thought of giving it back. Confiscated property was one of the fringe benefits." He ran his thumb along the edge of the blade. "Those Finns really know how to make a knife." He shoved the implement back into the sheath and stuck it into his belt. "Who'd Marve try to cut? He was drinking, I suppose?"

"He wasn't drunk that I could see. He got in a mix-up with a kid from the Club over in Thunder Bay."

Adam bent to scoop up another basket of rice. "Ah, talk about things going in circles, I don't guess Grandpa'd have been overly upset about his knife being used on one of that bunch of assholes."

"Walleye was hardly alone in those sentiments," McIntire commented. "Did your grandfather have something against the Clubbers? Something that was out of the ordinary, I mean."

"It was one of them shot him in the foot. He was only a kid, maybe about Marve's age, when it happened. It was his first day back home after he got out of the boarding school. He didn't realize that the lake he'd fished all his life had got to be part of their private territory. He met up with some vacationing banker and ended up losing two toes."

A distant look came into Wall's eyes and he sat down heavily on the chair, cradling the basket in his lap. "God, do you realize how long ago that was? When my Grandfather was born, the Civil War hadn't ended yet. This was a different world then, a...*primeval* world. Life had gone on the same here for thousands of years. But think of the changes that old man saw in the time he spent on this earth. Not all of them good." His fingers caressed the bone handle of the puukko. "Hardly any of them good." He looked up with an apologetic smile. "Anyway, he always wanted to get back at the son-of-a-bitch that shot him. Maybe it's his spirit just now getting around to it.'

"His spirit might have picked a more likely avenging angel than your brother. As you might have noticed, Marvin got the worst of this battle."

Wall looked quickly down, stirred his rice and picked out a stray pine needle. "Oh, well, Grandpa'd take revenge anywhere he could get it. He was an adaptable guy. He knew how to make the best of most any situation that came along. I guess that's why he got on so well in the world, changes or no. Even losing those toes had its bright side, he said. He had to fill out his shoe with wool, and that foot always stayed nice and warm even when his other one was freezing." He stood up, dumped the rice, and asked, "You know what started the fight?"

"Just ordinary horsing around. The Club kid throwing his weight around, girls, the usual." No need to mention the "redskin" ingredient. Adam Wall could surmise the meaning of "usual."

"You sure about that?"

"Why? Do you think it might have been something else?"

"No. Hell, how would I know? I wasn't there." He gazed thoughtfully toward the sun. "It's only that Ma always taught us that if we were going to use a knife on somebody we'd better have a damn good reason." McIntire felt his jaw drop slightly. Adam Wall's contemplative aspect was obliterated by a broad grin, and McIntire wondered if the day would ever come when he was no longer such a perfect patsy for his neighbors' ribbing.

Still he couldn't help but remember that Adam Wall spent four years of war on active duty, and undoubtedly had 'damn good reasons' for using a weapon plenty of times.

A trio of mallards sailed low over the water, thought better of making a landing, and lifted off again. A wise move. It was past time they should be long gone.

McIntire followed their example and turned to leave. "Well, keep an eye on your brother. The other kids see he's got a temper, and they're gonna bait him every chance they get." It hadn't escaped McIntire's notice that Marvin was lending neither hand nor foot to the rice processing. He glanced toward the trailer. "Hope he got home okay last night. I went to fetch Guibard to look at his nose, but he took off before we got back."

Adam Wall picked up the old pillowcase containing his rice and poured a short stream into the tub. He replied with his back to McIntire. "I haven't seen Marve. He'd have stayed with Ma. He wouldn't walk out here in the middle of the night."

He stepped into the tub, and McIntire left him to his jitterbugging.

If someone wanted to murder Charlie and Eleanor Wall in their beds, they would have only to circle around the barn and approach the house from the rear. The canine sentries had nothing against those who didn't arrive by the main road. They thumped their tails in tandem when McIntire stepped onto the porch to tap on the elder Walls' door, thinking to check on the state of Marvin's nose. He got no answer. Marvin had either gone with his parents or was keeping out of sight.

He felt more relief than disappointment. He'd done his job now and could get back to his own life.

As he walked back to his car, a movement in the trees at the edge of the yard caught his eye. He guessed what it was and checked himself in time to keep from turning. Twyla Wall, Walleye's widow and a living ghost. He knew that if he looked in her direction she would evaporate like a fragment of mist. McIntire kept his head down and studied her in his rearview mirror. She stood watching him over her armload of firewood, a shadow within the larger shadow of a giant pine. How could anyone shrouded to the ground in a tattered brown wool coat appear so ephemeral? Wisps of pale hair floated about her head like a halo of spider's webs loosed from a braid that dangled over her shoulder and hung almost to the coat's hem. Walleye's life may have been a story of acquiescing to change, but his wife had not succumbed. She had somehow managed to carry that "primeval world" with her, maybe by simply refusing to acknowledge any other. McIntire had once asked Charlie if his mother spoke English. "I don't know," he'd answered, "she doesn't like to talk."

He lifted his head and raised his hand in salute. The sharp black eyes met his for the briefest possible span of time before the old woman, with no discernible movement, vanished, leaving McIntire to wonder if she'd been there at all. Maybe she really *was* a ghost. Would death alter her existence in any way, or would she simply continue as she had in life, alternately materializing and fading until her spirit finally tired and dissolved forever?

He started up the Studebaker and made for home and his fly rod.

# IV

*How much quieter are the bright sunny days
than the dark nights under whose wings beasts
of prey hunt and owls hoot.*

*Fullkomlig.* Done to perfection. Inge Lindstrom leaned on the
Misto mop and allowed herself a moment of unabashed pride.
The previous night's dancing had loosened a year's worth of
grime from the narrow maple floorboards, and Inge had come
back that morning to attack it quick, before it could settle
back in. Better than three hours she'd been here, sweeping and
scrubbing, waxing and polishing. Now the sight of the tall windows mirrored in the glassy perfection of those beloved planks
made her forget her burning knees and lobster-claw hands.

The town hall floors were Inge's own special territory. Not
that she needed to beat off the other ladies with her broom.
When she'd left them gabbing at the back of the church that
morning, only Grace Maki had offered to help. Inge resisted
suggesting that Grace's time might be better spent tending to
the scuffed linoleum in her own kitchen and assured her that
she could handle it by herself, as usual.

She smoothed a few straggles of hair into the bun at the
back of her neck, took a quick glance out the windows,
slipped off her shoes, and waltzed the mop across the gleaming expanse to stow it in the closet. Humming to herself as

she straightened the "Please Wipe Your Feet" sign, she left the hall, lingering in the doorway for one last look. It wouldn't be this way long. Like a field covered in the first snow of the year, pure and bright and glorious, it would soon be trampled to ruin by the feet of people who had no consideration for the labor that went into such handiwork, be it God's or Mrs. Lindstrom's.

"Well," she lifted her eyes ceilingward and spoke aloud, "it'll look halfway decent for a day or two, anyhow."

Backing the dusty Chevrolet down the drive, she caught sight of the woodshed door standing partly open. One good blast of wind would rip the thing right off its hinges. She sighed, turned off the engine, and climbed out of the car.

Before hooking the door, she peeked inside on the chance that she might be locking in some critter who'd wandered in looking for a winter home. Or, more likely, a liquored-up Norwegian sleeping off the effects of the last night's over-doing.

The space was about half filled with split and stacked maple, nowhere near enough to supply both the hall and the school for the winter. Somebody'd better get off their backside. There was nothing else, and no one else, that she could see. She was about to close things back up when she noticed that the trap door leading to the attic storeroom also hung open. The door was in a far corner and could only be reached by clambering up and over the stacked wood. Which was just the kind of thing that would appeal to youngsters looking to hide out for awhile for one reason or another. Inge was tempted to pretend she hadn't noticed. She had her own home and her men to take care of, after all, and she didn't much like climbing woodpiles even when her knees hadn't been torn to ribbons by scrubbing floors all morning. But, in the end, conscience forced her to yank up her skirt and mount the shaky pile to make her way to the opening. If kids had been up there, who could say what they might have left behind to attract mice or even rats? Or to build up a head of steam and explode, for all she knew. Arnie Johnson had once told her about a jar of sauerkraut that blew up and cost his mother's cousin her right eye.

Standing on the wood, Inge could reach just high enough to poke her head through the opening. The air was still and warm as bath water and, as she had feared, filled with a sour odor that might be spoiling food or—she stiffened her jaw—vomit. The rectangular vent up near the roof peak let in a narrow shaft of light. The heavy buzzing told her it also let in plenty of flies looking for a warm spot on this fall day. Probably bats, too. She pulled her kerchief forward and knotted it more securely under her chin.

It was dim in the attic, almost dark. As her eyesight adjusted, she made out a kerosene lantern on the floor. Beside it an enameled tin plate held a pile of crusted-over baked beans and a few curled shreds of ham, and next to that—Inge rubbed her eyes and looked again—a pair of oxford-clad feet, ankles crossed and twisted with a length of heavy cord.

She sucked in her breath, grasped the makeshift ladder that was nailed to the wall, and hoisted herself through the opening. Keeping her face turned away from the feet, she skirted a pile of discarded textbooks and torn window shades to reach the wide double doors at the end of the room. The padlock on the hasp hung open. She threw it aside, wrenched the iron handles and gave a vigorous shove, jumping back to keep from sailing out through the opening.

The doors swung open with a clank. Mid-afternoon sunlight splashed across four decades' worth of collected junk. In its midst, a young man sat slumped forward in a cast-off double desk like some dozing student of bygone years. But Inge could see that no ringing of bells was going to wake this loafer to send him scrambling for the door and freedom.

The cord that bound his feet ran up his body like a growing vine to coil about his wrists, wind several times around his waist and bind him to the seat. A red bandana was tied around his head and stuffed between his jaws. It pulled back his lips to show a row of gleaming white teeth and pale gums. But the most ghastly thing, the thing that she would forever see in her nightmares, was not this grotesque grin or the staring brown eyes. It was his head above that knotted handkerchief. Where it rested on the desk, short reddish-brown curls fanned out over the scarred wood, but the other side, the part turned up to the honey-colored sunshine, was only a ragged patch of blackened blood, crawling with fat blue flies.

# V

*Weary are the ways of men's wanderings over
the earth.*

"Bambi."

Dr. Mark Guibard suspended his ardent probing to look
up. "What's that?"

"His name, if he was to be believed, and I don't know
why anybody'd lie about a thing like that, is Bambi. Bambi
Morlen," McIntire told him. "He was here last night. At the
dance. He…left early."

They were the first words McIntire had uttered since he
and the coroner had climbed the ladder into the stuffy attic.
He struggled to hold the kerosene lantern steady while keeping his arm extended to its full length. In his other hand he
held his less than immaculate handkerchief, flicking it periodically in a vain attempt to keep the flies at bay. The sight
of the arrogant youth, his smugness stilled forever, filled him
not so much with horror as with an agonizing sadness. How
could it happen so quickly? How could a moving, breathing,
annoying member of the human race become, overnight,
decaying food for flies?

Guibard grunted and bent to roll back a trouser leg, revealing one of the bound ankles. "He doesn't look familiar."

"He said he's from Connecticut. His family's been spending the summer at the Club."

"You've talked to him then? I take it he was mixed up in that scrap with Charlie's kid."

"He's the one broke Marvin's nose," McIntire said, "and now he ends up dead and…"

"Scalped," Guibard stated. He inserted a forefinger under one of the cords. "You think Marvin Wall did this?"

"Well," McIntire hesitated, "it kind of seems improbable that it would be only coincidence…but I took Marve's knife."

"There are plenty of knives around."

"That's what *he* said."

The doctor bounced up and pirouetted around to face his reluctant assistant. Neither advanced age nor the most trying of circumstances could dampen Guibard's aura of Fred Astaire *savoir faire*.

"John, believe me when I tell you that neither the Walls nor the tribe from which they descend has a history of lifting people's hair."

As usual, McIntire wasn't quite sure if Guibard was verbally slapping his hand or laughing at him. Somehow the doctor always managed to reduce him to a state of subservient defensiveness. He half expected to be addressed as "Johnny."

"I'm not a total moron, Mark, but it was Marvin Wall's being a 'redskin' that was at the bottom of the fight, and a kid could get the idea…you know, *You want a redskin, I'll show you just how redskin I can be!* Sort of an adolescent version of poetic justice. Marve was pretty steamed. Although," he let his gaze drop to the blood-caked curls for a brief moment, "this hardly looks like a kid's prank."

Guibard prodded the ragged edge of skin around the wound in a manner that made McIntire wince and look quickly away. "John," he said, "Marvin Wall's been skinning out mink and muskrats since he was knee high to—I don't know what—a mink or a muskrat. He wouldn't have done this kind of half-assed job." He motioned for McIntire to move the light nearer.

"I had his knife," McIntire repeated. "Maybe he had to make do with what he had."

"And I'll tell you something else," Guibard went on, "head wounds generally bleed a whole lot. It looks ugly, but there's really not much blood to speak of here. This pitiful scalping was done some time after death."

"Well, I sure as hell hope so!" McIntire nearly retched at the thought of such mutilation being inflicted on a living victim. "He had to have been already dead. Even trussed up like this, the kid would hardly have meekly laid down his head to have his hair surgically removed."

Guibard didn't comment on McIntire's hysterical stating of the obvious, only gave a delicate sigh, and went on, "When his heart quit beating, he would have stopped pumping blood out, but, even so, if the skin had been taken off before the blood started to congeal there would have been more than this. I'm saying that this looks like it was done a considerable time after he died. And if you look closer—"

"No thanks."

"If you *did* look closer, you'd see that there's more than just the scalp removed. There's a kind of hole here."

"A what?"

"A circular depression. Scraping down into the bone. Like someone tried to make a hole in the skull."

"Tried to…?"

Guibard stooped until his nose was nearly touching the wound. "It's not drilled all the way through, but it looks for all the world like somebody gave it a good try."

"Christ! Why? How—?"

They both looked into the shadows where a wooden toolbox sat balanced atop a leaning three-legged chair. Its hinged lid lay open, and a tray containing rusty nuts and bolts was pulled aside to reveal a few hand tools.

"Christ!" McIntire said again.

Guibard once more bent over the corpse. He pushed back the drooping lids to expose glazed eyeballs, shining his pencil-sized light into their depths. "The scalp wound is the only trauma I can see, and like I said, that wouldn't have killed him," he continued. "But it does really look like…well, I'll be able to tell more when I get him into the morgue."

"Too much to drink?" McIntire asked, glancing at the pool of dried vomit..

"Could be. It wouldn't be the first time a kid died from alcohol poisoning, but that doesn't explain the ropes and gag… or the scalping."

McIntire waved the lantern toward the pile of discarded window shades. "Looks like that's where the cord came from. Maybe kids fooling around, and he choked to death?"

"And they tried to revive him by drilling a hole in his head?"

Their conjectures were interrupted by a growl of an engine that might belong to a Sherman tank. Guibard and McIntire looked at each other. Guibard nodded. A car door banged shut, then another, followed shortly by a screech of twisting wood issuing from the ladder they'd placed against the outside wall. Such a vehement protest could only mean that it was being subjected to the weight of Sheriff Pete Koski. McIntire felt a momentary urge to lunge for the doors, shutting out the sheriff and everything he represented. Somewhere inside him a tiny spark lived, a vague idea that any drama needed the cooperation of all its players. Maybe if he and Guibard simply closed the door and walked away, refused to enact their roles, the ugly event would disappear, and this conceited boy, who had not been a part of their lives when alive, would not be allowed to inflict his dead presence upon them.

The moment passed, the outside light was eclipsed, and Koski's bulk appeared in the doorway. He ducked into the room, bringing the world with him and ensuring that the show would go on and dozens of lives would be changed forever.

The sheriff was followed by his baby-cheeked deputy, Cecil Newman, trailing a length of electric cord and carrying two trouble lights.

Koski remained near the door, huffing slightly, for some minutes before he turned to Guibard. "You through here?"

The doctor nodded. "I've pretty much done all I can. Leave his coat on and the gag in. No obvious cause of death. There'll have to be an inquest, of course."

"Got an I.D.?"

When Koski heard that the victim was a "kid from the Club," he sucked in his breath, but his only response was, "Well, we'll look things over and take a few pictures, then he's all yours." He motioned Newman forward and took one of the lights.

McIntire blew out the flame on his lantern and moved toward the door. Dying wasn't a township offense. The sheriff's department and the state police could take over from here. Thank God the victim wasn't a local resident. If it turned out to be homicide they might get lucky and the murderer wouldn't be either. There'd been plenty of strangers around last night.

Koski froze in the act of reaching to hook his light on a convenient nail. He stood arrested, lamp raised aloft, looking toward the open doors. A thin and distant wail grew until the blare of sirens ripped through the air. The sheriff lowered the light and gave a resigned groan. "Oh, shit, nothing like announcing things to the world." He turned to McIntire. "Wanna try and head off the crowd, Mac? And chase Mrs. Lindstrom out of here before she starts getting badgered for gossip. Tell her not to say a word to anybody, and let her know I'll come over to her house later." He hung the light and switched it on.

The shell that was Bambi Morlen appeared to shrink with illumination—a forlorn heap slumped at the sheriff's thighs. McIntire felt the sadness again. Here was somebody's son, maybe somebody's brother. A young man at the center of a circle of people; people who loved him, possibly people who disliked him, maybe even hated him; people who wouldn't recover from his wounds any more than Bambi himself had. Koski seemed to read his thoughts.

"Keep a lid on who this is 'til I get hold of the family," he said. "Clubbers, are they? Maybe you could ride along? I'd better leave Cecil here to keep an eye on things, 'til the state guys show up, and I'm short a deputy since Billy Corbin went back to selling shoes. Besides, you probably speak Club better'n I do."

He reached into the dead boy's rear pocket and extracted a brown leather wallet. He flipped through a small sheaf of bills. "Scratch robbery as a motive, anyway."

McIntire descended to the ground just as the ambulance screamed up to the door. He waved the driver to stay put and crossed the grass to where Inge Lindstrom sat hunched in the passenger seat of her car. McIntire's wife was behind the wheel. At his approach, she rolled down her window and stated in a voice that showed she was leaving no room for argument, "I'm taking Inge home now, John. You tell Mr. Koski if he wants to talk to her he can come to her house."

McIntire waited while the sheriff finished his business and the yard steadily filled with the curious, the fearful, and those who "just happened to be driving by." McIntire informed them each that, "Yes, there had been a death," and "No, it wasn't anybody from around here."

It was just as well that they'd come. It took a half-dozen men to lower the body, shrouded and strapped to a stretcher, to the ground.

# VI

*Had conversation here conjured up this woman?*
*One misfortune always brings another.*

Her newspaper hit the floor, and Mia stretched out, head pillowed on one of the worn davenport's arms and feet dangling over the other. She pulled the afghan up over her head and spent the final few seconds before she closed her eyes marveling at the kaleidoscope of overlapping circles produced by light passing through the spaces in the weave.

What should she dream about? Her drowsy contemplations of that blissful question were squelched by the sound of a car on the nearby road. Mia held her breath. The car slowed. She crossed her fingers, but fortune was not on her side. With a splatter of gravel, the vehicle turned in at the driveway. Maybe it was Nick home early...or Harry Truman out to recruit a new Secretary of State. Each was equally likely.

With a groan, she threw back the cover. Mia and Nick weren't on the regular Sunday afternoon visiting circuit. Still, neighbors showed up every now and then. Often enough to ensure that Mia maintain the habit of baking every Friday and keeping a supply of fresh cream on hand for the coffee.

She pulled herself up and tried to peer inconspicuously through the lace of the curtains. Whoever it was, they didn't *have* to know she was home. The car was unfamiliar, a convertible, not something often seen in this land of eternal winter, a deep maroon color. Mia squinted. It could be a Cadillac…classy, anyway. The top was up; she couldn't see inside. Maybe it *was* Truman.

She picked up the newspapers, shoved them into a rough stack on the coffee table, and had just time to fold the afghan before the knock came at the door.

At her first glimpse of the elflike creature standing on the porch, Mia thought Halloween might have sneaked up on her. The woman was tiny, with skin freckled as an overripe banana and a pixie cap of fox-colored curls. Circular spots of rouge decorated her cheeks. Only her eyes, the same emerald green as her dangling earrings, held a note of familiarity.

"Mia?" The woman smiled, turning her crow's feet into ostrich tracks. "I don't suppose you'd remember me." The husky voice came from somewhere around her silver belt buckle. "It's Siobhan McIntire…Siobhan Henry, now."

Mia could only gape.

"Colin's half-sister. I was —"

"Siobhan, of course I remember you! It's just…It's been so long…nobody knew where…" Mia took a breath and started over. "Come in. Forgive me, I'm only a little…"

"A little shocked at seeing me still alive?" She gave a throaty un-elflike guffaw and entered.

Mia led her guest into the kitchen, installed her on a chair, and filled the coffeepot. She slid a plate of blackberry-filled cookies onto the table and took a chair opposite. Now that she knew who she was looking at, she realized that the former Siobhan McIntire hadn't really changed all that much since she'd last seen her, which must have been at least twenty years before. More like twenty-five. Despite its wrinkles, the heart-shaped face maintained its childish tilt, and the eyes still seemed to hold some delicious secret.

"Well," she tried to begin again, "well, Siobhan…and how have you been?"

Siobhan's blood-red talons glittered as she reached for a cookie. "Ooh, let's see...I had pneumonia in 1932." Her lumberjack laugh burst out once more, so out of keeping with her appearance that Mia felt she was conversing with a ventriloquist's puppet. Siobhan chewed and swallowed before going on. "Sorry to barge in on you like this, but I've been to Colin's, and there doesn't seem to be anybody around. I didn't want to go all the way back to Chandler. And I wouldn't want to be sitting there when they get home and give anybody a heart attack! I thought maybe I could wait here? If it wouldn't be a bother."

Mia suppressed a smile. Bothering her, and John, had once been Siobhan's favorite pastime. But as to that heart attack...

"Of course it's no trouble. And we have plenty of catching up to do. But...I hate to have to tell you this, Siobhan. Colin is dead. He's been gone about three years. I know Sophie tried to find you and your mother when it happened, but..."

"Oh, God." The spark left her eyes, and Siobhan McIntire sounded weary. "What happened? How did he die?"

"Came out of Touminen's sauna and dived in the lake. He died instantly, massive coronary."

"Good lord! How awful! We didn't hear anything about it. A heart attack? When I said that, I...Colin? It seems impossible. He was always so..."

"Indestructible."

Siobhan took a crushed pack of Winstons from her shoulder bag and shook one into her hand. "I can't believe I won't see him again. If I had thought..." She tapped the end of the cigarette against her palm. "So Sophie's alone?"

"Sophie's moved to Florida. John's living in the house now."

Siobhan paused with the lighter flickering in front of her nose and snatched the cigarette from her mouth. She stared as if Mia had told her the Widow McIntire had eloped with the pope. "John? He actually came back here? To St. Adele? No.

I can't believe it." She completed the lighting procedure and inhaled deeply. "Good God, he didn't take over the tavern, did he?"

"Hardly! He stayed in Europe, London mostly I guess, all this time, since the first war. Didn't come back, even for a visit, until he retired last year."

"He stayed in the army?"

"Absolutely."

"John is the last person on this earth I could see as a soldier."

Now it was Mia's turn to give a bark of laughter. "He wasn't a soldier exactly. He worked as a translator. Or so he *says*."

The sooty penciled arches above Siobhan's eyes lifted, and Mia lowered her voice. "He was involved in *intelligence*."

"You mean like a spy? John? Well, I guess I shouldn't be too surprised. He always was kind of snoopy."

John was snoopy? Now there was a prime case of the pot calling the kettle black, if Mia had ever heard one. She shrugged. "Who knows? But hang on for this one. Last spring he was elected township constable."

Siobhan's hand trembled slightly as she drained her cup and returned it to the table. "So what does he do? Bore the bad guys into giving up?"

A twinge of the old protectiveness crept in. "He was kind of tricked into it, but people seem to think he's doing a fine job."

"No kidding? Well, who'd a thunk? And he stayed away all that time? Long disappearances must run in the family. Or," the eyebrows went up again, "was he possibly nursing a broken heart?"

Mia refilled the cups. "How's your mother?"

Siobhan gave another short laugh. "Okay, be that way." She dumped a spoonful of sugar into her coffee. "Ma's just hunky-dory, so far as I know. Believe it or not, she's married to a Lutheran minister. They live in Colorado. I don't see a whole lot of them."

So there was an ecclesiastical union in the mix. How Bridget McIntire might have snagged a Protestant man of the cloth sounded like a story in itself. Well, Bridget's marriage to John's Grandpa McIntire had shown she was resourceful. But Mia couldn't quite see Siobhan as the pastor's daughter.

"Did your husband come back with you?" she asked. "You did say you were married?"

"That's exactly right, I *was* married. Not any more, I'm happy to report."

"Only once?" Mia didn't want to appear to be prying, but the carnival worker in whose company Siobhan left St. Adele had definitely carried a much more colorful last name than Henry. Her curiosity went unsatisfied.

"Once isn't enough?" Siobhan asked. "Believe me, marrying for money isn't all it's cracked up to be." She smiled and leaned forward. "But I remember *your* husband very well. Is he still as handsome as ever? If he's got fat and bald I don't want to hear about it."

"No, he's the same old Nick, fit and hairy as ever. He'll be home soon and you can judge for yourself."

"I can't wait." The tiny hand darted out for another cookie. "What a doll he was! I used to wait by the mailbox every day, and he'd give me a ride to the corner on his motorcycle. The mailbag was on the back, so I had to sit in front of him. With his arms around me." She smiled contemplatively at the cookie, then took a sharp bite. "I also had to walk all the way back, but it was worth it. I cried myself to sleep for a month when you two got married. God, was I jealous!"

"You were ten years old!"

"That was the problem. If I'd been a couple years older, you'd never have gotten him away from me."

Remembering Siobhan at twelve, Mia didn't argue. "What brings you back, besides the torch you're carrying for Nick?"

She took a long pull off her cigarette. "I guess I just got homesick. I saw an article in the *Saturday Evening Post*. My divorce had become final, and I thought, why not?"

"Oh ya, the uranium story."

"Has anybody actually found anything yet? Enough to mine?" Siobhan sounded as eager as if she was planning to indulge in a little prospecting herself. Or possibly some secondhand gold-digging.

"Not that I've heard," Mia told her, "but if they haven't it's not for lack of trying. Like the article said, some guy from Minnesota found uranium over on the river, by the gravel pit. That was last summer. Since the snow melted this spring, we've had a regular gold rush. The woods are crawling with prospectors. There are more Geiger counters than guns out there this fall. But, so far, the only people making their fortune seem to be the bar owners. I imagine John's kicking himself, wishing he *had* taken over that tavern."

Mia found herself disappointed that there wasn't more of a story to tell. "And," she remembered, "the county's collected about five thousand dollars in back taxes. Nobody wants to take a chance on losing their land if some lucky prospector finds the mother lode on it."

"What happens," Siobhan asked, "if somebody does find uranium, if it's on land that doesn't belong to them?"

Mia wasn't too sure. "On state land you can just snoop around. If you want to dig you have to pay twenty-five bucks for a permit. If it's somebody else's private land, I guess you'd have to work it out with the owner. Most of the land out there is owned by logging companies. I suppose they wouldn't be above branching out into mining."

The telephone jangled, the two short rings that signified that the Thorsens were wanted. Mia felt an irrational grip of alarm that arrested her movements and must have shown in her face; Siobhan regarded her with a confused frown. Mia put down her cup and forced herself to cross the room to the phone. She listened to the calm and sensible voice on the line, murmured an assent and replaced the earpiece. She turned to Siobhan.

"That was Leonie McIntire, John's wife. There's been a death, and John's with the sheriff. Inge Lindstrom found the body, and she's pretty upset. Leonie's staying at her house until Ben gets home. She asked if I'd go over and take her roast out of the oven. You might as well do the honors."

When the dusty convertible had turned out onto the road, Mia went back to the phone. She'd better let Leonie know that she had company. For a second she shook off the darkness that had enveloped her on hearing of the death and pushed aside the memory of that imagined wound over a young man's ear. She laughed aloud. What she wouldn't give to see John McIntire's face when he came home to find that spoiled brat, his Auntie Siobhan, all grown up and fixing his Sunday dinner.

# VII

*She had been proud, rich, happy, and in one minute she was cast into such endless misery.*

Despite their grim errand, McIntire would not have wanted to miss this chance to visit the private retreat where Bambi Morlen's family had been spending its summer. Famous, and infamous, since before McIntire was born, the preserve had been established near the end of the last century when the holder of huge tracts of railroad land found himself needing support for a Senate bid. When the ink was dry, thousands of acres of prime forest and a mile and a half of Lake Superior shoreline, along with some twenty inland lakes, had ended up in the hands of a group of vote-producing capitalists. The Shawanok Fishing Club was born.

McIntire had heard stories of adventurous locals who had surreptitiously entered the grounds to bring back reports of the sumptuous lodge and private cabins owned by the Club's members, as well as the questionable activities indulged in by some of the more notorious. But no one he knew personally had ever gotten past its gate, guarded, it was said, by an armed and uniformed attendant twenty-four hours a day. The single exception, it now seemed, was Walleye Wall, who'd come in by the back way and lost a few toes for his trouble.

Over the years, the Club had boasted the membership of some of the country's most prominent robber barons and entrepreneurs. For half a century and more, those Clubbers had been the most universally despised group of people in the three-county area. Pete Koski had never made a secret of the fact that his feelings were no exception.

He swore extravagantly during the three tries it took to start his treasured new vehicle, the Dodge Power Wagon. McIntire didn't figure it was all directed at the recalcitrant engine.

The engine roared and the wagon trembled like a spirited horse eager to charge across field and forest leaping everything in its path. It was a deception. Koski let out the clutch, and they rumbled sedately out onto the road.

Koski proposed to take the shortest course, northeast through swamp and jungle-thick forest on roads hardly more than the ruts left by logging trucks. Since the alternative would have been the hundred mile or more route through Marquette, McIntire didn't argue. Not that the sheriff would have paid any attention if he had.

"This baby will climb a pine tree," Koski assured him. Not today, McIntire hoped.

The roads were in better shape than McIntire expected. It took only about thirty minutes of plowing through mud, rolling over exposed roots, and unscheduled braking that effected some painful collisions of McIntire's knees with the dash, before they emerged onto the sandy Gray Wolf Plain.

The Plain was only now beginning to recover from its most recent logging and resembled the aftermath of a forest fire. A few deer wandered among the stumps, bounding off to a safe distance at their approach, then turning to stare for a moment before continuing to nibble at emergent seedlings. As they clipped along, McIntire shouted over the jackhammer staccato of sand splattering the wagon's underside to relate the story of Bambi's scuffle with Marvin Wall.

"But," he concluded, "Marvin disappeared the minute I turned my back. Which was only a few minutes after Bambi left. And we don't have any way of knowing for sure what time he got home. *If* he got home. He didn't go back to Adam's place, and he didn't seem to be anywhere around when I stopped at Charlie's about noon. Unless he was just lying low, or sleeping late."

The track dropped into forest again and, after a few more hairpin turns and bruise to McIntire's shins, connected with the road that came from the east and led to the Club compound. This route was diabolically planned to be bad enough to discourage regular use by local residents without destroying the Club's supply trucks and the occasional Cadillac of its members.

"What was the kid like?" Koski downshifted to chug through a stretch of loose sand.

"Like he needed a good kick in the pants," McIntire answered. "Cocky, smug, arrogant."

"Sounds like a great guy."

"Probably his mother loved him." The ill-thought-out remark served as a reminder of the reason they were making this trip. They traveled on for a time in silence but for the low snoring of the German shepherd, Geronimo, stretched out on the back seat. "Odd, though," McIntire said, "Marvin stuck out his foot and tried to trip Bambi when he left the hall, and it didn't seem to bother the kid at all."

Koski accelerated around a curve and nearly collided with a five-foot-high cast iron gate. It cut straight across the road and was fastened by a four-inch padlock. To its right, a blocky log building topped off with a slate roof and complete with stone chimney crouched in a nest of cedars. Through an organdy curtained window, a gray head was visible. Koski waited exactly ten seconds before giving a prolonged blast on the horn. The plank door burst open, and the owner of the grizzled pate appeared.

Legend said that the Club's guards were recruited from murderers paroled from the state prison—in early years even a notorious stagecoach robber. The man who confronted them was disillusioning. He appeared as neither a menacing thug nor the fabled armed and uniformed figure. His costume consisted of a workman's green coveralls, and he was equipped with only a stick of gnarled willow. He hobbled toward them, his face clouded with anger or possibly arthritis. Koski gave McIntire a chagrined look and hefted himself out of the car. After a quick conference, bending almost double to shout into the old man's ear, the sheriff opened the gate himself, and they drove through.

The narrow road meandered under birch and maple for another quarter mile before the woods opened into farmlands. Sleek Holsteins wandered to the fence along the road to observe their passing. The road traversed fields of oat stubble, potatoes, and dried corn stalks, before turning to the north and again entering forest. Another ten minutes of driving brought them to the Club proper, a collection of unpainted log buildings that made up a village. But for the Red Crown gas pump, it could have been a scene from a hundred years past. McIntire had to admit it would be a pleasant place to escape from the world, although their mission here furnished proof that the world could find you where and when it chose. A little further on stood what must have been the main lodge. It was disappointingly modest, a rambling two-story structure of weathered wood and slightly sagging porches. Koski drove past.

"It's Mr. and Mrs. Wendell Morlen," he said. "Their place is the fourth one on the upper side, the old boy says. He called it a *cottage.* Another half mile or so."

The track wound further along the lakeshore and through the trees, passing a half-dozen private lodges ranging from simple cabins to structures the size of the Lincoln Memorial. This was more what McIntire had expected to see.

The Morlen summer hideaway also lived up to his expectations, and then some. The "cottage" hugged the earth on a stone foundation. Its lower portion was of cedar logs, tightly fitted and varnished to a subtle glow. Perched on this rustic base, like a birthday cake resting on an orange crate, was a second story of pale yellow fish-scale siding, a high peaked roof, and dormers with leaded windows. It could have held McIntire's house twice over.

Koski drove a short distance past the cabin and pulled off the road. He took a few deep breaths before switching off the engine, then rolled down the window, removed a pack of Camels from his shirt pocket, and stuck one between his lips. In spite of the chill air, his forehead and neck were damp with sweat. It was a natural reaction to the task ahead, but one that, nevertheless, surprised McIntire. They waited. A splash sounded as a golden retriever hit the water off the end of a nearby dock.

"Oh, hell. Let's get to it." The sheriff stuffed the unlit cigarette into the ashtray, wiped his hands on his twill-clad thighs, and wrenched open the door.

The cabin's front door stood open and the sound of an unaccompanied operatic aria issued forth. Rossini maybe, McIntire thought, Italian anyway, and not half badly done. As they approached, the singer abandoned her high-brow theme and launched into a musical lament about how she couldn't help loving that man of hers.

Koski rapped on the door frame. The song trailed off and steps sounded on hardwood floors. A dark, plumpish woman in a kerchief and flour-dusted apron appeared in the entryway and spoke through the screen. "Yes?"

The sheriff introduced himself with more formality than McIntire thought he had in him. "I'm Peter Koski, sheriff of Flambeau County, and this is Constable John McIntire. Are Mr. and Mrs. Morlen at home?"

The woman wiped her hands on her apron and pushed open the screen door. "I'm Bonnie Morlen. How can I help you?" The rich, melodic voice was steady, but her eyes, wary as a mother hen, betrayed the trepidation that an unexpected visit from the law is always likely to inspire.

Some seconds passed before Koski responded. He had no doubt expected the housekeeperish woman to present them to a Grace Kelly lookalike lounging in a brocade-covered chaise munching bonbons and sipping champagne.

McIntire was himself a bit nonplused. The personification of domesticity who stood before them was no more in keeping with the sophisticated image of the Club than was its unimposing lodge. She was equally hard to picture as the mother of the precociously urbane Bambi. But the full cheeks and mahogany curls peering from under the kerchief left him in no doubt.

She led them to a living room that commenced with a baby grand piano and stretched thirty or forty feet to a fireplace of unpolished granite at the far end. "Please, sit down, and excuse me for just a moment." She directed them to a deep green plush sofa and disappeared through a swinging door.

The furnishings of the cottage showed the same eclecticism as its architecture. The floor was strewn with rugs both Persian and polar bear. Spindly-legged tables vied for space with benches fashioned from split tree trunks. Dim landscapes in ornate gold-leaf frames hung on the lacquered log walls. These bucolic scenes of misty pastures were lackluster compared to that viewed through the four square windows. The sun had not quite sunk into the hills behind the cabin. Its low rays turned the water to a coral slate framed by fire-colored trees.

The moment stretched into real minutes. The distant grumble of an outboard motor grew louder, then died abruptly. The sun completed its plunge, and the room went from dim to dark. Koski rose to his feet and switched on a lamp. He was beginning to make for the swinging door when

Mrs. Morlen bustled back into the room. She'd shed the apron and head cover and carried with her a towel-covered crockery bowl the size of a small bathtub. She placed it on a table near the chimney, spent an inordinate amount of time fussing with the towel, and finally turned to the sheriff.

Baking bread. Were these Clubbers far more down-to-earth than was generally believed, or was Mrs. Morlen some sort of modern-day Marie Antoinette, playing at her own version of milkmaid?

"Is your husband at home?" Koski asked.

"I'm expecting him soon. Is there something you wished to talk to him about?" She picked up a basket from the floor, extracted a snarl of yarn and began pulling it apart, winding the free end around her hand, in a patently artificial show of unconcern.

But there was nothing counterfeit about Bonnie Morlen's reaction when she learned that her son was dead. She doubled over, yarn-tangled arms wrapped about her mid-section as if she had received a physical blow. Her breath came in short gasps, then seemed to cease completely. She might have been strangling on her horror. Koski looked helplessly at McIntire over her head. Why hadn't they thought to bring the doctor? McIntire racked his brain for what he knew of treating severe shock. Nothing at all.

The slam of a door came from the back of the house, and steps sounded in the kitchen.

"What the hell is this mess? If you have to indulge in these house-wifey pursuits, you could at least clean up decently." A short silence followed, then, "Bonnie, I've told you…." The door swung open.

Wendell Morlen was lean and tanned. He was dressed in neatly fitting tan trousers and wore a tweed sport coat over his casual shirt. His expression of annoyance changed to one of confusion, and he covered the length of the room in a half dozen strides.

"Bonnie, what's happened?" His gaze darted from his wife to the sheriff's uniform. "Is it Dan?" He knelt before his wife and gripped her arms. "He was old. He had a great life. You know how he's been since your mother died." Mrs. Morlen shrank as if she'd been struck and again struggled for air. He shook her slightly. "Bonnie, please! Stop this now! He wouldn't want you to carry on like this."

She released her breath with a great outrush and a violent twist out of his grasp. "It's not Daddy, you greedy bastard. It's my baby!"

In the vacuum of silence that followed, she rose to her feet and turned to the sheriff. "Please take me to my son now."

# VIII

*Her father...lived in the splendor of her glowing existence.*

The pine tree–climbing-wagon, with Pete Koski at the wheel, rolled into the yard and made an about-face that sent the Barred Rock hens scuttling for cover. McIntire dumped the dregs of his coffee into the sink and grabbed his coat and hat from the chair by the kitchen window. The sheriff stood by the open car door kneading the small of his back—if anything about Koski could be called small. As McIntire watched, he bent at the waist, first back, then to each side, and finally forward to place his hands on his knees. This posture he held for so long that McIntire wondered if he might be stuck there. At last he straightened up, completed the ritual with a few fascinating hip rotations, and stuffed himself back into the car. All this did not bode well for the constable. If investigating this death was going to involve frequent trips to the Shawanok Club, McIntire had a pretty good idea who might be doing it. He could hear it now: *You wanna take a run out to the Club, Mac? You're a hell of a lot closer than we are.* When Koski's back started to protest, and there were mundane errands to run, McIntire seemed to live a hell of a lot closer to the whole county. But, come to think of it, he'd much prefer making this trip on his own to going as Sheriff Koski's silent, and considerably narrower, shadow.

He closed the screen door behind him, careful not to let it bang shut. Leonie was still sleeping, not an unusual circumstance. His wife considered anyone who rose before ten hopelessly provincial. "I know," she'd say, "if I wanted to avoid provincial, I've married the wrong man. But I do what I can to maintain some standard of gentility."

Nor had his aunt yet emerged from the spare bedroom—his own childhood sanctuary—where Leonie had so eagerly tucked her in with that ominous, "Now, dear, we expect you to stay as long as you like."

When he'd returned home the previous evening to find Siobhan stretched out on the wine-colored plush sofa with the venerable spaniel, Kelpie, warming her feet, and smoke rings dancing over her head, recognition had been immediate. She might have walked out only the day before. Except for the web of fine wrinkles that lent her forehead the patina of crazed pottery, the impish face was much as it had been when he'd last seen her, when she was nine or ten years old. She was still slim and straight and her curls were as red, if not suspiciously redder, than ever.

He'd never known Siobhan well or thought much about her. She'd always been a bothersome, and vaguely sneaky, kid, one he did his utmost to avoid. Apparently this was not the case with Pete Koski. The sheriff eyed the dark red Lincoln convertible parked next to the barn. "Your rich uncle die?"

"Might very well be. The car belongs to my aunt." McIntire yanked in his right foot and pulled the car door shut as Koski stepped on the gas. "She's as alive as ever though, and from the looks of all the baggage she hauled into my house last night, she plans to stay that way for quite some time."

"Your aunt, eh? Pretty flashy car for an old lady."

"Old lady? I don't expect she'd care much for that designation. It's my father's half-sister. She's considerably younger than I am."

The car gave a lurch that left McIntire with a lump on his forehead and a new perspective on Pete Koski. "Siobhan? Siobhan is back?"

"You knew her, then?"

Koski's expression was as close to that of a dream-struck schoolgirl as could ever be imagined on the face of a six and a half foot John Wayne doppleganger. "Yeah, you might say that. Down!" This last was aimed toward the back seat, where the sudden stop had brought Geronimo leaping to attention. "She didn't bring her husband?"

"I understand she's not married at the moment." At Koski's satisfied grunt, McIntire added, "Though, last time I looked, you were."

The road through the trees hadn't gotten any smoother, straighter, or shorter overnight. And the Power Wagon hadn't gotten any easier riding, or faster. McIntire slumped down to keep his head a safe few inches from the roof and changed the subject. "How'd things go last night?"

Bonnie Morlen had insisted on identifying her son's body. After futile argument, the Club steward had turned chauffeur and driven her and her husband, following the sheriff, to the mortuary in Chandler. They'd been accompanied by—they might have guessed—the Club's full-time resident doctor.

"She held up okay when she saw the body," Koski said. "Guibard covered the boy's head, so she didn't see the scalp wound. They don't know about that. They can hear all the details when the autopsy's done. Damned if she didn't faint dead away afterwards, though. When she looked at his stuff."

"His stuff?"

"His personal junk. Wallet, shoes, jacket, that kind of stuff. We asked her to look at it to be sure that everything belonged to her son and sign for it, in case it's needed as evidence. She picked it all up, one thing at a time, said it was all his, and then"—he moved his arm in a sweeping arc—"timber!"

McIntire remembered when he was eighteen years old, entangled in the First World War. The body of a boy from St. Adele, Sandy Karvonen, had been brought into the camp in France where he was stationed. He'd gone to see him, something he felt he had to do. The lifeless body was so far removed from the Sandy he knew, that he felt nothing more than confused incomprehension. Later, back at his job of translating mail for army censors, McIntire had been handed Sandy's final letter to his parents. For the first and only time of that war, maybe of his whole life, he'd cried for hours.

"Things caught up with her, I suppose," he said.

Two cars were pulled off the side of the road near the Club's entrance, each with an unkempt-looking man dozing behind the wheel. When Koski came to a stop at the gate, the drivers woke up quickly enough and galloped to the car. The windows stayed rolled up, Geronimo growled deep in his throat, and the guard limped out and waved them through. The iron gate swung closed behind them with a clang.

"Reporters!" Koski gave the word the inflection he might had it been *cannibals*. Election time was almost four years away, and he could afford to slam gates in faces, or car doors on fingers if it had come to that.

McIntire was more sympathetic. "They've been hanging around all summer waiting for the Big Story. If they can't get Henry Ford or uranium, maybe murder's the next best thing."

"Probably even better."

They were met at the Morlens' door by an elderly man whose exhaustion was evident from the gray circles under his eyes, but who nonetheless had the strength and confidence to flatly refuse them entry.

"My daughter can't possibly see you now. I know this is a backward place, but I would think even here you'd have the civility to allow a mother a little time to grieve for her son."

So this was the Daddy whose supposed passing had filled Wendell Morlen with such poorly disguised glee.

For a moment Koski seemed on the verge of retreating as bidden. Then he looked down from his dominating height and spoke with uncharacteristic deference. "Sir, from all appearances your grandson was murdered. We really don't have time to wait around. We'll try to be considerate, but we'll need some information from your daughter and her husband."

The man kept his foot planted behind the door as if he expected them to bring on the battering rams. "Wendell isn't here. He's gone to make arrangements for the transfer of my grandson's body. And Bonnie's been sedated, so you'll simply have to come back some other time."

He was pushing the door into the sheriff's chest when Bonnie Morlen appeared at his back. "Don't bully the sheriff, Daddy. Come in Mr. Koski, Mr. McIntire." She looked gray and groggy. Her voice was a hoarse whisper, and her words came deliberately, as if speech had been something painstakingly learned instead of coming naturally. "I want to find out what happened to Bambi at least as much as you do." Her father stepped obediently away from the door, but stayed by her side as she wandered, like she was finding her way for the first time, back toward the living room, leaving the men to follow.

A sofa piled with blankets and pillows had been drawn up before the fireplace. Maple logs blazed, belting out heat and sucking up oxygen, leaving the room still and stifling. A sour smell rose from the towel-covered bowl that still sat near the hearth.

Bonnie introduced her father as Daniel Feldman. He nodded but didn't offer his hand, instead picked up a patchwork quilt and bundled it around his daughter's shoulders. She pulled it more closely around herself, sat down and croaked, "What is it you want to know?"

Koski sat quietly for a time before responding, maybe savoring the uncommon circumstance of being offered a chair big enough to hold him in comfort. He exhaled a great sympathetic sigh and began, "Mrs. Morlen, weren't you concerned when your son didn't return home from the dance on Saturday night?"

"No. It's a long drive from St. Adele on bad roads. I wasn't expecting him until yesterday afternoon." She cleared her throat. McIntire winced at the rawness of the sound. "I was making cinnamon rolls. Bambi loved my cinnamon rolls."

Mr. Feldman leaped to his feet and carried the bowl off toward the kitchen.

"Where was he planning to stay the night?"

Bonnie stared at the sheriff for a moment, then responded. "Oh, I guess you wouldn't know. Bambi wouldn't have been here anyway. He's been working this summer with a man from Minnesota, a college professor looking for uranium, Mr. Carlson. Professor Carlson stays in a cabin on the Salmon River. Bambi's been spending quite a bit of time there." She smoothed the quilt over her knee and, with a stubby finger, began tracing its pattern of bell-shaped blossoms. "This was to be their last week. Greg—that's the professor's name, Greg Carlson—has to go back home in a few days. We planned to leave soon, too. We've only been here this long because Wendell has to finish up some legal work he was doing for the Club. It's been taking longer than he expected." She pulled at a loose thread. "Another week or two and we'd have been safe at home. None of this would have happened."

So the victim wasn't just the only son of a privileged family. He was a uranium prospector, too. Maybe the reporters' perseverance was going to pay off.

"How did your son get involved with this crew?" the sheriff asked. "Was it arranged before you came here?"

"It wasn't a crew," she said. She shifted to make room for her returning father and continued, "only the professor and another boy about Bambi's age who sometimes helped, too. My son met Mr. Carlson here. Ran into him in the woods, actually. Bambi was interested in what he was doing, and

Mr. Carlson said he needed someone to help with surveying. It seemed like it might be a good experience for Bambi…at the time."

"And this other boy?"

"He and Bambi were quite good friends, I believe. He lives somewhere nearby, so he didn't stay in the cabin. His name is Ross, Ross…something…. I don't remember. We've never met him."

"Ross Maki?" McIntire asked. He was acquainted with the Makis, having played a few hands of cards with Mike and utilized his sauna on occasion. He knew his youngest son only as an unassertive but amiable young man who sometimes made deliveries for Mia Thorsen. Of late, he had been largely responsible for running the family farm, since his father had broken his leg in a slide off the barn roof. That had happened in midsummer and couldn't have left Ross much time for traipsing around the woods to ferret out uranium.

Bonnie swung her body around as a single unit to address McIntire. "That sounds right. Like I said, we've never met him."

"And the man they worked for?" Koski spoke, and Mrs. Morlen rotated to face him again.

"What about him?"

"Have you met this Mr.…?"

"Carlson. They didn't really work *for* him, they weren't paid. At least Bambi wasn't paid. I couldn't say about the other boy."

"Have you met him?" Koski persisted.

"Oh, yes. He often came home with Bambi for a day or two. To get a bath and a good home-cooked meal." McIntire was amazed to see a definite flush spread over the pallid cheeks. Could even death not dull this woman's pride in her domestic skills?

"Mrs. Morlen," Koski asked, "what about your son's other friends, kids he went around with, kids here at the Club?"

"I can't tell you any specific names, I'm afraid. They're all gone now, anyway. They'd be back in school."

"There must be a few who've come here for hunting season."

"No doubt there are. How would I know? If you want to know who's in residence, ask Baxter. Or knock on doors. What difference does it make who was at the Club? Bambi wasn't." Bonnie's words showed some spirit, if her demeanor did not.

She leaned even closer to the flames. "Mr. Koski, why are you so sure that my son was killed deliberately? You've said you don't know how he died." She swallowed. "He didn't look… injured. Couldn't it have been from some natural cause?" Her fingers found a loose thread on the quilt. "I don't like to think it, but I'm not naive, maybe he drank too much, or perhaps it was some illness that we didn't recognize."

"That could be," the sheriff admitted, "but he was found tied up. He didn't do that himself."

"Someone could have done it as a prank, or it might have been part of a game and Bambi couldn't get loose and died of exposure." She gave a sharp tug on the thread and looked surprised when it snapped off. "It was so cold Saturday night. He wasn't wearing a coat when…when I saw him."

"He had a heavy jacket on when he was found. The doctor took it off. You'd have seen…" Koski's voice trailed off. Remembering Bonnie Morlen's reaction to examining her son's possessions, McIntire guessed. "Of course it's possible that this was an accident. That's why we're trying to find out who he went around with, his friends."

"Friends don't kill people. Maybe you should concentrate on his enemies." Her voice was beginning to tremble and she brought the quilt up to her chin.

McIntire wasn't at all sure of that. Murder was as likely to be committed by a friend, if not more so. The sheriff asked, "Did Bambi have enemies?"

"If what you say is true—that someone murdered him—he must have had, or *we* must have had. Friends or enemies, maybe sometimes it's hard to tell the difference."

"Are you saying that Bambi might have been killed to hurt you and your husband?"

"Well, if so, it certainly worked."

Koski didn't respond, and she went on. "Has the doctor learned anything at all yet?"

"He was still doing his examination when we left. If he finds anything obvious we'll know by this afternoon. He'll be sending samples to the laboratory in Lansing. Those results are going to take a few days."

McIntire noticed the usually blunt sheriff's avoidance of the word *autopsy.* How long did he think he could shield the family from knowledge of the scalping and the fight with Marvin Wall? If they weren't told soon, they'd hear of it some other way.

Koski changed the subject. "We understand that Bambi drove his own car to the dance. What kind of car is it?"

"He'd have been driving a British sports car. A Morgan." Mrs. Morlen turned to her father. "It's Daddy's, really. He and Bambi drove it out from Westchester together this spring, and Daddy left it here for him to use."

Mr. Feldman asked, "Hasn't the car been found?"

Koski shook his head. "Not yet. My deputies are searching the back roads. We need the license number and a description to get the word out."

"It's a dark green color. It won't be hard to recognize. There aren't many of them around." McIntire didn't doubt it. "I'll get you the number," Feldman added, without budging from his daughter's side.

The sheriff leaned back and crossed his legs. McIntire could only imagine what that attempt at a relaxed attitude had cost his back. "Can you tell us about your son, Mrs, Morlen? What kind of person was he? What were his interests? What were his plans for the future? Has he talked about people he might have met around here, other than Ross Maki and this Mr. Carlson? Anything you can tell us will help."

"Bambi was the kind of son any mother would sell her soul to have." Bonnie Morlen's voice choked and she buried her head on her father's shoulder. Feldman folded his arms around her and glared, and Koski gave in. "We'll leave you now, Mrs. Morlen. But we'd like to take a look at your son's room, and can you give us directions to the camp where he stayed with Mr. Carlson?"

Bonnie pulled herself free of her father's grasp, but continued to lean against him. "The camp? The cabin? It's.... No, I'm sorry I can't help you. I don't think Wendell knows exactly where it is either." Her voice choked again. "I'm so sorry. What kind of a mother would let her child go off and live in the woods and not even know where?"

"Bambi wasn't a child, Ma'am."

"I didn't want to let him go! I did everything to keep him here! But he was eighteen. I couldn't stop him, and Wendell thought it would be good for him. He didn't think there'd be any danger, and it would keep things.... I let my own child go...."

"He wasn't a child," Koski repeated.

"He was a child to me. And now he always will be."

The sheriff appeared to be gathering himself to exit his chair. McIntire interrupted.

"Was there some kind of...strife between Bambi and his father?"

Koski's head jerked up, but Mrs. Morlen didn't look surprised at the question. "Maybe a little. Nothing out of the ordinary. I suppose some disagreement between young men and their fathers is to be expected."

"Was it over anything in particular?"

Feldman coughed. Bonnie hesitated and then answered, "No.... No, as I said, only the usual struggle for independence."

The sheriff once again prepared to hoist himself to his feet. McIntire kept going. "Is that why Bambi left?"

"My son didn't *leave*. He was only off working. He came home on weekends quite often. What has this got to do with anything? Are you trying to accuse Wendell of driving my son to his death?"

McIntire didn't really know what his questions had to do with anything. "Certainly not, Mrs. Morlen," he said. "It's only that the more we know about Bambi and the people around him, the easier it will be to find out what happened."

Bonnie Morlen turned to the sheriff. "I'll show you his room." She struggled to her feet and, still rolled in her chrysalis, led them down a short hallway to the stairs. With her foot on the first step, she hesitated, then retreated. "Forgive me if I don't take you up. It's the first one on the left."

Bambi's room had the air of having been readied for a guest who hadn't showed up. It was neat, dust free, and arranged with every comfort a young man could desire, but unused.

A braided rug covered the grey-painted planks of the floor. On pine-paneled walls, a rack of fishing tackle vied for space with a bookcase stacked with boy-oriented classics, Mark Twain and Jack London. In contrast to the unscratched rods, the books were obviously used and, besides the fiction, included a variety of wilderness survival–type manuals.

The closet revealed rows of lovingly pressed chinos and polo shirts. McIntire would bet even the kid's undershorts were ironed. He pulled open a bureau drawer. They were, and each pair was folded in tandem with a dazzlingly white T-shirt. Two framed photographs stood on the chest's top. One was a studio portrait showing a young Bambi, stiff between beaming parents. Next to it was a shot of Bambi, squinting in the sunshine, extending at arm's length a sacrificial offering to the camera god, a shimmering lake trout.

A cursory search of the remaining drawers turned up only a few articles of heavier clothing and a couple of rolls of unexposed film. McIntire turned to the rest of the room.

A pair of prints showing Labradors transporting dead ducks hung on either side of the single window. Over the bed's solid headboard was a shelf massed with highly polished trophies accrued in various athletic activities.

"Holy shit! Would you get a load of this?" Koski stood nose to nose with the disembodied head of a sixteen-point buck. McIntire guessed it was love at first sight. Siobhan move over!

Bambi Morlen had apparently not been without a sense of humor. A gilded medal on a blue and white ribbon hung around the severed neck—first place in high hurdles.

Koski removed the sacrilegious object and placed it on the shelf with the rest of the booty. If there had ever been anything of a personal nature in the room, it had fallen prey to Mama's relentless pursuit of domestic perfection. The real Bambi was more likely to be found in that prospector's cabin.

# IX

*Deep in the wood lay the cottage where the boy lived. A hilly path led to it; mountains closed it in and shut out the sun; a bottomless swamp lay nearby and gave out the whole year round an icy mist.*

The camp wasn't hard to find. McIntire should have realized that Koski would have made it his business to know which of the abandoned cabins in his province were occupied, and by whom.

It wasn't hard to find, but that didn't make it simple to get to. The gauntlet of reporters had grown, and Koski was compelled to placate them by agreeing to make a statement back at his office in the Chandler jail. He neglected to mention that he wouldn't be going directly back to that office, a subterfuge that necessitated driving in a manner calculated to leave the trailing press corps well behind before he turned off onto the track that led to the Salmon River. It wasn't easy. The reporters were not faint of heart. McIntire was, and he willed his bacon and eggs to stay down as Koski fishtailed around mud-slicked corners and took ruts, roots, and potholes head on. Geronimo's rhythmic snoring didn't miss a beat. It wasn't much on speed, but the Power Wagon proved its worth. The tortoise trundled in where hares feared to tread. When their pursuers had been left to continue leaderless into Chandler, Koski slowed to an even more sedate pace. They meandered through a maze of twisted tracks and logging roads.

"How the hell do you know where you're going?" McIntire asked.

"I didn't spend the last thirty years sipping tea at the British embassy."

McIntire hadn't either, but it was a nice thought.

The road came to an abrupt end in a mucky stream bed. A black panel truck was wedged into a semi-cleared spot. Otherwise all was alder brush and stunted cedar.

Koski left his wagon in the middle of the road. He made a careful circuit of the panel truck, Geronimo at his side anointing each tire.

McIntire walked a short distance back the way they'd come. In places, the tread marks of the truck were obliterated, not only by the tracks of the Power Wagon, but by those of a vehicle with a much narrower wheel base. Bambi's Morgan had been here, and gone, since the truck had been parked.

They waded through the mud to the higher ground. A trail took them another quarter mile to a hut of narrow cedar logs, positioned vertically in the Finnish style. It sank into the earth on one side, and its roof was covered with a thick bed of moss. A narrow pillow-ticking mattress, rain-soaked and mouse-nibbled, lay in the weeds outside the door.

The professor was nowhere about, and, after a single thump on the cabin's door, Koski lifted the latch. The interior was too dim to see much and too low to stand upright. They stumbled toward the middle of the room where the roof rose up to meet its center beam. Koski yelped when his head struck a kerosene lantern hung on a nail.

"Good work, Pete, you've found the lights. Got a match?"

The flame flared and smoked. McIntire turned down the wick and let the chimney drop into place. The yellow light revealed a single crowded room, a cast iron stove, unpainted wood table and two chairs, an iron daybed, and a set of narrow bunks built into the far wall. The lower bunk was obviously the source of the discarded mattress. It was heaped only with rumpled clothing. The top one supported a pad similar to the one outside the door, only slightly less chewed, and a rumpled army blanket. The space that wasn't taken up by furniture was filled with what McIntire assumed to be the implements of prospecting, among them shovels, a surveyor's transit, and the now-familiar Geiger counter. Both the table and the rumpled daybed were strewn with maps of every imaginable sort: survey maps, topographical maps, geological maps, maps showing vegetation and soil type, and township plat maps. Mingled odors of bacon fat and unwashed socks hung in the air. McIntire unhooked the lantern and put it on the table.

"All the comforts of home. No wonder the boys kept Mama away."

A stifled gasp sounded from the doorway. A sturdy-looking man stood in the opening, a pail of water dangling from one hand and a slingshot from the other, looking as if he didn't know whether to bolt or faint. Koski stepped forward before he had a chance to do either.

"Pete Koski," he put out his hand, "sheriff of this county."

The professor remained in the sunlight long enough to hang the slingshot on a nail and give McIntire an impression of relative youth, a sunburned nose, and eyes a curious shade approximating turquoise. He shifted the pail of water to his left hand before shaking Koski's bear-sized paw. The shock at encountering them had appeared to pass, and, in the dim light, his eyes showed only curiosity. At the sheriff's introduction, he nodded to McIntire and mumbled "Greg Carlson."

Koski said, "We understand that you're acquainted with Bambi Morlen."

"He's been helping me out this summer. What's wrong? Has he gotten himself into some kind of trouble?"

"The worst kind," Koski said. "He was killed yesterday."

Carlson's face went from ruddy to pale, and he shifted his stare from Koski to McIntire and back again. His chest rose, popping open the top button of his shirt.

"Killed? He's dead?"

Koski nodded. "I'm afraid so."

The prospector sagged against the door frame. His eyelids dropped. "Thank you for coming to tell me. This isn't an easy place to get to. Shit! The kid didn't have the brains of a jackrabbit when he got behind the wheel." He stood upright. "Was anybody else with him?"

"It wasn't a car accident," Koski told him, "and we didn't come here just to inform you of the death. Bambi Morlen was found dead in the upper floor of the town hall woodshed. He was bound, gagged, scalped, and had a hole drilled in his skull."

If the sheriff was trying to evoke some stronger reaction with his blunt recital, he got it. Carlson's mouth opened, then closed again. Water began to slop over the edge of the bucket. McIntire took it from his hand and lifted it onto the stove. Koski steered the man to a chair and brushed aside a pile of paper to make a seat for himself on the bed.

"It happened some time during or after the dance at the hall on Saturday night. Were you there?"

Carlson didn't respond, and Koski repeated, "Were you there?"

"Where?"

"Were you at the dance at the St. Adele town hall on Saturday night?"

"No."

Koski waited, and Carlson finally added, "I'm not from around here. I don't really know anybody."

"But you probably knew that Bambi was going."

"I heard about it."

"Did he talk about his plans? It would be helpful to know who he was with, where he was earlier in the day, anything you can tell us."

"I don't think I saw Bambi at all on Saturday. Not after we had breakfast. Bambi sometimes goes home on weekends, but he stayed over because they were going to go to that dance. I expected that Ross—that's Ross Maki—would be here sometime during the day, but I was out early and didn't get back to the shack until around five or six. It was dark. It's not like the two of them were working for me or anything. They were interested in prospecting. Like lots of boys, I imagine. I showed them what I could, and they helped me with the surveying. Quite a bit of the time they just went off by themselves. Most of the time it was only Bambi. Ross was needed at home a lot." He turned to McIntire as if for reinforcement. "They're not kids. I didn't figure I had to be responsible for them."

"No one's saying you did." McIntire took the opportunity to put in a few words of his own. "We want to find out whatever we can about who Bambi ran around with. Did he have any other friends that you know of? Bring any other kids here?"

"I never saw him with anybody else," he said. "Only Ross. They made a pretty strange pair."

"How's that?"

"Well, Bambi's a kind of snobby, city-type kid and Ross is the typical farm boy, hardly speaks English. Bambi pretty much led Ross around by the nose, in some ways. Could convince him to go along with any crazy scheme that came to mind. But he depended on Ross to do anything that took the least bit of common sense. I suppose Bambi was used to having somebody take care of him. He talked big, but he wasn't too well prepared for real life." Carlson smiled a feeble kind of smile. "Bambi had a lot of goofy ideas about woodlore, as he called it. Ideas he got mostly from books. When I didn't have work for him, and Ross wasn't here, he spent quite a bit of time poking around by himself, doing woodlore stuff, I guess. I worried about him at first. I couldn't manage to convince him that getting lost was a real possibility and a real danger, and he never bothered to let me know where he'd be. But he always seemed to make it back to the cabin before dark."

He hadn't made it back on Saturday, and Carlson hadn't sent out any search parties.

"Did you ever visit their homes?" Koski asked.

"Not the Makis. I was invited to the Morlens from time to time. Course they didn't have to twist my arm. What a place. That's the way to live, eh?"

McIntire broke in again. "Makes you wonder why Bambi chose to leave."

Carlson smiled. "I sure wondered that myself, plenty of times. I suppose if you're used to that kind of life, it doesn't seem all that special. Especially if you can go back to it any time you want. Roughing it can be fun, if it's not compulsory." He pulled a red bandana from his pocket and rubbed at the grubbiness on his hands. "I think he really didn't care much for fishing, and when he was home his father figured he should spend half the day in a boat."

McIntire nodded. He could well understand how a combination of boats and fathers could send a young man off to the bush. "Did Bambi say how he got along with his father?"

"Not so well, I think. But he didn't talk much about it."

Koski took over again. "So you were expecting Bambi to come back here last night? Didn't you wonder when he didn't show up?"

"No."

The sheriff waited.

"He might have decided to go home, or stayed somewhere closer to St. Adele, Ross' house maybe. Or tied one on and slept if off in his car."

"Did you go anywhere yourself Saturday, or Saturday night?"

Carlson appeared to be concentrating hard on this one. He didn't look, or smell, like someone whose social calendar was so full he couldn't remember two days past. "No," he answered. "No, I haven't left here in the last week."

In a surprising show of tenacity, he dug in his muddy heels and refused Koski's request to look around his cabin. He was sympathetic, he said, but pleaded the necessity of confidentiality where uranium was concerned. If they wanted to search they'd have to come back with a warrant.

The sheriff wasn't too upset. As they hiked back to their car he said, "If he wanted to get rid of some kind of evidence, he's had two days to do it in already. Besides I've got a date with Marvin Wall. And maybe the car's turned up. You ever see a Morgan?"

McIntire shook his head. "Not that I've noticed." He asked, "What about Ross Maki?"

Koski jumped on it. "Right. Good idea. You know his folks? Why don't you take a run over to the place and see what he's got to say? Once the state police go after these people we won't get a damn thing out of them."

That wasn't exactly what McIntire had intended. Ross could easily turn out to be more than just a source of information. And if somebody was going to go after him, he'd as soon have it be the state police.

# X

*She is of a melancholy, Madonna type.*

A screech of wood on wood was followed by the crash of splintering glass. Mia paused, breath arrested, paring knife suspended. A stream of Nick's favorite frustration-relieving words sounded through the screen door, and she exhaled. He was conscious, anyway. She stepped onto the porch. "You okay, Nick?"

Her husband stood at the base of the ladder, his right hand pinned to his side by his left elbow. He delivered a kick to the shattered storm window. "Ya, ya, I'm okay. I just lost my grip on the damn thing, that's all." He grimaced. "I got a hell of a sliver off it."

"Let me see." Mia took his tentatively offered hand. An inch-long splinter of wood protruded from the base of the thumb. She held the hand in both hers to stop its shaking. "You're freezing. No wonder you dropped it. Come on inside and I'll get a tweezers. Supper'll be ready soon. I can get Ross to do the storms."

Nick snatched the hand away. "I can change the damn windows! I dropped it, that's all." He stuffed his hands into the pockets of his plaid mackinaw and spun around to head across the yard. "I'm going to town to get some more glass."

The hardware store would be closed long before Nick got there, but Mia didn't try to stop him. Nick would manage to find something to occupy his time once he got to town.

She picked the window up from the grass and placed it with the others leaning against the gray asphalt siding. They should be painted before they were put up anyway. Maybe she could do it tomorrow.

The sound of Nick's Dodge puttering off to Chandler had barely faded when another rumbling took its place. A black Ford rolled into the yard with Boy Deputy Cecil Newman at the wheel. What now? Nick had hardly been gone long enough to get himself into trouble. Newman exited the car and yanked off his hat as he walked toward her.

"Hello, Cecil," Mia said. "If you're looking for Nick, he just left."

"Ya, I saw him on the road." His gossamer hair clung to his head like a monk's tonsure where the hat had rested. "It's you I've come to see."

She moved close enough to be looking down at him. "Me? But it's my husband that's the criminal."

His eyes glazed over in confusion for a few seconds before he emitted a forced chuckle.

"Come inside, Mr. Newman. It's too cold to stand out here."

Cecil stood awkwardly by the kitchen door until she pointed him to a chair. She didn't sit herself, but stood over him while she picked up the knife and resumed peeling the potatoes. He coughed, twisted his hat, and coughed again.

She relented and dropped into a chair. No need to work off her exasperation with Nick by intimidating this child. Cecil Newman wasn't enough of a challenge to make it satisfactory anyway.

"You know there was a murder after the dance here on Saturday night?"

Oh lord, how could they be bringing her into that? Unless they thought Ross had something to do with it. "I know a boy died. I didn't know it was for sure murder. But I don't think there's anything I can help you with."

"Mrs. Lindstrom—"

"She found the body. How awful for her."

"Ya, sure it was. But she was at the dance, too, working in the kitchen."

Mia nodded. "She generally is."

"She says that for awhile you were outdoors, behind the hall, that you'd gone out for some fresh air."

"Inge doesn't approve of anyone deserting her post, but I didn't think she'd report me for it."

This time Cecil actually laughed. "She says you went out right after the fight. It would work out to be about the same time the victim, Bambi Morlen, left. We're wondering if you saw anything."

So that was it. "I did see him leave," Mia admitted. "I saw him come around from the front of the hall and go to his car."

"Was he alone?"

"A couple of kids were by his car, waiting for him, it looked like."

"Did you know them?"

"I couldn't really see very well," Mia said. "They were in the dark on the other side of the car."

"Boys?"

"It sounded like a boy and a girl."

Cecil's questions were short and direct. He must have been listening to *Dragnet.* "Could you hear anything they said?"

Mia picked up a potato and resumed her dinner preparations. "No," she said. "I just heard them laughing."

"Okay, then what happened?"

"They got in the car." She concentrated on removing the potato's skin in a neat spiral. "That took a while, it was a kind of miniature car. But they managed to fit in at last, and they drove away."

"Think hard," Newman said. "Did you see anybody else in back of the hall?"

"Well sure, there were a lot of people at that dance. A few of them were hanging around by the cars. Kids mostly, I'd say. I didn't pay much attention."

"Did you notice Bambi talk to any of them? Even just say hi?"

"No. I didn't see him with anybody except the kids he left with." Then Mia remembered. She put down the knife once again. "He did talk to somebody though. Before he came around the corner of the hall, before I could see him, he said hello to some woman—sort of."

"Sort of?"

"Well, he said it in a kind of sarcastic way. Said 'Good evening, Ma'am' and then he laughed."

"Who was the woman?"

"I don't know. Whoever it was kind of huffed like she was startled. But she didn't say anything back or come around the corner to where I could see her."

Cecil screwed up his mouth and rubbed his baby-smooth chin. "But," he asked, "if you didn't see either of them while they were talking, how do you know that it was Bambi you heard? Couldn't it have been somebody else? Maybe Bambi coming around the corner at that time was a coincidence. Did you know his voice?"

Mia shook her head. "No, I'd never seen or heard him before." So how did she know? "He said something like, 'Good evening, arriving a little late, *Ma'am?*' and then laughed. He was still laughing when he came out where I got a look at him."

"You think the person he was talking to must have been a grown-up woman? Could Bambi have called a girl, ma'am? As a joke, maybe?"

"I guess he might have," Mia said. "I don't know. I never met the kid."

"Never?"

"Of course not. Why?"

The deputy leaned back in his chair and looked into her eyes. "When I asked if you saw him leave, you said yes. You didn't ask for a description or anything. How do you know the young man you saw leaving was Bambi Morlen?"

Cecil Newman might not be quite so naive as he looked. What could she say? *I knew it was the boy who died because the side of his head was covered with blood from the wounds he was going to get later that night?*

She stood and picked up the paring knife. "I don't know," she said. "I'm just guessing."

# XI

*Many were in great want, but life was often*
*made easier by a light and glad temper and an*
*inborn hardiness and capability.*

The ax came down with a crack, and Grace Maki dropped the
pullet onto the wood chip-strewn ground. A yellow tiger cat
leapt gleefully upon its severed head. McIntire averted his eyes
until the fowl's mad flopping ceased and Grace had reached
out with a long hook to snag one of its unsuspecting mates
by the leg. She held the second doomed bird by the feet and
pointed McIntire to a low-roofed henhouse.

Inside, her son industriously forked manure into a rusty
wheel-barrow. His energetic digging stirred up a fine, acrid
dust. He wore a faded plaid muffler covering his mouth and
nose below swollen, red-rimmed eyes. His friendly "Hi. Pa's out
in town," demonstrated that he had temporarily forgotten that
aside from being a neighbor and Pa's partner in the occasional
game of whist, John McIntire was St. Adele's version of a law
officer.

McIntire's "I wanted to ask you a few things about Bambi
Morlen" obviously reminded him. His hand shook as he
stabbed his fork into the earthen floor and stepped outside.
Ross Maki was not very tall, but his thin frame gave him
an awkward gangliness. With his bristly hair and oversized

clothing he had always put McIntire in mind of a cheerful scarecrow. Today he more closely resembled Sad Sack of the Sunday comics.

He pulled the scarf down around his neck. "I don't know who killed Bambi. If I did I'd of told somebody."

"Were you at the dance on Saturday?"

"Sure."

"So you saw the fight?"

Ross nodded.

"Did you see what started it?"

Here the young man hesitated and the pink of his eyes spread to his cheeks. "I think Marve might of been bothering one of the girls."

"And Bambi decided to put him in his place?"

"No. I mean, it was Marve started the fight. He went nuts, lit into Bambi like a wild man."

"Without provocation?"

"What?"

"Had Bambi done anything to get Marvin mad?"

"He might have said something to him, that's all."

"Something about bothering Karen Sorenson?"

"Yeah." He blew his nose on the rough wool of the scarf. "Marve's got a nasty temper. He carries a knife. Someday he's gonna hurt somebody."

"When did you last see Bambi?"

The flush grew to encompass the boy's forehead and throat. So was there more to his previous blushing than his gentlemanly sensitivities over Karen Sorenson's plight?

"He left right after the fight."

It didn't answer McIntire's question, but he followed it up, "And he didn't come back?"

"Well," Ross responded, "he must of got back sometime if he ended up in the woodshed."

"Did you see him return?"

"No."

If McIntire was getting more out of Ross than the state police could, he was going to quit paying his taxes. Maybe he needed to go at it differently. "Did you notice anybody going into the shed during the dance?" he asked. "Did any of the kids spend time there?"

"Are you out of your mind? It was cold, and there ain't any lights in the woodshed. Why'd anybody want to go there?"

Ross Maki was either not particularly imaginative or an Oscar-level actor.

"Did you and Bambi drive to the dance together?"

"No. I took Ma over early to set up. I helped out some, but I had to come home to do the chores. I didn't get back there until about nine-thirty."

McIntire went back to his unanswered question. "What about later? Did you see or talk to Bambi anywhere after he left the dance ?"

After more coughing, spitting, nose blowing, and a further change of complexion, paler this time, Ross lifted up his chin and looked McIntire in the eye. "Well, I saw him...ya."

"Where?"

"I went with him. When you kicked...when he left the dance. He dropped me off home."

"Did he take you straight home?"

"Ya."

"So you got home about what time?"

"Early, maybe eleven-thirty or so."

"Did Bambi say he was heading back to Carlson's camp after he dropped you?"

Ross' shrug and sudden interest in his cracked work shoes opened McIntire's mind to new possibilities.

"Was anybody else with you?"

McIntire had to lean down to catch the boy's response. "Karen Sorenson."

More new possibilities. "Was Karen Bambi's girlfriend?" McIntire asked. "Were they going together?"

"No! She wanted a ride home, that's all."

"Who did Bambi drop off first?"

"Me."

McIntire fell to studying his own shoes. He hadn't talked to Karen that night. He'd been unready to embarrass both the child and himself by questioning her about Marvin Wall's attentions. If he'd been the snoopy busybody that he was elected to be, could he have prevented this death? He didn't want to think about it.

"Can you think of any reason somebody'd want to kill Bambi Morlen, somebody besides Marve Wall?"

Ross looked toward the darkening sky as if for inspiration, then back down at his shoes. "Well," he said, "other Indians...Adam Wall maybe...they wouldn't like the way he beat up Marvin, and maybe they'd have other reasons...."

"What other reasons?"

"How would I know? I just said *maybe* they'd have other reasons." He blew into his hands and rubbed them together. "Bambi had a lot of money."

That was something McIntire hadn't considered. There'd been a few dollars in Bambi's wallet. "You mean he was carrying money with him? Are you saying he might have been robbed?"

"Nah, I just mean he was rich. Rich people are always getting killed for their money."

Unless Bambi Morlen had a scheming wife or a bunch of greedy nephews hidden away somewhere, that didn't have a hell of a lot of relevance. McIntire gave the boy a light clap on the shoulder. "The sheriff will be wanting to talk to you, so try to see what more you can remember."

As he turned back toward the house he saw the curtain on the kitchen window drop. Seconds later Grace Maki emerged out the back door.

"Stopping for coffee? I just made fresh."

McIntire would have accepted gratefully even if he hadn't been as anxious to talk with Grace as she obviously was with him. His outdoor interview with Ross had left him chilled to the core as well as mystified. He could see that Ross might believe his friend had been killed by Marvin Wall, but why these other Indians with their other reasons?

His shoes, already caked with mud from his walk to Carlson's camp, now had an aromatic overlay of chicken manure, but Grace waved away his move to leave them on the kitchen steps. "Oh, don't bother with that. I haven't mopped yet today."

Or this month, McIntire guessed. Grace Maki did not participate in the competitive housekeeping that occupied so many of her neighbors. She led McIntire through the porch crowded with shelves of tools and bric-a-brac to the kitchen table, swept aside nails, soda crackers, and magazines, and poured him a cup of what he would have assumed to be tea if she hadn't told him different. But it was hot, and he held the cup near his face to absorb the warmth of the steam.

Four paralyzed chicken feet protruded from a bucket on the floor. A blue enamel canning kettle filled with water simmered on the stove.

"Isn't it a terrible thing about that boy? Do you have any idea who did it?"

McIntire shook his head. "I was hoping your son might remember something helpful."

"Ross is pretty down in the mouth. Bambi and him were like brothers, you know."

"I heard they spent a lot of time together—looking for uranium, right?"

Grace gave a throaty chuckle. "Pie in the sky, I know. But it's supposed to be out there, and I guess Ross has as good a chance at finding a big heap of it as anybody. Better, maybe, with the professor to show him what's what."

McIntire hadn't heard of anyone finding so much as a teaspoon of uranium, let alone a heap of it, but he couldn't blame Ross for looking or Grace for hoping. What did families like these live on? Sell a little cream for pin money and eat what they could raise, McIntire supposed. But you couldn't raise chickens or pigs without feeding them, and that took money. Mike Maki hadn't been able to do much since he'd taken that dive off the roof in July. And he hadn't pulled a paycheck since being laid off from his wartime job at Ford's glider plant.

"Had they come across anything promising?" he asked.

"To tell the truth I thought they might of. Ross started acting pretty excited about a month ago, not saying anything for sure, but dropping a few hints, you know. With Bambi gone, though, I guess that's that. Ross needs to find something. He'd like to stay here and keep on farming, but there's no future in it." Tiny spatters of blood made an intricate trail across the once-white daisies of her apron. "I feel it was an act of God that he wasn't with Bambi, and didn't end up dead, too."

"So Ross came home from the dance early?"

"Well, we didn't get out of there until about one-thirty, maybe closer to two. Ross was already in bed by then." She gave an indulgent motherly shake of the head. "I tripped over his shoes when I came in the door. The sauna was hot so he'd been home for awhile. He said he came home early because he wasn't feeling so good. He did look kind of *kipia* all day yesterday. I didn't ask any questions, but I wasn't born yesterday. Well, maybe he learned a lesson."

McIntire had never seen Ross looking anything but *kipia*. The lid on the canning kettle began to bounce. Grace slid it to the rear of the stove, grasped one of the birds and dunked it into the scalding water. Then she lifted it out, slapped it on the table, and began stripping it of its feathers. The aroma of wet chicken feathers is nothing, McIntire knew, to compare with the sickly odor unleashed by the evisceration process. It was getting darker, and after determining that her husband's recovery was progressing satisfactorily, McIntire left Mrs. Maki to prepare her dinner in solitude.

# XII

*Why so many words and so much perplexity?*

McIntire took time for one more stop before heading home. The windows at the front of Mark Guibard's blue-painted house were dark, but the glow of a back porch light spilling across white sand and inky water told him the doctor was at home.

McIntire tapped on the door and went in. He found Guibard, as he'd expected, in the darkened living room seated in a chair drawn up before a window. Outside, a trio of raccoons tussled over a pan of table scraps. They reminded McIntire of overweight rats dressed for winter, but the doctor seemed enthralled by their activities. He waved McIntire to a chair and waited until the creatures toddled off with the last morsel of chicken skin before switching on a lamp and getting to his feet.

"I suppose you want to know every gory detail."

"Suppose again. Just give me the highlights. What did he die of, some kind of poisoning?"

Guibard walked to the kitchen and returned with a glass. He poured in a carefully measured three fingers from the bottle on his chair-side table and handed it to McIntire. McIntire accepted it with much greater anticipation than he did Grace Maki's coffee. The doctor, as a self-proclaimed reformed teetotaler, compensated for years of abstinence by buying, as he put it, "excellent booze."

Guibard added a dollop to his own glass, took a sip and sat down. "I can't be positive until I get some test results. But if I was forced at gunpoint to give my opinion, I'd go out on a limb and say that the contents of that boy's stomach showed enough *Lobelia inflata* to knock over a horse."

"Lobelia what?"

"Inflata. Old Sadie LaPrairie used to take a dose of it for everything that ailed her, smoke it even. I'll never forget the smell. Couldn't stand it. But it isn't all that strong. The smell, I mean. Bambi had to have had a real pile of it to be able to detect the odor. And to make the stomach contents alkaline as they were."

McIntire nodded. He'd expected as much.

"There wasn't much in his stomach," the doctor went on, "a few bites of ham, some brandy, microscopic bits of leaf and the definite odor of a variety of lobelia commonly known as Indian tobacco."

"*Indian* tobacco? This is starting to sound like a bad joke." Not that McIntire felt much like laughing. "I figured it must be some kind of poison that killed him."

"Well, it wasn't."

"Now you lost me."

"Lobelia takes a long time to act. And it's a powerful emetic. Anybody consuming lethal levels would probably upchuck it before it did much harm. Regardless, Bambi Morlen died before he absorbed enough of it to have an effect."

"And, of course, he did vomit some of it up," McIntire remembered.

"Somebody vomited, but it wasn't Bambi."

McIntire waited. Guibard sipped his drink and returned his glass to the table.

"There was no sign that anything that boy ate went any direction except down. The person that puked on the floor in that loft wasn't Bambi. But whoever it was might also have partaken of the poison." He paused. "Possibly."

"Then what did kill him?"

"He bled to death."

Now McIntire put down his glass. "How'd you figure that? I didn't see a drop of blood except on his head, and you said he was already dead when that happened."

"The bleeding was internal."

"His brain?"

"John! No, not his brain. He was stabbed. A small wound in his back, only a bit of a poke. It closed up right away, but the weapon nicked the pulmonary artery. He bled to death internally. Seeped to death is more like it. It might have taken quite a while. He could have been up walking around in the meantime. For sure, he put his coat on after he was stabbed. It didn't have a hole in it. He maybe lived as much as an hour, possibly more, depending on how active he was. Might not even have realized he was injured until he started getting woozy."

"Not realize it? Wouldn't the fact he'd just been stabbed in the back give him a clue?"

"There's not a lot of sensation for pain there. He'd have probably felt the whack, but not necessarily know it was anything more than a blow. "

"So it might not have happened in the woodshed?"

"No. It could very well have happened somewhere else. If he was active, say walking, or involved in a struggle with his attackers, he would have bled quicker. But if he was just sitting in a car, driving...who knows? Like I said, the rest of it—the binding and gagging, the mutilation—all that was done some time after he died. There was no bruising or scrapes from the cords and no sign that he'd put up any fight against them. Anyhow, the way they were tied a two-year-old could have gotten free."

McIntire figured he was, after all, as thick as Guibard took him to be. All was not being made clear. After a short hesitation McIntire asked, "You said something about a hole in his skull?"

"Not quite a hole, but it was like I figured. Someone tried to drill right through the bone using a bit brace. The human skull is pretty tough though. Whoever did it may not have put a lot of effort into it. At any rate he didn't make much headway, so to speak."

"Your unfailing sense of humor is a marvel." McIntire didn't want to think about that hole, inflicted after death or no. "Did you find anything else of importance, a few stray bullet wounds, maybe evidence of strangulation?"

Guibard laughed outright. "Well. He did have a bit of abrasion on his neck, but I doubt it contributed to his death. Unless the young lady responsible was one of those women scorned."

McIntire felt another twinge of guilt. Karen Sorenson again.

"So," the doctor continued, "all you and your fellow Keepers of the Peace have to do is find out who poisoned Bambi, who stabbed him, and who tied him up and tried to drill his head like a coconut. Maybe you'll get lucky and they'll be one and the same."

"When you put it that way, it sounds like a mob attack." Bambi probably hadn't been out of the woods often enough to make an awful lot of enemies, or friends either for that matter. Had he met Karen Sorenson before Saturday night? Was she the object of a long-standing rivalry between Bambi and Ross Maki? "But the drilling," he asked, "can you think of any reasonable explanation for that hole?"

"Shit, no. I can't even think of an unreasonable one." Guibard drained his glass. "Aren't you going to ask me the time of death?"

"Could you get an idea of the time of death?" McIntire was obedient.

"Hard to say. It would have been down close to freezing in that shed when he died, but it heated up good during the day with the sun on the roof. Body was cold. Rigor had mostly passed off. I can say that he died some time in the night. At least an hour after he was last seen, but two or three hours before sunrise."

"I'm more interested in the weapon, the *stabbing* weapon, that is."

"I can't tell you that either. It was small. The wound was a little less than three inches deep and narrow—a simple puncture, some pretty heavy bruising around the edges. Something with a thin blade and a very sharp point, used with a considerable amount of force. Not a knife."

"An ice pick?"

"You've been listening to *The Shadow* again, I take it. Why is it always an ice pick? I don't think I've ever even seen an ice pick. I'm not even sure what one is. Well, I suspect this *was* some kind of household implement, but I can't think what."

"Not something you'd bring along on purpose if you were planning to commit murder?"

"I'd say not."

"But poison…poison sounds premeditated."

"That it does."

McIntire sipped the last drop of the brandy. When an offer of a refill wasn't forthcoming, he got to his feet.

"Thanks for the information, Mark."

Guibard didn't escort him to the door. "Don't mention it. And, by the way, Pete's been griping about his back again. I expect he'll be finding you very handy to have around for the next few weeks."

# XIII

*Do you think that you have to lie stiff and
stark with a coffin lid nailed down over you to
be dead?*

Four cups of coffee might be overdoing it, but McIntire felt
the need for externally imposed courage, and it was a bit
early in the day to break into his meager store of liquor. He
pushed back his plate and stood to get the pot from the stove.
Keeping his back to his wife he spoke in as casual a voice as
he could muster. "Has she said anything about how long she
intends to stay?"

His query fell into a chasm of silence, and he turned to
find Leonie staring at him over her pan of chokecherries with
the anticipated wide eyes and dropped jaw.

"John, she's your family! You've hardly spoken a word to her
since she arrived. I've never known you to be quite like this.
What's going on? Are you only getting crotchety and more
anti-social than ever, or is there something about Siobhan
herself that you don't like? You haven't seen enough of her that
she could have done anything to offend you, and now you're
wondering when she's leaving. You might at least spend an
hour or two with your aunt before chucking her out!"

"Murder kind of eats into my time."

"That murder can get along without you. It's not your lookout."

Leonie's response was unlike her, and unfair, in McIntire's opinion. Well, maybe it was unfair of him to saddle her with the total responsibility for the entertainment of his aunt. He sat down. "I'll try to be more hospitable, but after all, Leonie, I hardly know the woman. Matter of fact, I *don't* know her. The Siobhan I knew was a child, and not a very pleasant one at that. Always sneaking around. Snooping. You never quite knew what she was up to. I still don't."

Leonie didn't comment, only tilted her pan to let a small river of fruit tumble into an aluminum colander, picking out the odd bug and dried leaf as she went.

"And she might not have *offended* me—well, that perfume she wears is pretty obnoxious—but you have to admit it's getting damn annoying the way she's taking over the place. Stockings in the bathroom, half cups of cold coffee all over the house, and…." He picked up the ashtray piled with lipstick-coated cigarette butts and dumped it in the trash.

"A shabby habit or two doesn't necessarily mean she's up to something" Leonie looked pointedly at the mountain of books and papers McIntire had shuffled into a pile and stacked on a kitchen chair. "Maybe," she said, "there was something lacking in her upbringing." Her smile faded, and she looked into her husband's eyes. "Or perhaps it's simply that she reminds you of your father."

McIntire choked and narrowly avoided demonstrating further his hereditary slovenliness by spraying a mouthful of coffee over the oilcloth-covered table. "No, my dear Freudetta, she's nothing at all like Pa. She doesn't look like him and doesn't act like him. If she was like Pa, she'd be right here, telling you don't know what the hell you're doing and making that jelly herself!"

"She did leave me with a few basic instructions last night."

McIntire laughed. "Well, rest assured that she doesn't remind me a bit of my father. The fact is she's the very image of his mother, and I was crazy about my Granny McIntire, so there goes your theory."

"Well, I can't quite work that out. It's true, the Irish do all sort of look alike, but why should she particularly resemble…" Leonie's forehead crinkled, "her father's first wife?"

It hadn't struck McIntire before that perhaps some of his antipathy toward Siobhan might have its roots in her connection to the grandmother he'd loved so dearly and lost when he was so young. He found there was still some soreness in the memory. "Siobhan's mother was my grandmother's sister," he said. "When Grandma was dying, she made Grandpa promise to take her body home to be buried in Ireland. He didn't do it, but he did go back to visit her relatives. When he came home a few months later, he had a new wife, Grandma's baby sister, Bridget. And shortly after that—real shortly, if you get my drift—Siobhan was born, the most spoiled kid on the planet."

Leonie held a dish towel to the edge of her pail and waited while a fat black beetle climbed onto it. "John," she said, "I never dreamed you had such an interesting family. It's like a radio soap opera." She carried the towel to the door and flicked the beetle into the bushes. "I don't have to be Mrs. Freud to see your difficulties. Grief, betrayal, and a big helping of jealousy as well."

McIntire had no chance to respond; the phone on the wall jangled and he jumped for it. "Mac, Koski here. The plot is thickening, as they say. I just got a call from Baxter, the caretaker, pardon me, the *steward*, at the Club. Morlens' got," McIntire waited while Koski chose words to send out over the six-party phone lines, "something they'd like us to see. I figured maybe you could go pick it up and bring it in. I'd send Cecil, but I think you'd handle it better. And you're a damn sight closer."

McIntire noticed Leonie's curious stare and tried to look exasperated. "Sure, okay, I can go. Did you get anything out of the other kid?"

A faint click sounded on the line, followed by a hollow hum. Koski responded, "Nothing much, I'll let you know when you come in. Make it as quick as you can. I've got a date to play strip cribbage with the mayor's wife this afternoon." He was rewarded by a muffled squeak and a louder click.

Leonie carried her strainer of cherries to the sink. "You're going to that Club?" she asked and looked up as the floor-boards creaked in the bathroom overhead.

McIntire nodded.

"I wish I'd known. I could have baked something."

"It's all right. The autopsy's done. I imagine the Morlens'll be taking off before the day's out."

She nodded, then said, "I'm sorry, John."

"Sorry about what?"

"Ah," she smiled. "A man with poor eyesight, *and* a short memory. I am truly blessed!"

She turned on the tap. A feeble stream trickled out over her berries. A humming in the pipes signified the filling bathtub. McIntire couldn't be sure, but he thought he detected a tiny sigh of irritation. He bent to kiss his wife's forehead. "Have a pleasant day," he told her.

Only when he was traveling along the road that separated the Club's pastures from its potato fields, did he begin to speculate on the nature of the article he would be collecting. If it was something found in the Morlen cottage, did that mean it pointed to a member of the Club, even to a member of their own household?

A vehicle came toward him out of the light fog, careening around a bend in the road. McIntire swung the wheel and swerved toward the ditch. The paneled truck he'd seen at Greg Carlson's camp screeched past with the prospector himself at the wheel. Carlson waved apologetically but didn't stop or slow down. Paying a condolence call? Turned back at the gate? Fleeing an irate Daddy? McIntire's stomach clenched at the image of Bonnie Morlen wrapped in her anguish before that stifling fire, waiting alone.

Death was supposed to be followed by a flood of obligations major and menial, calculated over the centuries to keep a bereaved family temporarily numb to its loss. The Morlens sat here in Northwoods limbo. No parade of neighbors with spice cakes and tuna hotdish to feed a horde of shirttail relatives; no funeral; not even their son's body to grieve over. Well, they should be getting that soon, and then, no doubt, as he'd told Leonie, they'd go straight back to Connecticut. Then what? How would an investigation proceed with the main players fifteen hundred miles away?

The news vultures had moved on. Only the geriatric guard leaned against the gatepost, his pipe dangling from his teeth. He swung the gate open and, with a nod and a scowl, allowed McIntire to pass through.

A ruddy-faced woman who introduced herself as Mrs. Baxter—"My husband is steward here."—answered his knock at the cottage door, and took him through to the front room.

Bonnie Morlen was an afghan-swaddled silhouette before the gray rectangles of windows. Her first words confirmed his speculations.

"Wendell has gone with my father to see the sheriff and arrange for taking my son home. We'll be leaving as soon as we can. May I offer you some coffee?" Her voice was flat and her manner detached, as if she'd reached the limit of what she could feel and had shifted onto some other plane.

McIntire declined more coffee. She moved to the sofa and switched on a lamp at its side.

"It came in the mail this morning." She didn't touch the letter that lay on the coffee table, only sat down stiffly, her eyes locked on the scrap of paper as if it was some disgusting tarantula poised to attack.

McIntire pushed his glasses up onto his nose and leaned over the single sheet. The note was composed from printed material, single letters, entire words, and phrases cut from newspapers, magazines, and typewritten copy. A few letters stood out. Larger than the rest, brilliant yellow on a black background, they'd been snipped from the familiar wrapping of a bar of Palmolive soap. The note informed the Morlens that if they ever hoped to see their son alive, they should leave $17,525.00 behind the old lighthouse at St. Adele on Wednesday. Wendell Morlen should come alone at midnight. If there was any "funny business" Bambi would die. It was signed *Seeker of Justice*. Such a cliché should have been nothing more than a joke.

The paper was cheap, the kind that came in a large pad with an Indian in a headdress on the cover and sold for five cents at the dime store. Paper mainly used by children. McIntire slid the sheet away and straightened up. "Do you have the envelope?"

Bonnie Morlen turned to the hovering Mrs. Baxter, who hustled to a spindly drop-front desk and returned holding a white envelope by its corner.

"People usually come to my husband's office to pick up their mail, but as soon as I saw this, I brought it straight over. I thought it looked funny." She dropped it onto the table next to the letter. "I tried to be careful, because of the fingerprints. Can you get fingerprints off paper?"

"Sometimes," McIntire said. He didn't really know for sure, but he doubted that whoever had gone through all that cutting and pasting would have been so careless as to leave fingerprints behind. The envelope was addressed in the same manner as the letter had been pieced together. *Mr. and Mrs. Wendell Morlen* was cut from typewritten copy. *Shawanok Club* and *Michigan* came from newsprint.

So it looked like Ross Maki might have been right. Bambi had been killed for his money.

"Have you heard anything yet?" Mrs. Morlen asked. "Anything about how…about the results of the autopsy?"

McIntire might be a lackey for the sheriff, but he wasn't going to be the one to impart autopsy information to a bereaved mother. "It was done yesterday," he hedged. "Mr. Koski will give the details to your husband. He most likely wouldn't want to do it over the phone."

"We don't have a telephone. The Club doesn't allow them. Baxter went in to Thunder Bay to call the sheriff about this." Her hand fluttered toward the letter. "Mr. Koski didn't tell him anything about the autopsy, but he said that they found Bambi's car last night. It was off the road, back in trees, several miles from the town hall where he was found. They think he was convinced, or forced, to drive there and...." She shook her head as if to clear away the fuzz. "But why would kidnappers have killed him, and so soon? It doesn't make sense. We'd have paid. We'd have paid anything."

McIntire had to agree. It didn't sound reasonable. But then kidnappers might be somewhat less than honorable or reasonable. They could have bargained that the ransom would be paid even if they offered no proof that Bambi Morlen was still alive. The cords that bound him weren't well knotted and Bambi hadn't struggled against them, so Guibard thought he hadn't been tied up until after he died. The stabbing was only a poke, according to the doctor. Something to scare him into compliance, without intent to do major harm? But what if, after that poke, and by the time they got him into that loft, Bambi was already too weak from loss of blood to put up a fight? And had then died on them? They might still have taken a shot at collecting the money. The fatal wound was deep and delivered with considerable force, but, unless the killer was extremely knowledgeable about human anatomy, it was largely chance that Bambi had died from it. Likely it hadn't been an act planned in advance. On the other hand, there was no way the poisoning could be construed in that light, although if Guibard was correct, Indian tobacco was also unlikely to cause death.

Bonnie hugged a crocheted cushion to her breast. "He must have been so terrified. I've been thinking maybe he was so scared he couldn't live with it; maybe he simply died of fright." There was an eeriness in the monotone voice and dullness in her eyes that were so at odds with her words and the emotion that must have inspired them.

In two world wars McIntire had seen fear do a great many things to men. But, while there were times that it might have been a mercy, he'd never known anyone to die from it. Maybe he should tell her the truth. Let her know about the stabbing and get it over with. Mrs. Baxter was here. They had that doctor.

"Bambi was a pretty tough young man, Mrs. Morlen," he said. "It took more than a scare to kill him."

The pillow dropped to her lap and a transient spark of life leapt into her eyes. "You knew my son?"

It was a bit late to deny it now. McIntire tried to sound offhand. "I spoke to him during the dance. Only for a few minutes."

Mrs. Morlen wasn't to be put off. "In the line of duty?"

There was no point in equivocating. "Your son was involved in a fight," he told her. "There's usually a mix-up or two at these dances. No one takes it too seriously."

It was not a good choice of words. She sounded not so much angry, as uncomprehending. "My son gets in a fight and dies, and no one takes it seriously? Why wasn't I told about this?"

"It was only a minor scuffle. He wasn't hurt at all. I don't think the other boy got near him."

"Was *he* hurt then, this other boy?"

"Slightly," McIntire said. "He wasn't the kind to make a fuss over it."

"What did you do about it?"

"I sent them both home."

"Bambi never got home."

McIntire nodded.

Mrs. Morlen placed the pillow squarely on her knees and looked into McIntire's eyes. "Let me understand this. My son got the better of another young man in a fist fight. You kicked him out and when he left, *somebody* ran him off the road, abducted him, and killed him. Why wasn't I told this before?" she demanded. "Do you see no connection here?"

McIntire had been seeing that connection since he'd first viewed Bambi Morlen's mutilated head, but the note on the table had changed things. "That letter took time to piece together. The kidnapping wasn't done on impulse."

Somewhere inside the zombie shell, Bonnie Morlen appeared to be reasoning well enough. "So maybe the fight was planned in advance, too," she said. "My son could have been baited into getting involved so he'd have to leave before everyone else…and he'd be alone."

It was true. Someone planning to abduct Bambi would have a better chance being unobserved if they did it early. If he'd been left to leave on his own, when the dance broke up, the roads would have been crawling with possible witnesses. Not a bad theory, but not borne out in reality.

"But it didn't happen then, Mrs. Morlen. Bambi didn't leave by himself. He gave Ross Maki a ride home."

"So Ross Maki was the last person that we know was with him before he died?"

"No, he wasn't. Bambi took Ross straight home. When he dropped Ross off, your son had a girl with him."

Bonnie silently traced the stitching of the pillow for a moment before speaking again. "Have these people been interrogated? Does that sheriff know what he's doing?"

"Koski and the state police have been questioning everybody that might be even remotely connected to your son," McIntire said. "I talked to Ross myself."

The look on Bonnie Morlen's face clearly demonstrated her level of confidence in the constable's powers of detection. "So it would seem that Bambi was abducted by someone he knew, someone he trusted?"

"But that could be most anybody. Your son would have had no reason to think he was in danger. If he was approached by a stranger asking for a lift or some help with car trouble, he'd have probably done it without thinking twice."

McIntire used the tip of his index finger to pull the note closer. "It seems kind of strange, asking for such a definite amount, seventeen thousand—."

"What difference does it make what the amount is? Seventeen million won't bring my son back."

"Still, it's a very specific amount and that might have some significance. Something that might lead to a particular suspect." It also might be significant that the extortioners hadn't found it necessary to combine numbers from more than one source to request the $17,525. It had come as a unit. Of course they could have typed some of the words, and those numbers, themselves, before snipping and pasting. "Do you have any idea what the amount might signify?"

Bonnie shook her head. "I can't really think now."

McIntire tried to sound in command. "The details of this note should probably be kept quiet for the time being. Has anybody else seen it? Greg Carlson?"

"What? Why? I don't know what you mean."

"Greg Carlson. Did you show him the letter?"

"It only came a few hours ago. I haven't seen Mr. Carlson since…. I don't know, it's been some time."

"I met him on my way in. I assumed he'd been here."

Mrs. Morlen was clearly mystified. "Greg was here?"

The steward's wife looked up from her post by the window and cleared her throat. "I didn't think you were ready for visitors," she shrugged. "I suggested he come back another time."

Bonnie Morlen threw aside her pillow and wrappings and struggled to her feet. "Mrs. Baxter, I'll decide for myself what I'm ready for. Please don't do that again."

The chastised woman turned and left the room. Bonnie plodded to the desk and rummaged for a few seconds through its drawers. She came back carrying a manila envelope, a ballpoint pen and a small book. "You can put the letter in this," she said, "and I'll need a receipt."

McIntire dutifully took the book and pen. *Received from Mrs. Wendell Morlen*…what? Ransom note? Threatening letter? *Letter dated October 14, 1950.* He signed it, *J. McIntire, Constable, St. Adele Township, Michigan.* Bonnie studied it carefully, tore off the carbon and handed it to him. She stood for some time staring at the letter, squinting a bit, seemingly reluctant to let it go, as if by looking at it long enough, she could somehow detect the source of the evil that had pieced it together. Finally she shoved it toward McIntire.

"Think if he hadn't been found," she said. "If I'd waited to pay the money and thought I'd have him back, when all the time he'd been dead in that loft." She turned away and selected a length of split maple from the basket next to the fireplace. "Mr. McIntire, are murderers executed in this state?"

"No," McIntire told her. "Michigan was the first state in the union to abolish the death penalty. That was over a hundred years ago."

She gripped the log like a cudgel and pitched it onto the dying fire, not flinching from the barrage of sparks that danced around her ankles. "Thank you for coming," she said without turning. "If you see my husband, tell him to please hurry."

Mrs. Baxter returned with McIntire's hat and guided him through the maze of furnishings. She surprised him by stepping out onto the porch and closing the door behind her.

"Mr. McIntire, I didn't want to say anything with Mrs. Morlen there. Maybe I shouldn't say anything at all.…"

In McIntire's experience, those who expressed reticence were often the most eager to speak. He waited while the steward's wife twisted the doorknob.

"On Saturday night—or Sunday morning, it would be, I think you should probably know…I heard Wendell Morlen's car drive in. It was after three."

That was indeed something they should probably know. McIntire asked, "Does the guard work that gate twenty-four hours a day?"

"Certainly not," she said. "The members have their own keys. Nobody else gets in after ten o'clock. That's why I took notice of a car coming in at that time of the night."

"Did you see it? It must have been pitch dark. Are you sure the car was Wendell Morlen's?"

"There aren't too many people staying here right now with their own cars. Mostly only staff. I recognized the sound of Mr. Morlen's. Ask Sam. He'd have heard it, too."

"Sam?"

"Sam Keller, the guard."

So that was the old coot's name, not one McIntire recognized as an infamous murderer or bank robber, but then he'd been out of touch for awhile.

"Thank you, Mrs. Baxter," he said. "You were right to let me know." He would have liked to add a request that she keep an ear to the keyholes to see what else she could pick up.

McIntire got out of his car and interrupted Keller on his laborious hobble to unlatch the gate.

"Mr. Keller," he said, "I wanted to ask you about Saturday. About anybody who might have gone in or out during the night."

The furrows of wrath on the guard's face appeared to be a permanent fixture. "I don't open the gate at night. You ain't got a key, you don't get in, or out, neither."

"But you sleep here in the gatehouse, I understand. Surely someone couldn't drive in without you hearing them."

"After ten o'clock, worrying about who goes in and out ain't my job. I don't pay no attention." He leaned against the gate and shook his cane for emphasis.

"Mr. Keller, we're not talking about somebody's granny sneaking in after a midnight pinochle game. A resident here has been murdered. Try to remember, did anybody go through the gate late Saturday night, about three or three-thirty?"

Sam Keller straightened his stooped shoulders. "I really couldn't say. And you can tell that horse's ass sheriff if he's plannin' to send somebody out here, they ain't gettin' nothin' out of me, so he might as well not waste his Goddamn time."

McIntire assured Mr. Keller that he'd pass that information along.

# XIV

*You were all beauties, ever bright, ever young,*
*ever lovely and gentle as a mother's eyes as she*
*looks down upon her child.*

A light mist had begun falling, droplets of liquid ice that were somewhere between fog and honest to god rain. John McIntire, driving a non-tree-climbing Studebaker, decided to exercise discretion by staying off the most primitive of Koski's shortcuts and made for home on a road that at least had been intended for cars. As he rolled through an intersection, he glanced at his gas gauge. Less than a quarter tank, not enough to get him all the way into Chandler. If he wasted a few hours by running out of gas maybe Koski would get off his royal backside and make the trip himself next time. Well, he'd make damn sure he got his fifteen cents a mile for these little excursions.

He braked and pulled over. He sat for a time, listening to the rhythmic thump of the windshield wipers. Then he switched off the engine and let the drizzle close him in with himself.

Why was he reacting this way? Why was the death of this young man more irritation than tragedy? A major irritation to be sure, but still, he wasn't experiencing the sorrow and outrage that such an event should inspire in any compassionate human being. Were these people and the kind of life they led so foreign to him that he could feel no empathy? Was it some underlying sense of envy? Did the detachment of the victim's mother communicate itself to him?

Maybe Leonie was right, and he was growing self-centered and grumpy. Perhaps it was the deep-seated Scandinavian sense that delving too deeply into the private griefs of others was simply unseemly. His wife was certainly correct about something else. He had no real professional interest in the situation, outside of being a damn sight closer to it than Pete Koski. It didn't directly concern him. A constable wasn't elected to solve murders, and it wasn't like the Morlens were his bosom buddies. There was no reason he should have a personal involvement.

Perhaps that was the crux of his unease. He couldn't stick his nose in if he didn't care, and if he did care, he couldn't keep his nose out of it. He sat in the cell a minute longer, then turned the key and put the car into reverse for the few yards necessary to swing it onto the main street of the hamlet of Thunder Bay—one tavern, a general store, a monster sawmill, a sawmill owner's mansion, and a sixteen-room hotel.

The store also boasted a gas pump. McIntire pulled up to it and got out of the car. A rosy-cheeked girl in a shabby letter sweater that proclaimed her to be *Judy* trotted out and began filling his tank with the requested two dollars' worth. McIntire left her applying a rag to his windshield and went into the cluttered shop.

The pump jockey looked as though she ought to be in school, and possibly she was; the girl seemed to have the ability to occupy two places at once. Here she was, perched on a stool behind the counter, bottle of orange Nehi at her elbow, leaning over a movie magazine. McIntire peered over the rack of paperback fiction to look outside. Judy was gamely swabbing the leavings of seagulls from his windshield.

A closer look at the young lady on the stool, and, in particular, her sweater, told him that this was *Joyce*. "Twins?" McIntire was no dummy.

Joyce tore herself away from the delights of Frank Sinatra and began an elaborate heavenward roll of the eyes, arrested when she reached McIntire's face at close to the elevation of that metaphorical paradise. McIntire smiled, and introduced himself as being from the Flambeau County sheriff's office.

He supposed he should exchange a few preliminary pleasantries before diving right into nosy questions, but what could one say to a child that didn't sound artificial and patronizing? Nothing McIntire could come up with. "You see many people from the Shawanok Club here?" he asked.

"Sure," she answered. "Once in a while. This is the only place between here and Marquette to buy gas."

"They have their own pump."

"That's mostly for the Club trucks."

McIntire hadn't come to talk about petrol. "You probably know that a young man from there died on Saturday," he said. "Maybe you've seen him. Drove a fancy sports car."

"Bambi, yeah."

"You knew him? He stopped here, then?"

"I s'pose he might've been here. He would of had to put gas in that car now and then, but I knew him from the Club. We work there summers, me'n Judy, waiting tables. Bambi Morlen was around for a while, but then he took off and mostly only came back weekends. Is it true then? Was Bambi murdered?" Her eyes showed the delicious morbid curiosity of youth.

"It looks like that could be," McIntire answered. He went on, "Did they allow you…." How could he put this? "Did you spend your free time with the residents?"

"Free time? They worked our hinders off sixteen hours a day. Did the Clubbers let their kids hang around with us lowlifes, you mean?"

McIntire supposed that's what he did mean. He nodded

"They didn't like it much, especially any boy-girl thing, you know. But," she gave a meaningful cough, "they couldn't watch us all the time."

"Did you get to know Bambi Morlen, enough to get an idea of what was he like?"

Joyce screwed up her nose. "Well, a little. I practically dropped dead when I heard he was staying somewhere back in the woods in a camp. Bambi was *not* the outdoorsy type. He tried to make out like he was a real whiz at sports, tennis and swimming…softball, that kind of stuff. He was a show-off, but mostly stood around griping about mosquitoes and flies, and he didn't like fishing or taking the boats out."

Chalk one up for Bambi.

She sipped from her bottle and giggled. "Once he put a chipmunk in Mitzi Haggerty's underwear drawer. She about died." She pursed her lips in a sugary smile and bobbed her head. "Course being one of their little darlings, *he* didn't get in any trouble."

"He got caught then?"

"He got caught hiding under my sister's bed so he could take a picture when Mitzi opened the drawer. Judy almost got canned for letting him in the girl's dormitory." The mincing smile came again. "But not our darling little Bambi." She drained the pop. "Well, he swore Judy didn't know a thing about it. So he wasn't so bad, I guess. Too snooty to suit me, though. He always had that camera with him, drove everybody nuts worrying about *composition* and *lighting*." This was something new. "He used a lot of big words, and he wasn't very…thoughtful, you know."

"In what way?"

"He didn't care much about people's feelings. Mitzi wasn't so scared by the chipmunk, but she was only wearing…." She paused and a flush spread up her cheeks. "She wasn't quite dressed, and she has a big birthmark on her back. It's shaped kind of like a rabbit. Bambi teased her about it afterwards and made her cry. It was in the dining hall where everybody could hear. Typical stuck-up rich kid—thought his shit didn't stink."

"Aren't all the Club kids rich?"

"They're not all stuck-up. Some of them are nice guys." Another blush indicated that she might have had a specific nice guy in mind.

"Would you know any kids that Bambi especially hung around with?"

"Naah. He wasn't there that much, and when he came home he usually had that guy with him, the one he worked for. They always stuck together."

"Not always." The bell over the door jangled, and Judy scooted in, shaking off water and blowing on her hands.

"What?"

"They weren't *always* together." She took the bills McIntire proffered for gas, and the dime for two Milky Way bars, and punched the keys on the cash register.

Joyce shoved her magazine aside. "Cripes, I never saw Bambi turn up without that guy. They were like...twins."

"Maybe so, but the guy did turn up without Bambi."

"He couldn't. He's not a member. What are you talking about?"

"I saw him." Judy turned away to hang her dripping jacket on a coatrack by the door. "He was poking around down by Deer Horn Lake. All by himself. No Bambi."

"And just what were *you* doing at Deer Horn Lake?"

"Fishing."

"Well, now isn't that just ducky?" Joyce responded. "And with who, may I ask?"

"Never mind."

"Bruce! You jerk! Did you pretend you were me? What did he say? What did you *do?* You better tell the truth or—"

"Wrong!"

Joyce's eyes narrowed. "There's nobody else at the Club that would give you...and what would your precious Dougie say if he knew you'd been fooling around with a...?"

Judy's only response was a smug smile, and Joyce let out a squeal that left McIntire's ears ringing. "Gads, you sneaked him in! You could of got us fired!"

The conversation was fascinating, but McIntire broke in before the two came to blows. He'd had more than enough of battling adolescents, and this wasn't his jurisdiction. "Was Professor Carlson looking for uranium on Club grounds?"

"I don't know if he was looking for anything," Judy said. "When I saw him he was sitting on a rock, writing in a notebook."

"Did he have a Geiger counter?"

"What's it look like?'

Where had this girl been for the past year? "It's kind of like a metal box, about yay big"—McIntire sketched out a foot square with his hands—"with a strap to carry it."

"Nope," Judy answered. "I didn't see anything like that. He had a knapsack, but it wasn't big enough to hold something that size."

"How could he have gotten past the gate?" McIntire asked. "Would Mr. Keller have let him in?"

"Sam might have opened up for him *if* he'd come through the gate. He was used to the guy being with Bambi. But he didn't go through the gate." She lifted her eyes to the ceiling and whistled a short tune before adding, "There are other ways."

"Sure, you *would* know!" Her sister exploded. "He could of come in the same way you sneaked Doug in. You coulda got us fired!"

Judy blew on her fingernails and rubbed them on her shoulder. "You're just jealous."

"Jealous? Of you and that pimply-faced creep?"

McIntire figured it was time to leave.

# XV

*He must go, the good son who had never given
his parents a sorrow.*

Maybe one more coat. It was a waste of time and energy, she
knew. The polish job was as near to perfection as she'd ever
done, and more wax wouldn't add a smidgen to the depth of
the wood's luster. But it was an excuse, something to keep her
sequestered here in her workshop, wrapped in the comforting
scent of wood shavings and the warmth of the fire. Something
to keep her out of the house.

The feeling was a familiar one. It came every fall, when
the unused rooms grew cold and the creak of their shrinking
floorboards echoed through the house, a sorrow that crept into
her life with the regularity of dropping leaves and migrating
geese.

She should have long ago passed the stage where those
empty rooms were a mocking reminder of loss and failure.
She should by now be reconciled to the knowledge that she
herself would be the final child to take its first steps on that
kitchen floor. Well, she could always die soon, and give Nick
a chance to marry some fertile young thing and fill the place
with a covey of Italian babies. It was dopey that the thought
still caused such an ache. And pointless. Right now there
might well be little Nicky Thorsens romping over half the
state of Michigan. To her horror, Mia felt tears stinging her

eyes. She wiped them away on her sleeve and picked up the jar of wax.

Maybe it was only that she was getting older. No children when she was twenty-five meant no grandchildren now. When she was gone there'd be nothing left of her in this world, except the occasional blanket chest and clock case.

She spread the paste evenly over the walnut surface and capped the jar. Papa's secret recipe. Not a secret any more, but it still smelled as bad as ever, a combination of skunk and sauerkraut with a hint of stale sweat.

The geese in the yard set up a squawk, and Mia crossed to peer out the door, grateful for the distraction. Ross Maki walked up the drive. He had the determined stride of one who is afraid that, if he slowed down for a second, he'd change his mind and head back the way he came. He looked like he'd lost his best friend, which, she remembered, he had. He also looked completely exhausted. The past months of running a farm, as well as doing her bidding and trying to make his fortune in uranium, had taken their toll.

"Come on in, Ross. Close the door to keep the dust out. I have to buff up this final coat. But it's done at long last. You can make the royal presentation to *Madame* Hollander on Saturday. I only wish I could be there for the unveiling."

The boy stepped inside but made no response other than a tiny nod, and Mia regretted her brusqueness. "If you feel up to it," she added.

"I've been drafted."

It didn't come as a surprise to Mia, as surely it hadn't been to Ross. Nevertheless it was a shock, partly because of the realization of how much she'd come to care about him. She'd miss him—his willingness, his habitual expression of bewilderment, and the sudden smile that could wipe it away.

"When do you have to go?"

"A few weeks. The middle of November. I can still take the clock to Dearborn."

"I didn't mean that," Mia said. "The clock's not important. *Madame* has waited six months. She can hang on a little longer. But Ross, you must have known for a while now. Didn't you tell anybody?"

Ross shifted from one foot to the other. "No, only...well, no." Of course, he'd told Bambi Morlen. "I told Ma this morning."

"Oh, your poor mother! How's she going to manage without you? Maybe you could get some kind of a hardship...dispensation, or whatever it is, get out of going for now."

"Nah," he said. "Pa's doing okay. He still limps some, but he's getting around fine. He just got in the habit of not doing much." There was a two-inch hole in the sleeve of his mackinaw, and he began pulling at the frayed threads. "Anyway, I want to go."

Mia laughed. "Oh sure, I can see that."

"I might as well go. There ain't no reason for me to stay around. I'll be glad to get out of here."

Ross might be right about that. And it wasn't like he had any choice in the matter. Maybe taking an optimistic view was for the best. "At least the business in Korea is about over," she said.

"Pa says it ain't." Ross sounded anything but optimistic. "He's got plenty of time to listen to the radio and read the papers. He says Tibet is only the beginning, and the Red Chinese are gonna be trouble."

"Tibet?" Mia asked. Oh lord, was there something new?

"They invaded Tibet. Pa says it's just a start."

Mia hadn't heard anything about that. The papers all said the war was over. She couldn't believe Mike Maki knew more than the president. She hoped not, anyway. "Well," she said, "not everybody gets sent to Korea."

"Almost everybody."

"Just don't volunteer for anything."

"Not me! I don't want to die. But...."

"But?"

Ross lifted his eyes to her face, then looked down, bit his lower lip, and coughed. "Do you think that maybe…in a war or something like that…. Well, not everybody dies…."

"No, some are only maimed for life."

He didn't smile, and why should he? Mia pledged to herself once again to learn to curb her gallows humor.

He nodded earnestly. "But some aren't hurt at all. Do you think it could be that it's not just luck? There *has* to be some people dying—in a war, I mean. Do you think maybe God takes the ones that need to be punished…the ones that have done something really bad?"

"Are you saying that soldiers who are killed might be ones that deserve to die?" Was this really coming from someone supposedly mature enough to become one of those soldiers?

"Maybe…something like that."

"What about the good-die-young theory?"

"Bambi wasn't all that good."

Bambi? Bambi had hardly been killed defending his country.

"You think Bambi Morlen's death was punishment?" she asked. "Punishment for who? Bambi's in no pain now. It's his family, his mother, and his friends, that are suffering."

"I suppose." The young man didn't sound convinced.

"Ross." Mia waited for him to look into her eyes before continuing. "Ross, even though I'm an ancient gray-haired crone, I don't know quite everything. But I can tell you this for sure, death doesn't play favorites. It takes the totally innocent right along with the wicked." It was a truth she knew for damn sure, but not something she cared to dwell on. She patted his arm. "But if you want advice about magic charms and avoiding curses, you'll have to go to Lucy Delaney."

This time Ross did laugh. "I think Lucy only *puts* hexes on people. Pa's still suspicious about how he came to fall off that roof." The smile transformed his face and once again he was the Ross she would miss so dearly. "Maybe that's what happened to Nick," he said. "He probably passed by Lucy without offering her a ride."

Brother, what next? Mia kept her voice light. "What kind of fix is Nick in now?"

"He's gone in the ditch, over by the old sawmill. That's why I'm here, for the truck and a chain."

"Well, you know where they are."

Ross nodded and stepped out the door, but Mia stopped him in his trek toward the toolshed. "Ross," she said, "you knew Bambi Morlen better than anybody around here. Do you have any ideas about what happened? About who might have killed him?"

Mia immediately regretted asking. Ross Maki's face resumed the hangdog look, and he went back to enlarging the hole in his sleeve. His words were almost lost in his turned-up collar.

"He got in that fight with Marvin Wall. Marve can get pretty wild when he's crossed. And there's his brother. They say Adam Wall did a lot of killing in the war." He lifted his head and shoved his hands in his pockets. "He made it back in one piece though."

Only when the young man was rattling down the driveway in her delivery van, did Mia begin to wonder what Ross himself might have done, or felt he'd done, that was so bad as to sentence him to death in battle. She did seem to recall that he walked off with a plate of food at the dance without paying the twenty-five cents.

# XVI

*You can never know how angry a man is*
*to the bottom of his soul when he hears of a*
*woman's infidelity.*

It was midafternoon when McIntire's car chugged up the hill
to the Flambeau County sheriff's office. The drive from the
Club had taken nearly two hours and had left his beloved
Studebaker Champion mud-spattered and once again low on
gas. A disconcerting clatter issued from its nether regions. A
loose muffler was the only theory McIntire, with his minimal
automotive experience, could come up with.

The parking area behind the courthouse was crammed
with vehicles, including, in a far corner, an alien-looking low-
slung two-seater that could only be Bambi Morlen's Morgan.
A disheveled-looking man walked slowly around it, snapping
pictures with a battery of cameras hanging from his shoulder.
He turned at the sound of McIntire's slamming car door, stared
for a moment, and loped for the courthouse steps. McIntire
followed with a sinking feeling as to what this reaction to his
arrival might augur.

The sheriff's outer office had been stripped of its furniture,
leaving only a gray metal file cabinet and coordinating desk.
The desk was strategically stationed before the door which
was closed on Koski's inner sanctum, and Marian Koski, her

duties as the sheriff's wife extending beyond the domestic, sat behind it, telephone to her ear. She waved McIntire to come through.

He plunged into the swarm of uniformed officers and eager-faced youngsters clutching notebooks.

Clayton Beckman, owner, editor, printer, and chief reporter of the *Chandler Monitor*, leaped into his path. The rest of the troop formed up behind Beckman, pencils at the ready.

"John, is it true that the sheriff has some new information?"

Beckman obviously had not taken time to shave or to partake of a swig of Lavoris that morning. McIntire backed out of exhalation range. "I might be able to tell you that after I've seen him. So if you'll just let me…."

McIntire didn't suppose the man stayed in business by letting himself be intimidated by township constables; the editor moved in again. "You've talked to the victim's mother. How's she holding up?"

Had the grimy state of the Studebaker given him away? A headful of brown hair, limp and dandruff-dusted, appeared at Beckman's left shoulder, and a feminine voice broke in. "Is there any truth to the rumor that the body was mutilated?"

The clamor in the room was shut off like a tap. Every eye turned to McIntire. Pencils were poised. The restrained elation was palpable.

It would be for the best if the whole story came out before the mutilation took on far greater proportions than the removal of a couple square inches of skin. But that wasn't McIntire's job.

He looked down at the young woman. "The boy was left dead. That constitutes mutilation in my book." The pencils dropped, and a quick sidestep got him through to Pete Koski's office.

It was nearly as jammed as the reception room. A third of the space was consumed by the scratched oak desk that ordinarily faced the smaller one out front. It wasn't often the sheriff wished to lock himself away from his constituents.

The desktop was usually concealed by the tattered map on which Koski plotted out his fishing expeditions. Today the map stood in a corner, rolled and fastened with a rubber band. The desk was a cliché of overflowing ashtrays and dribbly coffee cups. Koski sat surrounded by a cluster of men standing or seated on straight-backed chairs. The only one McIntire recognized was Wendell Morlen. Haggard, rumpled, and clearly agitated, he started up when McIntire entered. "It's about time!"

Sheriff Koski took the envelope from McIntire, removed the note and handed it to the bereaved father without reading it.

No one moved while Morlen squinted at the paper, then spread it on the desk, produced a pair of spectacles and stood to read the message. The chair screeched and slid across the floor as he dropped back into it.

"The sons-a bitches! How did those bastards think they'd get away with pulling shit like this?" He bellowed again, "The sons-a bitches!"

The murmur of voices outside the closed door ceased.

A stocky man with the insignia of a Michigan state police lieutenant on his hat—a hat held up by the biggest pair of ears McIntire had ever seen on anything not of pachyderm persuasion—spoke into the silence. "You know who wrote this?"

"Yes, I sure as hell know who wrote it." The rage in his eyes faded to bewilderment, and again he rose from the chair. "But why would they go after *me?* I only work for the place." He extended the letter to the lieutenant, his hands shaking so the paper rattled. "What you said…about Bambi's head…. God! The bastards!"

The policeman studied the paper and handed it to the sheriff. "I don't understand. How can you tell from this—?"

"It's the money," Morlen said. "So we'd know. He wanted us to know…."

Koski herded Wendell Morlen back to his chair. "Take it easy, Mr. Morlen. What is it?... who is this *he?*"

Morlen leaned back and took several deep breaths. "Like I told you, my family has been here because I'm handling some legal transactions for the Club. One of those transactions involves the purchase of a section of land, twelve hundred some acres. It started out complicated and has gotten more so. There's a dispute over ownership. Most of the property is state land, tax forfeit. But there is a claimant saying that he should have first rights to purchase it at the value the state sets."

"Seventeen thousand, five hundred twenty-five dollars."

Morlen nodded.

Koski picked up the phone.

"We'll need to talk more about this, Mr. Morlen."

"Just make it quick. Shit, it's all a matter of public record. You don't need me. I want to get out of here. I want to take my son home."

McIntire had remained silent through the entire exchange, and maybe now wasn't the right time to speak up. And he probably wasn't the right person to do the speaking up. But in a matter of hours, maybe minutes, Wendell Morlen would be long gone.

"Mr. Morlen," he said, "a witness at the Club says you came in late Saturday night, or rather Sunday morning, about three o'clock."

Three superior levels of law enforcement glared, and Morlen looked genuinely confused. "The eagle-eyed Mrs. Baxter, no doubt. Well, she'd better get those beady little eyes checked. She's wrong."

"She was pretty positive. Says she recognized the sound of your car."

"Then it's her ears need looking into. I spent Saturday night in Lansing. I came home on Sunday. You were with the sheriff at my cottage when I got there."

Pete Koski managed to nod to Morlen and send McIntire a ferocious *What kind of bullshit is this?* message at the same time.

But Lieutenant Dumbo was all business. "Witnesses?" he asked.

"Shit, yes, there are witnesses. I went with Jim Harrington. We met with half the lawyers in Michigan."

"Did you take your car?"

"We took the train from Marquette. Jim drove from the Club to the depot. And he drove us back on Sunday."

"Could someone have used your car while you were gone?"

Morlen shrugged. "The keys were in it. I guess anybody could have taken it. Maybe somebody borrowed it. You'll have to ask my wife."

"Could your wife have been driving it herself?" McIntire chimed in again.

Morlen looked like he'd bitten into a rotten apple. "You'll have to ask her," he said.

# XVII

*Others may listen to tales of lovers and sun-
shine. I choose the dark night, full of visions
and adventures, bitter destinies, sorrowful suf-
ferings of wild hearts.*

Siobhan's Lincoln was gone, and the house was blessedly silent.
Even the pall of cigarette smoke had lifted. McIntire lit the
burner under the coffee pot and lifted the lid from the cookie
jar. Peanut butter, his favorite. Leonie hadn't made them
before. He took a tentative nibble. When his wife attempted
something new it was always best to be cautious. He smiled.
His own mother couldn't have done much better. Taking up the
pot, a cup, and the cookie jar, he settled himself in the dining
room with *The Story of Gösta Berling*. It was time to begin.

McIntire had never taken on such an ambitious translating project before. He'd never done much of any work that
fell into the realm of literature. But the small jobs he did for
the defense department weren't enough to keep his hand in
or to put much stimulation into life since retirement. He'd
always said when he retired he'd do something *real*, something
important. This was as good a place to start as any. He'd put
it off long enough.

He'd read it long ago and hadn't found it to be the world's
most exciting piece of fiction. A year in the life of a nineteenth-

century Swedish settlement, although quite a frenzied year, at that. Maybe his past year in this community would give him a new perspective on it, a greater appreciation of these stalwart Scandinavians to whom anguish and guilt seemed to be mother's milk. Perhaps the title character, the defrocked priest, and his exploits could chase some of his own demons away. At least the systematic process of converting one tongue to another might clear his brain to think more logically about some of what he'd learned today.

Bonnie Morlen said that her son had become acquainted with Greg Carlson when he'd met up with him in the woods. That must have been on Club property. Why would a uranium prospector be poking around on the grounds of the Shawanok Club? There'd be no chance of developing a mine there. And he hadn't had his Geiger counter with him when Judy had seen him. It was remotely possible that he'd wandered in by accident, but unlikely; Greg Carlson was well supplied with maps, and it would take some effort to spend much time on Club grounds without being politely asked to get the hell out. Apparently Carlson had been there on his own more than once.

With the book face down on the table in front of him, he hesitated. Once he began, it was going to consume his life, trespass on his every waking thought. Did he have time for that now? Time? It would be a blessing! He flipped it over and fanned the pages. A word caught his eye. *Förkastad.* Outcast. Pariah. He read, *If you only knew what it means to be an outcast. One does not stop to think what one does.* Was that true in Marvin Wall's case? Was he so cut off from human society that society's rules didn't matter? Lord, it was starting already! With a single word Gösta Berling was insinuating himself into McIntire's life. He turned to page one.

He had barely picked up his pencil when a draft of cold air, bordering on a breeze, swept down from the stairwell. He sighed, stuck the pencil in his book, and trudged upstairs, nearly colliding with the pull-down attic ladder intruding into the hallway. Leave it to Siobhan to walk off with doors wide open. He folded the steps. The springs gave out with a twang.

His actions were greeted with a husky, "Hey, I'm not finished up there!" resounding from below. He let the door pop into its place in the ceiling. If Siobhan had opened it once, it wouldn't be beyond her strength to do it again. What had she been doing in the attic anyway?

He descended to find her in the room that had been his parents' bedroom and was now Leonie's library. As a child, McIntire's visits here had been limited to being tucked into the bed in the daytime on a few occasions when he was sick. Aside from that it had always been off limits, and he still felt the thrill of the forbidden upon entering. He'd never been able to bring himself to work here, despite Leonie's best efforts at a scholarly and masculine decor.

Siobhan stood with her back to the window. Her hair, thanks to either the setting sun or a fresh dye job, radiated with the glow of a new penny. Around her shoulders she wore a fringed shawl that had probably once been equally flamboyant but was now badly faded. She spoke with real sorrow in her voice.

"He's not here."

"No," McIntire replied, "he's mostly at the bar."

He'd known immediately whom Siobhan referred to. And she was right, no vestige of the late Colin McIntire's formidable spirit resided here in his house. It had been a great relief to McIntire when he'd taken over his father's home that he hadn't met up with his ghost around every corner.

"When Pa was alive, he only came home to eat and sleep, and sometimes not even then. If you're looking to get in touch with him, the Waterfront's your best bet."

An aroma of India ink and age sprung from a stack of paper-stuffed boxes on the table. "What's all this stuff?"

"Pictures," Siobhan told him. "Leonie said she didn't mind if I brought them down. Looky, here's you." Siobhan handed him the stiff cardboard-mounted photograph. Indeed, there he was, a stringbean in a doughboy uniform.

"Well now, I figured Pa'd have hung that up in the tavern for dart practice."

"He did put it up in the tavern, *above* the picture of *our* dad shaking hands with John L. Sullivan."

That came as a news to McIntire, and he wondered if it was true.

"John." The melancholy look was still there in Siobhan's Granny Kate eyes. "Colin was so proud of you it could make a person cry, but you never had a good word to say about him, not when you were a kid, and, Leonie says, not even now. I know you didn't always get along, but that was a long time ago. How can you stay so bitter?"

McIntire's reconciliation with his dead father was one of Leonie's favorite crusades. Had she now enlisted his aunt in the cause? "I'm not bitter," McIntire said. "I'm realistic. My father might not have outright hated me, but he came damn close. I was a weakling and a misfit and a complete disappointment to him. If he pretended to be proud it was only to save face."

"You shouldn't have stayed away like you did. You never gave him a chance."

"I gave him seventeen years, and he made every minute of it hell."

"But you left when you were so young, and when *he* was still young. He still had power over you. If you had come back that might have changed. You'd have grown up, and he'd have grown old." She made fists of her tiny claws in her effort to elaborate. "You put him into a kind of suspension...to you, he always stayed just as he was when you were a boy. You never saw him weaken."

"And you did?"

"I saw him sobbing into my mother's dish towels the day your ship sailed."

McIntire flatly didn't believe that. He'd never seen his father anywhere close to tears. Not even when the man's own mother, McIntire's cherished grandmother, died.

The ancient spaniel, Kelpie, toddled into the room. Siobhan lifted the animal in her arms and dropped onto the tweedy sofa and tucked her feet under her body. She stroked the dog's ears.

"Colin was the best brother a girl could ever have," she said, "like a father to me after Dad was gone."

"Ah, so that's why you, too, flew the coop when you were seventeen."

"I was sixteen. By the time I realized my mistake I was too ashamed to come back. I couldn't have expected much of a welcome. But Colin used to talk about you all the time. He made the priest in Aura pray for you every Sunday. It is just so terribly sad that you went away and never spoke to him again."

"Well, as a matter of fact," McIntire told her, "I did speak to him. We spent six weeks together in Ireland in nineteen thirty-eight."

"And?"

"And he was a total stranger to me. But he sure as hell wasn't in any way weak."

Siobhan stood and tucked her gypsy costume around the dozing Kelpie. "Okay, then, let's go."

"To Ireland? It's almost supper time."

"You said I'd find my brother at his tavern. You wouldn't expect an innocent maid like myself to go unescorted? Besides your wife's gone to Marquette in my car."

"For what?"

"She's gone to the nursing home to see Wylie Petworth. I don't know how she can stand it."

McIntire didn't know either. Leonie was about the only person in St. Adele who regularly visited Wylie. Maybe it was easier for her, since she'd never known him well. McIntire meant to accompany her someday. But after all that had happened, seeing his childhood friend locked in paralysis wasn't something he was ready for. Once one admitted to being a coward, life became so much simpler.

Siobhan went to her room and returned carrying an armload of soft brown fur.

"Won't you be a little overdressed for Pa's old beer joint?"

Siobhan placed the cape around her shoulders, gingerly, as if expecting it to go for her jugular. "No point in having it if you don't show it!"

# XVIII

*He came home again without wound or*
*injured limb, but he had been changed for life*
*by the battle.*

The Waterfront Tavern was crowded by Tuesday night regulars, and McIntire was amazingly popular by constable standards. A half dozen men found him a stool in their midst, fixed him up with a Pabst, and began the inquisition. When he came forth with no new information, the unaccustomed attention quickly turned to his exotic aunt. McIntire left Siobhan at the bar, renewing old acquaintances and forming some new ones, and approached Adam Wall where he sat alone in a booth near the back door.

Wall sat up straighter and dropped the dart he'd been twirling between his fingers onto the table. He nodded at McIntire's approach, but he didn't smile. "If you're planning to grill me too, save it."

"Had a visit from the sheriff, have you?"

"The sheriff, two deputies, that state police guy with the big ears. I'm expecting J. Edgar himself to show up any time now."

"I'd have thought it would be your brother they're paying court to."

"Oh, they got Marve scared shitless, but they haven't neglected the rest of the family." He laughed. "Elephant Ears even tried to question Grandma, can you beat that?"

"I find it hard to believe that he could even catch her."

"Cornered her in the pump house. She disappeared in her usual puff of smoke and left him holding his notepad." Adam Wall stood. "Hang on a minute." He picked up the dart, and walked the few yards to the line. McIntire winced when the dart stabbed neatly into the bull's-eye. He'd sent the board to his father from Ireland. A fiftieth birthday gift bought, after interminable nagging and haggling, from the pub in the McIntire family's home village.

Wall came back with two more beers. One bottle he placed in front of McIntire. He always insisted on a glass for his own, and he held it at a tilt to pour the beer carefully down the side.

"Talk is the kid was being held for ransom," he said.

McIntire could see no reason to keep it a secret. It would be common knowledge soon enough. "Morlens got a note in yesterday's mail."

"Asking, I take it, for seventeen thousand five hundred twenty-five dollars."

McIntire felt his jaw drop. Adam grunted, "Pete Koski asked me three times what the amount was that the Shawanok Club was paying for sections nineteen and twenty. I didn't figure he was interested in bettering their offer."

Why Adam Wall should be privy to the real estate dealings of the Shawanok Club was a bit of a mystery. "Wendell Morlen went through the roof when he heard the amount," McIntire said. "Koski hustled him off to a corner to get more information. Are you saying you know what this is all about?"

"It's about twelve hundred acres of land, give or take a few, and two lakes," Wall told him. "The Club boys don't figure their playground is big enough, so they're buying a little more from the state. I suppose I've been the Man of the Hour because I've been trying to throw a few roadblocks in their path."

"Morlen mentioned that somebody else is claiming to have first dibs on it." The light flicked on. "And that someone is...."

Wall gave a modest bow. "One hundred and sixty acres of that lakeshore should be mine."

For an unemployed Indian, Adam Wall seemed to be doing okay for himself. He'd already managed to get one nice hunk of Lake Superior shoreline and was now apparently working on another. McIntire drank from his bottle and waited for the explanation.

"My great-grandfather, that's Grandma's father, was a member of the First U.S. Sharpshooters, in the Civil War. He was also a volunteer scout and made a bunch of forays into enemy territory. They gave him a medal for his services and also a hundred sixty acres of land of his own choosing. He picked the land at the mouth of the Potato River where his family had fished for...centuries, maybe. He lived there the rest of his life. Greatgrandpa died in nineteen-hundred. In nineteen-oh-two, Grandma and her brother sold the land to a member of the Shawanok Club."

"So the land already belongs to the Club?"

"They sold it to a *member*, not to the association itself. The guy who bought it is long dead and it passed to his son, who is also dead. So it belongs to the son's widow. She lives in San Francisco."

"A good story," McIntire commented. "But it doesn't explain why you figure it should be yours. Are you saying Twyla wasn't mentally competent when she sold it?"

"Grandma is competent as all hell. Although I don't imagine she did have any idea what she was signing. But what I'm arguing is that in nineteen-two it was the custom for Indian lands to be held in trust by the federal government. An Indian didn't get title. I'm saying that neither Grandma or her brother had title to the place so they didn't have a legal right to sell it."

It sounded good on the surface. "But if Twyla's father was given the land outright, not a part of an allotment program, is it still considered Indian land?" McIntire asked. "Does simply the fact that your great grandfather was Indian give him no right to hold title to land? Would the government have even known that he was Indian when the piece of land was granted?"

"You should go to work for Morlen," Wall said. "That's what he's arguing, that it wouldn't have mattered. In some ways I'd like to believe that. But there's no record of a deed to the property before it changed hands in nineteen-two. Only a couple of certificates, one signed by A. Lincoln himself."

"Okay, it sounds like a nice piece of land. But it's only a hundred sixty acres out of what? Two entire sections?" Wall nodded, and McIntire went on, "Like you said, over twelve hundred acres. Why's it causing such a brouhaha?"

"It's the northeast quarter of section twenty. That's the only place where the section joins Shawanok Club property."

"So you're saying they have to pay you off to get access to the rest of the section?"

"No," Wall replied. "I'm saying that as an adjoining land owner I have the first option to buy the entire section. At the price the state sets."

"Seventeen thousand five hundred and twenty-five." McIntire understood, at least in part. "But everybody's got to know you don't have that kind of money. So why would the Club be going to all this trouble to...I don't get it."

"Don't matter. They won't see my check bounce until *after* I put in the bid. And allowing me to make the bid is admitting that I have the right to do it—admitting that the one hundred sixty acres deeded to my great-grandfather is legally mine."

"No offense, but why would anybody at the Club, or the state government, be taking anything you say seriously?"

"Just another worthless Indian, you mean?"

McIntire shrugged.

"Well, you're right. I've filed suit with the Indian Claims Commission, but they don't deal with individual claims, only those of tribes. They wouldn't even open my mail, if it was only me. But it happens that when I was off saving the world for democracy, I also saved the ass of one Mikey Sanders.

That's Mikey Junior. Mikey Senior is Federal District Attorney Michael J. Sanders."

"Ah…."

"Ah, is right. I don't suppose it's going to make any difference in the long run. The Clubbers have no shortage of friends in high places. Shit, most of *them* are in high places. That's how they got that ridiculous valuation put on the land, to get it way out of my price range. Sure, they're going to a lot of trouble for nothing. Hell, fifty bucks would of taken me out of the bidding."

"Maybe Lincoln's autograph is worth something."

"Not seventeen grand."

"But if you should be given title to that land…."

"That ain't gonna happen. I'm not looking for justice here. The Clubbers will get the land in the end. But Sanders ain't making it easy for them, and he's making them pay every penny he can. He's kept their hotshot attorney jumping."

"Wendell Morlen."

"Bingo."

McIntire said, "I'm surprised you're not sitting in jail right now. What with the ransom amount, and the fight, and the sca…."

"The what?"

McIntire tried to hide his embarrassment with a long pull on his beer. "You know…the fistfight with your brother and the…evidence…at the scene."

Wall put his own glass down. "So there was something more."

"Bambi Morlen was…in a way…scalped."

"Scalped? Are you saying…?" Wall looked quickly around the crowded room and spoke low. "The kid was *scalped?*"

His usually inexpressive voice was filled with incredulity that sounded not only uncharacteristic but, if McIntire had been forced to make a judgement, feigned.

"Sort of. A feeble attempt anyway. And," there was no point in holding out now, "he had a hole drilled in his skull."

*"Trepanation?"* The table rocked, and McIntire grabbed for his bottle.

"What?"

Adam Wall shook his head. "Nothing…a fancy word for brain surgery. I shouldn't have said it. This isn't a time for joking."

Wall hadn't sounded like he was joking. And Guibard hadn't mentioned any similarity to surgery. McIntire felt a poke on the shoulder. Siobhan gave him an airy wave as she pranced by and swung out the door on the arm of a silver-haired stranger.

McIntire nodded and turned back to Wall. "Is anybody else involved in this little real estate diversion? Other Indians? Your parents?"

"Hell, no! Pa'd be the last one to make any trouble. He promised Ma he'd give up being Indian the day he married her."

"But did he know the amount of the ransom? I mean, know the valuation of the land?"

"Sure, I told him. Are you hinting my old man's a kidnapper?"

"Can't you just picture it? *Charlie Wall, America's Most Wanted.* But your dad does get around, and he likes to talk. He might have mentioned the sale, and the seventeen thousand, to somebody."

"Well, it's not a secret," Wall pointed out. "Anybody might have known. It's a matter of public record."

"But how many people pay any attention to public records? I hadn't heard about this. The Club people probably kept it as quiet as they could. Especially with the price they were paying being so high. No," McIntire said, "I'd be willing to bet that the only people in St. Adele who were aware of the price of that land, or even that it's being sold, are you and your family."

Wall abandoned his scruples and drank the last of his beer from the bottle. "What about Wendell Morlen and his family?"

# XIX

*Women are not so saintly as they seem.*

"Ya, what about Wendell Morlen and his family? Damn good question." Pete Koski pushed himself back in his chair, slamming it against the wall and setting the windows to rattling. "They're about the only ones we're gonna find out anything from, and they've folded their tents and slipped back to Westchester. I told them to keep in touch. That's all I could do. *Keep in touch*. Hell."

"Are you saying you think Bambi's parents might know something about his death?" McIntire took a seat facing the sheriff and tried to find someplace to put his legs.

"They knew Bambi, I should hope…. At least as well as anybody knows a kid that age." Koski's eyes wandered to the desktop photograph of his dark-eyed adolescent daughter, and his massive shoulders gave a tiny shiver. "Knowing about the kid's life might help us figure out why he died. And it ain't like his old man's not involved. You can hardly ignore the seventeen grand that 'seeker of justice' demanded…or the fact that Wendell Morlen came here to face off against Adam Wall."

That seemed way too simple for McIntire. "The ransom business had to have been a ruse of some sort," he said, "a way to confuse the issue or to implicate Adam. He'd never be such a moron as to commit a murder and basically sign his name to it."

"Unless he didn't start out to commit murder. He might have figured he had a way to make his point and nobody would get hurt. You know those people ain't big on thinking too far ahead."

If skill in plotting chess moves was any indication, Adam Wall could think well into the next millennium without so much as a headache.

"And," Koski went on, "it don't look like the kidnapper planned on stabbing the kid."

"No, just poisoning him."

"Well, ya," the sheriff conceded, "there is that."

"Did you have a chance to talk to the parents again before they left?"

"We kept Wendell here all afternoon on Monday and got his wife in before they left yesterday." Koski shook his head. "For such a big shot lawyer he sure can be dumb as a stump when it suits him. Had no idea where his son was staying, what he was doing, why he wasn't back at some swanky Ivy League college…or why that housekeeper heard his car pull in at three-thirty in the morning."

"Bonnie?"

"So she finally admitted, when Ryan mentioned that baby blue Cadillacs aren't all that common around here either, and we'd be asking at filling stations."

"Ryan?"

Koski grasped his ears to pull them away from his head as he continued, "Says she went to Marquette to do some shopping. She decided to stay for a movie and got lost going back to the Club. Ended up on the Triple A road, she says, took hours to find her way out of the woods."

"That doesn't seem wildly implausible to me. Those roads are like a rabbit warren, and in the dark…."

"What's wildly implausible is that Mrs. Morlen would have even been *on* those back roads. Or that she would have gone to Marquette for anything in the first place, when the punch of a button would have sent good old Baxter scurrying to meet her slightest need." His eyes took on an expression both thoughtful and slightly lascivious. "Except maybe one."

"You think Bonnie Morlen was stepping out?" McIntire was dumbfounded. "She hardly seems like the type."

"How can such a man of the world be so naive? One thing I've learned in this line of work, they're all the type." He again cast an uncomfortable glance at his daughter's smiling image. "Did you notice the look on Morlen's face when you mentioned Mrs. B. hearing his car come in? That was not the face of a man thinking, 'Oh, the little woman must have been taking in a movie.' But she must have been telling the truth about driving around for a while. She filled up her tank in Marquette. The kid in the filling station remembered her. She went through an entire tank of gas that night, so maybe she *was* lost."

McIntire remembered Morlen's exasperation over finding a nearly empty gas tank when he prepared to leave the Club on the trip to identify his son's body. He'd been out of cash, and McIntire had paid the four dollars.

"And, speaking of Wendell Morlen," the sheriff was saying, "his alibi didn't turn out to be quite so watertight as it seemed."

"No?"

"No, indeed. He did take the train to Lansing on Thursday afternoon with one James Harrington III. Borrowed money then, too. Harrington lent him the train fare. But they didn't have any meetings after Friday. Our civil servants don't work weekends. After they left the depot, Harrington didn't see Morlen again until they were on the train going home."

"So he stole a car, drove all the way back here, stabbed his son, and got back to Lansing in time to board the train to Marquette?"

Pete shrugged. "Who knows what one of those types might do?"

McIntire knew to which of "those people" categories Koski had assigned Adam Wall, but Morlen?

"Ambitious, dog-eat-dog types."

McIntire nodded. "I guess anything's possible. What do we really know about either of the Morlens?"

Koski pulled a typewritten sheet from the folder on the desk. "This much, for a start. Wendell is the son of a street car conductor. Worked his way through college and law school at New York University. Got a job with a firm that handled Feldman and Levinson, jewelry importers and wholesalers. Then pulled off the big stunt. Married the boss' daughter. In a manner of speaking, anyway. He still works for the law firm, Petry and Bigelow, but hasn't moved up in the ranks much. Was young enough to be drafted into the war, but got out of it, four-F."

"He looks plenty healthy to me."

"Yeah, well, maybe money can't buy health, but it can buy a convenient disability if you know the right doctor." He scanned down the page. "Other than that, not much more to say. He's got a big place in a snooty suburb of New York City, compliments of Daddy. Most of what they have is compliments of Daddy, by the looks of things. Wendell has a good income, but nowhere near enough to live as high on the hog as they do."

"Did Morlen tell you all this?"

"Nah. State police got it." Koski flipped to the next sheet of paper. "I ain't got time to do shit since Billy quit." McIntire wasn't about to make any comment acknowledging Koski's dearth of flunkies, and after a sigh or two the sheriff continued, "Bonnie is the only surviving child of Daniel Feldman. She had a younger brother who died when he was a baby, and her mother died two years ago. Looked like she might have a career as a singer until she gave it up for marriage. Six and a half months later, when bouncing baby Bambi came into the world, it wasn't hard to see why she'd made the sacrifice."

"How'd they get to be Club members?"

"Shit, they ain't members. Like I said, Morlen ain't in the Club league, and all the money in the world wouldn't get Daddy Feldman in. Wendell got to know one of the Club's officers. He hired Wendell to handle that sticky land deal and threw in his cabin for the summer."

McIntire said, "I guess if you have to have in-laws, Feldman's the kind to have."

"You could do worse," Koski agreed. "Funny thing, Daddy was kind of in the same boat as Wendell. He came into his money by marrying it. He's a partner in the jewelry business and makes a ton, but nothing compared to the Levinson estate, which was controlled by his wife."

"What did that amount to?"

"Four or five million." The sheriff reached into his shirt to scratch his chest. "The lion's share of it left by Grandma Feldman in trust to—"

"Her darling grandson."

Koski smiled. "At twenty-five he'd have gotten the whole shit-load."

"Who handled it in the meantime?"

"Feldman. And if Bambi died before reaching the age where he'd inherit, it all goes to Bonnie. The Feldman-Levinson clan liked to keep things in the family."

Maybe so, but Bonnie's inheritance would effectively put a fortune in her husband's pockets.

Koski shuffled the papers into a neat stack and leaned back in his chair. "I see your aunt's still in town."

"You bet," McIntire assured him, "and shows no sign of taking off soon. At least not so long as I have a drop of water left in the well."

"I saw her last night." Koski yawned. "She was with some old gray-haired guy I didn't know."

If the sheriff was referring to the matinee idol type in whose company Siobhan had left the Waterfront, he was indulging in some real wishful thinking.

"Yeah," McIntire said, "I never saw him before last night, but when I mentioned it to Leonie, she knew who I meant."

Koski cleared his throat. "Well, I don't suppose you came here to engage in idle gossip. What brings you all the way to town?"

"I wanted to find out what you heard from Karen Sorenson."

"Feeling a little guilty, are ya?"

For someone who physically resembled the proverbial dumb ox, Pete Koski could be quite perceptive.

"I should have talked to her that night," McIntire said. "I should have found out what started that fight right then and there. But I figured it was only some kids' squabble."

"That's about what it was. Marvin Wall found something that belonged to her, one of those things women have with the mirror and powder in it."

"A compact?"

"Christ, you *are* a man of the world. Anyway, according to Marve he found it on the ground and went to give it back. Bambi saw him talking to her, told him in colorful language to get lost, Marve got mad and took a swing at him, and the rest is…you know what."

"What about later?"

"Karen left with Bambi and Ross Maki. They dropped Ross off and Bambi took her home."

"Immediately?"

"Shit, I take it all back. You're an innocent lamb. No, not our Bambi. He parked at the gravel pit. Made quite a big play. Said he'd be gone soon, and they might never have another chance."

"Did she…er, succumb?" McIntire remembered Guibard's mention of abrasions on the victim's neck.

"I didn't ask. Her mother was there." He snorted. "In that car, I don't see how the hell she could have. But regardless, she's heartbroken now. Figures he must have had some premonition of his own death. And she thought he was just talking about going back east."

"What was her version of the bothering incident?"

"About the same as Marvin's. She was outside with some of her friends, and Marve came up to give her the compact. Bambi came along and made a fuss, and Marve tried to hit him. She was none too pleased with Bambi for embarrassing her that way, said she tried to tell him it was nothing, but he wouldn't listen. Said she left with him and the Maki kid because everybody was looking at her. It was cold at the gravel pit, and they didn't stay long. She also said she left her purse behind in his car."

"Was it still there when you found the car?"

"Nope. It was in the Sorensons' mailbox Monday morning."

"Any idea who put it there?"

"She figured it was Bambi. Except that she says things were all messed up and some stuff was missing. Including that damn...what did you call it?"

"Compact?"

"Ya. It was gone, along with some fingernail junk and a picture of her with a couple of other girls."

"Fingernail junk?"

"For fixing up fingernails—files, clippers, junk like that—in a case."

"So maybe the murderer, or whoever, just threw the purse alongside the road, and some things fell out."

"The picture was in her billfold." Koski swivelled his chair toward the window, and for the first time McIntire could see the lines of exhaustion in his face. "The billfold was still there. She had an identification card in it. It gave her name, and her address, and said who her parents are. Anybody could of left it in the box, and it could of been any time between Saturday night and when Ma Sorenson went out to get her mail on Monday."

"No money taken?"

"She didn't have any."

"I suppose it was checked for fingerprints?"

The sheriff nodded. "The purse and everything in it had been wiped. But we did find a few. Karen's own and one that probably came from one of her girlfriends or maybe her mother. It was small. Too smudged to get a positive ID."

Koski regarded McIntire with an expression of bemused exasperation, and McIntire suddenly realized what he'd been hearing. "I suppose," he asked, "that the fingernail junk included a scissors?"

"You suppose right."

"About three inches long with a slightly curved blade?"

"Something like that. Karen got the kit from Monkey Wards. I got Marian to send for another one."

Was it possible that Bambi died as a result of an ill advised pass at Karen Sorenson? McIntire asked, "Did Karen say what time she got home?"

"Around midnight. Maybe a little later. Her mother backs her up."

"A mother would."

"Well, your switchboard operator, and Karen's friend Diane, and Diane's father who wasn't overjoyed when the phone woke him up at one in the morning, also back her up. So the big question is, where was Bambi between midnight and the time his car ended up off the Townline Road."

"What *did* you find in his car?" McIntire asked.

"Not a hell of a lot. Well, I don't mean that exactly. We did find a hell of a lot of crap. The kid seems to have been living out of his car most of the summer. But there was nothing in it of any obvious significance, as our man with the ears would say."

"What kind of crap?"

"You name it. Clothes, cracker crumbs, candy wrappers, beer cans. Ma wasn't around to tidy up after him."

"Was all the clothing his?"

"Ma says so. And it wasn't the kind of stuff any of the kids around here would be able to afford."

"Anything that didn't belong to Bambi?"

"A few things left over from Feldman." Koski ticked them off on his fingers. "A pair of reading glasses. A couple of programs from concerts that Mrs. Morlen said were probably his. Feldman's a big music fan, too. Plays the violin, she says. That's about it…a tin of aspirin."

"Fingerprints?" Why did he have to ask every single question? Couldn't Koski just once come out with something without his asking?

"Oh, a whole shit-load. Bambi might not have been the most popular kid around but his car sure was."

"The most popular kid?"

"Eh?"

"Never mind," McIntire said. "Anything else? Lipstick on cigarette butts?"

"No cigarettes or butts."

The howl of an angry baby sounded from outside the office door. Seconds later Marian Koski appeared pushing a stroller that barely contained a squirming toddler. "Eileen Kruger would like to talk with you." She stepped aside to usher in an anemic-looking redhead carrying the squalling infant.

"How are you, Eileen? Little shavers growing like weeds, I see." Koski shoved the only empty chair toward the young mother and lifted the child from the stroller to his knee. The boy gave a gasp, and his chin began to quiver, but he made no sound and no attempt to free himself from the giant's grasp. "Seems like only yesterday I used to see *you* running around about this size. How old's the baby now?"

The girl smiled. "Six months." She had a pronounced lisp, making it come out, *thickth month.* "Her name is Caroline."

McIntire wondered if he should leave. Maybe Eileen had some confidential business, but neither she nor the sheriff seemed concerned about his presence.

The little boy bravely whispered, "Horthie," and Koski's knee began a rhythmic bounce. He leaned toward the baby. "Well, Miss Caroline, is there something we can do for you and your mother?"

The child stopped crying and began to suck furiously on its fist. Eileen giggled. "No, not for me. I've come about the car."

The flush suddenly spread up the girl's neck and she waited for Koski's nod before continuing. "The car behind the courthouse. The one that belonged to the kid that was murdered."

The horthie halted in mid-canter.

"I don't know if it's important, probably not, but I thought I should tell you. I was cutting across in back of the courthouse, on the way home from Mom's, and I saw the car, and Cecil was there, so I asked if it was his, and he said no, it belonged to the boy that died, and…. Well, it's probably not anything you're interested in." She started to rise.

McIntire resisted taking her by the shoulders to shove her back into the chair and asked, "What is it, what about the car?"

"I saw it. I was up with the baby Saturday night, or more like early Sunday morning. She's getting teeth, and she's been so fussy. Patrick was such an easy baby. I never missed a night's sleep, but—"

"Eileen, the car?"

"I was rocking Caroline. I had the lights out and the drapes open so I could look out. Sometimes deer come out on the road, and I like to watch." She removed a soggy fistful of her blouse from the baby's mouth. "I saw that car go by."

Koski was oblivious to Patrick's squirming in his tightened grip. "What time was that?"

"Sometime between three and four. She woke up about three, and I know it was past four o'clock when I got back to bed."

"Are you sure it was the same car?"

Eileen stared at the sheriff as if he were indeed that proverbial ox. "It's not the kind of car you see every day."

"Could you see how many people were in it?"

"I didn't notice nothing about who was in it, just the car. It went by, heading toward downtown, and came back again only a few minutes later. I was surprised at seeing anybody drive by so late. Usually it's only the deer."

The infant set up another squawk, and Eileen stood and rested the child on her hip. "I better get her home before she eats her fingers. I was just walking by, and I thought maybe I should tell you."

"You were right about that, Eileen. You've been a big help." Koski popped the toddler into the stroller and wheeled it to the door. "Say hello to your folks."

He returned to his desk and sat staring morosely at its paper-strewn surface.

"What's the problem?" McIntire asked. "You don't look like you've had big help."

"What? Oh," he shrugged. "You know, John, that girl is only two years older than my daughter…and with a husband and a couple kids."

Considering the guard her father kept over her, Marcie Koski would be lucky to ever experience motherhood, or her first date.

"Well," McIntire said, "that pretty much lets Bonnie Morlen off the hook, if she was ever on it. At the time Mrs. Baxter heard her come home, her son was alive and well, tooling around Chandler."

"His *car* was tooling around Chandler. And Mrs. Morlen's claim to have been tooling around in the woods sounds pretty flimsy to me. But what the hell difference does it make? The whole fam-damnly has spit the hook, flown the coop, done a bunk. However you want to put it, we've seen the last of that bunch."

# XX

*The old people were always so careful of the young woman. Never could they bear to hear any evil of her.*

Another murder, the woods full of patriotic prospectors eagerly seeking uranium to make their country's bombs, one more crop of boys being shipped off to die...ah, life. Mia scratched around in the nest of quack grass until she found what looked like the shriveled leaves of a rutabaga plant. She gave a yank. The pale, bulbous root popped up easily. She used the tail of her shirt to wipe off the bulk of the dirt and dropped it into a basket with its garden-mates. That should be the last of them. The harvest of her vegetable patch's feeble bounty was complete. Mia's weed-choked quarter acre was the scandal of the neighborhood, but it generally came through with enough produce to fill her needs. And when she got caught short, her neighbors were only too happy to supply her with their extra.

Leonie McIntire planted flowers—dahlias, glads, chrysanthemums—right in with her squash and carrots and beans. The sight of Leonie's exuberant plot had given Mia her first ever twinges of garden envy. She'd like to try it herself, but she didn't want to be a copy cat.

Anyway she'd have a hard time passing off her garden as being for show. She lifted the basket onto her hip.

Another war—oops, *police action*. How could it be happening again so soon? And this time with a bomb that could wipe them all out in a few seconds, like pouring gas on an anthill and setting a match to it. Poor Ross. Usually there was enough time between wars for the survivors to get old and start putting a romantic gloss over things to prime the next generation. But Ross Maki and his kind wouldn't be so easily bamboozled. Their notion of war wasn't formed by some doddering grandfather spinning tales of adventure, valor, and loose women. They'd seen their own brothers come home, if they'd come home at all, withdrawn at best, often tormented.

What an ungodly pack of fools men were. Mia kicked a clod of earth. Maybe women, herself in particular, were even bigger idiots for letting themselves get so dependent on that pack of fools. She looked at the storm windows, still leaning against the house, shedding flakes of paint into the grass. Her gaze traveled to the delivery van parked next to the workshop, dejected and Rossless.

As much as she hated ladders, she could handle the storms if she had to, but she'd never driven a car of any kind. If she needed something from town, Nick picked it up, or they'd go in together on a Friday night. Most of what they used came mail order. Nick handled that, too.

Mia had always managed to find a willing kid to drive her father's old van to pick up wood and other supplies for her cabinet making and sometimes to deliver the finished product. But they never lasted long. They grew up, got married, went away. Once in a while one of them even found a genuine job. In between she fell back on Nick. And Nick…Nick was starting to show his age.

Mia had faced the fact long ago that her husband wasn't going to grow up. Maybe that was why she'd expected him never to grow old. Nick wasn't always reliable, but he'd seemed invincible. Now the years were catching up with him. The drink was catching up with him. The level of brandy in the bottle was decreasing more slowly than usual, but Nick was showing its effects in ways he never had before. His ending up in the ditch was nothing new, but in the past driving the car off the road had usually followed some extenuating circumstances. Snow, mud, or an early Monday morning. Nothing like that had been going on this last time. And he was getting shaky, stumbling now and then.

She carried the basket of vegetables to the porch steps and walked across to the van. The door gave a screech when she opened it. It could stand a squirt of oil. She smoothed the old rug that covered exposed springs in the seat and slid behind the wheel. An absurd thrill of daring, almost guilt, beat in her chest. Like a high school girl smoking her first cigarette. With one hand on the shift knob, she began ticking off the bank of dials and buttons before her. Gas gauge, starter, choke, speedometer, lights, windshield wipers, heater, radio—ah, those two she could handle—gear shift, gas, brake, or was that the clutch? Horn.

She'd never liked cars much, never liked riding in them and never had the least desire to drive one herself. She could still remember her first automobile ride. Well, why not? It hadn't been all that long ago. Nick had owned one of the first cars around, a Model T Ford bought in 1927 to replace the team and sleigh, and the notorious motorcycle, he'd used on his mail route.

The motorcycle…even that didn't seem so long ago. Her introduction to motor vehicles had been her maiden voyage on that 1909 Indian cycle. They'd been married a week before Nick managed to talk her into it. She made sure there was no one around to see. Nick showed her where to put her feet. She tucked up her long skirt and climbed up behind him, seating herself on the platform he'd had welded on to carry the mailbag. Her knees came halfway to her chest, exposing her spider-thin legs almost to the garters that held up her black stockings. And then the thing took off. The machine shook until her jaws ached from the effort of controlling her chattering teeth. The wheels spit gravel into her eyes. She'd wrapped her arms around Nick's leather-protected chest and promised God that if she survived she'd never again skip her nightly prayers. She'd made it to the lake and back alive and, surprisingly, had always kept the promise. Three decades of marriage to Nick made prayer second nature.

A knock on the window sent her heart leaping and her elbow into the horn. Leonie McIntire beamed in at her, crimson-nosed below her kerchief-covered curls. Mia opened the door.

Leonie leaned on her bicycle, puffing. When John McIntire's fascinating foreign wife had turned up on that bike it had been the talk of the neighborhood. The sight of a middle-aged woman pedaling around the sandy roads had been a source of entertainment for weeks. Now it was only good for the occasional snicker. Too bad you couldn't haul many boards on a bicycle.

"Don't let me hold you up, Mia, if you're off somewhere. Are you having trouble with the lorry?"

"Oh, no," Mia assured her. "I was just…checking things." She got out and gave the hood a knowledgeable pat. "Come on in the house. You look like you could stand warming up."

"I could that, but unfortunately I can only stay a minute, I'm sorry to say. I'm off to get the paper sorted out. I just popped over to see if you have any news for this week."

Mia couldn't help her. No out of town relatives visiting, no birthdays. She and Nick hadn't even taken that Friday-night trip to Chandler. "Afraid not, Leonie. You'll have to depend on more sociable people than me for your headlines." It wasn't unusual for Leonie to pop over to get her latest news. Though she usually called first, to see if it was worth her while. Mia wondered what this unannounced visit might mean.

They walked together to the front porch. Leonie leaned the bike against the rail and sat down on the steps.

"But what about you?" Mia asked her. "Do you have news? Have they found out anything about the murder?"

"Not that I've heard. The Morlens took their son's body home on Wednesday. They went on an airplane. John's been running himself ragged for the sheriff, pretending to hate every minute of it. They still don't have a new deputy to replace Mr. Corbin."

Leonie removed her kerchief and gave her blond curls a thorough fluffing. "I feel a bit mean to say this, but I do wish John had more time to spend with his aunt. She's come all this way, and he hardly does more than nod to her. I do my best to entertain her, and it is nice to have someone to help exercise the horses, but she didn't come to see me. She seems sort of at loose ends. Wanders about the house, does a lot of bathing." Leonie rolled her eyes ever so slightly toward the treetops. "Goes out every night. I don't know where. Into Chandler, I imagine."

"Nick says she was with John at the Waterfront the other night."

"They went together. He came home about tea time without her."

"She has turned up since, I take it?"

"Oh, yes. But was out rather late, I believe. At least I didn't hear the water running until about three in the morning." She smiled and donned her kerchief. "She'd gone off with...somebody."

Mia wondered if the hesitancy in Leonie's voice meant that the somebody was Nick. Her next remark answered the question.

"A chap John didn't know, but he said they looked pretty chummy. From his description I think it was that man...the one that was at the dance. You know, the one that Evelyn Turner was so taken with."

"Evelyn wasn't the only one," Mia said. "Leave it to Siobhan to make the big catch."

Leonie stood and made to mount the bicycle, then let it fall back against the rail and plopped back onto the steps. "Mia," she asked, "how well do you know Siobhan?"

Mia shoved the basket of garden produce aside and joined her. "I *knew* her very well, a long time ago. She was an aggravation. Kind of a sneaky, secretive kid. She drove me crazy then, but, looking back, I have to feel sorry for her. She had an…unusual life. Her father was so much older, and, as you can imagine, there was quite a bit of talk when he married his sister-in-law and plenty of jokes when Siobhan was born so soon after. There weren't any other children her age around. She spent most of her time alone or tagging after us older kids. She was man-crazy from the time she was nine years old. Her mother couldn't do a thing with her, and her father, Jeremiah—that was John's grandfather—thought she could do no wrong. She pretty much ran wild. The old man died when Siobhan was sixteen or seventeen. A few months later she left with a man she met at the county fair, a gypsy."

"Did you say *gypsy?*"

Mia nodded.

"There are gypsies here?" Leonie looked around as if she expected to be ambushed that very minute by dark-skinned chicken thieves lurking in the lilacs.

"They travel with carnivals, running rides and games, things like that."

"And Siobhan was taken by them? Didn't anyone look for her? Try to get her back?"

"She wasn't kidnapped! She left a note. Sure, somebody should have gone after her. She wasn't old enough to make that kind of a decision. Colin tried to find her for a while. But that was in the twenties, remember. It was pretty easy for people to disappear if they didn't want to be found. Siobhan's mother, Bridget, got a letter now and then. But Bridget didn't stick around for long after Jeremiah died either. Went to St. Paul, I think. So Siobhan really had no reason to come back here."

"Until now," Leonie observed, with what might have been a note of suspicion?

"She said she got homesick after reading that magazine article about uranium," Mia said. It did seem a little strange that Siobhan had turned up after all this time and with no apparent plans to leave in the foreseeable future. Mia asked, "Leonie, has Siobhan said anything about where she's been all this time? Doesn't she have a home somewhere?"

"She's mentioned California now and again. She doesn't seem to want to talk about herself, and I don't care to pry."

A Siobhan McIntire whose favorite topic of conversation wasn't Siobhan McIntire did indeed sound suspicious.

Mia had the feeling that Leonie would like to tell her, or ask her, something more. But after a few throat clearings, her moral code, *only if it's fit to print*, obviously won out, and she rose to her feet.

"Can't I give you some rutabagas, Leonie?" Mia asked. "I planted way too many."

The panic in Leonie's eyes was at odds with her gracious smile. "Why thank you, Mia. That would be lovely. I can't carry many on a bike." She eyed the misshapen vegetables. "Maybe two." Mia retrieved a paper bag from the kitchen. Leonie chose two of the smallest and popped them into the basket on her handlebars. "*Rutabaga.* That's the funniest word I've ever heard," she commented. "But I imagine referring to them as 'swedes' around here could generate some confusion." She swung the bicycle around and walked it to the end of the rutted driveway. Mia turned back to her truck.

At least she could clean the thing up. Madame Hollander wanted her clock case, and Mia wanted Madame's money. Ross was still around, and it was time to make that delivery.

She opened the double doors at the back and pulled out the chains that Ross had used for Nick's recent rescue. The bed of the van was covered in clumps of dirt and sand, not hospitable conditions for transporting highly polished furniture.

In addition to saving drunken mailmen, Ross must have been using it in some of his uranium-hunting forays.

After the chains came a peach crate containing a couple pairs of yellow work gloves and—eureka!—a chisel she'd been looking for. Her jubilance faded when she saw its ragged edges. Had Ross been chipping rocks with her wood chisel? She shuddered.

The crate landed with a thud in the grass next to the chains. An unfamiliar object rolled across the dirty truck bed toward her, a dark leather cylinder about two feet long. A case for fishing rods? Didn't John McIntire have something like that? A twist opened it, revealing not rods, but rolled papers. She pulled them out and let them unfurl. Maps. A confusing maze of black lines and incomprehensible symbols.

She walked to the front of the truck and spread the maps on the hood. A network of penciled-in lines and X's dotted the two-dimensional landscape. Each sheet bore the name *Morlen*.

The case had the soft patina of age. Her fingers traced its intricate engravings. It looked expensive. Maybe it was an heirloom. It should go back to the family. Ross had probably forgotten that he had it.

She returned the maps to the tube and laid it in the grass next to the peach crate. It would have to be turned over to the sheriff, she supposed. Taking it to John McIntire would be easier.

As she pulled out the scrap of carpet that covered the truck bed and carried it to the clothesline, she whistled a little tune.

# XXI

*No one, you know, worships unpunished the*
*god of wisdom.*

"She's back."

McIntire stuck a pencil between the pages, closed his book, and regarded his wife's flushed cheeks and bright eyes. Her newswoman's face. "That doesn't surprise me a hell of a lot," he said, "but I didn't realize that she'd gone."

"No, not *her*. Bonnie Morlen has come back, and her husband, too, I reckon. She's moved into the Ford mansion and she's brought along one Mr. Melvin Fratelli." Leonie paused on the verge of an old-fashioned swoon. "He's a private detective from *New York City!*"

"A private eye? That should make quite a scoop for you. You'd better hotfoot it over to welcome her with a pie or something before Beckman beats you to it."

"I have done, actually. You'll be having cheese for dessert tonight." Her voice deflated, and she placed the bulky parcel she had been clutching to her chest gently on the table. "And to no good purpose. When Mrs. Morlen discovered I'm married to you, she wouldn't let me past the entrance hall. And frankly," she added, "for a place that calls itself a mansion, it's not much of a hall."

McIntire doubted that Henry Ford would be allowed to own a home not deemed a mansion whatever the condition of its front hall. "I wouldn't know about that," he said, "but it's a pretty strange choice regardless. Why not just stay at the Club? It's been years since anybody's lived in that house. Matter of fact, I don't know that it's ever been lived in. Their modest little fishing club has everything anyone could possibly want and more."

"Except telephones," Leonie said. "And it is pretty isolated. Any day now they could get snowed under 'til June. But from what I've heard, once the Club members got a look at Papa Feldman, they decided the Morlens probably weren't their kind of people. Wendell received a rapid demotion from guest to hired help."

The canceled stamps on Leonie's package were testimony to the source of her information. McIntire had to admit that things might move along faster with Nick Thorsen as the detective.

"You might have casually mentioned that you also put in a few years married to a man who wasn't the Club sort," he told her. "Mrs. Morlen might have overlooked the fact that your current husband is the town snoop."

"Believe me, I tried, but I couldn't come up with a way to work it into the conversation on such short notice." Leonie removed her hat and stroked its improbably blue feathers. "I don't think it's your snoopiness that's bothering her. Before she chucked me out the door she said her detective would be coming to see you."

"What is the problem then?"

Leonie shrugged. "I've not the foggiest. She was all graciousness when she came to the door, but the minute she heard my name, she said I simply had to excuse her, because she needed to frost a cake, like it was a dire emergency."

"So you sacrificed a blackberry pie for nothing." McIntire plunged into the depths of gloom.

"Don't remind me! That pie represented about fourteen hours of hard labor, not to mention the scratches and bug bites." Leonie's aspect brightened when she turned her attention to snipping the string from the brown paper-wrapped box. A delivery from Montgomery Wards.

"You finally get some Wellie boots?" McIntire asked.

"Not quite." Leonie grinned and spread aside the tissue to reveal a pair of heavily engraved high-heeled western boots, remarkably similar to those sported by Pete Koski when election time drew near.

"Going into politics?"

"Just going riding." Leonie kicked off her pumps and, with the aid of a grimace or two, tugged the stiff boots onto her feet. She did a quick turn to the kitchen door and executed a tap dance on the linoleum. "How do I look?"

The boots were brown with spangled cutouts and squared-off pointy toes. In her blue flowered dress, Leonie looked like Annie Oakley on washday. McIntire responded with, "How do they feel?"

"Smashing." Leonie sat again. "They may need a bit of breaking in." She extended both feet and flexed her ankles. "You're probably wondering how much they cost."

The question had crossed McIntire's mind.

"Fifteen dollars and some odd cents."

McIntire hoped he managed to keep his expression bland. It was roughly half his weekly retirement pay. Not that it mattered. Leonie had money of her own. He'd often wondered how much. That not-the-Club-sort husband had done okay. He'd been well enough off to fly his own airplane, not something McIntire had ever envied him, since it was that piloting experience that led to his being the second of Leonie's husbands to lose his life in a war.

"I wanted to get some for Chuckie, too," Leonie said, "but children's feet grow so fast, and shipping is so slow. By the time he got them they might already be too small." Her eyes took on the wistful glaze that always accompanied a mention of one of her grandchildren. "I'll send a hat." She poked the frayed spine of the three-inch-thick volume under McIntire's hand. "What's this?"

"I had it sent from the university library in Marquette." He flipped the cover so she could read, *Neolithic Peoples of the Western Hemisphere*, by M. Gordon Hannah.

"To what purpose?"

"Trephination, or, more accurately, *trepanation*."

"Which is?"

"Drilling a hole in the skull. As in brain surgery, or as practiced by various primitive peoples of the earth, including certain Indian tribes of," he swept his hand over the chapter heading, "Central and South America."

"This is neither Central nor South America."

"No, but curiously, some of the scarce evidence of North American natives engaging in the ritual has been found right here in Michigan."

"Does it mention any names?"

McIntire laughed. "It was a long time ago, a couple of thousand years, and it's not a tradition among any modern tribes."

"So far as Mr. Hannah knows."

"I'm not looking for any ancient skull drilling cult among the Walls. But whoever tried to make that hole in Bambi Morlen's head must have known about this procedure."

Leonie went back to admiring her feet as she asked, "But is there some connection between the hole in Bambi Morlen's skull and the Walls or any other Indians? Would those ancient people have done it to young men? Was it a means of killing people? Some sort of sacrifice? What was the original purpose?"

"Well, my dear, that's the big question. M. Gordon here seems to think it was to let out evil spirits, or maybe let good ones in. Sometimes it appeared to be therapeutic, following injury, say. The patient did survive quite often. Other times it was done after death. Like it was with Bambi Morlen."

"So Bambi's murderer did him the favor of letting out the evil spirits after he died?"

"Tried to. He didn't finish the job." McIntire closed the volume with a thud. "Adam Wall's been putting an awful lot of energy into, as his father puts it, learning to be Indian. His last years in the army he had plenty of time for reading. He could have stumbled onto something about this." He slapped the book. He couldn't bring himself to mention that Adam Wall was also the source of his introduction to the term trepanation. "Well," he said, "somebody knows about it. That's for sure. And then there's that Indian tobacco."

"Is that for certain?"

"It is. Guibard got some of the test results back yesterday. They confirmed an alkaloid substance that would be the same as that in *Lobelia inflata*."

"Is that something Indians actually use?" Leonie asked.

"I don't know," McIntire said. "Guibard says somebody named Sadie LaPrairie did. LaPrairie is a fairly common Indian name. Maybe it doesn't matter, if the common name connects it to Indians."

"But that's exactly why it does matter. If it's something generally used by the Indians in the here and now, then it turning up here could point to an Indian culprit. But if it's not, if Indian tobacco is simply some old name that stuck, then whoever used it could be trying to frame an Indian."

*Frame.* Leonie had been listening to *Boston Blackie* again. "Or maybe it could be an Indian wanting to make a point," McIntire said.

"I'll get you some fresh." Leonie stood up and reached for the cold coffee pot. "John, you don't have to do this, you know. You can just forget about it and get back to Gösta."

McIntire pushed his chair from the table and turned to his wife. "I hate to admit this, Leonie, but my first thought when I saw that poor boy's body was, 'Thank God, it's not one of us this time.' And for some reason I figured if the victim was a stranger, we'd get lucky and the murderer would be, too. I'm not at all sure that'll turn out to be the case."

"Well," she put a hand on his shoulder and leaned to kiss the top of his head, "maybe you can leave it to that detective. He doesn't know *anybody*."

As if waiting in the wings, a slowing engine and scraping gears sounded from the direction of the mailbox. McIntire turned to the window. Daniel Feldman's Morgan pulled into view, gave three hops and jolted to a stop. The mud it had collected in its travels with Bambi had been washed away, and areas not coated with rust were waxed to a gleam that would have done Inge Lindstrom proud. The driver, who could only be the imported private detective, stepped nimbly out, smoothed the lap of his brown serge suit, and looked around. He made a few notations on a small pad while staring down Leonie's brown leghorn rooster, then pocketed the pad and pen, and strode to the front door, glancing back toward the strutting fowl at prudent intervals.

McIntire stepped outside. "Ah, Mr. Fratelli, we've been expecting you." Rather than being impressed with McIntire's powers of deduction, Fratelli only smiled stiffly and shook the extended hand, no doubt accepting as his due that his reputation, and name, would have preceded him.

McIntire led the detective to the dining room, shoved *Neolithic Indians* aside and invited him to a seat at the table. Recalling every P.I. movie he'd ever seen, he offered his guest a choice of coffee or scotch. A begging-dog look came into the gray eyes, but the response was, "Coffee'd be fine," and the man got right down to business. "I've been engaged by Wendell Morlen to investigate his son's murder."

McIntire nodded.

"I understand that Bambi Morlen was kidnapped, stabbed, and poisoned, and that the body was mutilated."

McIntire nodded again. Put that way, it sounded positively tawdry.

"And no progress has been made in finding the killer?" He had a radio announcer's voice, smooth and unaccented. His name should have been *Smith* or *Jones*.

McIntire added a splash of the whisky to his own coffee and took a sip. It wasn't tasty, but he wanted to show this city boy the kind of people he was dealing with. "You'd probably be able to get more information from the sheriff or the state police," he said. "They're handling the investigation."

"But the sheriff is miles away. You live right here. You know these people."

"I live here right enough, but the Morlens don't. Before this happened, I'd never met any of them."

Fratelli was undeterred. "I mean you know the others involved, the ones who might be considered suspects. And," he ran an unremarkable hand over his medium brown hair, "I thought you might be able to tell me where I could get a Geiger counter."

"A Geiger counter? So far as I know they're no help at all at detecting murderers."

Fratelli's indulgent smile reflected the feebleness of the joke. "Well, I was hoping to kind of blend in. If it looked like I was here hunting for uranium...."

"It's getting a little late in the year. People are beginning to give up and go home."

"Then it should be fairly easy to get a Geiger counter."

That was true enough. "Just go into Chandler and ask at any bar or café," McIntire said. "You'll have more prospecting equipment than you'll know what to do with."

"No question about that," Fratelli laughed. "I wouldn't know what to do with any of it. I figure to lug it around and, like I said, blend in."

McIntire had to admit that in a place like New York City it wouldn't take much to make this man disappear. He doubted that he'd ever seen such a forgettable face. Melvin Fratelli might have been a dictionary illustration for *Homo sapiens*. All the components were there—arms, legs, nose, eyes, chin—but the combined effect was completely indistinctive, like he'd been pieced together from a kit.

His nondescript looks no doubt served him well in his native cosmopolitan setting, but here in the Upper Peninsula, where individuals were so dissimilar as to be almost separate species, his bland handsomeness would single him out like a turd in a punchbowl, as Arnie Johnson might say.

And if the investigator thought he could gather more information by posing as a uranium prospector than he would by owning up to his considerably more intriguing profession, he had a lot to learn.

Fratelli pulled the notebook and pen from his breast pocket. "Mind if I ask a few questions?"

McIntire found that, for some reason, he did mind, but he nodded. Morlen had brought this guy all the way from New York. He was probably paying him a bundle.

"Was this an annual event?"

"Murder?" McIntire asked. "Or kidnapping? Murder's been semi-annual. We've gotten short-changed on our ration of abductions lately."

The watered-down smile again. "The dance, the night Bambi was killed?"

"Oh. You betcha. The Hunters' Dance is *the* annual event."

"So the kidnapper knew there'd be a crowd…maybe a lot of confusion…?"

"Might well have," McIntire agreed. "But Bambi wasn't abducted from the dance. He left on his own at about eleven o'clock. We don't know what time he ran into his kidnappers, and they couldn't have known in advance that he'd be leaving so early." Unless that fight with Marvin Wall had been set up some way.

"Could he have been followed?"

Followed, on mostly deserted roads, to Maki's, the gravel pit, on to the Sorensons' house without being noticed? "No." McIntire was sure of it. "It seems likely that Bambi stopped for some reason. That somebody thumbed him down for a ride or faked car trouble."

"How much is uranium worth?"

McIntire had been mentally girding himself for an interrogation pertaining to these people that he supposedly knew so well. This question took him by surprise. But he was ready with the answer. "A ten thousand dollar finder's fee and about three-fifty a pound forever after, last I heard. The government buys it."

Fratelli gave a whistle. "So if Bambi had found a…vein of uranium and somebody knew it—"

McIntire headed him off. "That's in theory so far as I know, nobody's actually gotten the ten grand. You don't simply fill your pockets and head into town. Uranium's not just lying out there waiting to be picked up. It's in ores, ores that have to be mined by the tons to glean out a few pounds of uranium oxide. It wouldn't be cheap."

"So you don't figure the boy was killed because he'd struck gold, in a manner of speaking?"

"There's gold out there too, but it's every bit as hard to get out of the ground. I think you're getting way off the track. The motive might have been money all right, but ransom, not claim jumping."

Fratelli didn't ask for it, but McIntire spent a few minutes recapping the events of that dismal evening as he saw them. If the detective was going to be hanging around he might as well have more information than he'd probably gotten from Wendell Morlen.

Fratelli jotted *Sorenson* on his pad and doodled the S into an arrow shape before he responded. "So the killer was somebody who knew Bambi Morlen and knew he came from a wealthy family, knew he'd be at that dance, knew his old man was buying a piece of land for seventeen grand, knew where to find him after he took the girl home, knew something about poison plants, and was familiar enough with the neighborhood to stick him up in that shed."

Add *and knew that the neolithic Michigan natives were given to drilling holes in heads*, and that would about sum things up. "You forgot 'and was seeking justice,'" McIntire said.

Fratelli grunted. "This isn't a major metropolis. How many people can that fit?"

Not many, McIntire had to admit. "It's not that simple," he said. "Bambi was stabbed an hour, or maybe more, before he died. We can't be absolutely sure that he received that wound from his kidnappers. Or that he was stabbed by the same person that poisoned him."

"Right. That Indian kid could have been skulking around, seen the whole thing, sneaked in after Bambi was bound and gagged, and stabbed him in cold blood."

McIntire couldn't quite picture Marvin Wall skulking around the town hall at three in the morning or seeing much of anything in the pitch dark. He went on, "It's possible that Bambi wasn't killed intentionally. The stabbing looks to be a spur of the moment thing, and the doctor says even though he had a hefty dose of the poison, he probably would have vomited it up before he died from it. Or," McIntire hadn't really seriously considered this before, "it's possible that it didn't start out as an abduction at all. If Bambi's death was unplanned, the murderer, or accidental killer, would have had all day Sunday to concoct that letter and get it to the post office in Chandler, just to muddy the waters."

"Well." Fratelli flipped his notepad shut. "I'm not interested in what might have happened. I'm here to find out what *did* happen."

The man's arrogance was begging for a pie in the face, but McIntire had lost his pie to Bonnie Morlen, and he could grudgingly admit to seeing the guy's point. There wasn't much to be gained by conjecture. It wasn't a puzzle where if you got the right combination you'd be rewarded with bells and flashing lights. They could hash over possible scenarios until the cows came home, but it wouldn't change the facts, or give them any further knowledge of those facts.

A shriek sounded from the second floor. McIntire waved the scrambling investigator back to his seat. Half a minute later Siobhan appeared from the stairwell.

"There's no water." She spoke in a tone similar to that used by Roosevelt announcing the attack on Pearl Harbor. "I turned on the tub and nothing happened."

McIntire sighed. "The pump's probably not getting any juice. Most likely a fuse," he said. "I'll get it in a bit."

Siobhan's "But—" was interrupted by her notice of the visitor. She snugged up the belt of her fuzzy blue robe, replaced her peevish frown with a smile and stepped forward.

"Oh, I'm sorry. I didn't know you had company." She smoothed the hair over her ears. "Never mind about the fuse now. Maybe I'll just get a cup and have some coffee." She backed through the kitchen door and was back in record time with a cup, a saucer, and freshly applied lipstick. McIntire performed the introductions.

"A private investigator! How exciting! I bet you could tell stories that could scare the pants—" she giggled—"that could scare the bejeebers out of a girl."

Since there was nary a girl in sight, that didn't appear to be a problem. Fratelli pulled out a chair and offered a cigarette for Siobhan's empty tortoiseshell holder. McIntire filled her cup with coffee and went off to the pump house to change the fuse.

# XXII

*She was leaving life, the real life, but it did
not make much difference to her, she who
could not live but only act.*

The Ford mansion wasn't a particularly impressive building.
It was big, Mia would grant it that, but even the seven white
pillars that held up the roof of the porch—it probably had a
fancier name than porch—couldn't keep it from looking like
a small-town schoolhouse. It had stood for close to twenty
years, facing an expanse of white sand beach, furnished and
tidy, ever ready for its celebrated owner who, so far as anyone
knew, had yet to spend a night under its slates.

Mia remained a short while under the trees waiting for her
courage to grow, wondering if she'd be greeted by some pickle-
faced housekeeper or a gaunt and tortured bereaved mother.
Maybe Mrs. Morlen wouldn't be home, and it would be the
husband. That thought was about to send her scurrying back
down the drive, when a shadow moving across a window told
her she'd been spotted.

The woman who answered her knock *was* dressed in a
house-maidish manner, in a plain gray dress with a white
collar and a sparkling white apron. She admitted, though, to
being Bonnie Morlen. Her far-from-gaunt features showed
no emotion other than a mild look of surprise at seeing her

visitor. It was a reaction that Mia, standing just a hair under six feet, had long been accustomed to.

"I'm Mia Thorsen," she said. "I heard you'd moved in. I just came to see if there's anything I can do for you." The woman's expression remained static, her gaze fixed, and Mia struggled with the urge to make a quick retreat. "And," she continued, "to tell you how sorry we all are for your loss."

Bonnie stared for a moment longer, then gave her head a shake. "Forgive me, the doctor has been filling me full of pills that seem to do nothing more than slow down my brain. Please come in. How kind of you to visit." Her voice was beautiful, soft and full. But without feeling.

Taking Mia's elbow, she led her into a high-ceilinged room. It was Scarlett O'Hara's worst nightmare. The dark papered walls and carved, white-painted woodwork battled with chairs and tables fashioned from pine logs, sofas draped with Hudson Bay blankets, and a polar bear rug whose sparse fur hinted that its original occupant might have frozen to death. The single piece of furniture in keeping with the home's southern plantation elegance was the baby grand piano that stood before a bank of tall windows.

"Please sit down. I've made cocoa." Mrs. Morlen directed her to a seat facing a blazing hearth. The fireplace was large enough to have easily held the rough hewn settee, and Mia would have been hard pressed to resist the temptation, had she been the tenant. A varnished wood fish-box, serving as a coffee table, was already laid with a tray holding a pair of plain white pottery cups. Mia folded her hands in her lap as her hostess filled the cups with steaming cocoa from an ornate china pot. Was the woman clairvoyant, or was she expecting someone else?

"If this isn't a good time…."

"No. No, please. I'm grateful for the company." The words were welcoming, but Bonnie Morlen's tone was empty. Maybe that was the pills, too. "Excuse me one moment, while I get some fresh tarts." Bonnie picked up a plate of tiny pies and walked out of the room. She returned with the same plate containing what looked to be the same pies.

"Thimbleberry," she said. "I hadn't heard of thimbleberries before. I hope you like them."

On such short acquaintance, Mia felt it might not be appropriate to say that she would rather eat a dead rat, maybe even a live one, than a thimbleberry. She smiled, "They're lovely." They were. Perfectly formed, golden, and decorated with a berry-shaped dusting of sugar.

"Do you live nearby?" Mrs. Morlen asked.

"Over on the Swale road, a little north of the town hall."

Bonnie shook her head. "I'm not that familiar with the area, yet. Maybe you could help me get better acquainted. Have you been here long?"

"All my life. I live in the house I was born in."

Bonnie sipped her drink and cocked her head to one side as if assessing its suitability. It apparently passed the test; she sipped again and smiled. "Really? How interesting. In this day and age one hardly expects that, does one?"

Mia supposed that one didn't. She tasted her own cocoa. It was delicious. Unlike anything she'd ever gotten out of a Hershey's can. She placed her cup in its saucer and looked up. Bonnie Morlen's gaze was locked on Mia's hand—the hand which had only four fingers.

"An accident with a wood chisel," Mia told her.

"How awful for you. It must have hurt terribly." She gave a shudder and went on, "I imagine you must know nearly everyone around here?"

Mia nodded. It was a rapid change of the subject, for which Mia could only be grateful, and she could see where it was leading. She saw no reason to make Mrs. Morlen squirm. "Are there things you'd like to know?"

Bonnie put her cup on the table and folded her hands in her lap. "Mrs. Thorsen, I've come back here to see that my

son's murderer takes up residence in Hell. There are a great
many things I'd like to know."

The woman's bluntness, counterpoint to her prim demeanor,
was disarming.

"I'll help however I can," Mia assured her.

"Bambi's friend, the boy who prospected with him, do
you know him?"

Perhaps, Mia thought, she shouldn't have been so eager.
"Ross Maki. He works for me."

The look on Bonnie's face was similar to the one she'd
worn upon seeing Mia on her doorstep. "Works for you? At
your home, do you mean? Farm work?"

"I build furniture. Ross makes deliveries for me, picks up
supplies, things like that." Bonnie Morlen's eyes widened
again. Her continual astonishment getting tiresome.

"Mrs. Morlen," Mia said, "Ross Maki is a good natured,
hard working boy. I've never known him to lose his temper
or behave badly in any way. I'm sure he couldn't have had
anything to do with your son's death."

"What's his financial situation?"

"What?"

"Did he need money?"

"I guess we all need money."

"But here's a young man, out of school—?"

Mia nodded. "He graduated last spring."

"—a young man, out of school, with no support except
doing odd jobs for a…cabinet maker? It sounds to me like
he'd need money more than most."

"Not much more than most people around here." Bonnie
Morlen needed to know that the Shawanok Club was not the
Upper Michigan norm. "This is a poor community. There are
no jobs for young people. Ross would have left last spring,
but his father fell off the roof of their barn and broke his leg.
Ross needed to help his mother with the farming. He's been
working like a dog, at home and for me, in addition to his
prospecting jaunts."

"But not making any money."

"That's beside the point now. Ross has been drafted."

"Is he looking forward to the service?"

"No."

"So what he really needs is a *lot* of money." Bonnie picked up her cup, clutching it in both hands and nodding to herself like a down-home Jane Marple. "Oh, I know a boy like that probably couldn't have carried off the abduction by himself, but he'd have been in the perfect situation to help somebody else do it."

"But who?"

Misery leaped into the dark eyes, and was gone just as quickly. Bonnie Morlen frowned into her cup. "What do you know about the Indian that attacked him?" she asked.

Indian attack? It sounded like the Saturday movie matinee.

"Marvin Wall," Mia prompted.

"Do you know him?"

"I know who he is. I can't say I'm that well acquainted with any of the kids around here, except Ross. But Marvin's parents have lived here for years. They've been good neighbors."

"Even though they're Indian?"

Mia couldn't help herself. "I'm Indian, too, Mrs. Morlen."

Bonnie apologized without a trace of embarrassment. "I'm sorry. I only meant…."

"I know. The Walls are pretty much a part of the community like everybody else. But you're right, most of the Indians around here keep to themselves. My mother did."

That wasn't quite true, the ostracism of Mia's family had more to do with her father's German roots and the First World War than her Potowatami grandmother—great grandmother, actually, which didn't make Mia all that Indian. The only thing truly Indian about Mia was her given name, inherited from her grandmother when she was five years old, Meogokwe, and no one ever called her that. But she was beginning to feel an antagonism toward Bonnie Morlen that she didn't quite understand. The woman had just lost her son, for God's sake; could she be blamed for being suspicious?

Bonnie nibbled the precisely fluted edge of a tart. "What did you do with the end of it?"

"Pardon me?"

"Your finger, what did you do with it?"

What should she say? I fed it to the cat? I wear it on a chain around my neck? The inquisition came to a merciful end with a knock at the door. Bonnie pulled her apron off over her head, draped it on a birch-twig chair, and excused herself. Mia took the opportunity to pour herself another half-cup of the intoxicating chocolate. She wondered if it would it be rude to ask for the recipe.

Bonnie's voice carried through from the entry hall. In contrast to its earlier flatness, it sounded strong and expressive, like an actor on a stage. "Why, hello. How kind of you to stop. My husband has gone out, I'm afraid. But do come in." Mia gulped the chocolate and stood up as Bonnie returned with the newcomer. He was youngish, an impression enhanced by the blond hair combed flat to his skull and the scrubbed flush of his face. And like a child, a faint ring of grubbiness remained above his collar. Surely not an acquaintance from the Club.

Bonnie introduced Greg Carlson. Mia put out her hand. "I've heard about you from Ross. Found the mother lode yet?"

He looked blank for a moment, and Mia once again felt that she'd overstepped the bounds of etiquette. Then he smiled. "I haven't even found the baby-sister lode." An uneasy silence descended, and he stood shifting from one foot to the other.

"I see there's a piano here," Mia floundered.

"It's my own," Mrs. Morlen responded. "I never go any-where without it."

That must prove to be inconvenient at times. She should have taken up the harmonica.

"Daddy had it brought from the Club," she added.

"Is your father here with you?" Carlson glanced toward the door, as if poised to flee should the answer be yes.

"No." Bonnie turned to the instrument and ran her hand over its polished wood. "He wanted to come back with us, but I needed someone to stay home with my son. I couldn't leave Bambi all alone, back in that cemetery."

There was no possible reply to that, and Mia took the opportunity to make her escape, despite feeling slightly mean at abandoning the awkward caller to their hostess.

Mrs. Morlen accompanied her into the front hall. When they reached the door she put her hand on Mia's arm and pleaded in a low voice. "I do hope you'll come again, Mrs. Thorsen. It's lonely here with no family or friends. Please, come soon. Tell me if you hear anything. You must understand how difficult this is, the not knowing."

Mia did understand, and she relented slightly. "Certainly, I'll help any way I can. But anything I hear would be just gossip. If you want real information, you'll need to talk to the police or the sheriff, and maybe your...." Mia hesitated. Possibly it was supposed to be a secret. Well, Bonnie Morlen might as well know that secrets aren't easily kept in places like St. Adele. "Your detective."

"Melvin Fratelli has his mind on uranium. He spends more time looking for that mother lode than Mr. Carlson does. His *cover*, he says."

"Maybe if your husband—"

"Wendell is here very little. That's mainly why he accepted when Mr. Fratelli offered his services. He thought I might need protection. And that sheriff has done nothing, only keeps complaining that he needs more deputies. Your constable probably knows more than he does."

Strange that Mrs. Morlen should express more confidence in a township constable than she did in either the police or the detective for whose services she must be paying through the nose.

"Would you like John to come and see you?"

"No!" It was almost a shout. Bonnie glanced over her shoulder and lowered her voice again. "No, please, I don't feel like facing any of those people now. Or any more men."

Mia could appreciate that. Having to deal with a crew of men out to prove what they could do was often more exhausting than it was worth. Bonnie went on, "I suppose you're well acquainted with him, with Mr. McIntire?"

Mia nodded. "He and his wife live near us."

"Maybe you could talk to him for me. Find out what's going on...." Tears glittered in the corners of her eyes. "And let me know."

Mia surrendered. "If you want me to."

"And could you please ask him if he can find out what's happened to Bambi's belongings?"

"Is something missing?"

"Personal belongings. The police say there was nothing much in his car, and Mr. Carlson has turned over everything that was at the camp, but much of his clothing and personal things hasn't turned up. I'd be so grateful." The eyes teared up again.

"I'll see what I can do," Mia told her.

Bonnie Morlen gave her a misty smile and opened the door. Mia wondered what she'd gotten herself into, and why she hadn't mentioned Bambi's map case.

# XXIII

*I do not think that there was anything hidden
or forbidden in their hearts.*

Wolves snapped at the heels of the trusty Don Juan as he
galloped through the night pulling the sledge carrying Gösta
Berling and his latest kidnapped bride. Small wonder Don
Juan knew his stuff. Fleeing into the night, with or without a
female companion, was becoming a habit with Gösta, and was
beginning to wear about as thin as the ice over which he sped.
Ah, abductions were not what they used to be. No longer a
convenient and romantic escape from a bothersome life. The
fictional tribulations of the mad priest held scant interest for
McIntire this morning, and as his mind wandered, his eyes
followed. So he saw Mia coming long before she reached the
house.

She strolled along the path that ran next to the pasture
fence. Her plaid skirt fluttered around her knees, showing a
bit more leg than it would have on a woman of less stature,
and more of Mia's legs than he'd seen in over thirty years. They
hadn't changed much.

The two quarter-horses, true to their inquisitive equine
natures, trotted to the fence to observe this novel approach of a
stranger. She stopped to scratch them under their bristly chins
and embedded her face in the thick winter coat on Traveler's

neck. Or was that one Spirit? Whichever, his companion began to nibble at the single braid that hung down her back. McIntire wondered how old Mia would have to get before she abandoned that childish coiffure. Gray hair, even that silvery color, wasn't suited to pigtails. It was suited to Mia, though, prettier than the dishwater blond it had been. As he watched, she laughed and tickled the animal's nose with the tail of the plait, causing it to curl its lip in a horsy sneer. When she turned toward the house, McIntire left the window, feeling almost voyeuristic, and met her at the kitchen door.

"Dressed in your Sunday-go-to-meeting duds just for me?" he greeted her.

"No!" She spoke as if appearing in the skirt rather than her usual costume of cast-offs from her husband needed a vigorous defense. Her smile was more of a grimace. "I've been paying a 'welcome to the neighborhood' call on the Morlens. Bonnie Morlen, that is. I didn't see the mister."

"Oh, so you only put on your glad rags for snobby Easterners?"

"Lay off it, John. You want to hear about Bonnie or not?"

Mia liked to get to the point, but was generally not quite this brusque about it. McIntire smiled and swept the door wide. "I surely do want to hear about Mrs. Morlen. Step right in."

Mia handed him her coat and slipped out of her canvas oxfords. She carried a pillowcase containing some long object, which she did not immediately hand over. McIntire led her to the dining room.

"Want coffee? I could use some myself. I was too lazy to make any earlier. The water system's on the blink at the moment, so I have to carry in the water."

"I thought from the way Leonie's been talking, all your water went to keep Siobhan looking fresh and lovely."

"She does use her share. The pump keeps blowing fuses. Maybe if it keeps up, Siobhan'll move on to wetter pastures."

"Well, tell her to stop in and see me one of these days." Mia looked at the paper-strewn table. "What's all this?" she asked.

McIntire filled her in on Gösta and company.

"John, I hate to dampen your enthusiasm, but I tried to read that once. I got enthusiastic after I saw the movie, and, well, I stuck with it for about three chapters, then gave up."

"It was a movie?"

Mia's smile was one of genuine satisfaction. "I can't believe it! For once I can tell you something that you don't already know. Nick and I saw it in Houghton. *The Saga of Gösta Berling*. It was Greta Garbo's first movie."

McIntire couldn't believe it either. "It was Swedish, then? Were you able to understand it?"

"Oh, sure, every word."

She'd caught him out again. There would not have been much of a language barrier involved in Miss Garbo's first movie.

"Anyway," she said, "it beat the book all hollow."

"When you've read the McIntire translation, you'll change your tune. Now what about the Morlens? Why'd they come back?"

"I don't know about Mr. Morlen, I didn't see him around, and his wife says he's not home much. But Bonnie's come back for the obvious reason, to find her son's murderer and to see him—How did she put it?—residing in Hell." She went on, "I suppose you know she's brought her own detective."

"Yes, we've met."

"Well, she doesn't seem to think he's doing much."

"Then I'd say Mrs. Morlen's no fool. So why doesn't she send him packing?"

Mia shrugged. "I didn't ask. She wants your help."

"Mine? What does she think I can do? Anyway, when she found out Leonie's married to me, she all but booted her out the door. Does she figure I'll just come trotting along when she whistles?"

"Mrs. Morlen doesn't want you to trot up to the mansion. She wants you to trot around and find out who killed her son and then trot over to tell me, so I can tell her, and she can see that he takes up residence in Hell. She also wants you to find some of Bambi's belongings."

"What belongings are those?"

"She didn't say, only that some of his stuff is missing, and she's not happy about it."

"Ross?"

"Maybe." Mia produced her pillowcase package. "At least I know he had this."

She tipped a leather cylinder out onto the table. "Maps. Maps in a case. I didn't think I should handle it any more…fingerprints, you know."

"Ross had this?"

"It was in my truck. I suppose both Ross and Bambi used the maps, but the name 'Morlen' is on them. And they're all marked up, so maybe they can give some hints about…you know," she smiled and lowered her voice, "clues."

McIntire shoved Father Berling out of the way, pulled the papers from the tube, and spread them on the table. There were two geological survey maps showing the sectors south of St. Adele roughly extending from the Slate River on the west all the way to the Huron on the east. The top map was crisp and pristine. The one underneath, that covering the area where Carlson's camp was located, was older. It was smudged, water spotted, and overlaid with a maze of pencil-drawn trails.

McIntire inverted the case. A pencil and another, smaller cylinder landed on the table. He pounced on it. A roll of film.

"Bambi was an enthusiastic photographer, I've heard. Maybe his mother's right about things missing. I haven't heard of a camera turning up." McIntire tried to keep the kid-in-a-candy-store excitement out of his voice. "Looks like it's been exposed."

"Talk about clues. Good thing you're the detective here. All I found were the maps."

"Did you ask Ross about this stuff?"

Mia's answer was long in coming. She pulled out a chair and sat. "No."

McIntire nodded. Murder didn't only take a life. It left the living looking over their shoulders.

"He's been drafted," Mia said. "He's scared stiff."

McIntire looked up. "When?"

"He didn't say when he got the greeting. It must have been a while ago. He goes the middle of November." She stood up and slipped her arms back into her sleeves. "I better get going. Nick will be home soon. If he's not wrapped around a tree somewhere." Mia generally referred to her husband's foibles with at least feigned good humor, but this time her tone had a bitter edge to it. McIntire generally avoided making any comment related to Nick at all and did so now.

He walked her to the door. Before she left he attempted to make amends for his earlier transgressions. "I was just kidding before, Mia, about the dress. You look very nice."

She didn't respond, but bent quickly down to tie her shoes. Her braid, the color of a lake on a hazy day, swung forward and swept the floor. As she stood and turned to the door in one movement, McIntire was appalled to see what looked like tears shining in her eyes.

# XXIV

*He who will see how everything hangs together
must leave the towns for a lonely hut at the
edge of the forest.*

No one had accused the professor of being absent minded,
but he looked genuinely befuddled when McIntire told him
his reason for making the trek to his camp. He also looked
like he'd been on a three-day toot. His eyes glittered indigo
from dark hollows in an ashen face. His faded shirt was damp
under the arms in spite of the frosty weather. He'd been sick
all night, he explained. The worst was over now, and he was
feeling better but not well enough to be doing any work. Nevertheless, he leaned on a shovel, maybe only to keep himself
upright. The slingshot protruded from a back pocket of his
baggy trousers.

"I brought the stuff Bambi left here back to the Morlens
right after he died," he said. "There wasn't much."

"Mrs. Morlen seems to think there should be more."

"Well, talk to your boss, or the state police. They ransacked
this place like the Gestapo, and took whatever they damn
pleased." His expression showed exactly in how much esteem
he held the position of township constable. "I'm not holding
out on you. I have no use for Bambi Morlen's old socks."

McIntire couldn't think of any reason to disbelieve him. If Bonnie Morlen didn't even know where her son was spending his nights, it was hard to imagine that she'd know what he kept there. He felt a little foolish. "Any idea where his camera might be?"

"He always kept it with him. I'd guess it was in his car. It was a pretty fancy gadget. Worth stealing, I'd say. Find his camera and you might find his killer."

"We've alerted places that deal in used goods, pawn shops, outfits like that. If anyone tries to sell it we'll nail him." McIntire had only now thought of it, but it seemed like a good idea. "How's the prospecting going?"

Carlson's grip on his spade relaxed. "Oh, we never tell." He then burst out in a hearty laugh. "That hard-boiled detective has taken to it like a duck to water. He showed up yesterday all decked out in Levis so stiff it took about five minutes to unbend himself out of that shrunken excuse for a car, which he's been making pretty free with. Questioned me for about three minutes. Well, basically, he asked if I knew who'd killed Bambi. I said I didn't, and he ambled off into the woods. I haven't seen him since."

Come to think of it, McIntire hadn't seen him for some time, himself. "You don't suppose he's still out there somewhere?"

"Oh, I'm sure Bonnie—Mrs. Morlen—is keeping tabs on him. She'd sound the alarm if he turned up missing."

"Is she here alone? Didn't her husband come back with her?"

Carlson's clammy brow became even shinier. He covered his mouth with his hand and turned away. McIntire could hardly blame him. Wendell Morlen could have that effect on a person.

Carlson wiped his sleeve across his mouth. "Sorry. Wendell's here, too, of course. He might still be spending quite a bit of time in Lansing. I guess that's why he took Fratelli on, to keep an eye on Mrs. Morlen."

Mia had said Bonnie Morlen told her much the same thing, that Fratelli was there for her protection. Of course "keeping an eye on" could have other connotations, especially where a wife was concerned. Mia had also told him that Fratelli had been the one to approach Wendell with an offer of services, services that he didn't seem to be providing to any extent. Maybe he just wanted free room and board and a Michigan vacation. But why were the Morlens willing to put up with it?

There was nothing about Greg Carlson that seemed even remotely crafty or devious. But McIntire couldn't help but feel that there was more to him than was apparent at first glance. Why had he been snooping around at the Shawanok Club? And why was he still here? The sheriff hadn't spent much time on him and neither had Fratelli.

Carlson leaned more heavily onto his shovel. "I miss having the kid around. Besides that, it's good seeing another human now and then. He had a good eye, and was a real help mapping things out." He laughed, a laugh that was cut short with a grimace of pain. "Not to mention that the cabin is being overrun with mice since he's been gone."

"Bambi was a mouser?"

"He was quite handy at catching small critters of all sorts—mice, squirrels, a weasel or two. Devised some pretty ingenious traps. He let them go alive, so they probably came right back in as soon as it got dark. Which gave him the great pleasure of outsmarting them again. And he wasn't above capturing something in my boot or the cracker tin now and then. Gave me a bit of a jolt. The kid got a real kick out of it."

"Our Bambi appears to have been quite the jokester at times," McIntire commented and wondered if the young man's pranks always involved small mammals. "But right now we're trying to trace his whereabouts between midnight and about three in the morning on the night he died. We think he was still alive at that time. Did he come back here after the dance?"

Carlson turned his back to lean the shovel against the cabin wall. "No, he didn't come back."

"Were you here all night?"

"Sure, where else would I be?"

"Maybe he came back for a short time and you slept through it?"

"In a place this size?"

"What can you tell me about these?" McIntire pulled the maps from his jacket pocket. "Maps, Bambi Morlen's."

Carlson gave a derisive snort. "Hell, I might have known."

"What?"

"Bambi kept his maps in a fancy leather case. Said it once belonged to Cyrus McCormick. One of those damn cops walked off with it."

"It turned up somewhere else. It's being looked at for fingerprints. But right now I'm more interested in the contents." McIntire unrolled the most obviously used of the maps and spread it against the log wall of the cabin. "Do you have any idea what they've marked here? Possible uranium deposits?"

Carlson moved the map into a sunnier spot and studied the markings. "I don't think so. This isn't anything we did together, and the boys didn't have a Geiger counter. This is an old map, and shows some things that aren't marked on newer ones, trails and roads that aren't much used any more. These," he pointed to some treasure-map style X's, "are old mine sites, gold or silver. They had big plans to rediscover some abandoned gold mine and strike it rich."

"Which begs the question, why would such a mine have been abandoned?"

Carlson chuckled. "Actually plenty of them were abandoned, gold intact. Getting the ore out cost too much. It's even more expensive now, so I don't expect Bambi and Ross Maki would have done any better. But they had a good time hunting."

"How did they know where to look?" McIntire asked.

"I investigated mineral rights before I started this project, and let them have the legal descriptions of the locations of some mines and claims. So I recognize some of these places. Not all of them. My guess is that where X marks these other spots, there's an old mine they just stumbled onto."

McIntire looked at his watch. It was still early. "I might like to see some of these for myself. Do you by any chance have a compass?"

"I'm loaded with them."

The reply came from behind, and both McIntire and Carlson whirled to behold Melvin Fratelli, Private Eye, resplendent in rigid denim and flamboyant plaid flannel.

Carlson greeted him. "Find anything yet? Pitchblende? Murderers? Poison ivy?"

Fratelli ignored the question and repeated his assertion that he was well supplied with compasses and was chomping at the bit to see a gold mine.

McIntire was glad for the company, so didn't mention that any mine they found would probably amount to a couple of rotted timbers and a weed-covered pile of dirt.

He turned to the now-shivering Greg Carlson. "If we're not back by dark, call out the militia."

# XXV

*...and if one should chance to meet him in the wood, one must not run, nor defend one's self. One must throw one's self down on the ground and pretend to be dead.*

They followed the track past the cabin to where it picked up a logging road that had long ago deteriorated into a foot trail. The terrain was hilly, but not rugged, and the path had been well trodden by Carlson and his ilk. Only a few of the more resilient mosquitos had survived the frosty nights. So at the beginning they set a good pace, despite the stiffness of Fratelli's trousers. Along the way the detective pummeled McIntire with questions. "What's that tree? Should we be on the watch for bears? Have people really made millions in gold mining around here? What *does* poison ivy look like?" None of which had anything to do with the murder of his client's son.

Each time McIntire walked in these deep woods, his spirit shed another layer of the claustrophobia of Europe. With every step on the musky earth, his senses awakened. He moved along in his own world, letting his companion's ramblings blend into the background noise of the breeze and the chatter of red squirrels.

After a little more than a mile they dipped into lower ground and crossed a small creek, where a pencil line on the map indicated that they would find a trail branching off to the south.

"It should be just to the left." McIntire walked slowly, peering into the thick undergrowth. "It might be an old, overgrown trail, or it might be one that Bambi and Ross cut through themselves. Either way we should recognize it when we see it." If they saw it. So far he saw nothing but alder brush. "Maybe we've gone too far."

"Well, you go ahead and scout around. I'll just check things out a bit." Fratelli unshouldered his Geiger counter, clipped a set of earphones to his head, flipped a few switches, and ambled off along the meager stream.

McIntire held the map at arm's length and turned to face the direction his borrowed compass told him was south. They'd encountered no other creek. This had to be the one. And it certainly looked to be the right crossing spot. There were no other routes they could have taken. According to Bambi's map, they should walk straight across the stream and just keep going. McIntire walked a dozen paces further on. The ground rose gradually, and the growth of alder nearer the water petered out to thimbleberry and bracken fern. The leaves were shriveled and brown but untrammeled. He was about to turn back when, "Halloo, over here!" sounded from upstream and Fratelli's red deer hunter's cap showed through the brush. McIntire found him standing at the head of a narrow path cut into the muddy bank. So those who passed this way had disguised the fact by walking a short distance up the creek before cutting back into the woods. McIntire had no need for such secrecy, and would just as soon leave an easily followed trail for the return trip. He plowed up the hill.

*Cliff* would have been more accurate. The way was steep and, gravity being what it is, was clogged with an accumulation of fallen trees. The route was clearly marked, however, in the manner of one who'd spent some time studying a book on woodsmanship. White blazes, slashed with a hatchet, stood out clearly on tree trunks, and the more easily moved debris had been cleared away.

When they once more stood on level ground, McIntire's heart was pounding. He was relieved to hear Fratelli puffing as well.

The terrain here was more forgiving, but traversing it not so simple. This portion of Bambi's trail was not well marked, and McIntire had to abandon any hope of following it and rely on his navigational skills. If Fratelli had believed that in hooking up with McIntire he was getting an experienced backwoods guide, he was in for severe disappointment. When McIntire stopped for the tenth time to consult his map, the detective said mildly, "I thought you knew your way around here."

McIntire surreptitiously consulted his watch. It was still before noon. "So far as I can recall, I've never been in this spot before in my life."

"But you said…. I understood that you were born here."

McIntire rolled up the map. "I was born in St. Adele. When I was young every tree within a forty-mile radius had been chopped down. Things looked completely different. I left when I was seventeen years old. I only came back last year." Fratelli froze. Philip Marlowe would never have let such panic show in his eyes.

"You could spend your whole life in these woods and you'd still need a compass to get around," McIntire said. "We've got a compass *and* a map. If Bambi knew what he was doing when he drew in these trails, we're okay. The tricky part is reckoning how far we've come. It's always going to feel like we've walked about three times the distance we really have."

Fratelli didn't appear convinced. "I should have known," he said. "You don't talk near so funny as everybody else around here."

"I'll be glad to oblige with an 'uffda' or two if it'll make you feel better," McIntire told him. "Now," he mentally crossed his fingers, "according to my calculations, one of these mines should be right past that pine tree!"

He led the way to a small rise that grew up from the forest floor about fifty yards to their left. His reputation, and, judging from the glower on Fratelli's face, possibly his life, was saved. Rusted remnants of iron gears, a teepee of hand-hewn timbers, and some freshly turned soil showed that they'd located one of Bambi's abandoned mines.

The old excavation had caved in, or been covered over, long ago. It was clear that the two boys had not put much effort into exploring the site. Except for a couple of shallow holes, nothing was disturbed.

"Okay, Bwana, how far to the next one?" Fratelli lit up a Chesterfield and leaned against the trunk of a beech tree.

McIntire perched on the axle connecting a pair of rusting wagon wheels and spread the map on his knees. "There's one more nearby, over in that direction," he waved to the west, "and another about a mile and a half south, farther into the mountains. It looks like it's near a small lake, or maybe a beaver pond, so it should be easy to find. And a half mile or so beyond it there appears to be a major trail going out, seems to connect up to a road of some kind, so we won't have to go back the way we've come."

"So why in hell didn't we drive there first?"

McIntire scrutinized the map. He was beginning to get a blurry idea of where they were relative to the larger world. He folded the map and tucked it into his pocket. "Nothing wrong with a bit of exercise," he said.

The next site was much like the first, without the rusting equipment. Only a slightly dug-up mound of earth. It would hardly have been noticed by the casual passer-by, if casual passers existed here. The area around it was open and sunny, feeling twenty degrees warmer than the deeper woods. Fratelli observed that it might be a good place to stop for lunch.

"You didn't think my employer would send me off unprovisioned?" He removed the knapsack from his back and knelt next to a wide beech stump. He then proceeded to set out an array of waxed paper-wrapped packets—roast beef sandwiches,

deviled eggs, tiny sticks of carrots and celery. And to top off
the feast, coconut cake and a thermos of coffee.

"Sorry, she only packed one cup. We'll have to take
turns. I'll go first." Fratelli uncorked the thermos and filled
the cup. "And only one napkin." He sat on a fallen log and
spread the square of sparkling white linen on his knees. "An
amazing woman," he observed between bites. "Bakes all day,
plinks away at that piano all night. Don't know that she ever
sleeps."

"A damn strange woman," McIntire said, helping himself to
a sandwich. "She's hell-bent to see her son's murderer caught.
She's hired you, after all, and she's pretty disappointed that
there is no chance the guilty party will be executed in this
state. But she'll have nothing to do with the police, or the
sheriff…or me, for that matter. Well, maybe she doesn't have
a lot of faith in our ability."

Mia had said that Bonnie didn't express much confidence
in her P.I. either. And didn't seem too concerned about it.
Even more strange.

"Who do you think did it? The Indian kid?" So Fratelli
was still centering his suspicions on the Walls.

"Oh, I doubt it," McIntire said. "If it'd been Marve, I
figure we'd have found some smudges of war paint and a few
feathers on the scene."

"That's a good one!" Fratelli gave a whoop and a grin which
quickly faded to an *are you laughing with me or at me?* look.

"But," the detective continued, "it seems plain as the nose
on your face. Walls planned to kidnap Wendell Morlen's son
to settle a score and maybe make a little cash in the bargain.
They drug him to knock him out, but he puts up more of
a fight than they expected, and they end up stabbing him.
They get him into that loft and tie him up. Then he surprises
them by dying."

"So they scalped him, so we'd be sure to give credit where
it's due?"

Fratelli sprinkled salt from a screw of waxed paper onto an egg. "Don't forget the hole."

"Right," McIntire replied. "That hole is the really curious part."

"Why?" It happened every day in New York City, no doubt.

"It's true that some Indians and other societies did that, a few thousand years ago. But it's one of those little-known facts. I doubt even Arnie Johnson knows it."

"Who?"

"Never mind. The point is, who else would even have heard of such a thing."

"That Indians used to do it, you mean? What about your Swede back there. Sounds like it's something in his line of work."

"Carlson? He's an—"

"Anthropologist. He's no more looking for uranium here than I am. A damn sight less, if you get right down to it."

"How do you know that?"

"I'm a detective." He dusted his lips with the napkin and smiled. "Shit, it didn't take a lot of sleuthing. I called the university where he works. He's a professor of anthropology, currently on a year sabbatical to study—let's see, what was it?—ancient copper people of the western great lakes."

"Well, hell! So why's he keeping it a secret?" It sounded like Fratelli might have a few secrets of his own. For instance, that his profession was, in truth, private investigation.

"That I couldn't say."

It switched on at last, the first glimmer of light since the boy had been murdered. McIntire reached for an egg. "So that's why Carlson was buddying up to Bambi, sneaking into the Club."

"Why?"

"There's supposed to be a big rock of some kind there, a sort of prehistoric monolith. The Clubbers live in fear of the world finding out about it and beating a path to their door."

"What's that?" The detective leaped to his feet, sending an intricately sculpted radish skipping into the fallen leaves. McIntire strained to hear a distant barking. He listened as the sound came nearer, a cacophony of yipping.

"Geese," he said.

Fratelli stared in disbelief until a great V of migrating birds came into view, their white underbellies barely clearing the treetops.

"They wouldn't be this low on such a clear day if they weren't going in for a landing," McIntire said. "Maybe that means this pond, and the next mine, are not too far off. Follow that bird!"

Before setting out, he took a turn at having a cup of the lukewarm coffee, while Super Sleuth did a tour of the area with his Geiger counter.

The birds did not wait around, so the two men followed a mostly dry stream bed that seemed to head in the right direction. McIntire let Fratelli take the lead and was rewarded for his courtesy by a yelp that told him the detective had stumbled onto, and into, the body of water near Bambi's third X.

It was a good-sized pond, inky black, with jungle-like brush around its edges that contributed to Fratelli's sudden discovery and his wet feet. It appeared to be a permanent feature of the landscape, not the temporary result of a beaver dam.

According to the map, the mine site itself was on the opposite side of the pond from where they stood, and once again they could find no discernible trail. They spent some time scrambling around the swampy eastern shore, and trudging uphill deeper into the woods, before finally coming across a weak path that led them straight to the spot.

Even at first glance, it was considerably more interesting than the previous two mines. Heavy log timbers formed the frame of a doorway. A fresh mound of dirt showed where soil had been removed to reveal the adit in the steep hillside. Fratelli reached into his sack and pulled out a flashlight.

"Jeez," McIntire said, "ain't you the regular boy scout."

"Lucky for you." He stepped aside to let McIntire enter first.

The cave-like space was low, but wider than McIntire expected. The light on the walls and ceiling showed up no heady glints of gold. When Fratelli elbowed past him, McIntire put a hand on his sleeve. "Wait, let me see the torch a minute." He played the light over the floor. The earth was covered with footprints. "Look at this." McIntire aimed the beam into the back of the recess. A dark mound rested against the wall.

"A body," Fratelli whispered and once again attempted to charge past him.

McIntire snorted, "Look again. Looks like blankets to me."

The P.I. reclaimed his flashlight and dropped to his knees. "We don't want to mess up these prints. Looks like at least two separate sets."

"Dr. Watson would be proud of you. But I don't think there's much doubt as to who they belong to."

"What's that smell?"

McIntire sniffed. "Kerosene." He pointed to a box-shaped heater with a stovepipe extending through the earthen ceiling. A metal box with a padlock sat next to it.

They stood in the center of the space and examined the floor and walls. It was clear that the boys, or possibly someone else, had spent time here, but there were no obvious signs that they had conducted any further excavations after clearing the opening. Fratelli advanced toward the dank, low recess at the back. McIntire let him go alone.

"I'd as soon think this over out in the open." McIntire stooped to exit the cave, blinked at the sunlight, and found himself staring into the twin barrels of a twelve-gauge shotgun.

"Straighten up and get the hell out of there." The voice was harsh and raspy. It bore nuances of French. McIntire straightened up and got the hell out of the mine, not exactly in that order.

The butt end of the gun was planted firmly into the shoulder of a small man with fidgety black eyes and sparse, tobacco-yellowed whiskers twitching at the corners of his mouth.

"Get your buddy out here."

McIntire didn't turn. "You heard him, buddy. You better get out here!"

"What the hell!" Fratelli's response was muffled. McIntire felt himself bumped from behind and heard the detective's sharp intake of breath.

The grating voice rang out again. "What's your business here?"

"Who the hell do you—"

McIntire stepped back onto the imprudently mouthy detective's foot. "Good afternoon," he said, in a voice that he hoped sounded composed. "I'm John McIntire. I believe you're Esko Thomson?" Then McIntire did what any good Catholic boy does when faced with imminent bodily harm. He invoked the saints. "I think you knew my father, Colin."

A degree of the craftiness passed from the eyes. "You Col's boy? Well, I'll be!" The gun barrels sank below the level of McIntire's forehead, then rose again. "You don't look much like him."

"No," McIntire acknowledged, "I took after Ma. In looks."

"What're you doing out here?"

"Scouting a place to put up a deer stand and got a little turned around, as they say. Keeping your bearings can be tricky around here."

"Not if you got any sense a-tall, but I remember you ended up being a city boy." He tucked the gun under his arm, and his voice dropped to a less strident pitch. "Thought you were a couple of them gol-damned uranium hunters. I've had to per-suade a few of them to hunt elsewhere." He arced a stream of tobacco into the bushes. "What about your buddy there?"

"Pa's cousin's son, Paddy McIntire, all the way from County Cork."

Fratelli coughed and put out his hand. "Top o' the day t'ye."

Thomson grasped the hand in his own grubby paw and gave a satisfied nod. "Now you *do* favor the McIntires." He pulled a plug of tobacco from his shirt pocket, stripped back its brown wrapping, bit off a generous portion, and extended it to Fratelli. "Chaw?"

The P.I. showed his mettle. "It's after my own heart you are." He took his medicine without so much as a tear. As a city boy, McIntire figured he was safe in declining.

"Come on down to my camp, and we'll have a little warmer-upper." Thomson stowed his tobacco. "I couldn't let Col's boys run off without a bit of hospitality. And I know no real McIntire would turn *that* down."

McIntire took one look at the persuader under Thomson's arm and, like a real McIntire, followed him through the trees.

Fratelli hissed through his chaw, "But what about my—"

"Forget the damn Geiger counter!"

# XXVI

*He would have liked to fill the castle with
whirling wheels and working levers. He wished
to be a great inventor and improve the world.*

The trip to Esko Thomson's camp followed no direct path.
After scrambling through the brush for forty-five minutes,
they climbed a ridge, descended its other side, and emerged
in a clearing occupied by a bizarre conglomeration of wood
and metal. The industrial revolution run amok. Every square
foot of space among the trees, as well as half of the trees themselves, contained some motley assemblage of timbers, angle
iron, pulleys, and rope.

The purpose of some of the contraptions was evident. The
hand pump enthroned on a platform six feet off the ground—a
series of gears converting its operation to a crank at ground
level—would send water down a twisting chute to the cabin.
The iron wedge attached to a length of steel would drop like
a guillotine from its tripod of upright logs to split even the
most recalcitrant hunk of firewood. The use of other devices,
like the one consisting of the top of an oil barrel and a rusty
mallet, both tethered to a tree limb, was unfathomable.

In addition to the Rube Goldberg apparatuses, raw materi-
als were stockpiled neatly under makeshift lean-tos. Car parts,
wagon wheels, plumbing supplies, containers from lard cans to

stock tanks. Each species of cast-off had its own spot. How in hell had the scrawny old coot gotten all this stuff back here?

In the center of this backwoods mad scientist laboratory, a corrugated metal roof rose up, distinguishing Esko Thomson's home from its junk-yard surroundings. The structure was about sixty feet long, the former center of a lumber camp. For a building of its age, and one which hadn't been constructed for the long haul, it stood reasonably straight and square for about a third of its length. From there on it ran downhill both figuratively and literally.

Its undulating roof descended at a steep pitch to meet a set of eaves-troughs with downspouts converging into a single dented conduit. This pipe angled down to spill into a galvanized washtub perched on a boxy cast iron stove. The stove sat on its own concrete pad next to a stack of firewood as high as the cabin. It made an innovative method for collecting and heating water, but the resourceful Esko hadn't stopped there. Copper tubing ran from the base of the vat and ended in a spigot bolted to the side of a chipped claw-footed bathtub. To complete the cycle, a rubber hose extended from the bathtub's drain down the gentle slope to a good sized garden plot. The entire complex was tucked into a spot sheltered by buildings, lean-tos, and stacks of enough firewood to last until well into the next century, protecting it from wind and possibly even the bulk of the snowfall. McIntire had to give Esko credit. Most people would have settled for a sauna. But from the appearance of the back of his neck, of which McIntire had an all too clear view, the old man didn't appear to give his bathing facilities much use. Well, it had been a dry autumn.

McIntire wondered if the stove and copper tubing were leftovers from Esko's infamous still. Maybe the bathtub had been used for gin. Esko had been Colin McIntire's main supplier during the long arid years of prohibition and had provided the occasional jug even before that. As far as McIntire knew he'd gotten out of the business. Not much market for home brew these days. He might still produce some for his own use, or, a chilling thought, for entertaining guests.

Behind the tub was a pile of what resembled gigantic galvanized bowls, nested one inside the other. McIntire had heard of these, a kind of basin used in the gold extracting process. After the mines had closed down, local people had salvaged them to use as chick brooders. Supposedly someone had found that gold deposits could be recovered from them, and chickens were being evicted by the hundreds. Esko Thomson didn't look as if he'd made a fortune in gold.

A clothesline strung between two birches held a pair of much mended wool trousers. Not remarkable in itself, but the piercingly acrid odor emanating from them set McIntire's eyes to watering. Fratelli's shoulders shook as he coughed into his handkerchief. Neither of them risked a glance in Thomson's direction or in each other's. So the great woodsman had run afoul of a skunk. It had happened to Kelpie once. The smell had lasted until she grew a new coat of hair. Esko might as well give the pants a proper cremation and have done with it.

As they approached the building, three identical cats, long legged and gray, leaped from their sunny spots on the woodpile and disappeared into the brush.

Esko stopped just outside his door, a heavy carved oak affair which, aside from its peeling paint, McIntire quite envied him.

"Hang on a sec, boys." The little scavenger stooped to take an egg-sized stone from a yellow lard bucket and directed his attention across the clearing to his vegetable garden. A few rows of drying sweet corn still stood. One stalk swayed under the weight of a persistent crow struggling to strip a shriveled ear of its husk. Thomson drew back his arm and let fly. Crow and rock hit the ground together.

"That's one less."

He led them into a room crammed with more of the same, a veritable shrine to Sir Isaac Newton. In addition to the elaborate array of gravity-assisted appliances, a good share of the space was taken up by a stove whose Paul Bunyan proportions attested to a previous incarnation in service to a crew of lumberjacks. The room must have comprised Esko's entire living space; there was no adjoining door to the rest of the building. He probably used that for storage. Maybe the stuff stacked outside was only the overflow. It also looked like a good spot for hanging out of season deer. McIntire wondered if he should have a look. He had a look at Esko and his firearm and decided to leave it for now.

Esko stood the shotgun in a corner, lit a lamp, and poked up the fire. "Just sit anywhere. Make yourselves homely." His low chuckle didn't disguise the fact that it was more order than invitation. Fratelli dove for the pitted chrome kitchen stool, leaving McIntire to step over a galvanized metal chick feeder and hopscotch around several piles of magazines to a salvaged car seat. He sank into it, knees in the air.

Their host produced two crazed cups and a glass from a small cupboard, then dropped to his knees and crawled under the oil-cloth covered table. For a few minutes only his skinny twill-covered posterior was visible. Fratelli mouthed something that looked like, "We could take him now!" but McIntire shook his head. The skinny haunches went into motion. Esko backed out and stood erect with a grunt and a bottle. McIntire was relieved to see that, from surface appearances anyway, the warmer-upper was of the purchased variety.

McIntire's Son of Colin status paid off once again. Esko handed him the only glass, small but embellished in full color, the Road Runner trapped forever in his flight from that brush wolf.

The whisky wasn't only store bought, but was smooth, creamy, and definitely imparted a welcome warmth. McIntire accepted a second bump, leaned back against the seat, and listened abstractedly to Esko regaling cousin Paddy with tales of his illustrious American relative.

Esko's walls were decorated in keeping with the rest of his home. Objects both utilitarian and ornamental covered every inch. Traps for fur-bearing creatures in sizes ranging from weasel to wolf hung in a ragged row. Deer antlers held jackets, hats, and ropes. Pictures cut from magazines overlapped one another and provided a background for a collection of axes, fish nets, fish spears, fishing rods, fishing lures, and a peeling stuffed bass.

A framed photograph near the window showed the Esko Thomson that McIntire remembered, wiry, his face tanned dark but smooth and unmottled. He stood clutching a pick to his chest with both hands, surrounded by a cluster of fellow miners or prospectors. McIntire leaned closer. Of the seven men in the group, he recognized two besides Esko. On the far left, one of his father's regular customers, Jack Driscoll, was the only one to be smiling. Driscoll might have had more to smile about. He was reputed to have discovered some rich source of silver, but died before anyone could worm the secret of its whereabouts out of him. Next to him was Walleye Wall. Walleye had worked many years as a Huron Mountain guide and was probably with the group in that capacity rather than as a member of the prospecting crew.

There were a few other photographs, formally posed studio portraits, staid subjects in shades of brown. A wedding portrait, the bride's head level with her new husband's though he was sitting while she stood at his side, her hand on his shoulder. A small girl in buckled shoes and effusive curls swinging on a crescent moon.

The room was growing dim and comfortably warm. McIntire extended his legs, fitting them between a stack of encyclopedias and a glass churn. He had never thought of Esko as having a family. Well, everybody has to come from somewhere. McIntire felt his eyelids droop. Esko came from Canada. The old man's voice droned on, punctuated by an occasional *och* or *begorrah* from his rapt audience. The story had moved to a lurid recounting of rape and torture at the hands of orange men. Orange? Orangemen? Some Canadian political strife, McIntire imagined, no doubt considerably embellished by the intervening years. Did Esko still think of life north of the border? Not fondly, by the sound of things.

*Estella.* The word swam up from the depths of his subconscious. A hazy recollection of a conversation between his parents, heard the way Johnny McIntire had gotten most of his information, through the open grate in his bedroom floor. Esko had a sister. She'd died sometime before he fled French Canada for Michigan. Estella. McIntire had been fascinated by the sound of the name.

A bloodcurdling yowl sliced through his drowsing. McIntire's eyes flew open, and his feet hit the floor. "What in—"

Esko Thomson rose from his spot on a narrow cot and gave a yank on a knotted rope looped through a hook on the wall. "Still a little skittish, eh?" A hatch in the bottom of the door slid up, allowing the three rangy felines to slip inside. They sidled up to the chick feeding pan and sat, dark shadows, six topaz eyes glowing.

Esko zig-zagged through the room, pulled aside the flour sack curtain from a fruit crate cabinet and lifted a can of Carnation milk. He drew a jackknife from his pocket and stabbed a pair of holes in the can.

"If I leave 'em out all night, owls'll get 'em." He poured a thick yellow stream into a fruit jar and added an equal amount of scummy looking water from a vinegar jug. The cats waited without moving until he'd poured the concoction into the pan and stepped back. Then they fell upon it like hairy vultures.

McIntire wondered if he should try to put a few questions to Esko about who else he might have seen hanging around the old mine. Maybe Bambi and Ross had gotten involved with somebody Ross hadn't mentioned. Maybe they'd been involved with Esko himself, although if Esko had visited their hideout before today, McIntire was confident that the stove and supplies would have gone with him when he left. Unless, that is, the boys had cached a lot more gear, and Esko was there because he was making a second trip. Had he confronted Bambi and Ross? He didn't have much use for the uranium hunters. He'd never had much use for hunters of any sort poking around his place, but so far as McIntire had heard, he'd never gone so far as to eliminate any of them. And the mine was not all that near Esko's place.

Thomson pulled a white pouch of Peerless and a packet of cigarette papers from his pocket. Fratelli countered with an offer of his ready-made Chesterfields. Thomson drew a stick match across his thigh and lit up. He flicked the spent match toward the stove. It hit the lid but bounced off, narrowly missed a pile of newspapers, and smoldered out on the toe of a worn boot. How was it that the place hadn't gone up in smoke years ago?

The cats had licked the pan clean and were involved in the process of tidying themselves up. Then, one by one, they slunk off to a row of wooden boxes. McIntire's torpor abated a bit. He stared. Each of the boxes was rigged with rope that ran through a pulley on the beam overhead.

"What the devil is that?" The warmer-upper had rendered McIntire imprudently blunt as well as groggy, and he interrupted Thomson's tale of the elder McIntire's expert manhandling of three drunk, ax-wielding Swedes.

Thomson frowned, his eyes black marbles in the lamplight. McIntire waved apologetically toward the boxes. "Cat beds," he stated and made to turn back to Cousin Paddy.

"But why the block and tackle?"

"Like I said, if I leave 'em out—great horned supper! Can't stand to have them running around the cabin at night, though. Crawling all over the bed, hair on everything." He gave a fastidious shudder. "I tuck them in their beds and," he mimed pulling on the ropes," up to the ceiling, snug as bugs all night long."

"Speaking of night," McIntire said, "it's time we headed back while we can still see."

"It's pretty gol-damn dark already. Maybe you boys better stay over."

Was this another enforced invitation? Spend the night or face their host's wrath? Hadn't McIntire heard a story like this on *The Inner Sanctum*? He looked from Esko's shotgun in the corner to his stained and rumpled cot. He chose the lesser of two evils. "'Fraid we have to be going."

"Well, suit yourselves. Keep your eyes peeled for wolves." He smiled. The few teeth he had left were as yellow as the cats' eyes.

As they stepped out into the dusk, the creak of rope on pulley announced that the cats were on their way to being snug as bugs.

"How in hell are we gonna get out of here?" Fratelli demanded. "I didn't leave any trail of breadcrumbs along the way."

"Relax, Sherlock," McIntire told him. "I'm pretty sure I know where we are."

"*Pretty* sure?"

"Real sure." McIntire did know where they were. He'd visited Esko's camp with his father back when the little opportunist had first co-opted it, shortly after it had ceased functioning as a lumber camp. He knew where they were, but wasn't quite so sanguine about his ability to get them back to their cars at Carlson's cabin. He buttoned his coat up to the neck, led the way across the minefield that was Esko's homestead, and started down an overgrown track.

"Hey, this ain't how we got here!"

"You want to go back the way we came, be my guest. I'll take the high road. With luck when we get to it, we can hitch a ride back to our cars."

"I need to get my—"

"Forget about the damn Geiger counter."

"I paid two hundred bucks for that thing."

"You got snookered."

Once under the canopy of the trees, they proceeded without speaking, concentrating on finding their way in the darkness. Fratelli pulled out one of his fleet of compasses and turned his flashlight on its face. "Do you think there really are wolves here?" He twisted his wrist to let the compass to catch the light. "Where do you suppose that old codger got the Scotch?"

McIntire wasn't sure about the wolves, or the whisky either. "I can tell you for damn sure he didn't make it himself! It seemed okay to me."

"Okay? I guess! Johnnie Walker, gold."

"No kidding? Well, I doubt they sell it in Chandler. Nobody around here has that kind of money."

Fratelli stuffed the compass back into his pocket. "I imagine Morlen might be able to squeeze it into his budget."

# XXVII

*She was the gayest and most foolish of women.*

McIntire returned the handset to its cradle with a crack that threatened to rip the phone off the wall and brought Leonie scrambling from the living room where she'd been sequestered with the ironing board and the week's episode of *Tales of the Texas Rangers*. "What's happened?"

McIntire took a cup from the cupboard. "Nothing! Not one damned single, solitary thing has happened," he slammed the cup on the table, "and I'm starting to wonder why."

He sat down and stared into the empty vessel. "Bonnie Morlen comes galloping back claiming to be desperate to find her son's murderer. Well, just how eager can she be? She won't let the sheriff or the state police in the door, just hides out, tinkling away on that piano and plying Mia Thorsen with cocoa. That woman lied through her teeth when the state police talked to her, wouldn't admit to being out the night her son died until they forced her into a corner. Said she was afraid she'd get into trouble for not having a Michigan driver's licence. Talk about feeble excuses! Her personal private investigator is traipsing around the woods playing Yosemite Sam, while she packs tidy lunches to keep up his strength. And she's been pretty cozy with Prospector Imposter Carlson, the only person I can imagine would have known that ancient Michigan Indians were given to drilling holes in skulls."

Leonie rescued the cup. "That poor woman has had a terrible tragedy. I don't suppose she's being completely rational."

"Rational? Bonnie Morlen is a complete fruitcake," McIntire said. Leonie didn't disagree.

"And now," McIntire continued, "to top it off, I've been trying to call Pete Koski, and Marian tells me he's gone to see Adam Wall."

"What's wrong with that? You seemed pretty sure that Adam Wall might have known about his skull-drilling ancestors. Mr. Koski must consider him a suspect."

"Something is suspect, that's for sure. I called Ellie Wall to see if I could catch Koski before he left their place. She said Adam and the sheriff weren't back yet. They went to Fenster Lake for bass—again. Yes, that's what she said, *again*." He nodded as Leonie held out the coffee pot. "Thanks. Does anybody care at all that the boy's dead? What about his father? Is Wendell Morlen ever even around?"

An unearthly squeal sounded from the front yard. Leonie smiled and patted her husband's arm, "Well, love, from the sound of those grinding gears, I'd say that Melvin Fratelli, P.I., is on the job after all."

"He probably wants my advice on where to get another blasted Geiger counter."

"You're both wrong." Siobhan swept into the room on a wave of cigarette smoke and Prince Matchabelli. "He's here for me. We're going to Chandler to see *Sunset Boulevard*, and then perhaps out for a little Halloween celebration." She turned her back and looked over her shoulder. "Are my seams straight?"

Siobhan didn't wait for a judgement. She was out the door before Fratelli had chance to beep his horn. Or change his mind, McIntire reckoned.

"Halloween?" Siobhan's chatter suddenly registered in McIntire's mind. "Oh, lord! This can't be Halloween?"

"No," Leonie told him. "You've got until Saturday to gird your loins for the big night. And gird you better had. Don't forget what happened to Sally's milk cow last year."

McIntire didn't need to be reminded. Opal had shown up on All Saints' Day painted an unimaginative purple. It had been mildly amusing at the time. Dealing with the culprits had been Walleye's job.

"I'll worry about colorful cows and tipped outhouses another day. Right now I have weightier things to sort out. But it's late, and I can do it better after I've washed off the residue of Esko Thomson's delightful abode." He stood and tossed the dregs of his coffee into the sink. Boys would be pranksters, he guessed, but he'd rather they didn't do it on his time.

"I wonder if he'd do an interview." Leonie's expression was one of unashamed avarice.

"Are you talking about Esko?"

"Naturally. How many people have lived a life like that? In this day and age! It would make a fantastic story. I might be able to sell it back home. With photographs, a magazine might take it! Maybe *Picture Post!* The man's an original."

"Not all that original around here," McIntire said. He took both her hands and kissed the fingers. "No, my dear one, I think this time you'd better forget it. Esko and Old Bessie don't take kindly to visitors." How true was that? Thomson had been eager for McIntire and Fratelli to stop for that warmer-upper, even to the point of suggesting they spend the night. Leonie echoed his thoughts.

"He took kindly to you."

"He was ready to let Old Bessie have her way with me until I called on Pa to save me."

"Well, it's only natural for him to be suspicious," she argued. "Out there all by himself in the forest. No protection but his own wits—and that shotgun."

"You make him sound like Daniel Boone. Esko Thomson is a grubby little scavenger."

Leonie's eyes still had that newswoman's gleam. "You have to admit it is rather romantic."

"*Romantic?* He lives in complete and utter squalor. He's got cats hanging from the ceiling, for God's sake! It ain't exactly the American Dream."

"But, don't you see," Leonie said, "that's exactly what it *is*. Freedom. He's found a way to do exactly as he pleases, without asking for anything, living on what nature provides."

"Or what other people leave lying around unguarded."

"Well, you wouldn't understand, because you haven't had to be dependent on anyone else. If you were a woman, you might see things differently. You might appreciate how that sort of self-sufficiency is a rare and special thing." She seemed to notice that she still held McIntire's empty cup. She grimaced and returned it to the table with only slightly less force than McIntire had used earlier. "It's not really fair."

"How's that?"

"A woman wouldn't be able to live that way. She'd end up locked up somewhere."

"As she probably should be! Same goes for Esko." McIntire leaned forward and kissed his wife's nose. "You're not dependent on me, Leonie."

"I know," she said. "That's why I married you."

McIntire turned once again to the stairs.

"I'd wait a wee bit if I were you." For someone who had recently declared her independence, Leonie's voice sounded uncharacteristically timid.

"Why?"

"Siobhan spent the last hour in the tub. I doubt there's hot water left."

# XXVIII

*She could conceal her anger, preserve it fresh and*
*new for years. She was a richly gifted person.*

"Boston cream pie."

Mia accepted the proffered plate and balanced it on her
knee.

"You could use a little meat on your bones."

Mia forced a smile. She wondered what Bonnie's reaction
would be were she to reach for the cake on *her* side of the tray
with a, "I'll just take that, Dearie. You could do with a bit
less padding on your bottom." Strange how it was considered
perfectly acceptable to comment on her thinness. Well, Mia
supposed she had the better of it. She could assuage her hurt
pride by consuming innumerable pieces of Boston cream pie
with impunity.

"Have you spoken to Mr. McIntire?"

Mia nodded. "He said he'd check with Greg Carlson and
the sheriff. See if they know where your son's things might
be." Once again she didn't mention the maps she'd found in
her truck. That probably wasn't the kind of belongings Bonnie
was looking for, and they were out of her hands now.

"But you haven't heard anything?"

"I'm sure if anything turns up, John will bring it to you."

"Oh, I'd really rather he didn't." She gave a short, self-
deprecating laugh. "I know this might sound…silly, but I

absolutely can't bear to deal with those policemen. They bring everything back. I see the sheriff or Mr. McIntire and…all the pain…they were the ones who told me about…."

"Of course," Mia said. "I understand." She didn't really, didn't understand why Bonnie Morlen hadn't pitched her tent on the courthouse lawn, why she wasn't making Pete Koski's life hell. "I'll ask John if he finds anything to let me know. Course I can't do that with the sheriff."

"You're all so *tall*."

It came from nowhere. Mia fumbled for a response.

"You…Mr. McIntire…that sheriff is a giant. Is everybody here so large?"

Mia laughed, but suppressed a shiver. The question was almost childlike. "We pretty much come in all sizes."

"Is your husband big, too?"

"Not especially. You've probably met my husband. He delivers the mail. Nick."

Bonnie's genuine smile indicated that she'd indeed met the mailman. "Oh, yes, a very nice man. So helpful. I'm afraid he's gotten a few things mixed up though. Left mail in the box that wasn't meant for us. I suppose since we're new here…."

"Oh, new has nothing to do with it. He's been at it for thirty-five years. Everybody's pretty much used to it. Nick claims he's doing the neighborhood a favor by shuffling the mail a bit. Forces people to keep in touch with the folks down the road."

"Really? How interesting."

Did this woman have any sense of humor at all? Mia instantly felt ashamed. How much gaiety could one expect from a woman whose only child had been kidnapped, murdered, and mutilated? Although, as chagrined as she felt, Mia couldn't bring herself to like the little Betty Crocker opposite her. She might be all Boston cream fluff on the outside, but rare glimpses of the inner Bonnie hinted that the chocolate and cream disguised a core of strychnine. Maybe she was trying to play Nero Wolf, sitting home and eating while Mia took care of the Archie end of things.

Bonnie cut off a piece of the cake with her fork, then paused with it halfway to her mouth, eyes bright as any gossip-seeking housewife. "Have you heard any talk? Is the sheriff closing in on anybody? How about those Indians?"

It was galling, but Mia managed, "I understand that Mr. Koski has been spending quite a lot of time with the Walls."

Bonnie gave a satisfied nod. "Before we came here, Wendell used to joke that he was heading west to do battle with Indians."

Could Adam Wall and his lawsuit actually have had something to do with the murder? Mia hadn't seriously considered that before. "Did Bambi know about the lawsuit?" she asked. "Would he have heard about it from his father?"

Bonnie opened her mouth, hesitated, then seemed to make up her mind. She put down the fork. "My husband is not Bambi's father."

Her triumphant expression said that she wouldn't have been surprised, or disappointed, to see her visitor faint dead away from such a revelation.

"I see," Mia stumbled, "...everyone just assumed...I guess you can't do that these days."

"I married Wendell before my son was born," she said. "Bambi never knew."

Mia could think of no response to this, and Bonnie didn't wait for one.

She began making precise folds in the starched napkin on her lap, creasing them down with her thumbnail as she spoke. "I was expected to be a musician, a singer. I *was* a singer. I started performing when I was three years old. And I was good. Not quite good enough to have the career my mother wanted for me, in opera, but I didn't care. When I was fifteen, my aunt took me to opening night of *Showboat* at the Ziegfield Theatre. It was a Christmas gift. After that, I wanted to do nothing but musical comedy. But my mother wanted Aïda, not Ado Annie. She hired the best teacher she could buy. He was older, incredibly handsome, sophisticated—and married. Mama didn't get Aïda. She got a grandson."

Bonnie continued to fold as she talked. "Wendell worked for my father. He was young, single, reasonably presentable, and ambitious. I'd met him a few times. I was in no position to argue. We made a bargain and we both stuck to it. My mentor got a quick trip to California, I got a husband, Wendell got my daddy's money, and my son got a father." She spoke without bitterness. "And he was a good father. Wendell never treated Bambi as anything but his own child."

Wendell's record as a husband may not have been so illustrious; once again acid oozed from the sugary crust. "But Bambi doesn't need a father now, and that man is not going to get one penny of my mother's money!

"The money," she explained, "that Bambi would have come into when he turned twenty-five will now go to me. And I'm going to make sure that Wendell never gets his hands on it!"

The naked rage in Bonnie's voice was painful and spellbinding at the same time, like watching a burning building.

"My husband was well paid to marry me, and he's more than collected in full. But it's never been enough to suit him. He's been waiting like a vulture for my father to die. I could have lived with that. But I'll be damned if he's going to profit from my son's death!"

She placed the napkin, now a jaunty linen sailboat, on the table. "I came back here to see that the people responsible for killing my baby suffer for it. But before I left Westchester, I instructed my attorney to file for a divorce."

Divorce was for movie actors. Mia had never known anyone who'd been divorced. Except possibly Siobhan, now that she thought of it. She steeled herself to ask, "So are you separated from your husband now?"

"No more than usual. Wendell works a great deal. He's often away from home."

"But your husband *is* here in Michigan? Not back in Connecticut?"

"He's still trying to get that Club business straightened out. That keeps him in Lansing most of the time. Otherwise, yes, he's here."

"Even though you've asked for a divorce?" Mia couldn't conceive of that kind of situation. She also couldn't believe that she had actually been so ill-mannered as to question her hostess about it. Well, Bonnie had brought the subject up herself.

"Wendell thinks it's the grief talking, or one of my little whims. He thinks I'll get over it." Mia could understand the bitterness that underlay Bonnie's words.

Bonnie took the napkin back in her lap. "Mrs. Thorsen, do you have children?"

She'd expected it, had figured it would come sooner than this, but Mia, as always, flinched at the question. For once though, she didn't sugarcoat the response. "I had three children," she said. "They all died shortly after birth."

"Oh, I'm sorry." She reached forward to give Mia's hand a perfunctory pat. "Then you can't know what it's like to lose a child you've raised."

The anger and tears were too close to the surface. Mia put down her cup. "I really have to go now, Mrs. Morlen."

"You'll let me know—?"

"I'll call you if I hear anything."

The gate left smudges of rust on Mia's coat where she leaned against it. After a short hesitation, she pushed it open and walked through. Her steps made no sound on the thick golden carpet of pine needles as she crossed to stand before the single stone that marked the graves of her parents. She tried to appreciate that the bodies of the two people who had created her were there under her feet, tried to feel their presence, to realize that if the earth was removed she could look on what was left of them. But it was something she couldn't grasp. Strange that she had only to slice into a loaf of fresh bread or catch a whiff of Fels Naptha soap, and her mother would be beside her again, still brown-armed and strong. Charlotte Fogel's death at forty-one had ensured that she would stay forever young. It had overnight transformed her vigorous husband into an old man.

Mia knelt and brushed the needles off the small white slab embedded in the soil. The stone contained an engraving of a single lady slipper over the inscription:

> *Nicola Ramona Thorsen*
> *May 6 1925 - May 10 1925*
> *Age 4D 8H*

The only one of Mia's and Nick's three children to live long enough to be given a name and a place in the town's cemetery. The daughter Mia had held, and suckled, and sung to, even while every trace of those hours was being erased from her brain by fever. It was the ultimate cruelty, letting her keep her baby for nearly five days, almost a whole week, only to wipe that perfect life from her memory forever.

Maybe it was selfish, but she found it hard to sympathize with a woman who'd had her child for close to two decades.

She heard the soft closing of a car door and looked around to see Nick walking toward her. He leaned against a nearby headstone. "You shouldn't come here, Meggie. It only makes you sad."

Mia turned back to the stone. "Mostly it makes me angry," she said. "And I intend to keep that anger good and fresh, until I meet God face to face."

"You shouldn't say things like that." His voice trembled.

Mia reached for his hand and let him pull her to her feet. "Nick, you'd better see a doctor."

"What are you talking about?"

"You're shaking, you're stumbling…you're driving in the ditch."

"That's nothing new."

"I think maybe it is."

"I could lose my job."

"Now, *that's* nothing new. You've been on the verge of losing your job since nineteen-twenty. If you're sick, getting sicker isn't going to help you keep working. You have to see a doctor."

Mia had expected her suggestion to be met with anger, but there was only weariness in Nick's response. "There's nothing wrong with me. I just need to slow down a little. I'm getting older, that's all. We're all getting older."

Mia didn't comment, only knelt to sweep the blanket of gold back over the tiny stone.

# XXIX

*What is so certain of victory as patience?*

Pete Koski chewed and swallowed the last bite of his pasty. He pushed the plate aside to make room for the one containing half an apple pie. McIntire wondered if the sheriff ever ate anything that wasn't encased in a crust of some kind.

Koski downed a few more bites before he said, "What makes you think the bottle came from Morlen?"

"Somebody was setting up housekeeping in that old mine, and Bambi had the mine prominently marked on his map. It was most likely him and Ross Maki. Besides nobody else I know of could afford it."

"Well, I'll ask Wendell," Koski said, "if I can track him down."

"Hasn't he been in touch? Isn't he at the mansion?"

"I don't know where the hell he is. He left the phone number of a hotel in Lansing, but so far he's never been there when I've called. And he doesn't call back."

"Can't his wife tell you where to get hold of him?"

"I'd have to get hold of her first!" He pulled a cigarette from the open pack on the desk and contemplated its tip. "What do you suppose the two kids were up to in that mine? And why?"

"The provisions included blankets, so they must have spent some time there or at least been planning to. Carlson hasn't mentioned Bambi being out overnight, other than when he's gone home. We didn't get a chance to look around much before we received Esko Thomson's kind invitation to take tea. Maybe they were going to explore the mine more and wanted to be comfy. Maybe they were just playing Neanderthal. I'd say Ross Maki should be able to tell you."

"But Ross was running a farm. He didn't have all that much time to play Neander-anything. Milk cows get up early. He couldn't have been away overnight, even if Bambi was. Bambi did quite a bit of his poking around on his own. How far in is this place? Any chance that Bambi was there the night he was killed?"

"None at all. It would have taken all night to walk in and make it back to the town hall in time to die there."

The sheriff nodded. "Sure wish Billy Corbin was still around. Well, I'll send Cecil up to have a look. Unless you want to go back?"

McIntire might have liked to see what else Bambi had stowed in his hideout but had no wish to continue the role of surrogate Billy. "You could probably talk Fratelli into it," he said. "He'll be wanting his Geiger counter."

"Thomson's most likely cleaned the place out by now anyway." Koski put down his fork, a definite sign that something significant was in the offing. "I got a package in the mail today," he said, "from that stiff-necked butler at the Club."

"The steward? Baxter?"

"Baxter, Jeeves, whatever the hell it is. He sent me a couple of magazines."

"Thoughtful chap."

"They were high falutin' cooking magazines." Koski gave a snort. "The guy called it *cookery*. Can you beat that? Took me a while to figure out what the hell he was talking about. Anyway, his wife found them when she was cleaning the main lodge."

McIntire was beginning to see where this was leading.

"When Mrs. Baxter went to whip up a batch of *cremm* something or other, she found part of the instructions missing." Koski picked up the fork again, but only tapped it on the table. "The magazines had been left in the main lodge, but they were addressed to Mrs. Wendell Morlen."

"So? Mrs. Wendell sure seems like the recipe clipping type to me."

"No shit, but this wasn't only the recipe. It was whole pages. And the paper and print look suspiciously like the print in our ransom note."

"You think Bonnie wrote that note herself?"

"That woman is crazy as a loon. I wouldn't put much past her. But Bonnie wasn't the only one that could get to those magazines."

"The butler did it?"

"Looky here, Bambi's body showed no sign that he struggled with his kidnappers, and he was a tough little shit. He wouldn't go easy. He might have been poisoned, but he hadn't digested it, so he wasn't drugged into doing what they wanted. He went of his own accord. Guibard says he probably wasn't tied up until after he died. At least some of the raw material for the note comes from the Club. I'm guessing Bambi didn't put up a fight because he knew his kidnappers."

"And," McIntire reasoned, "those kidnappers were people who had access to the Club lodge. Which leaves out Ross Maki and Marvin Wall."

"And Adam Wall," the sheriff sounded definitely gloomy. "Unless he had an accomplice."

"Adam Wall with a buddy at the Club? That's going pretty far out on a limb."

"No stranger than Adam Wall with a buddy in the federal attorney's office. Besides, not everybody at the Club is upper-crust. There's plenty of peons working there." Koski uncorked a red thermos and added coffee to his cup. "Even one or two trusty Indian guides."

McIntire hadn't thought of that, and he didn't want any more complications now. He rose to his feet. "We'd be way ahead if we could be sure the person who wrote that note was the same one who stabbed Bambi in the back."

"Ya." Koski forked down the last morsel of pie and stacked the two empty plates. "You see quite a bit of Wall, I hear."

"Now and then." What was this leading to?

Koski went on, "Not especially law abiding, is he?"

"Nothing serious."

Koski sighed. "Billy got on pretty well with the Indians. He was a handy guy to have around."

Prior to his recent fishing expeditions, the sheriff had never been overly concerned about keeping on the good side of the local Indians. Well, it was quite a large segment of the population. Maybe he was expecting an uprising. More likely concerned about votes. Whatever the sheriff had on his mind, he didn't elaborate. He handed the dirty plates to McIntire. "Take these to Marian on your way out, will ya? And tell her to get me a couple aspirin."

# XXX

*An implacable fate is on this lovely spot. It is as if misfortune were buried here, but found no rest in its grave, and perpetually rose from it to terrify the living.*

"Aren't you coming to bed?" Leonie stood at the foot of the stairs, slapping her paperback western against her knee.

"No," McIntire said. "Tempt me as you might, I'm not budging. The minute I doze off, or not, if you insisted, the phone is going to ring, and I'll have to go get an elephant out of somebody's attic."

She clutched the book to her chest. "Well, Mr. Grey, I reckon it's just you and me." She looked at McIntire with raised eyebrows. "You sure? We might bob for—"

"I'm not stirring from this chair until at least…one o'clock."

"Fancy a cup of cocoa?"

"Sure. Thanks. Toss in a splash of brandy if you would."

Leonie brought the cocoa, along with the brandy bottle and two pieces of cinnamon toast. McIntire thanked God that his wife had become Americanized enough to learn that toast should be buttered and eaten on the same day it pops out of the toaster.

"Siobhan is out, you know," she said. "I expect she'll be quite late." He'd married a persistent woman.

"Well, it is Halloween," he said. "Fratelli is probably scaring the pants off her with tales of his daring exploits."

"John! That is no way to talk about your dear Auntie. Anyway, it's not Melvin Fratelli this time. She's gone off with that captivating stranger, the handsome Rudy Jantzen."

"Rudy who?"

"Jantzen. The good looking one. You remember. She left with him the evening you two went to the pub."

McIntire nodded. "It's the first time I've heard he actually has a name. I thought he just went by oohs and ahs. Quite the coup for Siobhan. I hope she's prepared to beat off the competition."

For a second McIntire thought he detected a smile that indicated his wife might be contemplating entering the fray. She replied, "He has created quite a stir. Even Lucy Delaney has taken to putting fancy barrettes in her hair when she goes to town."

"Well, he seems okay," McIntire said. "Kind of sissy looking, though. I'm not sure I trust a man with dimples."

Leonie rolled her eyes. "Have you seen anything of Wendell Morlen yet?"

"Not hide nor hair," McIntire replied. "But Koski's on his trail."

"Good. Mrs Morlen shouldn't be left alone this way." She kissed him on his retreating hairline and left him with only the radio for company. McIntire switched it on and listened with half an ear while he opened his own book, the year's hottest seller, Mika Waltari's *The Egyptian*. It was a gift from Leonie in its original Finnish. That was thoughtful of her, but for once McIntire might have preferred the translated version. Somehow he couldn't find the hot-blooded Mediterranean hero believable in the language of the earth's most sober people.

McIntire read to page eighteen, where those magic words, *Skull-borer to the pharaoh*, jumped out at him. He read on. So

Waltari's dashing protagonist made his living drilling surgical holes in the skulls of the ruling class. Every Finn in the world, and that world definitely included Michigan, would no doubt be familiar with the trepanation concept, if not the term itself.

McIntire poured another squirt of brandy into his cup and sipped. So what? That didn't mean they'd relate it to Indians. Or that the hole was meant to point to Marvin Wall. Well, Egyptian was one of the few nationalities not represented in St. Adele, and if the driller had meant to frame a Finn, there were simply too damn many candidates.

McIntire closed his eyes and settled back to think things over.

The radio droned. *This is The Mysterious Traveler, inviting you to join me on another journey into the strange and terrifying. I hope you will enjoy the trip, that it will thrill you a little and chill you a little. So settle back, get a good grip on your nerves, and...*

Before the dregs of the cocoa were cold in the cup, a tentative tapping at the back door insinuated itself into his dreams. McIntire groaned himself awake, plodded to the kitchen, switched on the porch light, and flung open the door. In the bulb's sudden glow, Ross Maki stood blinking like a startled toad.

"I think maybe you should go...."

The boy radiated an aroma of wood smoke and cheap beer. McIntire waited.

"Some of the guys...they're...." He glanced down, then up quickly. "They got Marve."

McIntire grabbed his coat from the peg by the door. "Where?"

"Down on the shore. By the old lighthouse. There's a path by the cemetery."

McIntire knew that. He also knew that the path led through about a quarter mile of swamp. He tied on heavy leather boots and stepped out the door.

Ross set out across the yard toward Mia Thorsen's truck.

"Where do you think you're going?"

"Home."

"Like hell! Get in the car. I'll see you safe home to Ma later."

Ross Maki's face turned pale with the terror of a snitch anticipating being on the receiving end of retaliation, but he obediently slid into the passenger seat of the Studebaker.

"How fast should I be going?" McIntire asked.

"Fast" was the reply.

"What's going on?"

"Some of the guys got together—"

"Only guys?"

"A couple girls. Mostly guys."

"And one of the guys was Marvin Wall?"

"Bugs Ferguson brought him along. Some guys thought if they got him drunk enough he'd confess."

McIntire didn't need to ask confess to what. "And…?"

"And Marve got pretty loaded. He passed out."

McIntire was reasonably sure Ross hadn't come to request that he escort a drunk home. He waited.

"Some of the guys thought it would be fun…well, not *fun* but…they kind of wanted to do to him what he did to Bambi."

"They're going to kill him?"

"No! Only, you know…his head."

"They scalped him?"

"I don't know! They were talking about it. That's when I came for you. There were girls there."

McIntire overshot the turnoff to the road that ran past the cemetery, braked, reversed, and skidded around the corner. The road was deserted.

"Is this where the guys parked?"

"No. Course not. Everybody would see the cars here. We went back in by the boat docks."

"Well," McIntire brought the car to a halt, "you and I'll take the short cut." He fetched a flashlight from the trunk and dug around for his official issue handcuffs. He'd never had occasion to use them, and hoped he wouldn't have to tonight. He wasn't absolutely sure he could locate the key.

He aimed the light at the ground and trotted down the trail with Ross dawdling a prudent twenty yards behind. The wide, sandy lane quickly gave way to grassy marsh with no discernable path. If there was a moon up there, the heavy overcast obscured it; outside the circle of the flashlight beam, the night was solid black. Wood smoke hung heavy on the air. Soon the glow of a campfire flickered through the darkness. McIntire loped toward it.

The spot had obviously been well used but was abandoned, and abandoned in a hurry. Empty Grain Belt cans littered the sand around the washed-up tree trunk that had served as a seat. The grumble of engines stirring to life sounded from the direction of the harbor.

"You can come out now, Ross, they're gone," McIntire called.

The young traitor ventured out onto the beach.

The engines died away. There was no breeze, no plash of waves on the sand. Only the soft hiss of the driftwood fire. McIntire turned to Ross. "Where—?" A sound half way between a groan and a tremendous hiccup interrupted his question. McIntire swung his light toward the shore. A short stone causeway ran out into the lake, leading to the spot where St. Adele's lighthouse had stood before a 1947 storm had reduced it to a pile of rubble. The causeway was bisected by an iron gate which, even in McIntire's early days here, had always been secured with a massive padlock, necessitating that anyone bent on vandalism or a romantic assignation go to the bother of stepping over its three-and-a-half-foot-high bars. From the center of the gate a dark figure hung, long arms stretched out and up, head slumped forward—a black silhouette resembling a vulture in its macabre dance celebrating death. McIntire stood mesmerized and let his light travel over the scene. One side of Marvin Wall's head had been crudely sheared, exposing sallow skin, scraped and scratched, and decorated with patches of ragged black stubble. Above his ear a quarter-sized spot of crimson glistened. McIntire moved forward as if in a dream to touch a fingertip to it. His hand came away stained and greasy. Lipstick. Lipstick had also been used to draw three parallel lines on either side of the misshapen nose, and to scrawl the word *killer* across the burlap bag that was the youth's only garment. The boy gave a snort that ended in a moan.

An echoing whimper sounded at McIntire's shoulder. He turned to see Ross Maki, eyes deep holes in his sheet-white face, transfixed with horror. That's all he needed, another unconscious kid.

"Give me a hand here."

Ross advanced a few steps. "He's not...is he dead?"

"No, but he's not especially lively." McIntire shoved the flashlight into Ross' hand. "What'd they do with his clothes?"

Ross didn't answer. A scraping of his coat collar indicated that he'd shaken his head.

"Put the light on him." McIntire opened his pocket knife and cut through the shoe laces that bound Marvin Wall to the gate. The boy slumped like a sack of oats onto the path. Ross leaped back. Marvin lay in a heap, his legs scrabbling in the gravel, making running movements like a dreaming dog.

McIntire untied his own laces and removed his boots and socks. He thrust his feet back into the damp boots and slipped the socks onto Marvin Wall's icy feet. Ross finally went into action, and together they pulled Marvin into a sitting position and grappled him into McIntire's jacket, which was just about long enough to cover the bony rear. Their ministrations did not revive the boy to the point that he was able to walk, or even stand unaided, but complicated matters by giving him enough strength to struggle ineffectually against them. McIntire and Ross locked arms behind his back and, struggling to prevent the skinny frame from slipping out of the oversized coat, managed to transport him to McIntire's car.

Once installed in the Studebaker's back seat, Marvin mumbled something that sounded like *pigshit* and collapsed into snores.

McIntire turned his attention to Ross. "He could have died. He still might."

"There's nothing wrong with him. He's just drunk." Ross was decidedly sanguine for one who'd been on the verge of collapse himself only a few minutes earlier.

"You don't know that. And people can die from drinking too much, you know, especially if it's cold. If he'd been left out there like that, naked, he'd have never lived through the night."

"He wasn't left. I came to get you." Ross lifted his chin. "A damn sight more than he did for Bambi."

"Why are you so sure Marvin Wall killed Bambi Morlen?"

"Who else? Look at all the evidence." Ross didn't sound nearly so confident as his words made out.

"Why'd you come for me then?"

Ross' reply was eclipsed by an explosive retching from the back seat. McIntire sighed and rolled down the window.

A light was burning in one of Guibard's upstairs rooms, and after an extensive wait, the doctor answered the door. He was covered only by a dapper silk bathrobe.

"I hope this is one Goddamned humdinger of an emergency," he said.

"I hope you're disappointed," McIntire told him. "I don't know how much of an emergency it is, but I didn't know what the hell else to do with him."

"Him?"

"Customer for you, beaten, falling down drunk, and half froze to death."

"Bring him into my office." Guibard slammed the door. At that instant another upstairs window began to glow. Either the doctor had some touchy wiring, or he had a guest. McIntire wished he had the luxury of time to delve into that mystery.

Ross Maki had taken the opportunity of McIntire's temporary absence to disappear. He was probably a mile down the road by now. McIntire opened the car door. Like a bear trapped in its den, Marvin Wall shrank into the opposite corner. McIntire walked around to yank open the driver's side door. He flipped the seat back forward.

"Out! Now!" The venom in the black eyes left McIntire wondering if the boy might have stabbed Bambi Morlen after all.

"Go to hell." Marvin's words came out thickly, with little conviction.

"You're in my car. Get out of it." That tactic proved to be an inspiration. Marvin swung his legs out. His feet touched the gravel and the rest of him slid off the seat to join them.

McIntire leaned on the warm hood of the car and contemplated the ragged heap at his feet, knobby knees scraped and bleeding, filthy with sweat, dirt, and vomit, the warpaint-smeared face. Marvin Wall was a most pathetic sight.

"Come on, son, on your feet."

Marvin opened his eyes. He seemed to notice his lack of trousers for the first time and tugged the borrowed jacket over his knees.

"It's all right, come on."

Marvin waved off McIntire's help and struggled to his feet. He proceeded with docility to the doctor's front door, not even protesting when McIntire lifted him bodily up the two steps. He stayed admirably on his feet, only stopping to lean against the wall twice in the trip down the short hallway to Guibard's cramped office.

He'd dropped McIntire's coat and was still erect, garbed only in his gunny sack and Leonie's hand-knit socks, when the doctor came in.

"So what have we got here?" Guibard looked at the lip-sticked inscription on Marvin Wall's chest. "A killer is it?"

Marvin must have rallied indeed. The punch he landed on Guibard's chin left the elderly physician flat on his back in a pile of shattered glass.

◇◇◇

It was past two o'clock when Cecil Newman showed up to cart Marvin Wall, in a pair of Guibard's gabardine trousers, off to spend the night in the county jail, sleeping off his excesses and awaiting the doctor's decision on whether to press assault charges. The boy had taken all McIntire's strength and ingenuity, as well as his keyless handcuffs, to subdue.

McIntire watched the tail lights of Newman's Ford disappear. The clouds had blown off and the night had turned from chill to cold. Frost transformed each blade of grass into a miniature silver sword. He postponed his own trip home long enough to walk to the end of Guibard's dock. The lake lay smooth, reflecting the cold green fire of a spectacular display of northern lights.

How had he come to this state? Why had he allowed this magnificence to be subjugated by ugliness? He'd let his dream of a life with a nominal amount of meaningful work and extensive leisure, conducted in a realm of woods and water, turn to a nightmare of petty errands and wasted time. And all for some nebulous goal of being accepted, being a good guy. Showing his father that you didn't have to be Jack Dempsey Junior to be liked. Now here he was, reduced to Colin McIntire's terms, alternately playing nursemaid and strong-arming drunks, and not doing a very good job of either. Even Ross Maki had enough sense of dignity to get the hell out of this sordid episode and head home when he had the chance.

Ross Maki. Why had the kid come for McIntire? At the same time, stubbornly sticking to his conviction that Marvin

Wall had killed his friend? Maybe Ross knew the side of Marvin that showed itself tonight. But Marvin Wall sure as hell hadn't pieced together that message from magazines he'd picked up while lounging about the Shawanok Club lodge. And McIntire didn't think the butler did it either, or Bonnie Morlen. But now he had a pretty damn good idea who had—and why.

# XXXI

*But it was not their lot to sleep in peace and quiet
until noon, as you and I might have done, if we
had been awake till four in the morning, and our
limbs ached with fatigue.*

As McIntire had predicted, it seemed his eyes were barely
closed when a second caller pounded on his door. He slipped
from the bed, grabbed up his glasses, and staggered to the
window. Adam Wall's pickup sat coughing next to Mia
Thorsen's van. Bad news travels fast. Maybe not all that fast;
the sun was high, and the clock on the bedside table showed
that even Leonie might be up soon.

McIntire took his time answering the door.

"Come on in and have a seat while I stoke up the fire."

"I'll only take a minute of your time." Adam didn't preface
his statement with any "Good morning," but then, neither
had McIntire.

"I'm not standing in the doorway, freezing. Get in here."
McIntire turned without waiting for Wall to enter and
descended to the cellar. He opened the furnace damper, stirred
up the embers, and threw on a few sticks of wood. When he
got back up to the kitchen, Adam Wall still stood stiffly by
the door, which was mercifully closed.

"Coffee?" McIntire asked. He began running water into
the pot to rinse out yesterday's grounds.

Wall shook his head. "Don't bother. I just came to thank you for getting my brother out of that fix last night." Wall was never easy to read, but nothing about the frozen features said *grateful*.

"And," he continued, "to ask why, when a kid gets beat up and left in the woods to freeze to death, you throw him in jail. What kind of horseshit is this? Where are the fun-loving boys who tortured my brother? How much time have you and Baby Face Newman spent rounding *them* up?"

McIntire was cold and groggy and in no mood to be told off in his own kitchen. "Your brother assaulted a seventy-year-old man. He was looped out of his mind. He needed to be put somewhere for his own protection."

"His *protection?*" Wall shouted. At the uncharacteristic display, McIntire put down the coffee pot and gave his guest his full attention.

"Marvin was a filthy mess," he said. "He was naked, he was sick, and he was violent. Would you rather I'd brought him home to your mother in that shape?"

"Better that than the shape he almost ended up in."

"I don't think those kids would have left him out there. If Ross hadn't come somebody else would have." McIntire wasn't sure about that at all.

"So you really haven't heard?"

"I guess I probably haven't. What?"

Wall gripped the back of the chair McIntire had shoved his way. "Sometime last night, while he was in jail where you so kindly put him for his own protection, my brother used that seventy-year-old man's belt to hang himself."

McIntire felt a buzzing in his ears and his heart pounding. "Marvin is dead?"

"No. No, he's not dead. No thanks to you. The kid screwed that up, too. Guibard's belt was a little longer than he figured. When he jumped off the bunk, his feet hit the floor. The noose didn't pull tight enough to block off his windpipe, only enough to keep him trapped there until Mrs. Koski came with his breakfast. Gave her quite a shock."

"Please, sit down."

"Sit down? *Sit down!* I tell you that because of you, Marve nearly died, and you politely invite me to have a seat? Planning to offer me a spot of tea, are you?" Wall wrenched open the door. "I want my brother out of that cell! And get him to a doctor that won't treat him like some lower form of life. If that's possible. And I won't be stopping for tea, thank you very much. I'll be out taking care of the assholes that tried to kill my brother!"

McIntire's yard was beginning to look like a used car lot, and he decided that Siobhan's Lincoln would suit him nicely. The Studebaker could use a spot of tidying up.

As he passed the Thorsens', he caught sight of Mia standing at the foot of a ladder leaned against her house. He might as well let her know where her truck was, and maybe find out if her *tête-à-têtes* with Bonnie Morlen had led to anything interesting.

Mia wasn't particularly concerned about the whereabouts of her vehicle, and it seemed that Bonnie had given off fretting over her son's missing articles.

"The woman is completely...." Mia made circles with her forefinger in the vicinity of her right ear. "I know I should be sympathetic to what she's going through, and I am. Really, I am. Maybe the drugs are affecting her, but she's so strange, kind of sneaky. And that baking! The house is full of doughnuts. For who? She seems to be alone all the time. Where the heck is that husband? I'm beginning to think he doesn't exist. She says she's planning to divorce him, doesn't want him to get his hands on Bambi's money, and, by the way, Bambi is not—"

She broke off. "John, I don't like doing this. I don't know if I feel like a spy or a dupe, maybe both, but I don't like it."

"So, how do you think *I* feel?"

Mia burst out laughing. "John McIntire, who do you think you're kidding? You are just about the nosiest person I ever met!"

"Well, it's starting to wear off." McIntire guessed that he'd have to postpone asking if Mia knew anything about Mark Guibard's possible love life. "But if you think Bonnie Morlen knows something that might make a difference, I hope you'll tell me." He'd heard enough about the Morlens and their troubles himself, and decided to change the subject. "What're you doing here?"

"Storms."

McIntire looked up at the high, and large, windows. Mia lugging those things up a ladder and putting them in place? Mia, who became woozy standing on a chair to reach a shelf? "Mind if I watch?" he asked.

"I notice you don't offer to help."

"Not me. I'm saving myself to do my own."

"Well, if you're nice, I'll teach you my system." She climbed a few rungs up the ladder. "See this?" She pointed to an eye bolt screwed to the backside of the storm window's frame. "I throw a rope out the upstairs window, tie it on, pull the window up from the inside, and tie the end to the bed, or whatever's handy. Then—*voila!*—all I have to do is climb the ladder and shove the window into place. No lifting."

"Esko Thomson would be proud."

"Esko Thomson. They'd make a great pair, Esko and Bonnie. Both lunatic hermits." Backing off the ladder, she stumbled and McIntire instinctively reached out to steady her. When his hands touched her shoulders, Mia froze like a startled rabbit. Her arms were as thin as they'd been when he'd last held them thirty years before, but now had a surprising layer of muscle. Her hair smelled faintly of lemons. For the shortest time imaginable McIntire tightened his grip. At Mia's quick intake of breath he dropped his hands.

"Mia," he groped to break the awkwardness, "what were you starting to say? About Bambi. You said, 'by the way, he's not.' Not what?"

She kept her back turned, scraping a few flakes of white paint off the window frame. "I was talking about Wendell. He's not Bambi's father. Bonnie got pregnant by a married man, and Wendell was paid off to marry her."

It gave McIntire something to think about, something other than Mia's shoulders, as he sought out Ross Maki.

Finding Ross was easy. McIntire spotted him splitting firewood. Catching him was something else. The boy looked up as McIntire drove into the yard and ducked into the outdoor privy.

McIntire waited. Ross couldn't stay in there forever. As time ticked by, McIntire began to wonder if perhaps he *could* stay forever, or if he might have tunneled his way out. He walked over and rapped on the door.

"I'm not feeling so good."

"You'll feel a hell of a lot worse if I have to set fire to this thing. Out! Now!" Sheriff Koski himself couldn't have done it better.

Ross finally crept out, but clung to the door as if ready for a quick retreat.

McIntire beckoned him to a more aesthetically pleasing location near the woodpile.

"Ross," he said. "I'm disappointed in you. I don't think you've been quite truthful with Sheriff Koski, or with me."

Ross shrugged and reclaimed his ax.

"I found the mine," McIntire went on, "and the sheriff has the magazines that were used to make the ransom note. Bambi's car was seen in Chandler the night he died."

Ross swung the ax and embedded it in a maple log.

"It was Bambi's idea."

# XXXII

*People have often been cruel and tortured one another with greatest hardness when they have trembled for their souls.*

"It was Bambi's idea." Ross Maki said again before his freckled face crumpled in a single convulsive sob. He dropped his head to his hands. Pete Koski lit up a Camel and waited.

They were the first words Ross had spoken since their original iteration in his parents' yard. On the forty-minute trip into town he'd turned to the window and made no sound other than the occasional throat clearing. In the car, McIntire had been able to switch on the radio. Here, the silence was like a physical barrier.

Ross lifted his head at last, drew a stiffly crumpled red bandana from his pocket, and blew his nose. "He said it was *his* money. His grandmother left it to him. He didn't want to hang around home until he was twenty-five, and he didn't want to go to college. He was fed up with his old man pushing him around. They gave him a big allowance, but he wanted to get some of the money so he could move out. An advance. Not the whole amount. He only wanted enough to live on. His grandpa would of gave it to him, too, and he could've talked his ma into it, but his old man threw a conniption." He wiped the bandana across his nose. "He said it was none of his old man's business. The money was from his grandma, and Wendell didn't have anything to do with it. Can I have…?"

Koski shoved the cigarettes and matches across the table. It took three tries for Ross to light the match, but his hand was steady as he held it to the cigarette's tip. He inhaled, coughed into his sleeve, and went on. "He knew if he was held for ransom, his folks'd pay up. And it was his money anyhow."

It was pretty much what McIntire had figured, but that was about as far as his conjecturing went. "So why try to pin it on the Walls?" he asked.

"We weren't trying to pin it on anybody. When it was over, and Bambi had the money, everybody would know Bambi wasn't really kidnapped. His old man was dickering over some land for the Club, and Adam Wall was fighting it somehow. Bambi thought it might be funny and a way of getting back at his old man, if we asked for the same amount of money the Club had to pay."

Koski stubbed out his cigarette. "So why the fight with Marve?"

"We didn't plan that. We were going to fight with each other. So we'd get kicked out, or, if that didn't work, we'd act like we got mad and leave early. We didn't know Marve would be there. When Adam Wall and Marve came in, I told Bambi who they were. He said how we should pick the fight with them to make it look really good."

"The both of them?"

"Bambi wasn't scared of anybody."

"But the fight was only with Marve."

"Adam wasn't there very long." Ross fidgeted in his chair. "Bambi said something to him."

"To Adam? Said what?"

"He asked him how many teepees he could put up on a hundred-sixty acres."

Bambi wasn't only not scared, he'd obviously had a death wish all along.

"And what did Adam say?"

"I don't know. I got the hell outa there. I told Bambi I wasn't going to have anything to do with getting on Adam Wall's...." Ross turned white. "Oh, God, he's gonna kill me."

Neither McIntire nor the sheriff had words of comfort. The boy's assessment was very likely correct.

"So how did it come about?"

"What?"

"How did Bambi lure Marvin into the fight?"

"Shit, that wasn't hard. Marve's got a nasty temper."

"How?"

"Bambi got something from Karen Sorenson's purse. She didn't want to carry the purse around, so he said she could leave it in his car. Bambi took something from it and gave it to me. One of those little boxes that opens up and has a mirror inside, and some powder."

"A compact." This time it was Koski who supplied the technical term.

Ross shrugged, "I don't know much about girl stuff." He took another pull on the cigarette. "I gave it to Marve and told him to give it back to Karen. Karen started asking where he got it, and Bambi jumped in." He looked at McIntire. "You know the rest."

"Did you never stop to think about what all this might do to Marvin?" McIntire took the opportunity to ask his own question.

"After we got the money and got away, we would of let people know we were okay. Nobody'd of gone to jail."

Koski gave McIntire a meaningful look and dragged things back on track. "So Bambi got in the fight and got kicked out. What did you do then?"

"I went with him. He dropped me off home."

"What time was that?"

Here Ross stuck with his original story. "About eleven-thirty. I put a fire going in the sauna and changed my clothes, so when Ma saw my coat and shoes she'd figure I was in bed. I sacked out for a couple hours, then I walked to where Bambi left his car."

"He left it?"

"We planned it all out ahead of time. We didn't dare have him come back to get me, in case Ma and Pa were home. So Bambi hid the car in that old garage where the blacksmith shop used to be. Then he walked across to the hall and went up into the attic of the woodshed."

"He wouldn't have gone back to the hall until everyone had left."

"Yeah, well there might still be a few people hanging around, but he could sneak in. I don't know what time he went back. Maybe everybody was gone. I was at home then."

"Still, if he dropped Karen off an hour or so after you, he must have had some time to kill before he could risk going back to the hall."

"I guess."

"Any idea how he might have spent that time?"

"No."

"Okay, go on. You went to Bambi's car…."

"I drove it into Chandler to mail the note. We didn't want to mail it in St. Adele." He looked up quickly. "The car was still kinda warm when I picked it up. Bambi hadn't been gone long."

The sheriff exchanged a glance with McIntire, then asked, "What if somebody saw you? Asked what you were doing? Wasn't that taking a pretty big chance?"

"Only if they could tell it was me, and not Bambi, driving. Then I was going to say that Bambi had disappeared, and I was looking for him. Anyway, I went on the old roads through the reservation. It was late. I didn't even see another car."

"Was Bambi planning to sit up in that woodshed until you collected the money on Wednesday?"

"We had a place for him to hide, back in the woods. We had food, and a stove, and sleeping bags." Ross looked at McIntire again. "You said you saw it."

McIntire nodded. "It was a long walk in."

"It ain't so bad if you take the old road that goes in by the sawmill. You have to walk through some water but it's shorter. But we didn't want to leave his car anywhere near there. Bambi figured it all out. While I was gone to mail the letter, he was planning to wait for me in the garage, but when we were at the dance, he saw the woodshed and thought it would be a better place. It was warmer, and we sneaked up with some food and a lantern. I was going to come back and pick him up and drop him off at the sawmill. He could walk on the old road in the dark, and by the time he had to cut through the woods it'd be getting light. After I left him off I was going to dump the car. But when I got back, Bambi was...."

"We'll get to that," Koski said. "After you picked up the money, what was the plan then?"

"I had to make a delivery for Mrs. Thorsen. To Dearborn. Bambi was going to hide in the back of the truck, and when we got there, we'd take the train to Denver. We were going to split the money, even up. Bambi wanted to go on west, to California. I figured I could come up with some excuse and come on back home when things settled down. And we'd of left a note in the truck saying we were okay. We didn't want people to worry." He looked up. "I was going to deliver the clock case first."

Koski was evidently not impressed with Ross' devotion to duty. "So you mailed the letter, then what?"

"I went back to the hall to get Bambi." Ross' chin began to quiver again, and he bit his lip.

"Did you take anything from the car?"

"No!" It was a yelp. Then he added, "Like what?"

"Like Karen Sorenson's purse?"

"She forgot it. I put it in their mailbox." A note of defiance crept into his voice. "Bambi gave Karen a ride home, too."

The sheriff leaned forward. "Is that the reason you killed him?"

"I didn't! I didn't kill Bambi!"

"Okay, don't get your water hot." Koski lit another cigarette himself. "Just tell me what happened."

"There was nobody left around the hall, so I put the car in back of the woodshed. It was pitch black inside, and I didn't have a flashlight. Bambi had one, and I thought he'd hear me coming and shine it down for me, but…he didn't. I had to feel my way to climb over the wood and up through the trapdoor. He didn't answer when I said his name. I thought he must not be there, but maybe he'd left a note or something to tell me. So I crawled up through the door. There was a lantern. It was turned down really low, so it barely made any light at all, but it made enough."

The sheriff handed Ross another cigarette. This time he lit it for him.

"Bambi was sitting at an old desk. I thought he was asleep. I tried to wake him up. But he didn't wake up." He faced Koski with a pleading look. "I never saw a dead person before. But I knew right away Bambi was dead. I could tell."

The sheriff nodded. "And then what?"

Ross took his time responding. Trickles of sweat made muddy tracks down his neck. "I didn't know what to do. I knew I'd be the one blamed. We left the dance together. I was driving his car. I mailed the note." He frowned. "I didn't see how he could be dead, sitting there with his head on the desk like that. He looked…normal, but he wasn't breathing…and his eyes didn't move. He was *dead*."

McIntire could keep quiet no longer. "He looked normal? What about the…cuts on his head?"

Ross closed his eyes and puffed the cigarette. His voice was barely a whisper. "I did it."

Koski's chair gave a screech as he sprang to an upright position.

"I didn't know what to do!" Ross looked frantically from one of them to the other. "I didn't want to go to prison! I knew Marve or Adam must have killed him after all, that the joke got turned around. I wanted them to get caught. Everybody knew about the fight, and the letter was in the mail. I couldn't get it back. There were some old window shades. I took the cords and tied him up."

Sheriff Koski only stared. It was McIntire who went on, hardly believing that he could say the words. "Then you wanted to make it look really good, so you scalped him?"

"Just a little. It was only a little bit. I didn't want anybody to think I was the one killed him. He was dead. It couldn't hurt him. Bambi was my best friend. I wanted Marvin to get caught. I looked at the spot on his head and not at the rest of him. I tried to think like it was a rabbit or a deer. I cut some of the skin from Bambi's head. I did it *for* him."

"You mutilated Bambi Morlen's body because he was your friend?"

"I didn't want to. It wasn't easy. I couldn't make myself do it at first. I had to…. Bambi had a fancy bottle, a flask, he called it. We had brandy in it. I drank some."

And likely got a dose of *Lobelia inflata* in the process. McIntire swallowed. "And the hole?"

For the next few minutes the only sound in the room was the boy's tortured sobbing. When it quieted, he didn't raise his head, but spoke into his folded arms. "Greg told us about it. That ancient people all over the world drilled holes in people's skulls, and nobody knows why. But in the United States only the Indians in Michigan did it. So if Bambi had a hole, everybody would think it had to be Indians that made it. They'd never think it could be me."

That was true enough. Even hearing it from Ross himself, McIntire still couldn't believe it.

Ross lifted his head. "I wanted people to know it was Marve that killed him! There was a bit and brace in the toolbox. I tried to make a hole, but the bone was too hard…. I threw up."

Koski came back to life. "Then what?"

"I left."

"What'd you do with the drill?"

"It's in the wall."

At the sheriff's questioning look, McIntire explained. "The floor in the attic doesn't go all the way to the wall. There aren't any inside walls, only the bare studs. So if you drop something down, it's gets caught between the outside and the inside walls below." Such construction was the source of several of McIntire's frustrating childhood experiences, having lost a ball or two, and once a shoe, that way in the hay mow of the barn.

Koski nodded. "And then?"

"I dropped off Karen's purse. I tried to wipe it, in case of fingerprints. Then I drove the car in the ditch to make it look like Bambi'd been run off the road. After that, I cut through the woods to get home and did the milking. Ma and Pa got up late. They thought I'd been there all along."

A new crop of sweat beads erupted on Ross Maki's forehead. "Are you gonna tell my ma?"

Koski was apparently rendered speechless once again, and McIntire was himself dumbfounded. Was this boy truly so naive that he did not know he'd committed a serious crime? Any number of serious crimes?

McIntire recovered first. "Where is Bambi's camera?"

"I don't know. I didn't take it!" There was a fair amount of irony in Ross' indignation at being suspected of petty theft.

"What did you take," McIntire continued, "from Karen Sorenson's purse?"

Ross looked confused. "I told you, that...thing you said. Bambi took it."

"I mean before you left the purse in Sorenson's mailbox."

"Nothing!"

Koski glared, and Ross' voice dropped again. "I took a picture."

"That's all?"

"Ya."

"What about a manicure set?"

"A what?"

"A kit for fixing fingernails. With a scissors. A scissors about this big." Koski held his thumb and forefinger about three inches apart. "One that somebody used to stab your best friend."

Ross' eyes widened. "Bambi didn't look stabbed to me. He just looked…dead. Stabbed?"

Koski ignored the question. "Bambi had at least a couple of hours to kill between dropping you off at your house and the time you picked up his car. Did he say what he planned to do?"

"No."

"Do you think he spent that time with Karen Sorenson?"

"No! He just gave her a ride home. Same as me."

"I've talked to Karen," Koski pressed. "She seemed to like Bambi quite a lot."

"She hardly knew him. Anyway she was pretty mad at him. About the fight with Marve."

"Was Karen your girl?"

"We ran around together some."

"Was Bambi Morlen cutting in on your time? Was that why you killed him? Was that what made you mad enough to take a bit and brace to his head?"

"I didn't kill him! I only did that with the drill because—"

"Did Bambi spend those two hours with Karen?"

"I don't know what he did." Ross hesitated. "Well, he might have gone…."

"Where?"

"When we were at the dance, he was mad because he forgot to bring his winter coat, and he was going to need it when he waited for me and for walking back to the cave. In the woodshed, when he was dead, he had it on. I think he must have gone back to the camp."

# XXXIII

*The old piano was her own…to it she could
tell her troubles. It understood her.*

Pete Koski returned from stowing Ross Maki away in the cell
recently vacated by Marvin Wall. "John," he grimaced while
kneading the small of his back, "I really hate to put you out,
but…."

McIntire pulled the keys to the Lincoln from his pocket
and waved toward the door. "After you."

Koski grabbed his hat, whistled for Geronimo, and recited
his litany. "The State police have pretty much robbed me of
my deputies, and we still ain't got a replacement for Billy."
He looked greedily at Siobhan's convertible. He peered into
the tidy back seat and fingered Geronimo's ears. The sheriff
was obviously in the throes of a monumental moral struggle.
"Never mind," he said at last, "we can take my car." He handed
McIntire the keys to the Power Wagon.

The engine turned over on only the second try, and McIntire tried not to look smug as he backed the vehicle out of
the lot while his passenger slid down into the seat, braced his
knees against the dash, and closed his eyes. A snuffling from
the rear told McIntire that the German shepherd was doing
a canine version of the same.

"Shit," the sheriff finally said. "Can't you just picture it? The innocent farm boy turning the lantern up barely enough so he could see, leaning into his best friend's skull with a bit and brace and…shit!"

McIntire had no desire to picture it.

"I've been sheriff here for sixteen years, and I've never come across anything even close to…and just an ordinary kid. Sheee-it."

"Ross was panic stricken, terrified, drunk, and disoriented from the mixture of brandy and lobelia in Bambi's flask." Even as he said it, McIntire couldn't believe that he'd taken the position of defending corpse mutilation. "And don't forget he'd been up all night. People will do bizarre things when they're deprived of sleep. It's my theory that half the brutality of war stems from soldiers being exhausted rather than barbaric."

"Shee-it!" Koski reiterated.

"Do you think he was telling the truth?" McIntire asked.

"Why in Christ's name would anybody make up a story like that?"

"I mean about not killing Bambi."

Koski snorted, as though it was a moot point.

McIntire continued, "Guibard says Bambi was probably stabbed an hour or so before he died, and he wasn't scalped for at least half an hour afterward. Could Ross have done both those things and still been in Chandler to mail the note between three and four in the morning?"

"Why not? We don't know what time the kid died."

"But if Ross had stabbed him, would he have come back and hour and a half later to scalp him? And if he did stab him, when could it have happened? Ross says he didn't see Bambi after Bambi dropped him at home. Not until he went back to get him from the woodshed attic."

"Are you trying to say our Ross would never lie?"

McIntire slowed the wagon from its cruising speed of forty miles an hour and stopped to await a porcupine lumbering across the road. "But would Bambi turn his car over to the guy that had just stabbed him? And continue on with their extortion plan?"

"They might have had some kind of tussle over the girl. Bambi gets poked with the scissors, but neither of them know he's badly hurt. They make it up and go on with the plan. When Ross gets back he finds Bambi dead and proceeds with pinning the blame on Marvin Wall. What're we sitting here for?"

"We're not." McIntire let out the clutch. "But that doesn't explain the lobelia in the brandy. And Ross drank it, so he probably didn't put it there."

"Nothing explains that poison. Course the kid conveniently chucked it back up."

"This puts things right back to the starting line."

Koski shifted in the seat and scratched an armpit. "If Bambi was on the road, walking to the hall from the old building where he hid the car, he'd have been fair game for almost anybody."

"Only anybody who had Karen Sorenson's scissors."

The sounds of Scott Joplin at his most exuberant indicated that Bonnie Morlen was at home, but their knock on the mansion door went unanswered. Koski gave it two more shots before pushing it open and calling out, "Mrs. Morlen, we have news for you!"

Bonnie Morlen appeared in seconds, rubbing her eyes. "I'm sorry, I must have dozed off a little. I didn't hear your knock." She positioned herself to block the door. "What is it?"

When the sheriff had made it sufficiently clear that he was not about to impart his news while standing outside the door, she walked before them into the dim front room and waved them onto a blanket-covered sofa. The aroma of gingerbread wafted through the air, but she made no offer of coffee or other refreshment. She sat on the piano stool, where she had seemingly been lately dozing, and gripped its edges. "Have you found my son's murderer?" Her voice was brittle, almost angry.

"Is Mr. Morlen at home?" the sheriff asked.

"Mr. Morlen is in Lansing." McIntire wondered if Wendell had accompanied his wife to St. Adele at all. No one he'd spoken to had actually seen him here. Bonnie asked again, "Have you found my son's murderer?"

"Possibly. We're not sure. What we have found is his kidnapper."

"Isn't that the same thing?"

"We don't think so." As she listened to Koski's story of the boys' extortion plan, Bonnie Morlen's face took on a greenish pallor. When she spoke her voice had a flat, breezy quality, as if she was dismissing nothing more than a misunderstanding about the price of eggs.

"No. I'm sorry sheriff. You're wrong. That…that boy, that *Ross*, is lying to save himself. Bambi would never have let me think he'd been abducted if he hadn't. He wouldn't have put me through such a thing."

The sofa's springs creaked under Koski's weight. "They were planning to leave a note letting people know they were okay, after they got away."

"Got away? Get away from what? My son had everything a young man could want. What could he be trying to get away from?" She looked belligerently from one of them to the other. When no response was forthcoming, she stated with finality, "Bambi would never have done what you say." She turned and placed one hand on the piano keys, picking out a lively tinkling melody that McIntire didn't recognize. A curious accompaniment to grief. "He couldn't have hated us that much," her words were almost drowned by the music, "not even if…."

"Boys can be thoughtless, Mrs. Morlen." Koski's breaking into Bonnie Morlen's speech was itself pretty thoughtless.

McIntire leaned forward. "Not even if what, Mrs. Morlen?" Was she suggesting that her son might have made the discovery of his parentage? Or possibly some other transgression?

Bonnie swung around and looked blankly at him.

"Was there something that might have made Bambi angry with you or your husband?" McIntire persisted.

"What are you talking about? My son loved me. He didn't do what you say. That boy's lying."

Her face flushed with anger, and Koski shifted uncomfortably. "It looks like it's true. The ransom note was written with letters cut from one of your magazines."

Bonnie raised a hand to her throat and swallowed. "My magazines. He took magazines from *my* house." It was not a question.

"Mrs. Baxter found them in the main lodge. But they were addressed to you."

"Anybody could get magazines from the lodge."

"The boys had a hideout fixed up in the woods. A place to wait out the days before they picked up the ransom money."

Bonnie flinched at this, but made no response.

"It's possible, maybe even most likely," Koski told her, "that your son's abduction and his death were not related. His murder may have had nothing to do with money."

"Can't you see how wrong you are?" she begged. "My son was killed for money. That other boy might have been behind some kind of scheme, but Bambi would never have put us through this."

The fact that Bambi had been posthumously mutilated by his friend seemed not to have made an impression. Bonnie could only steadfastly deny her son's voluntary infliction of suffering upon herself and her family.

"Young men are often in conflict with their parents," Koski said, "and they often end up suffering for it."

"What are you saying? That my son brought this on himself? That he's at fault for his own murder? You're too blind to see who did it, so you're putting the blame on Bambi himself?"

"Mrs. Morlen, Ross Maki admits that he, and your son, manufactured the evidence against Adam and Marvin Wall. He denies causing your son's death. He might be lying, but I don't think he is, and if he ain't, we're right back where we started from. In other words, you're right, we don't know shit about who killed your son. So if there's anything you know, or think you might know—if you have the slightest, the flimsiest, the fuzziest idea, I'd suggest you tell me!"

The sheriff's outburst had little effect. "Could you please go now? You've said what you came for." She turned back to the piano.

"Your husband—"

"I'll let Wendell know what you've told me. You can see yourselves out."

McIntire touched her arm. "Are you sure you'll be all right, Mrs. Morlen?"

"I most certainly am not all right! I won't be all right until the people who took my son's life are every bit as dead as he is." She moved away from his touch. "I want to be alone now."

"There's one more thing." Koski fingered the brim of his hat. Bonnie lifted dead eyes to his face. "We've been told that your husband was not Bambi's natural father."

McIntire tried to hold back the groan. Cross Mia Thorsen off as their final source of information.

Bonnie didn't look surprised or offended, only nodded.

"What was his father's name?"

She looked for a time as if she was trying to remember. "Anatole Pavil." The stool swivelled back.

Pavil. It was an unusual name, but hazily familiar. McIntire couldn't think why. Mia had said Bambi's father was a musician and had been exiled to California, but he was sure she hadn't mentioned his name.

The strains of *Maple Leaf Rag* accompanied their exit. "Quite a place." Koski closed the door with a thump.

"Looks like it was decorated by the firm of D. Boone and Farouk," McIntire commented. "Do you think she should be left alone?"

"Hell no, but I don't know that we have much choice."

"You managed to get hold of Wendell yet?"

"Not so far. The number he left is a hotel. He's checked out. The legal tussle with Adam Wall was wrapped up a week ago without ever going to court. Morlen got the Clubbers what they wanted, even if they had to dip into their extra pin money. He's had no more work for the Club. He hasn't been there, or at that hotel in Lansing, and from what we can tell, he hasn't been at home, not here or back in Westchester."

Koski looked back at the closed door and the pulled curtains. "Well, he ain't been reported missing," he went on, "and there's no law says he has to let us know every move he makes. But I figure it's time to smoke him out some way. There's something about this whole thing that don't smell right. His son's been murdered, for Christ's sake. He might try to at least fake some concern. At least if he don't care all that much about Bambi, he might want to take care of his wife."

"I'm led to believe that's what he's paying Fratelli to do."

"Ha!"

"Ha, what?"

"Far as I can see, Wendell Morlen hasn't paid his so-called detective one red cent."

McIntire waited for the sheriff to elaborate. He might as well wait for him to rip off his shirt and burst into a chorus of *Old Man River*. He asked, "How do you know?"

"Morlen has paid all his bills with checks written on an account at the First National in Marquette. He gets cash from the same account. There's no record of any payments to Fratelli. The last big cash withdrawal was the Thursday *before* the murder."

"Before Morlen went to Lansing."

"Yep. He left with three grand."

McIntire whistled. "Lansing is an expensive place, but… hang on a bit, I thought you said he borrowed the money for the train ticket from James What's-His-Name III."

"He did. So it seems he needed cash for something. And it was before he had any need for Fratelli that we know about. Like I said, it doesn't look like he's given his investigator a penny."

"Maybe the guy gets paid only if he gets results."

"If that's the case he must be one of those wealthy lords in the books, detecting as a hobby. He ain't been doing much to get results, but he's been plenty free with his spending. Wining and dining your aunt, for instance."

That did seem to be the case.

"I didn't suppose private investigators were all that flush," Koski went on. "*If* that's what he is."

"You have doubts?"

"He's got no license in the state of New York. Or anywhere else that I can find." The sheriff gave a short laugh. "Well, with the amount of investigating he's been doing, we sure as hell can't accuse him of operating without a license."

He also didn't seem to be sticking around much to stand guard over Mrs. Morlen, if that's what he was here for. She shouldn't be left alone now. McIntire thought of calling Mia, the one person Bonnie seemed to trust, or had before the sheriff brought up Bambi's parentage. The memory of that thin shoulder under his hand gave him a twinge of uneasiness. He pulled open the car door. "I'll ask Leonie to stop over soon as I get home."

# XXXIV

*The stone remained because it had already*
*lain there so many years.*

McIntire didn't get home soon. And when he did it was a bit
late for even Leonie to make humanitarian visits, especially to
someone who might well slam the door in her face.

Koski had demanded that they head straight to Greg
Carlson's camp to confront him with Ross' suggestion that
Bambi had returned there for his coat.

McIntire wasn't convinced that the trip was worthwhile.
"Why would Carlson lie about Bambi coming back?"

"Only one reason that I can think of," the sheriff said. "But
Carlson didn't say that Bambi didn't come back. He said that
he didn't *see* him come back. Maybe what he was lying about
was being there himself."

"He wouldn't have much reason to lie about that either.
Anyway the tracks of the Morgan were *over* the tracks of Carlson's truck when we were there on the day after the murder.
Bambi was the last person to drive in. So whenever he got
there, Greg was around, unless he'd left on foot."

"Or went off with somebody else," Koski said. "So figure
it this way, Bambi came back. They got in some kind of fight,
and Carlson stabbed him."

"With Karen Sorenson's scissors?" McIntire asked. "Where would he get it?"

"We don't know that it was Karen's scissors. She's not the only one with manicure scissors."

"So Bambi interrupted Greg Carlson trimming his toenails, and Carlson stabbed him."

"Well, maybe Bambi pulled the scissors first, and Carlson wrested it away from him."

A showdown with three-inch scissors. It was as good a theory as any, better than some. But McIntire wasn't ready to relent. "Guibard says that Bambi might have hung on as much as an hour after he was injured, but he thinks he'd have been petering out pretty fast. And that if he'd moved around much after he was stabbed, he'd have bled more and died faster. If he was stabbed at the camp, I don't think he'd have had the stamina to drive back to the blacksmith shop and still walk across to the woodshed. Going by what Guibard says, he must have been attacked after he left the car, or in or around the car before he left it."

"Well, let's go see what Professor Prospector's got to say."

It was not to be. The spot where Greg Carlson habitually left his panel truck was empty.

"You don't suppose he's gone back to…where ever the hell it is he came from?" McIntire asked.

"I told him not to leave without telling me. Doesn't mean he wouldn't. I can't quite figure why he's still here. He's taking a pretty big chance." McIntire had wondered about that, too. Heavy snow could happen any day. Carlson could end up buried until April.

Koski rolled the window down a crack and peered out. "Why don't you run on up and see if his stuff is still there?"

McIntire didn't trust himself to make a verbal reply, but his expression was apparently sufficient. The sheriff cranked up the window and leaned back. "He probably just went to town. I'll get Cecil on his tail." He mumbled something more—words that included "Billy Corbin" and "way the hell out in the boondocks"—and was soon snoring in harmony with his canine sidekick. He came to as they entered the outskirts of Chandler, but had nothing more to say until McIntire drove around to the back of the jail and pulled up before the entrance to his living quarters.

"Hang on a minute, Mac. Maybe you can run on over and lock up that blacksmith shop 'til I get a chance to take a look at it. No telling when that'll be. It's been really tough without—"

"Sure, okay." McIntire didn't need to hear the rest of Koski's lament. Locking up the blacksmith's garage, and taking a peek inside in the bargain, was one request McIntire was glad to oblige. "You still got those concert programs?" he asked. "The ones from the Morgan?"

The sheriff looked mystified, either at the request or the temerity McIntire showed in making it. "Yup," he replied.

"Could you check where and when they're from and see if the name Pavil turns up on them?" Koski shrugged and went inside. He was back in less than five minutes with a sturdy padlock and the information that both programs were for concerts given in 1949 by the Sacramento Symphony Orchestra, and Anatole Pavil was listed under *first violin* and *concert master*, whatever the hell that was.

So Pavil had wound up in California, and evidence of that had wound up in Bambi's car. Bambi had plotted his own abduction to raise money with the intent of going to California. It was a bit too much to be coincidence. Had he been in touch with Pavil? Or was he just planning to knock on the musician's door and introduce himself? Well, it would explain why Bambi didn't simply prevail upon Mum and Gramps to fund a trip out west. It didn't explain how he had learned the truth about his parentage. *Pavil.* There might be another revelation here.

"Pete," McIntire asked. "What about the ransom note? You still got that?"

"Hell, no. The state police grabbed it and ain't letting go. Why?"

McIntire tried to picture that note. Among the jumble of print, the canary yellow capitals had stood out from the rest. McIntire couldn't remember exactly what the letters were. Only that he'd recognized that they were cut from the wrapper of a bar of Palmolive soap. *Pavil.* It would fit. And would mean that it wasn't only Wendell who had received a coded message in that ransom note. Had Bonnie Morlen recognized that taunt, if that was the intent? Or had she been too distraught to notice? The real question was, if she had seen Pavil's name embedded in that letter, who did she think was responsible?

Koski asked again, "What you want the note for?"

McIntire told the sheriff, "Never mind," bid him good-night, and reclaimed the Lincoln. As he backed out into the street, his affection for the modest Studebaker was beginning to wane.

◇◇◇

Bambi's photographs should be back from developing by now. He might as well pick them up. With any luck, the kid had snapped a shot of a scissors-wielding maniac, and McIntire could go home to a good night's sleep, too.

As he left the drugstore, McIntire saw Greg Carlson's truck rattle to a stop in front of the Northwoods Inn across the street. He crossed over and followed the flannel-garbed professor inside. Pete Koski might prefer to have the first shot at the guy himself, but, if the sheriff was picky, he could damn well get himself another chauffeur. *Run on up and check.* Shit. McIntire wondered, as he frequently did, what kind of aspect he must present that led people to assume they could order him around like a feeble-minded apprentice…and what was the sheriff hoping to accomplish with all those not so subtle hints about the dear departed Billy and needing a deputy out in this godforsaken neck of the woods? It would be a cold day in hell when McIntire made himself Pete Koski's full-time lackey.

His quarry was seated at the bar, ordering a beer, when McIntire plunked himself down beside him. "—and whatever my friend here is having," Carlson finished. McIntire nodded and requested Scotch and water. "And better make it quick," he added, "while I'm still a friend." He turned to Carlson. "I stopped to ask you a few more questions."

Carlson didn't seem surprised but did appear inordinately eager to please. "Oh? You bet. Just step into my office." He slid off the stool and walked to an empty booth.

For someone who'd gone from academia to five months in the woods, losing one of his partners to murder, and ostensibly searching for something he hadn't found, he looked good, well fed and hearty. No trace of disillusionment showed in the turquoise eyes. And no trace of the nausea he'd been suffering on the last occasion they'd met.

"You ever drink any of Bambi Morlen's liquor?" McIntire asked.

"I never saw Bambi with any liquor."

McIntire let it go and went on, "When Bambi was found— dead—he was wearing a heavy coat."

"And that strikes you as strange? If he hadn't been, he probably woulda froze to death and saved somebody the trouble of killing him. Unless the coat was mine, what's it got to do with me?"

"According to Ross Maki, when they left the dance, Bambi didn't have the jacket. He says Bambi was peeved because he'd forgotten it at the camp. It looks like he went back to get it."

"What time?"

"After one o'clock…maybe closer to two," McIntire told him. If Carlson had been there the entire evening, why the concern about the time? "Can you explain how he could have come into the cabin without you seeing him?"

"It was dark." Carlson gave an exasperated sigh. "He didn't come in. I'd of heard him. The coat was probably in my car."

"In your car?"

"When the kids were out fooling around, they left a lot of their junk in my car. It saved them a trip up the trail to the cabin."

It made sense. McIntire could check it out with Ross. If true, it also meant that Carlson, or his vehicle, was indeed at home that night, at least after the time Bambi retrieved his jacket. They'd already concluded that Bambi's Morgan was the last car to drive into that spot.

McIntire sipped his drink. The whisky could not compare with Esko Thomson's brand. "Why haven't you let anybody know that your profession is anthropology?"

"Nobody's asked."

The classic answer. The classic evasion. "You've led people to believe that you're here to find uranium. Why?" McIntire persisted. "What is it you're really looking for?"

"I'm not looking for anything specific. I'm researching the primitive people of this area."

"So why keep it a secret?"

Carlson didn't answer immediately, only signaled for another round. Then he leaned forward as if eager to impart the secret. The academic shone through the dingy flannel.

"Copper." He looked over his shoulder and lowered his voice. "Copper was the first metal to be used by humans, beginning about ten thousand years ago, toward the end of the last ice age. Copper was used all over the globe, but this is the only place it was found in quantity just lying around at or near the earth's surface, waiting to be picked up. Here and on Isle Royale. Artifacts made from Michigan copper have been found all over the western hemisphere, and," he paused and spoke in a barely audible voice, "I believe, the eastern hemisphere, too."

McIntire assumed some response was expected. He raised his eyebrows.

"By three thousand BC, copper was in great demand in Europe," the professor went on. "Evidence is that the techniques used to mine copper here at that time were exactly the same as those used in the old world."

He ceased whispering, leaned back, and sipped his beer. "The copper here and at Isle Royale has been mined for centuries, but no one really knows who those early miners were. I'm convinced people crossed the Atlantic to acquire copper here thousands of years ago. They have to have left evidence, and I'm going to find it. But not everybody wants that kind of evidence found, not on their private land."

McIntire remembered that mystery rock on Shawanok Mountain. "Like the Shawanok Club?" he asked. "That's why you cultivated Bambi's acquaintance, to get onto Club land?"

"Not exactly. I ran into Bambi when I was on Club property. He was out taking pictures. I had my Geiger counter. He was interested in learning to use it, and I needed some help with surveying. But it didn't hurt that he could get me into the Club, more or less legitimately."

"Did Bambi know what you were really up to?"

"Up to? You make it sound like I was plotting a Communist invasion. But no, he thought it was uranium, same as everybody else."

He pulled out his wallet. "Take a gander." Like a proud father, he produced a couple of snapshots. "This," he said, extending the first photograph, "was taken in Wales." It showed a large, flat rock precariously balanced on three smaller ones, a sort of miniature Stonehenge.

"And this one," he slapped down the second, "this one was taken at the Club."

There it was. Perched on a slab of exposed bedrock. The notorious monolith. McIntire stared. Comparison to the thermos bottle resting beside it showed that the rock was slightly bigger than the average bed pillow and sat about six inches off the ground on three rounded softball-sized stones.

"That's it? That's what all the fuss is about?"

"It's a dolmen. They're found on hilltops all over the world. It might not look like much, but somebody built this structure. I plan to find out who."

"Structure?" McIntire said. "That is *not* a structure. That is a pile of rocks, and not even an especially appealing pile of rocks."

"But somebody put it there."

"I guess maybe somebody, or something, did. And it could have been anybody, at any time. A couple of bored loggers or reasonably strong Clubbers. It didn't take any great feat of either engineering or strength to set this up. Maybe it's a cairn of some kind, or an improvised picnic table, or just something dropped by a passing glacier."

"That could be. That's why I'm going to find corroborating evidence."

"But nobody here knows what you're looking for?"

"No." Carlson cleared his throat. "Nobody who would…. No." He swigged down the last of his Grain Belt. "Anything else?"

"I expect Koski will be looking for you. He thinks you might have taken a powder. How much longer do you plan to sit out there in the bush? Kind of tempting fate, aren't you?"

"Well, yeah, I gotta get outa there pretty soon. But you know how it is. We never really believe in snow until we're up to our ass in it. I might hang around for a while though, get a room here in town. I'm on a year sabbatical."

"And you want to spend it here? In winter?"

"You're here, are you not?"

McIntire could think of no good response to that.

The archeological revelations reminded him of the photos in his own pocket. As Carlson waved to Fergus behind the bar and swung out the door, McIntire pulled out the envelope. His heart beat faster as he opened it and removed the pictures.

McIntire did not consider himself an art critic, but he was impressed. The photographs mostly depicted people in those effortlessly candid poses whose seeming spontaneity belies the work and talent that went into their composition. Karen Sorenson and Ross Maki faced one another across the hood of the Morgan. A group that included Bonnie and Wendell Morlen milled about on the porch of the Club lodge. Greg Carlson looked intellectual next to his dolmen. So, despite Carlson's claims, there was someone who might have known what he was really looking for. And that someone was now dead.

A few were the more usual scenic shots of woods and water. A doe knee-deep in a stream; a longer distance shot that included a swimmer cutting through water, slim arm lifted above a white shoulder. All else was dark, water, tendrils of hair, trees edging the scene. Not Superior. One of the Club's smaller lakes and ponds.

McIntire had spread the snapshots on the table. Three rows of six, and one extra. Nineteen pictures. He removed the strips of negatives from the envelope. Five strips of four. Twenty negatives. Which meant that one of them hadn't been printed. In the dim light the negatives were only black squares. He gathered the snapshots and walked to the bar. "Fergie, you got a flashlight back there?"

McIntire returned to the booth with the torch and another drink. He passed the negatives over the light. At the end of the second strip there it was, no doubt deemed too prurient to print. A woman in bra and half slip, naked slim back, and a cloud of—McIntire transposed hues—dark hair. On the negative it was difficult to tell more than that this girl wasn't the Nordic blond Karen Sorenson. Her position in front of an open bureau drawer gave McIntire another clue to her identity. The unfortunate Miss Haggerty caught in her encounter with the chipmunk.

He stacked the pictures and contemplated the group on the Shawanok Lodge porch. Bonnie Morlen wearing ruffles and a cherubic smile. Wendell seated on a folding chair, relaxed and incongruously urbane in the rustic setting. Both so apparently satisfied, surrounded by affluence and.... McIntire aimed the flashlight at the shot. There, lounging casually against a pine railing, gazing speculatively at the back of Bonnie Morlen's neck, was Siobhan McIntire Henry's latest flame, the charming and debonaire Rudy Jantzen.

McIntire had no sooner began engaging in some speculations of his own, when he glanced up to see the object of those conjectures advancing toward him, with his Aunt Siobhan glued snugly to his side.

"Well, Siobhan," McIntire stuffed the photo into his pocket, "what takes you so far from my well?"

"If you want to keep your water to yourself, you might keep your hands off my car."

"Sorry. Mine needs some cleaning."

She wrinkled her nose. "So I noticed. Well, I tracked you down. If you want a career as a car thief you'll have to work on it."

She turned to her silver-haired companion. "Rudy, I'd like you to meet my...cousin, John McIntire. John this is Rudy Jantzen."

Jantzen's handshake was hearty. He smiled, showing square white teeth and the notorious dimples. "Great to make your acquaintance, at last. Siobhan's told me about you."

McIntire bit off a mention that Jantzen's reputation had preceded him, also. "What'll you have?" Both Siobhan and her escort requested beer, and McIntire made it three. He said as he slid back into the booth, "What brings you to our part of the world?"

"Business," Jantzen stated. He took Siobhan's hand. "And lately a bit of pleasure."

Siobhan smiled sweetly at him.

McIntire felt on the verge of retching. "What kind of business is it you're in?" he asked.

The question netted a look of warning from Siobhan, but Rudy answered smoothly, "Real estate. Development. I've been looking into the possibility of opening a marina here for pleasure boats. I have two on the west coast."

"Two boats?"

"Two marinas."

"This might not be the best climate for a venture of that sort."

"I'm beginning to find that out."

"You giving up on the idea?"

"Most likely. I thought of branching out into hunting lodges."

"That why you've been at the Club?"

The moment of silence was barely detectable. "Staying with friends," Jantzen said. "If you've got friends in a place like that, it'd hardly do to stay anywhere else, would it?"

"Oh, dear," Siobhan broke in, "Rudy, sweetheart, do you think you could be a dear and get me some cigarettes?"

Rudy Sweetheart nodded obediently and made for the bar.

"What the devil are you up to, John?" Siobhan was the fractious ten-year-old McIntire remembered.

"Only looking out for your interests, Cousin Siobhan."

"Just look out for—"

Rudy was back with the requested Winstons. Siobhan looked at her watch. "Oh, darling, I expect you need to go. I know you have to get out early tomorrow. I'm sorry to keep you so late. You just run along. John can drive me home. Or I can drive him home." Her expression said that John could easily end up walking home, if he gave her any more trouble.

McIntire averted his eyes from the fond farewell.

When they were alone he spoke more soberly. "What do you know about this guy, Siobhan?"

"Enough. I'm a big girl. I can take care of myself. I've been doing it most of my life."

"You only just met him."

"Well, I haven't run off to Las Vegas with him." She smiled. "Yet." She lit the cigarette. "What are you so suspicious about?"

"Did you know that he had been at the Club, that he was acquainted with Morlens?"

"I knew he was there this summer, sure. So what?"

"Why didn't you tell me?"

"Why would I? It wasn't some kind of secret. It's not a crime to know someone who dies, and it's not a cause for suspicion."

"Having a tryst with the married mother of a murder victim on the night he dies might be a cause for suspicion, or at least cause to question his morals."

"And you think Rudy did that?"

"Bonnie Morlen was out with somebody the night her son was murdered. Somebody who was not her husband. She was with him most of the night." He pulled the photograph of the group at the Club from his pocket. Siobhan gazed for a long time at the image of Rudy Jantzen with his eyes trained on Bonnie Morlen. She sighed and screwed the cigarette against the side of the ashtray.

"Rudy wasn't with Bonnie Morlen that night," she said. "He was with me."

"The murder happened before you came. You hadn't met Rudy Jantzen then."

"The murder happened the night before I came to St. Adele. I spent that night in the Chandler Hotel. I met Rudy right here in this bar. *We* were together most of the night."

# XXXV

*The mother could not die who had brought
down such misery on her child.*

"She's gone!" Leonie's voice on the telephone carried exactly
the same tone as her, "She's back!" had a little over a week
before.

"Well, she's not a prisoner, Leonie. Maybe she went into
town, or for a walk. I'd say it's high time she got out a bit."

"Her car's still here. She might have left on foot, but I
don't think she only went out for a stroll. Her oven's on, and
there's a pan of something that might once have been bread
rolls in it."

"You mean you're in the house now? When did you take
up breaking and entering?"

"I didn't break. But I did enter. The door wasn't locked, and
I smelled smoke. I can't believe she'd walk off and leave things.
Oh, God! You don't suppose she's been abducted, too?"

"Leonie...."

"Oh, I'd forgotten for the moment that Bambi kidnapped
himself. I still can't get used to it. I'm sure she couldn't either.
Do you think she might have done something to herself...?"

Whatever had made them leave that woman alone? "She
probably wasn't thinking clearly and forgot about the biscuits. Maybe she's gone somewhere with Wendell." It was as

much to reassure himself as Leonie. It didn't convince either of them.

"I think you should get here, straight away."

"You've got the car, remember."

"Take the bike or Traveler."

"Leonie, if some guy in a cape and a long mustache is in the process of tying you to a railroad track, or you're up to your belly button in quicksand, I might get on that bike, or even be convinced to saddle up old Traveler. Otherwise...."

"Oh, all right," Leonie relented with a sigh in her voice that said, *I married a panty waist.* "Start walking, and I'll meet you. Judging from the condition of these biscuits, she's already been gone for some time. They'd make excellent things for your ice hockey." McIntire heard a clunk which he took to be a wheat-based puck hitting a table top. "Hurry, John. It's freezing out there, and she could get lost."

McIntire penciled a faint check on the page to mark his progress with Gösta *et al.* He tugged his jacket on as he went out the door. It wasn't freezing—quite. It was damp and darkly overcast. A wind that had come out of Canada, and picked up speed over a couple of hundred miles of thirty-eight-degree water, hurled an icy mist into his face. He ducked back into the house for gloves and a cap with earflaps.

Leonie came bumping down the road before he'd made it much past the end of the driveway. "Just what did you say to that poor woman to make her take off like this?" she demanded when he opened the door. The car still exuded a faint aroma of *eau de Marvin Wall.*

"You don't know that she took off. And what makes you think it was something I said?"

The gears screeched as Leonie cranked the Studebaker around in a U-turn. "I didn't exactly mean you specifically. I was talking about all of you, the state police, and the sheriff as well. Has anybody considered what Mrs. Morlen's feelings must be? Well, maybe I *am* talking about you. And that Pete Koski, blithely telling her that her son died plotting the most cruel extortion imaginable and then simply walking out and leaving her on her own!"

"I wouldn't say we were exactly blithe. And we didn't have a whole lot of choice about leaving her alone. She practically threw us out." Leonie was right, and his intention to send his wife over was no defense. "She didn't answer the door when we got there," he added lamely, "and when she did, Pete had to force his way in. Now I think of it, I wouldn't be surprised if she saw you coming and was lying low 'til you got tired of knocking and left."

"Well, I'd be greatly surprised. I didn't only knock. I walked right in. And I didn't notice her cowering behind the piano. But we'd better check. If she is in the house she probably locked the door after I left." Leonie shifted down and turned into the mansion drive. "Why didn't you get Mia, for God's sake? She lives closer than we do, and Bonnie talks to her. She's gotten pretty chummy with Mia, actually."

McIntire's reasons for not summoning Mia Thorsen were self-centered and short sighted and not something he wanted to discuss with his wife.

Bonnie Morlen did not answer their rapping, and Leonie opened the unlocked door. McIntire wondered if the defense department was aware of the toxic gases that could be created by a few charred blobs of bread dough. A chair that looked as if its components had been produced by a family of beavers stood in the hall. McIntire shoved it in front of the door to hold it open.

Leonie called out, "Mrs. Morlen, are you here?" She turned to her husband. "I guess we may as well look around. She might be…sick or injured. You take the basement. I'll go upstairs." Her customary efficiency returned, and she stepped briskly to the staircase, then stopped. Her fingers tapped the polished rail. "It's a big place, maybe we should do this together."

McIntire was all for that. It was looking like he *was* a panty waist.

Once upstairs they did split up, each taking one side of the wide hallway. Nine bedrooms. Three were obviously in use. Wendell must return periodically, if not exactly to be welcomed with open arms. A fourth contained a rumpled bed but no other signs of regular occupancy. An overnight, or afternoon, guest?

Twenty minutes of innumerable closets and bathrooms later, they descended to the main floor—kitchen, pantry, living room, dining room, library. Mercifully, there was no basement. There was also no sign of Bonnie Morlen.

McIntire felt only minimal relief. If a conscientious housewife like Mrs. Morlen intended to take her own life, she might well choose not to mess up the rented house. And nobody could last more than a few minutes in that lake.

The combination of guilt and grief that Bonnie must be feeling could drive a far more stable person to drastic acts, of which suicide was only one.

"I'll look around outside," he told Leonie. "You better stay here in case she comes back."

"Don't be ridiculous. I'm not staying here. But we can split up. I'll carry on looking in the woods between here and the road, but I'll check the house every now and then in case she comes back."

McIntire nodded. "I'll take a walk along the shore toward Walls."

"Walls? What makes you think she'd go there?"

"If she thinks one of them is responsible…."

"But you told her that Ross Maki set things up to make it *look* like Marvin Wall."

"Because he was convinced Marvin killed Bambi, and he didn't want him to get away with it."

"Sounds more like he wanted to steer the suspicion to Marvin and away from himself. But I see what you mean. You think Bonnie would go after them? How? What could she do?"

"I think Bonnie Morlen is building up a head of steam that won't take much to set off. I suspect that this craziness all along has been aimed at getting to Bambi's killer before the law does."

"Why?"

"Maybe she wants to take charge of the punishment, make sure it's quick and severe. Or she might feel that personally avenging her son's death will assuage some guilt."

"Guilt over what?"

"Don't mothers always feel guilty?"

"No, they do not! Despite the best efforts of the psychiatric world." Leonie buttoned her coat up to her chin. "But she still thinks Marvin Wall killed her son?"

"I don't know who she thinks did it, or if she's zeroed in on anybody. But if she believes we're getting closer, who knows? Let's get a move on before we freeze in our tracks. If she comes back, give a couple of blasts on the horn."

McIntire took the short path through the trees to the lake shore. The wind, a stiff breeze in the shelter of the trees, roared itself into gale proportions over the open lake. Slate gray water churned into great undulating swells that exploded onto the sand with a steady cadence, obliterating any interruptions in its smooth, packed surface. Further from the water, as the wide expanse of beach crept toward the woods, undisturbed footprints wound through the litter of driftwood. Bonnie Morlen, and maybe her husband, had obviously walked here frequently. A well defined path ran parallel to the shore in the grassy ground between the woods and the sand.

McIntire's heart gave a jolt when he spotted prints leading from this upper path straight toward the lake. Small depressions ran in an unerringly straight line. The soft sand was damp and packed; the tracks were distinct. When he came near, McIntire could detect that the prints led from the water up to the path. Unless Bonnie was a mermaid, she'd been walking in the lake, or at least at its wave-washed edge. Why did this disturb him so? A brisk walk in the cold to sort things out after ghastly news wasn't something hard to understand. He'd likely do it himself.

The blast was close enough to make his ears ring. A gunshot definitely, but not the ubiquitous shotgun or deer rifle that punctuated the Upper Michigan autumn. A brief pop, three more following in quick succession, from the woods at his back. What the hell? Should he duck? Should he run? Dig himself into the sand like a crab? He yelled out "Hey!" and was rewarded by a sudden movement of blue among the trees. He hastened toward it.

"Mrs. Morlen." He nodded. "Good afternoon."

"I'm sorry, Mr. McIntire. Did I frighten you?" She clutched a small black pistol in both hands, pressing it to her starched ruffled chest. Little Bo Peep with a side arm.

McIntire moved away from what he reckoned might be the direct line of fire. "You should be wearing red, if you're going to be in the woods during hunting season."

"Oh? Oh…I'm sorry," she apologized again. "I'll try to remember that." She wore no coat, only a loose cardigan approximately the same shade of blue as her lips.

"Would you mind telling me what the devil you're doing with that thing?"

Bonnie looked at the gun as if she hadn't noticed it until McIntire pointed it out. "I'm getting some practice." She waved the barrel, in a way that made McIntire again consider digging a foxhole for himself, toward a row of bottles, all still intact, set up on a not too distant stump. "Mr. Fratelli brought it for me. Spending so much time here alone, I thought I might need protection. He showed me how to shoot it."

Thank you, Melvin Fratelli.

She stared bleakly at the bottles. "But it's hard to keep from shaking when it's so cold."

"We were worried about you. My wife came by to see if there was anything she could do."

For the first time in McIntire's acquaintance with her, Bonnie Morlen attempted a smile. Its effect was ghastly. "I told you and the sheriff, I'm fine. Why can't you understand that I need to be left alone?"

"You left your oven on."

Her face crumpled and she dropped the gun to her side and began shivering violently. "Oh, gracious, I—"

"It's all right, Mrs. Morlen. I took care of it." Leonie McIntire appeared. She slipped out of her coat and bundled it around Bonnie's shoulders.

McIntire took the gun from the icy fingers. He removed the two remaining shells and pocketed them.

Leonie kept her arm over the shaking shoulders. "We'd better go now. It's much too cold here."

"Yes, it must be nearly lunch time." Bonnie Morlen spoke through chattering teeth. "My husband will be home soon. I'll have to make more rolls. So silly of me to.... You must excuse me." She brushed a few grains of sand from the borrowed coat. "My gun please, Mr. McIntire." McIntire handed it back.

# XXXVI

*I have nothing new to tell you, only what is
old and nearly forgotten.*

McIntire left Leonie to lead Bonnie home and continued on
down the beach the quarter mile or so to Adam Wall's trailer.
It wouldn't hurt to let Adam know that his nearest neighbor
was out taking target practice, and that her aim wasn't all that
good. Mrs. Morlen's level of marksmanship might be good
news or bad depending on how Wall chose to look at it.

Adam Wall was nowhere outdoors, and he didn't answer
McIntire's knock. McIntire had not realized before how much
Wall himself was a part of his surroundings. Without his presence, his simple and inviting home was only the shabby and
dismal lodging of a poor man.

McIntire wondered if Adam might be around but still
holding a grudge over the fiasco with his brother. More likely
off hobnobbing with the sheriff again. When it came to Adam
Wall, Koski's investigative methods were taking an odd sort
of turn. Especially considering that the sheriff's relationship
with the Indian population of Flambeau County was far from
what anyone would call cordial.

The wind had died off, and the mist began to take on a
suspiciously substantial aspect. Feathery white flakes that hit
water and sand with a splat, dissipating on impact. McIntire

turned to take refuge on the wooded path that would take him to Adam Wall's childhood home.

He found Charlie, and Adam as well, seated in the kitchen eating a midday meal of frybread, fried potatoes, and ham, also fried.

The kitchen was small and crowded and heavy with the odors of fat and smoke. Its welcome warmth would soon become unbearably hot. Eleanor Wall stood at the wood-fired range. She nodded to McIntire, but didn't smile, and it fell to her husband to offer the constable a chair. She dipped a spoon into a bulky jar of lard, adding an egg-sized lump to the cast-iron skillet. As it melted, she twisted off a lump from the pillow of dough in a white enamel basin, patted it flat, and slapped it into the pan. It sizzled, and small hills began to grow on its surface.

"Marvin ain't home," she said.

A third syrup-smeared plate on the table told McIntire that Marvin very likely *was* home. He would probably be staying there awhile, at least until his hair grew out.

None of the Walls seemed particularly concerned about Bonnie Morlen's gunplay.

"She's waving that pistol around like a flag," McIntire told them. "I'd be careful about wandering too near her house. She's on the edge," he emphasized.

"Well, naturally she is!" Ellie yanked off another wad of dough. "If it was one of my boys that was murdered, I'd be shooting more than bottles!" She lowered her voice. "I'm seriously considering plugging that Maki kid. And look at the poor woman, all alone in that great big barn, no family, her husband gone most of the time. Only that," she raised her eyebrows, "uranium guy showing up now and then. I should think she'd have gone off her rocker before this." She gave the dough an extra whack.

Ellie Wall seemed extraordinarily well informed about the comings and goings at the mansion, and about what Ross Maki had been up to. How had that news gotten about so quickly?

"Well," McIntire said. "I just thought you should be aware of the situation."

Charlie and Adam Wall harumphed in chorus.

McIntire felt a movement in the adjoining living room. An amorphously shaped shadow lay on the linoleum floor, extending from behind the squat wood-burning heater. Twyla Wall. McIntire wondered what would happen if he suddenly stood and walked around the stove. Would she be at all distinguishable from her shadow?

Charlie cut his bread into pieces as small as his potatoes and stabbed a chunk of each on his fork. "Hear you been out prospecting with Sherlock Fratelli."

"I wouldn't exactly call it that, and I doubt that Fratelli will be doing any more prospecting for a while." McIntire told the story of Esko Thomson and the uranium guy's abandoned Geiger counter. He turned to Charlie. "I saw a picture at Esko's that had your father in it."

"Buncha miners?"

"I guess so. They had picks and shovels."

"Yeah, Pa guided for that crew, way back. I might of been there myself when that picture was taken. Ma went along, did the cooking. Hell, did most of the work, most likely. So I was probably there, too. They wouldn't of bothered taking a picture of Ma and me."

"Esko couldn't have been very old himself, at the time."

"No, Esko Thomson ain't a hell of a lot older than I am. Maybe six-eight years. Lived a rough life though. He came down from Canada, you know. Sneaked over, they say, on his own when he was only a kid, around thirteen or fourteen. Worked in the cook's shack at a lumber camp for one winter before he took up with that bunch prospecting for gold. When that didn't amount to anything, he just stayed on. He's been out there better than forty years. Building those outlandish contraptions and managing to stay alive." He turned to his son, "Maybe he'd take you on as an apprentice. I'd bet he knows stuff about living off the land that the Indians never even thought of." He chuckled at Adam's glare. "Is there more syrup, Ellie?"

Eleanor opened the door to the pantry. Cool cellar-smelling air invaded the room. She brought out a quart jar capped with waxed paper held in place with a rubber band. Charlie snapped it off and poured the maple syrup over bread and potatoes alike.

His wife scooped three of the crusty breads onto a plate and handed it to McIntire. McIntire drizzled on the syrup and cut off a piece. The syrup was better than his mother's had been, thicker and sweeter. He took a second bite. The frybread was better than Sophie's, too.

Eleanor began shaping the remaining bread dough into loaves. "What a sad story, to leave everything behind at that age and take off for a strange country. Makes you wonder how awful things must have been."

McIntire chewed and swallowed. "Well, this isn't such a bad place to be. But he must have left some family. He's got other photographs, a wedding picture, maybe of his parents. I remember Pa saying he had a sister that died. There was one of a pretty little girl."

Charlie laughed. "Can't be Esko's sister, then. He's about the homeliest guy I ever seen." He went on, "He always was a loner. I remember once, the men musta gone into town, and he stayed behind at the camp with Ma and me. He showed me how to make a whistle from a willow stick. But mostly he just kept to himself. Course I was too young then to realize that he was really only a kid, too. He was a grown man to me. He must have been a tough little nut. Still is! But when you think about a kid that age, especially one his size, coming without a penny in his pocket...managing to survive out there in the woods, like an animal, almost. Well. Not everybody coulda done it."

A hollow cackle from the adjoining living room put them all in suspended motion.

"*Weiejingeshkid!*" Twyla Wall's voice was soft and nasal. "*Weiejingeshkid,*" she said again and chuckled once more.

McIntire turned a questioning gaze to Charlie, who shrugged. "Don't look at me. I had that language beat out of me years ago."

Adam's expression was one of puzzled surprise, quickly replaced with a face as blank as his father's. It was hard to say with Adam, but McIntire would bet he had some inkling of what his grandmother was getting at.

They all knew better than to ask Twyla to explain. And any further discussion was arrested by the ring of the phone, two short jangles followed by a single long ring, a call for the McIntire household.

McIntire stood up. "Leonie's still with Bonnie Morlen."

"John?" Mia Thorsen responded to his hello.

"Hello." A second female voice eclipsed McIntire's reply.

"Siobhan, I wanted to talk to John."

"Oh, I'm sorry he's not here right now. I could—"

"I'm here, Siobhan."

"Where?"

"Never mind. Just hang up!"

"Okay." The line gave a click.

"What is it, Mia?"

"No need to get cranky."

"Sorry," McIntire said. "It's just the way that woman affects me."

"Could you come here? Please? It's important."

"I'm at Walls' right now. I don't have a car." He looked at Charlie and received a nod.

"All right. I'll be right over. Are you okay?"

"No. Not really." McIntire waited through a long pause. "I can tell you who poisoned Bambi Morlen."

"What? Who?"

Her answer was a muffled blur.

"I'm sorry Mia, I didn't get that."

The intake of breath was audible. "I said, John, that it was me."

# XXXVII

*He never left a ball until he had danced with everybody, from the oldest woman to the young-est girl.*

"Selma Maki came over this afternoon. She told me about Ross. She also said Ross wanted to apologize for taking a bottle of brandy from me. He got it from the cupboard on the porch where Nick keeps his hoard. That's where the poison came from." Mia stood with her back to the sink, furiously twisting the end of her braided hair. "Did I kill that boy?"

"Guibard says no," McIntire said. "Bambi died before the poison could have any effect. Who is it you were trying to kill?"

"Oh, John, don't be an idiot! I wasn't trying to kill anybody. I was only hoping to…." She twisted harder. "Lately, Nick's been drinking way too much."

"Lately? Mia, was there a time when Nick didn't drink way too much?"

"He's getting bad, John. He's getting older. He's got to quit. It's going to kill him."

In that case, why was she bothering with the poison? "Sit down, Mia." He pulled out a chair and held its back until she sat, then took one opposite her. "Maybe you'd better tell me about this from the beginning."

"In the beginning, I had a cavity."

"Mia!"

"I had to go to the dentist. Doctor Browning in Ishpeming. He kept me waiting for ages. He had a magazine in his waiting room. Well he had lots of magazines, but the one I picked up was about scientific stuff. *Science Digest.* It had an article about some kind of drug that's made from…well, it has something to do with rubber…or something like that. Anyway, it's a cure for alcoholism. When people take it, drinking makes them really sick, so they don't want to do it anymore." She looked at the ceiling. "It sounded worth a try."

"So you put Indian tobacco in Nick's booze?'

"Mama used to call it pukeweed. I crushed the leaves, tied them in a bag, and let them soak in the brandy for a few hours. I didn't know how much to use, so I started with only a tiny bit."

"Guibard says Bambi got enough to kill a horse."

"Well, it didn't seem to be bothering Nick. So I kept adding more. And letting it soak longer."

"And Nick never got sick?"

"Not that he mentioned. And my husband isn't one to suffer in silence. Do you think it was because I increased the amount gradually? That he might have built up a tolerance to it?"

"I suppose that's possible. I don't know."

"But if he had reacted to it…. Was I really giving Nick enough to *kill* him?"

"You might have been. But according to Guibard it would generally be vomited up before it could do much harm. Mia, what made you decide to do this? Nick's been a juicer for a long time." And he'd also been plenty of other things that might cause a wife to break out the poison.

Her voice had a pleading quality he hadn't heard in many years. "It didn't used to bother him so much. Except for banging up the car now and then. But he's been getting weak and shaky. You must have noticed. I'm afraid for him. I'm afraid for *me*. Lately he even walks different, kind of careful and stiff." She dropped the braid. "Oh lord, you don't suppose I've made it worse?"

McIntire stood up. "Get him to a doctor."

"He won't go. He's afraid of losing his job."

"What? Does Nick actually think that the U.S. Postal Service hasn't yet figured out that he's a drunk?"

A spark of anger leapt into the pale blue eyes. "You're talking about my husband, you know."

"I'm not likely," McIntire said as he went to the door, "to ever forget that."

Mia coughed, and McIntire turned. She hesitated, then said, "I see Siobhan is still here."

"Shows no sign of leaving. Not with Melvin Fratelli and Rudy Jantzen vying for her affections."

"Rudy who?"

"If you don't know Rudy, you're about the only woman in the county who doesn't. The silver-haired Adonis."

"Oh! Sure. I hadn't heard his name. Leonie mentioned Siobhan had been out with him. She'd better watch her back. He made quite a splash at the dance, especially with Evelyn Turner. And, I hear, with Lucy Delaney. No point in getting on *her* bad side."

"He was at the dance? You sure of that?"

"Oh, you betcha. Stayed 'til the last dog was hung. Had the ladies eating out of his hand." She laughed, "He'll be taking over Nick's…."

Tears welled up in her eyes. She swung around to busy herself at the sink, and McIntire reached for the door.

"Nick will be all right," he said. It sounded lame.

She turned with an expression similar to Kelpie's when she wanted to be lifted over some obstacle.

McIntire twisted the doorknob. "You'll be all right."

# XXXVIII

*But where had he been, the pale watcher of
the source of deeds, that night when she had
learned to know the fulness of life?*

So it was *Go Back to Start.* Unless Ross was lying about finding Bambi already dead—and McIntire didn't think that
he was—they were right back at the beginning again. The
scalping and the trepanation meant nothing. The poisoning
meant nothing. What did they have left? Even Bambi's trip
back to the camp was probably meaningless, if he had only
returned to get his jacket from Greg Carlson's car, and hadn't
been attacked until his return. Every inconsistency had been
explained.

McIntire shut down the circuit and opened the fuse box. He
unscrewed the burned-out fuse and dropped it onto the shelf
next to a can of rusty screws and bolts. The pump must have
some fundamental flaw, but McIntire knew no more about
electricity than he did about cars. He popped in a fresh fuse
and flipped up the switch. The pump hummed. Good enough
for now.

Leonie had been a good sport about it. Pumping water
by hand was no fun, nor was lugging it into the house and
heating it on the stove. Especially when one was entertaining
a guest to whom hot water was the elixir of life. McIntire was

frequently awed by his wife's fortitude, and not a little proud that she'd demonstrated that mettle by choosing him.

He latched the pump house door and walked back to the house and the work that lay in wait on the dining room table.

Yes, all the inconsistencies had been explained, except Bonnie and Wendell Morlen. Where was Wendell? Why wasn't he there, making a pest of himself, prodding the state police, harassing the sheriff? Wendell was a mystery, but McIntire felt that somehow the key lay with his wife. Bonnie Morlen sat alone in her opulent lodge, grief, guilt, and vengeance in equal parts. The vengeance McIntire could understand, but why guilt? For allowing Bambi so much freedom? He was eighteen years old. He could do as he pleased. Was it remorse over the circumstances of his birth, her marriage of convenience? Could she suspect Wendell? Wendell Morlen might be a horse's ass and the greedy bastard she'd accused him of being, but from all appearances he'd treated Bambi as his own, much better than some natural fathers. The few times McIntire had seen him, he'd seemed genuinely grief-stricken.

Or was Bonnie's regret brought on by her extended shopping trip the night of her son's death? Where *had* she been the night of that dance? It seemed pretty sure she was not panting in the stolen embrace of Mr. Popularity, Rudy Jantzen, if he was kicking up his heels right here in St. Adele.

That asinine affair! McIntire fervently wished he'd never heard of the Hunters' Dance. If the township hadn't needed a constable to stand guard at their annual bash, he could be off fishing right now. Or getting on with some real work. He picked up Gösta to find him whirling across the dance floor. He slammed the book shut.

Was there no end to it? Everything seemed to lead right back to that dance. Even Adam Wall was there and had been on the receiving end of that teepee building remark. Something he might not have been willing to overlook. When he took on the Shawanok Club, Adam Wall was going to an awful lot of trouble for what he freely admitted was a lost cause. Why? Only to demand that he be taken seriously. McIntire could understand that. But how far was Wall willing to go in his quest for respect?

Respect, uranium, relics of the past, freedom, murderers. They were all hunting for something. Which brought him back to Hunter in Chief, Bonnie Morlen. She was leading her own dance now. A butterfly, with Bonnie Morlen in the middle, munching pastries while she swung them all around her at ever more dizzying speeds.

McIntire left his spot at the dining room table to retrieve the envelope with Bambi's photos from the breast pocket of his jacket. He extracted the pictures he'd temporarily forgotten in the wake of Bonnie's target practice and Mia's revelations.

There he was, God's gift to the middle-aged woman, the suave Rudy Jantzen, gazing across that crowded room, or porch, appraising Bonnie Morlen with the same expression Leonie had on her face when she sized up a horse.

Koski had followed up Bonnie's story. The movie part was true as far as it went. She still had the ticket stub, and the girl selling the tickets had noticed her come in. Well, women wearing diamonds the size of marbles weren't all that common in Marquette. But the showing she attended was over before eight o'clock, and, in any event, no one reported noticing her leave. She could have gone any time. Getting lost would have been easy *if* she had taken the wrong road out of Marquette. If she'd gotten on the Thunder Bay Road, it couldn't have taken her anywhere except to Thunder Bay and on to the Club. If she'd accidentally headed east out of Marquette, she'd have to be a complete moron not to notice that Lake Superior wasn't on her right where it belonged. That left Number Thirteen heading south. Number Thirteen didn't go anywhere near the lake at all, a major tip-off that one might be straying a bit.

Who in hell was this Rudy Jantzen, and why had he been at the Club? More to the point, why was he now hanging around Chandler? Only for the pleasure of Siobhan's company?

Siobhan had lied like a trooper when she said she'd spent most of the night of the murder with Jantzen. The Siobhan that McIntire knew had never needed much of a reason to be economical with the truth, but for Rudy Jantzen? From what? Was she so taken with the guy that she'd lie to protect him from suspicion of murder?

Bonnie had met someone the night her son died, McIntire was sure of that, even if it hadn't been Jantzen. The assignation might have nothing to do with Bambi's death, but his death did make her an extremely wealthy woman and one who might no longer have reason to stay with the husband she'd married only to give her son a father.

But where had Bonnie been? She and her companion most likely hadn't engaged in an evening of making out in the back seat of a car. They'd have been visible at some time or other. Koski and his cohorts at the State Police had probably checked every restaurant, bar, gas station, and motel between Marquette and Ishpeming, but how far off that route had they gone? Bonnie would have had plenty of time to walk out on *Mystery Street* and drive well off the beaten track on her trip home. If she wanted to be invisible, where would she go? To some isolated tavern? She'd stick out like a sore thumb. Better to look for a place where she could get lost in a crowd—a crowd where unfamiliar faces were commonplace, and affluent women in fancy cars could pass without much notice. Like the resort area around Lake Michigamee? McIntire slipped the pictures back into his pocket, donned the jacket, and went out the door.

Pete Koski had been looking for a slightly chubby, slightly snooty, expensively dressed brunette. But that had been her description at five in the afternoon. What if the ten o'clock Bonnie had been wearing a coat? And maybe a scarf over those chestnut curls? What if she'd lost that confident, upper-crust air? Would she be only another non-descript middle-aged woman?

Two filling stations brought nothing, but the third time was the charm, in the form of the Timberlake Lodge. Its supper club was crowded with lacquered pine tables, a fair number of them filled even at four-thirty.

McIntire eased himself onto a vacant stool at the bar and ordered a Hamms. The husky bartender was engaged in refereeing a heated discussion concerning the workings of the minds of the Red Chinese as it applied to their recent invasion of Tibet. McIntire began tentatively, "I'm from the Flambeau County Sheriff's Department. Could I have a word?"

His question was lost in a barrage of groans and laughter from the two opposing factions.

"Hey, shut yer traps, will ya, so I can hear what this man has to say?"

A half dozen mouths closed and a dozen eyes turned expectantly to McIntire. With a disgusted look at the gallery, the bartender beckoned McIntire to the far end of the bar. "Now what can I do for you?" He leaned his beefy elbows on the bar with an eager air not often seen in a publican receiving a visit from the law.

McIntire hoped he didn't disappoint. "I'm looking for a woman who might have been in here in the past few weeks, specifically Saturday night two weeks ago, probably in the restaurant. Is there anyone here who might have been waiting tables then?"

"Might be. My wife would have been working then, but unless the lady you want has two heads, I doubt she's going to remember. It gets pretty busy here Saturday nights."

"Could I talk to her?"

The man shrugged, stretched his torso across the bar, and bellowed within inches of McIntire's ear, "Bernadette, can you help this man a minute?"

A woman wearing an apron over a navy-colored dress looked up from her pad, nodded, and turned her attention back to an elderly foursome. Her husband waved McIntire to a table near the kitchen and turned back to the bar with the opinion that "The Chinks can't do shit without the Russians to back 'em up."

McIntire was seeing the bottom of his second beer when Bernadette slid into the seat opposite him. She carried with her a carton of salt and an armful of empty shakers.

McIntire got straight to business. "I'm wondering if you saw a woman. On the fourteenth of last month. It was a Saturday. She might have been here, maybe with a man. Probably late in the evening, ten or eleven. I know you get very busy, and it was over two weeks ago, but try to think. Did you notice a couple that might have stood out a little, but kept to themselves. Maybe looked slightly out of place?"

She smiled. "Guilty? Furtive?"

"Well, maybe."

She laughed outright. "That would describe about half the couples in here. The legitimate ones stay home." She screwed the top off a shaker and tipped up the carton. Its illustration of a small girl carrying a container with her own image carrying that container never ceased to fascinate McIntire. The child with her umbrella and spilling salt spiraled inward to infinity....

Bernadette said, "It might help to know what these people look like." McIntire wrenched his gaze from the blue carton.

"I'm not sure about the man, the woman is short, brown hair, somewhat...plump...."

The waitress looked blank, and McIntire gave it up. "The person I'm looking for is the mother of the young man who was found dead in St. Adele, Bambi Morlen. I have her picture."

He reached into his pocket, but Bernadette put out a hand to stop him. "Oh ya, she was here."

"What?"

"She was here that very night. The night he died. But she wasn't with a man. She was by herself, and it was nowhere near ten o'clock. More like seven-thirty. We were still jammed with dinner. She wanted a table by the window and waited until one was clean. Then she only ordered pie and coffee. She left without finishing that. And a good thing. We needed that table."

A *Miss!* sent the waitress scurrying for the coffee pot to fill the cup of a plaid-jacketed diner. When she returned, McIntire asked, "How did you know who she was? Did she come here regularly?"

"I didn't know who she was, not then. Her picture was in last Sunday's *Mining Journal*."

"But why didn't you tell somebody?"

"I told everybody I know! It kind of creeped me out, me giving her pie maybe at the same time her son was being murdered. That boy was the same age as my own son." She removed her glasses, breathed onto the lenses, and began wiping them on the hem of the tablecloth. "He's in Korea right now."

"I'm sorry," McIntire said, and meant it. "It looks about over now. Maybe he'll be home soon."

Bernadette shrugged, and McIntire continued, "I meant why didn't you tell somebody in authority, the police or the sheriff?"

"Why would I? She wasn't committing any crime, poor woman." Bernadette dropped the tablecloth. "Or was she? Are you saying she's a suspect? Oh, I can't believe that!"

"We don't really have a suspect, I'm afraid, which is why we need all the information we can get, about anyone and everyone involved."

"Oh, that's right, you mentioned a man she was supposed to be with. Not her husband, I take it?"

McIntire nodded and asked, "I don't suppose you noticed when she drove away, which direction she took?"

"Oddly enough, I did. She took the Petosky Grade road, heading north. I noticed because I was clearing her table, and when I looked out she was walking to her car. There was a guy sitting out there in another car, like he was waiting for her to pull out so he could take her spot. But when she left he whipped around and went right behind. The Grade road is pretty desolate, and she looked like she had a little money...."

"Did you get a look at the driver of the car?"

"Not really. It was after dark and I could only see them because of the light by the back door. He had fair coloring, light hair. That's about all I can say."

McIntire reached again for the photograph and pointed to Bonnie Morlen, seated at her husband's side. "Is this the woman?" Bernadette replaced her glasses, glanced briefly, and nodded. McIntire went on. "Do you see the man here?"

She studied the picture for a long minute. "Could be. Like I said, all I know is that he had light hair. There are two men here with blondish hair." She pointed to Wendell Morlen, and then to Rudy Jantzen. "It could have been either of them. Or neither." She pulled the snapshot closer. "On second thought, maybe not. The guy in the car, his hair looked almost white. More like..." she indicated Jantzen again, "but that could have been only the light shining on it."

Rudy Jantzen had stayed at the town hall until—what was it Mia had said?—the last dog was hung. She didn't mention when he'd arrived. If he met Bonnie at seven-thirty....

"What about the car?" McIntire asked. "What did it look like?"

"Oh, nothing special, kind of beat up. I don't know the make. A panel truck, black."

So that explained the pink cheeks that cropped up at the mention of Greg Carlson and his delight in a home-cooked meal. When Ellie Wall mentioned Bonnie's visiting "uranium guy" she may not have been referring to Melvin Fratelli. Apparently Bonnie *had* spent the night her son died, or a part of it, necking in a back seat.

So now what? He'd probably have to go to Koski. With Bambi dead, all an enterprising young fella had to do to make himself a wealthy man was wrest Bonnie away from the greedy bastard she was married to. This affair wasn't something they could ignore.

Why was it that every time he learned something new, he ended up feeling less like an investigator than like a busy-body snoop? How could Fratelli live with it? Come to that, as far as McIntire knew, Fratelli hadn't learned one damn thing, and if he had, he sure hadn't told the sheriff.

# XXXIX

*She had her own ideas on many things, as one always does who sits much alone and lets her thoughts dwell on what her eyes have seen.*

The geese had taken shelter under the running board of Pete Koski's new station wagon. Mia envied its shiny maple side panels. Otherwise it was a clumsy-looking thing. Boxy with tires like a logging truck. It didn't look like it could move fast enough to catch many criminals.

She leaned against the table and stared out the rain-streaked window, limp as the dripping shirts on the clothesline. At least the sheriff had done her the honor of coming out to take her statement. She hadn't had to endure the humiliation of going into his office. Or infinitely worse, telling her tale to his nephew, Cecil Newman. Although it might have been fun to give Deputy Newman his day of glory apprehending another Mrs. Boston. Cecil was hardly out of diapers when the infamous Mrs. B. had eliminated that troublesome spouse. Koski had been in office then, though. Mia turned back to him.

"Am I going to be charged?"

"For what? Attempted cure of an alcoholic? I expect our eager-beaver county attorney is after bigger game."

"Husband poisoning's not big game? What's Mrs. Boston got that I don't?"

Koski looked as weary as Mia felt. "She had a few more husbands, for a start. I don't think you need to worry."

Mia wasn't so sure. Warner Godwin's term as County Attorney hadn't been all that illustrious so far. The perpetrator of the only serious crime committed since he'd taken office had been declared unfit to stand trial. He might be looking for a chance to show off. Well, maybe her distant cousin relationship with his late wife, and hence his daughter, would save her.

"Mrs. Thorsen." The sheriff cleared his throat and began again. "Mrs. Thorsen, you seem to be about the only person to get into Bonnie Morlen's good graces."

Mia nodded. "Oh, you bet. I'm her dearest friend. Not something I'm all that crazy about being."

"She needs somebody."

"I guess so."

Koski shifted on the spindly kitchen chair. "So do we."

"We?" What was the sheriff getting at?

"Mrs. Thorsen, it just ain't normal for the parents of a murder victim to behave the way Bonnie and Wendell Morlen do. I could understand if they'd stayed in Connecticut, but, dammit, they came all the way back here. Supposedly, they're interested. So why won't they talk to anybody? It don't make sense!"

"I don't know about Wendell, but making sense is not one of Bonnie Morlen's strong points."

"How often do you see her?"

"If I don't go over every few days, she calls."

"Have you ever seen her husband at home?"

"I have *never* seen Wendell, period," she said. "But I don't live in Bonnie's back pocket, and I don't go over on weekends. He could be around then."

"Does she say where he is?"

"No. She only says he's away, or he's finishing up that work for the Club. Can't somebody there help you?"

Maybe Koski didn't much care for Mia telling him how to do his job. At any rate, he didn't answer directly. "We can't make the Morlens tell us anything they don't want to," he said. "We got no legal right to question either of them, or even to know their whereabouts. But there's something damn funny going on."

Mia fingered her braid. "If I had to make a guess, I'd say Bonnie Morlen is, to put it politely, just plain nuts."

"And Wendell?"

"Like I said, I've never met him. But I couldn't blame him if he'd as soon spend his time in Lansing or anywhere but with his wife." She hesitated, then said, "It's not like Bambi was his own son."

Mia wasn't sure if the sheriff knew, but he demonstrated no surprise, only emphatic disagreement. "Yes it is. I spent hours with that man in my office. It is *exactly* like Bambi was his own son. Which is why it's strange that he's making himself so scarce, now."

The sheriff's unexpected show of empathy left Mia feeling a trifle callous. "Well, maybe he's been trying to lose himself in his work," she offered.

The sheriff nodded. "Could be. "

"So," Mia said, "I don't know any more about Wendell than you do. I'm afraid I can't help you. And when Bonnie finds out it was me poisoned Bambi, I don't suppose we'll be bosom buddies anymore."

"I wish you wouldn't tell her."

"Not tell her? Why? She's bound to hear anyway. How would it look if I didn't say anything?"

"Bonnie's not gonna be out gossiping with the neighbors. She won't hear, at least not for a while. It's good if she has a friend, someone she can trust."

It dawned on Mia that the sheriff might have more than Bonnie Morlen's social life on his mind. "Is there something you want me to do, besides keeping an eye out for Wendell?"

Koski smiled. "I want you to let Mrs. Morlen know that we're about to make an arrest."

# XL

*The lake lies spread out before it and close*
*behind it is the cliff, with steeply rising top*
*and a look of wildness and romance which*
*well suits an old mountain. But the smithy,*
*that is not as it ought to be.*

A litter of antiquated farm machinery and rusting motors created an obstacle course between McIntire and the entrance to St. Adele's former blacksmith shop. But in the tall weeds, the tracks of a narrow vehicle were clearly visible. It was the perfect hiding place. Although only a short walk to the town hall, it was completely screened from view thanks to debris, trees, neighboring derelict buildings, and, in the wee hours of the morning, darkness.

It was midday now. With no darkness to conceal him, McIntire looked around to assure himself that he wasn't being observed. No point in arousing curiosity. He pulled one of the double doors. It caught the edge of the concrete floor, and grated in a way that set his teeth to vibrating, but opened readily enough.

The windowless room was not much brighter than it would have been when Bambi was here. McIntire stopped worrying about being seen and pushed both doors open wide. The space was low ceilinged and airless. It smelled of old wood and dust. Hooks on the walls contained a few remnants of past days: the pitted rim of a wagon wheel; a 1932 calendar from a bank in Chandler; a cobweb-laced horse collar, its leather still smooth and uncrazed. The floors were largely bare but for the pale yellow stems of a few stunted weeds growing up through cracks. A darkened area showed where the forge had once stood. One corner was occupied by a tattered cardboard box. A heap of assorted rubble lay near the door.

There was little to show that this building had once housed a business that was a vital part of the commerce of St. Adele.

Papa Feldman's Morgan had brought in clumps of mud and dead grass. McIntire trained his flashlight on the floor to avoid treading on the traces of footprints that showed here and there and walked to the place he imagined Bambi would have stood when he got out of his car. No footprints here, only a small heap of gray ash.

If it was the perfect place to conceal a car, it was also the perfect place to attack its driver. Bambi wouldn't have dared to turn on his headlights. He'd have been a sitting duck for anyone laying for him. But he hadn't put up a fight. Could he have been meeting someone here? Had someone come with him? The theory that he'd been stopped on the road by an acquaintance or someone feigning car trouble was out now. He'd presumably gotten into this building in one piece and under his own steam, and he wouldn't have let himself be seen on his short walk across to the town hall.

McIntire shivered. He could understand why the kid had chosen to make that trip to the woodshed over spending the night in this dungeon.

He walked slowly around the building, shining his light into the corners, all of which were thick with dust and spiders' webs. No one had lain in wait for Bambi Morlen there. The box in the corner contained a store of paint cans, lidless and empty.

He returned to the door and the jumble of rubble off to one side. The usual trash. A single mouse-chewed felt boot liner, some yellowed newspapers. A gallon size gasoline can, still showing a few flecks of red paint, nested amongst a couple of pairs of ancient trousers and sundry other rags. Everything exuded an aroma of age and motor oil. McIntire gave the can a nudge with his toe. It met with unexpected resistance. He trained his flashlight beam onto it.

Around its handle, a few greasy smudges gleamed, but it showed no trace of the dust that had collected on its surroundings. Rags, paper, gasoline. Was Bambi an intended arson victim? Was this yet another failed attempt on his life? Or a plan to destroy evidence?

McIntire stepped out into the light and pulled the sheriff's padlock from his pocket. The door that had uttered the scrape when he opened it stuck fast, and he lifted it to swing free. The source of its recalcitrance lay in the weeds, a thin rod about ten inches long, formed with a loop at one end. The other end protruded through a tear-drop shaped lump of lead. The point extended about three inches, was slightly bent, flattened a bit, honed to a lethal sharpness, and covered with a flaking substance much the same shade as the rust on the gas can. McIntire broke off a stalk of goldenrod and ran it through the loop. He lifted the object into the sun. He didn't know its exact usage, but he knew what it was. Or had once been. A surveyor's arrow. And he only knew one person who might have such an implement.

# XLI

*He who will live in the wilderness should
have bright memories. Otherwise he sees only
murder and oppression among plants and
animals, just as he has seen it among men. He
expects evil from everything he meets.*

"Esko Thomson."

Sheriff Pete Koski leaned back in his chair and sighed.
"What the hell are you talking about?"

McIntire dropped the arrow onto Koski's fishing map.
"This handy-dandy...*instrument* has Esko Thomson written
all over it. Accidental poke, hell! It was cold-blooded, premeditated homicide. That demented runt's been working on
killing somebody for years, and he's finally done it."

"John, you're talking like you've got shit for brains. Esko's
about as harmless as they come."

"Harmless? Don't forget I recently spent a few hours facing
the business end of his shotgun."

"Oh, for Christ's sake. Like you said, Esko's a shrimp. It's
not like he can back up anything he says with muscle. He's
been waving that thing around since he was a kid. It's the only
protection he's got, and it's probably older than he is. I doubt
he even has shells for it."

"Which may be why he had to use other methods for getting rid of Bambi."

"What possible reason could Esko Thomson have for wanting to get rid of Bambi Morlen?"

"Bambi *was* one of those gol-damned uranium hunters."

"Was he? Well, not so you'd notice. And Esko wouldn't have known it. Besides, he hasn't bumped off any of the other five hundred gol-damned uranium hunters out there. And if he'd wanted to, he wouldn't of had to come into town to do it." Koski gave the object a shove with his pencil. "What the hell is that thing?"

"It's a surveyor's arrow. I don't know what it's for, exactly. The weight on it makes it double as a plumb bob."

"Where would Esko get surveying equipment?"

"Have you seen his place?" McIntire asked. "There's not much that loony bastard doesn't have. There's been no shortage of surveying going on along with the uranium hunting. He could have picked it up most anywhere."

"And sharpened it up to kill Bambi Morlen?"

"You bet!"

"Why?"

McIntire hadn't gotten quite that far. "I can't imagine why. Who knows what could be going on in his puny little louse-infested head? He's been out in the woods a long time." What motive could Esko have? "Well," McIntire offered, "so far as I know, he's a squatter. He doesn't own that land. If anybody did find minerals on it, he'd be out."

"But John, use your head. Esko wouldn't know those kids were looking for uranium, and even if he did, they'd be the last ones he'd figure to actually find it."

The sheriff was showing some logic there. "But the fact remains," McIntire insisted, "that somebody rifled through that car and through Karen Sorenson's purse. Somebody that left smudgy fingerprints. And the clincher, somebody dumped the ashtray and took the cigarette butts. Who else but Esko Thomson would have done that?"

"How do I know? The Wall kid was out running around loose. He probably ain't above smoking butts."

That was true enough, but Koski didn't wait for McIntire to admit it. "You think," he went on, "that Esko somehow figured out that Bambi would be in the blacksmith shop, waited there, jumped him and stabbed him in the back with this thing?"

"Not quite," McIntire said. "I think he threw it."

"Like a dart?"

"Precisely."

The sheriff was renowned for his proficiency at darts. McIntire could see him turning the possibilities over in his mind as he examined the weapon.

McIntire took his advantage. "I saw Esko nail a crow with a rock at thirty yards. He's a regular Dizzy Dean."

"How could he have known Bambi'd be in that garage?"

McIntire conceded that there were some gaps in his theory. "I don't know. But there might be somebody that does."

Koski pulled a ring of keys from a desk drawer and walked to the door. "Marian, get Ross out, will you?"

Ross Maki's face was plumped out and he had a bit of a blush on his cheeks. He looked better rested than he had in six months. A few more weeks in jail and he'd be in tip-top shape. All ready for Uncle Sam.

Koski shook a Camel out of the pack and offered it to the young man. Ross shook his head. The sheriff lit up and sat back. "He's all yours, Mac."

The sheriff was obviously prepared to have some entertainment at McIntire's expense. McIntire was only too happy to oblige.

"Ross," he began, "was there anyone else who knew what you and Bambi were planning?"

Ross lifted his gaze from the stained weapon on the desk and shook his head. "No, course not."

"Where did you talk over your plans?"

"Where?"

It seemed like a simple question, but McIntire elaborated. "Where were you? In Greg Carlson's cabin?"

"Oh. Sometimes there. In the car. When we were out doing the prospecting. Anywhere."

"What about the note? Where were you when you put it together? Could anybody else have seen it?"

"Bambi did the note at home. I s'pose somebody could have seen it. I don't think so. He'd of been careful."

"What about in the cabin?"

"There's nobody but Greg. Bambi put the note under the mattress on his cot. I don't think Greg would have looked there."

No, and he probably wouldn't have stumbled across it when he was changing the linen.

"Could Greg have overheard you talking about what you intended to do?"

"We didn't talk about it when he was around. If he heard, he'd of tried to stop us." He paused. "He mighta heard us if we didn't know he was coming, I guess."

"When you were prospecting, did you find anything?"

"Find anything? Like what?"

"Like what you were looking for, uranium. Or gold, silver?"

"We found the old gold mine." He shrugged. "I guess if it still had gold in it, somebody'd of got to it before we did."

"Could anyone have thought you'd found something?"

"I don't see how."

"When you were out, did you see any other prospectors?"

"Earlier in the summer they were all over the place." Ross glanced at the sheriff's cigarette and cleared his throat. "Not lately, though. There were quite a few people out during partridge season. Hunting, I mean, not prospecting."

"What about the gear you had in the mine. Any of it ever turn up missing?"

"You mean did somebody take it?" Ross shook his head. "Nah. We didn't have much. Lugging it back there was no fun. That stove was a bear! Nobody'd want it bad enough to drag it back out."

McIntire took a deep breath. "Did you ever see Esko Thomson?"

"Sure, I've seen him."

"I mean when you and Bambi were in the woods."

The boy hesitated. Possibly weighing how much trouble a further admission could add to his already precarious state. "We sneaked up so Bambi could take a look at his place," he said. "We didn't see Esko though."

"Did you snoop around a little then?"

"Shit, no! Esko shoots at people."

The sheriff gave a derisive snort but didn't interrupt.

"Bambi had a case with maps," McIntire said.

Panic showed in Ross Maki's eyes for only a second before resignation took over. "I got them. I didn't take them. Bambi left them in the van. Honest."

McIntire waved his denials away. "One of the maps had some old trails marked. It showed that you can get close to the mine a whole lot quicker if, instead of going from Greg Carlson's camp, or the old track in from the sawmill, you drive around and take the trail that goes by Esko's place."

"We didn't go that way. We didn't want anybody to see us. Anyway it would have been a shorter walk but a long drive from the camp, and we'd of had to leave the car along side the road. Bambi didn't like to do that."

It made sense. McIntire asked, "Might Bambi have used that trail to get to Esko's place when you weren't with him?"

"I don't think so…he wanted us to go back. He wanted to get pictures. But I doubt if he did. Bambi liked to brag. He'd of told me."

McIntire forged ahead. "When you picked up the car, the ashtray had been emptied. Would Bambi have done that himself?"

Some color rose in the boy's cheeks. "I emptied it," he admitted. "I needed a smoke on the drive into town. I didn't have any."

"So you picked out the butts and smoked them?"

Ross nodded.

"And threw the stubs out the window?"

Another nod; another dead end.

There was only one more thing. "Ross," McIntire said, "Bambi didn't decide to spend the night in the woodshed until you were at the dance. So you must have talked about your plans at least a little bit while you were at the town hall."

"Yah."

"Where were you then? Could you have been overheard?"

"We were outside. It was hard to get away from kids hanging around. Because of the car, you know. We walked over in the trees, by the men's can, so the girls wouldn't follow."

On a night when beer flowed like Niagara Falls, it was hard to believe that the two hadn't picked the most public spot possible to discuss Bambi's abduction. McIntire asked, "Were you close enough so someone inside might have heard you?"

"Nah, I don't think so. There wasn't anybody inside, anyway. The door was stuck. Bambi tried to fake like that's where he was going, to get away from the girls, but he couldn't get the door open. The light was off, so there wasn't anybody inside. Lots of guys just go out in the trees. And they wouldn't bother to shut the door if they went in, 'cause it sticks."

That was true. The door to the men's privy wasn't all that it should be. It was easy enough to kick it open from the inside, but once it was closed, anyone on the outside could generally only open it with the aid of a crowbar. One was kept hanging outside the door for the purpose. It was also true that it was unlikely anyone had been lurking inside with the light off, on the chance of picking up spare bits of conversation between teenaged boys.

Ross had the look of a guest reluctant to leave, wracking his brain for something to say that would extend the visit. Not surprising, and to no avail; Koski stuck his head around the door and summoned his wife to escort the prisoner back to his cell. Ross went willingly enough when Marian Koski appeared bearing a plate containing a slice of chocolate cake.

The sheriff stood staring out the window, massaging his troublesome back. "It just can't be," he said at last. "There ain't no way Esko Thomson could have known Bambi'd be in that shed."

"There doesn't seem to be a way that anyone could have known," McIntire said. "But obviously somebody did. And Esko's as good a bet as anybody. I'd say he was waiting when Bambi got there. He planned to hit Bambi with that arrow and burn the place down to conceal the evidence. He could have attacked him from behind, but, as I said, I think he probably threw it. It would have been pitch dark inside the blacksmith shop, but there was a bright moon. When Bambi went to the door, he'd have made a silhouetted target for anyone inside. Whichever it was, throwing or stabbing, the dart didn't go in as far as Esko hoped. Bambi surprised him by not dying or even appearing to be injured, and Esko high-tailed it out of there. He might have sneaked back later to clean out the car, and been interrupted by Ross coming back." What an appalling shock it must have been for the boy. Had Bambi known what was happening? Seen his meticulously planned adventure start its downward slide?

Koski didn't respond, only reseated himself, poked a pencil through the loop in the arrow, and lifted it onto a sheet of white paper.

"Bambi must have pulled that thing out of his back himself," McIntire said. He felt again the desolation of the young man, waiting alone in a cold, dark attic full of rubbish, while his life seeped away. "Damn!" He suddenly remembered. "It slipped my mind again. Did you ever ask Ross about that whisky?"

"I know where Thomson got the whisky." Koski must have been indeed weary. He exhibited not a trace of gloating, and he didn't wait for McIntire to beg.

He began to turn the paper, scrutinizing the weapon as he spoke. "I forgot about it, until Marian reminded me. It was at the county fair, a year or two ago. The newspaper sponsored a contest to raise money for something or other. Red Cross, March of Dimes, something like that. They had this big jar of jelly beans. You had to pay a dollar to guess how many were in it."

McIntire nodded and waited while Koski touched his finger to the sharpened tip of the arrow and frowned before continuing, "Beckman got businesses to donate prizes—blankets, dish towels, canned ham, that kind of stuff. Whoever came closest to guessing the number of jelly beans walked off with the whole shebang, including a bottle of expensive Scotch whisky." He rubbed his eyes and bent until his nose was within inches of the weapon. "And the jelly beans," he added.

"And Esko Thomson won?"

"Hell, no. A woman from down in the Lower Peninsula hit it right on the nose. She was passing through on her honeymoon. Making a trip all the way around the lake. It's a long ways." He swivelled his chair from side to side. "She had her husband along, naturally."

"Naturally."

"Thirteen hundred."

"Jelly beans?"

"Ya. And the distance around Lake Superior. Thirteen hundred miles. That's why she picked that number."

"Pete, are—"

"Okay, okay. I'll get to the point. They stopped to see the husband's aunt in St. Adele. On the way out of town, they 'got tired' and decided to take a so-called nap behind a haystack. They pulled the car off into some trees to keep it in the shade. When they got back, the loot was gone, down to the last jelly bean."

"Did you know it was Esko?"

"I do now. You saw the whisky."

"You suppose it could be coincidence?"

"What do you think?"

McIntire nodded. "Scurvy little thief."

# XLII

*There came over her suddenly an irresistible long-
ing for a married woman's titles and dignities.*

Siobhan mashed the end of her cigarette into a pool of egg
yolk. She pushed back her chair, gripped the belt of her green
robe, and fanned her face with its frayed end. "My, isn't it
hot in here? I think I'll simply have to take off my ring." She
waggled the fingers of her left hand, the third of which was
adorned by a thin gold ring bearing a small pearl. When neither of the McIntires did more than stare dumbly, she smiled.
"I'm announcing my engagement. Leonie, you can make it
front page news!"

"It's an engagement ring?"

"Rudy doesn't approve of diamonds. He says they're produced by slave labor." Siobhan polished the gem on her robe.
"And I think it's lovely."

Leonie recovered with her usual grace. "It *is* lovely, Siobhan.
You took us by surprise. We're very happy for you, aren't we
John?"

If it meant Siobhan would be setting up housekeeping in
someone else's abode, McIntire was prepared to be ecstatic.
"Are you planning to stay around here? Or in Chandler?"

"Oh, lord, no! We haven't decided for sure where we'll go
yet. Rudy has the business in California, and he's had the offer
of a position in San Antonio."

"We'll be sorry to see you go." Leonie really did sound sorry. How did she manage it? Maybe it was the potential for visiting the happy couple in Texas, or as Leonie might think of it, Mecca. She got up from the table and struck a match to the gas burner under a kettle of water. A bucket by the door and Siobhan's dry hairline were evidence that the pump was once again on the fritz. McIntire would have to get to the bottom of the fuse problem. He regarded his twice-daily bathing aunt. Maybe there was no hurry.

"Have you set a date yet?" he asked and hoped he sounded interested rather than eager.

"We got the license yesterday," Siobhan answered. "We're not planning to have a big wedding, just the JP. I'm hoping you'll stand up for me, Leonie."

"I'll be honored. But this is awfully sudden. And are you sure—?"

"Oh, positive!"

"Are you sure you want our Justice of the Peace to do it?" McIntire asked.

Siobhan paused in lifting her cup. "Why? Is there something wrong with him?"

"It's not a him," McIntire told her. "It's Myrtle Van Opelt."

"Myrtle…" Siobhan spoke hesitantly. "You're not talking about *Miss* Van Opelt?"

"The very same."

"How can that be? How can she even be still alive? And she's a woman…isn't she?"

"She says so," McIntire replied, "and I, for one, am prepared to take her word for it."

"But how did she get elected?"

"If Miss Van Opelt asked for your vote, would you turn her down?"

"Blast it." Siobhan frowned. "She probably doesn't approve of second marriages."

*Or third.* McIntire glanced at Leonie. "I doubt Miss Van O approves of any inter-gender fraternization," he said.

"Oh, lord, she's sure to remember the time…."

"Ah," McIntire nodded, "the cornflake and Karo incident. Even I remember that, and I was thirty-five hundred miles away when I got news of it."

"Well," Siobhan said, "marrying people is her job, after all. We've got the license. It's perfectly legal. It's not like she can simply refuse." McIntire and his wife both responded to the confident remark with a silent stare, and Siobhan clutched his arm.

"Can't you arrange it, John? Please! You were always Miss Van Opelt's pe—" Siobhan interrupted her plea with a judicious cough. "You always knew how to handle her."

"I don't handle her quite so well these days. She doesn't figure I bring her enough business."

"So now's your chance."

"All right," McIntire relented. "I'll see what I can do. Let me know the date, or give me a general time frame. The justice doesn't cater to whims." McIntire forced himself to look into his aunt's eager Granny McIntire eyes. "Are you sure you don't want to wait a while, Siobhan?" he said. "You hardly know this guy."

It was true. Rudy Jantzen might not be a kidnapper or murderer, but he was still a mystery. At the very least, he may have been influenced by Siobhan's conspicuous affluence. Maybe that was being unfair. Siobhan could be charming in her own way and was probably good company under the right circumstances. Jantzen didn't seem hard up, and Siobhan was not the gullible sort.

She'd obviously managed pretty well for herself so far. But still…. "Maybe we should try to find out a little more about him," McIntire suggested.

Siobhan spoke brightly. "I know him better than you could ever imagine."

McIntire didn't want to imagine. "Melvin Fratelli will be crushed."

Siobhan went back to admiring the pearl. "He'll live."

# XLIII

*For so is man, too weak to meet sorrow in all its bitterness.*

The five-mile round trip stroll into St. Adele to go *mano a mano* with Myrtle Van Opelt had done McIntire good. He had prevailed; the marriage would take place. At this point even the smallest success felt like a major triumph, and the defeat of Justice Van O was no paltry victory. The Studebaker was, once again, in its proper place under the white pine. Leonie was back from wherever she had so mysteriously disappeared to that morning. Some breaking news story, no doubt. A visitor from Ironwood, maybe, or a litter of puppies. The Lincoln convertible was absent. All was right with at least this small part of the world.

The door swung open from the inside as McIntire reached for the knob. Leonie stood smiling in the doorway. She put her forefinger to her lips and spoke brightly.

"Hello, darling. How nice that you're home. We have a guest."

Over his wife's blond waves, McIntire beheld, seated at his kitchen table, what had lately been Wendell Morlen, bleary-eyed, rumpled, unshaven, and not smelling very good.

"Mr. Morlen," Leonie's smile didn't fade. "I think you know my husband."

The saucer clattered as Morlen placed a dainty china cup into it. His nod was more of a tremor. He didn't try to rise.

"Mr. Morlen is feeling a bit under the weather," Leonie said. "I thought a cup of tea would be in order."

Morlen looked like a stiff shot of bourbon might do more to bring him around. When he spoke his hello, it was clear he'd already had a go at that method.

"Could you help me for a minute, Leonie? I have something in the car." McIntire turned to the ragged attorney. "You'll excuse us for a moment?" He took Leonie's arm and led her into the yard.

"Where in hell did you pick him up?"

Leonie looked over her shoulder to the door. "At the Sundown Motel in Hancock. The lady at the desk said he'd been holed up there for almost a week," she said. "I think he's been drinking."

That seemed like a safe assumption.

"How'd you know where to find him? And why didn't you just tell the sheriff?" *Or me*, he didn't add.

"Mr. Morlen hasn't committed any crime."

"Don't be too sure."

"He's lost his only son. He blames himself. He thinks Bambi wanted to leave because of him. So the boy planned that goofy scheme, and he ended up dead. Think how your father would have felt after you ran off to the army, if you'd been killed."

How would Colin have felt if his son had died a war hero? McIntire had no time to think about that now. Maybe he never would. "How did you find him? Koski hasn't been able to track him down."

Leonie wrapped her arms around herself and shivered. "He had to be somewhere. I didn't think he'd go too far away. I asked the linen man."

"The who?"

"The man who drives the lorry to pick up laundry. The American Linen Company. He stops at the filling station in

Chandler. And he goes to most all of the inns. I reckoned he'd notice if that Cadillac was parked at one of them for any length of time."

If the linen man and Nick Thorsen ever got together there'd not be a secret left in the county. Leonie's reporter's instincts had once again served her well. The next obvious question was why she had undertaken this search for the wandering Morlen. She answered it before he could ask.

"His wife needs him."

In McIntire's opinion, Morlen's wife needed a straight-jacket. "Well, before she gets him," he said, "I'm going to ask him a question or two."

"He's in quite a weakened condition."

"I'm counting on that."

Morlen hadn't moved. He had downed the tea, however, and Leonie hastened to refill his cup.

"Maybe we could have some coffee," McIntire suggested. "Please," he added in answer to Leonie's forced smile.

He didn't give Morlen or himself a chance to think. "Wendell, on the Thursday before your son died, you withdrew a pile of money from a bank in Marquette. Why?"

Morlen's head swivelled in an attempt to focus on McIntire's face. "It wasn't a pile. It was three thousand. I was going to Lansing. I needed some cash."

Three thousand constituted a pile in McIntire's book. A mountain. "You borrowed money from your friend Harrington for the train ticket."

"The money I withdrew was in big bills. Hundreds. They couldn't change it at the station."

It was quick thinking. So quick that it was likely the same line he'd used on Harrington. And it might well be true. But Morlen had known he'd be buying a train ticket when he took out that cash. The bank had plenty of small bills. McIntire persisted. "Where did that money go?"

"Cards."

"You lost it at cards? On a Thursday morning?"

"No. It was a stake. I needed three grand to get into the game." Morlen leaned his head against the wall and closed his eyes. "I didn't lose. I quadrupled it."

Quadrupled. Twelve thousand dollars. "You were broke when you got back to the Club."

"I had bills to pay." True. He still owed McIntire four dollars. The sunken eyes opened to slits. "I don't always win."

Gambling debts to the tune of twelve grand. Five or six times McIntire's annual army pension. There were times when he was not sorry to be a member of a less advantaged class. He ventured into more sensitive territory.

"Do you think Bambi might have found out the truth?" he asked. "Could he have known that you weren't his natural father?"

"He knew. He's known since he was twelve years old. I told him."

"You *told* him?"

"He was figuring it out for himself, and I thought it would be better if I just told him the truth. I didn't want him asking a lot of questions and Bonnie getting wind of it. It would break her heart if she had any idea that he knew. Anyway, it was during the war. My wife and I used to give blood. We were both type O. Universal donors. Bambi tested his own blood in science class. He was A." He rested his head against the heels of his hands. "I told him what happened, and that his mother would feel terrible if she ever found out that he knew."

"Did you tell him his father's name?"

"I was his father."

"Did you tell him Pavil's name?"

"No. No, of course not. Did he find out?" He didn't wait for McIntire's reply. "Bambi knew that the man was Bonnie's voice teacher. Learning his name wouldn't have been any harder than looking at his grandparents' check stubs."

Small wonder Bonnie Morlen was being eaten by guilt, if she'd recognized the name in the ransom note. Were all young people this thoughtless, cruel, even?

McIntire asked, "How much are you paying Melvin Fratelli?"

"Old Mel?" McIntire barely caught the rest of the reply. "Not one penny more than he's worth."

"How much is that?"

Morlen's chin dropped, and his head flopped back.

Mel? McIntire grasped Morlen's shoulder. "How much?"

The pink-tinged eyes opened wide. "Mel's been worthless since sixth grade." He folded his arms on the table and put down his head.

"John," Leonie had that *He followed me home, Mom, can I keep him?* look.

"Where do you want him?" McIntire gave up.

She regarded the wrinkled and stained clothing, wrinkled her nose, and also relented. "Perhaps the sitting room."

McIntire stuck his hand under Wendell Morlen's arm and led him to the living room couch. He fetched the Indian blanket from the library and tossed it over him. Morlen snugged it up under his chin. Kelpie, never one to miss out on a warm napping body, waddled over from her spot by the window. McIntire picked her up and popped her under the blanket. She made a rotating lump as she settled down in the vicinity of Morlen's knees. McIntire left the two of them snoring softly in the late afternoon sun.

Were Wendell Morlen and Old Mel Fratelli old friends? Or at least old acquaintances? Well, that made sense. The Morlens probably wouldn't have taken on a complete stranger who approached them with an offer of help to find their son's murderer. And maybe that was why no money appeared to have changed hands.

Leonie stood near the sink, slowly running her finger around the rim of her china cup.

"So," McIntire said, "you waltzed into a complete stranger's motel room and dragged him off."

She nodded and put the cup on the counter, apparently satisfied that it had survived its stint with Morlen unscathed. "I guess I did."

"Did you wear your boots?"

"John!" Her smile faded. "Darn, I wish I'd thought of it."

"Well," McIntire said. "Maybe next time. Any chance at all of his getting a shower?"

"Oh, I think so. The pump seems to be working fine now."

"Good. Might as well clean him up before we take him back to the missus. I don't suppose any of this will be easy on the poor man's ego."

"Oh," Leonie said, "I think Mr. Morlen's ego is big enough to look after itself."

# XLIV

*Am I not your wife? Is it not my right to expect
you to come to me with your troubles?*

The van gave a screech and a lurch and stopped dead. Mia
Thorsen put her forehead on the steering wheel. She was
too old for this. Or too stupid. She'd been at it a half hour
and had made it almost to the end of the driveway. Ross had
explained it all: *pull out the choke, push in the clutch, give it
a little gas, step on the starter, let off the hand brake, ease out
the clutch while you ease in on the gas.* One more time. Mia
inhaled, pressed the clutch to the floor and slowly let it out.
The vehicle hopped three times, effected a sideways leap, and
charged into the telephone pole at the side of the road. The
pole didn't fall, only leaned enough to leave the wire lying
across the slightly crumpled hood. She returned her head to
the steering wheel and let the tears flow.

Well, that did it. Ross was simply going to have to come
with her. He might not be the best teacher in the world, but
he could be more or less depended on to keep his mouth shut,
at least as long as she owed him money. Leonie McIntire had
offered, but the thought of having her ineptness exposed to
John was more than Mia could face.

She got out and slammed the door. The pole gave a creak
and settled gently against the windshield.

She went to the kitchen and shoveled a sizable slice of chocolate cake onto a plate. Before sitting down she added a couple sticks of wood to the fire in the pot-bellied heater. It had been ten years since they'd replaced her mother's old wood range with a shiny white gas-fired model. Mia hadn't been sorry to see it go, but she was glad she'd insisted on adding the heater. It was handy for burning trash and gave the kitchen a warmth that a blue gas flame couldn't touch. A warmth she needed today.

She sat at the window and contemplated the van skewed across the driveway, nose to the telephone pole. She'd have to figure out some way to get it out of there before Nick got home.

Her chance passed. Nick's much abused Dodge pulled into the driveway. It was not yet noon. He was hours early. He couldn't possibly have completed his route. Several minutes passed before Mia heard the thunk of the car door closing and saw Nick emerge from behind the van. He walked stiffly, in contrast to his usual arm-swinging stride. His slow progress toward the house was painful to watch. Had she done this to him? Guibard said no, but how could he know? In her fear of the future, had she been slowly killing it? Killing her husband?

He came into the kitchen with his coat on. "There any coffee, Mia? I ain't feeling so well."

If he felt anywhere near as bad as he looked, that was a colossal understatement. Mia turned to the sink. "I'll make fresh."

"Just give me what's there." She struck a match to the gas burner and slid the pot over the flame. Nick gripped the edge of the table as he sat down. "The Maki kid gone haywire?"

"Ross? Why?"

"Why's the truck holding up the telephone pole?"

"I put it there."

"You don't know how to drive."

"Obviously." She poured a short stream of coffee into a cup. It was the color and consistency of molasses. Nick would have to wait. She dumped the entire mess down the sink and dipped more water into the pot. "But it's time I learned."

"You need to go somewhere, I can take you."

"It's time I quit expecting you to do everything for me."

"Why? It's been good enough for you for thirty years."

She turned with her back to the sink and folded her arms. "You have to see a doctor, Nick."

"There's nothing wrong with me. I just need a little rest." His words were slurred. "And a little coffee!"

Mia picked up the cup and slammed it onto the table. "You're sick. Face it, Nick. You can get to a doctor, or I'm calling Guibard." She looked out at the wire dangling limp from the pole. "Tomorrow!"

"You don't need to bother." Nick was turned away, so that his expression was obscured, but the defiance was gone from his voice.

"Good." Mia pressed her advantage. "So do you want Guibard, or do you want to go to Houghton?"

"I don't need a doctor," Nick persisted.

"Nick—"

"I don't need a doctor to tell me what's wrong. I know what it is."

"You can get help for the drinking."

"I haven't had a drop in six weeks."

If Ross had taken much of the brandy, that could possibly be true. Nick hadn't been drinking his usual amount. Mia stooped to look into his eyes. "Why?"

"Why? Now there's a good one. You've been nagging me for thirty years about a little booze, and now I quit, you ask why?"

"Yes, why? Why now?"

"I wanted to see if it would help." He looked away. "It didn't."

"Maybe it takes a while. Maybe it's withdrawal."

"Withdrawal, be damned! It ain't withdrawal. It ain't booze. And it ain't something a doctor can do anything about. It's Parkinson's."

The second Mia heard him say it, she knew it was true. Anger welled up in her like she'd never felt before. She put down the coffee pot and kept her voice steady.

"How long have you known this?"

"Long enough."

"Why didn't you tell me?"

"What for? You'd find out soon enough."

"Not soon enough to do anything about it."

"What the hell do you think you can do about it? There ain't anything to do. I'll get weaker and weaker, and sooner or later I'll die."

Mia pulled out a chair and sat down. "I can't believe you kept this from me."

"I can't believe you thought I was nothing but a drunk!"

Mia felt a heavy knot in her stomach. If she'd cared as much about Nick's pain as she had about her own security and convenience, would she have realized that he was sick, really sick?

Nick stood up. "I'm going to lie down for a while. You might as well get used to having an invalid around the house." He pulled an envelope from his shirt pocket and slapped it on the table. "I brought you a letter from your buddy. She was putting it in the box when I came by. You can steam off the stamp and save yourself three cents."

She didn't recognize the handwriting, and there was no return address, but Mia had no doubt as to the identity of the buddy.

"Bonnie Morlen?"

Nick nodded.

The handwriting was strong but looked as if it had been written in a hurry. *Thank you,* it began, *for your friendship and your help. I see what I have to do and I must do it now. I cannot live with sharing in his guilt. And I can't die while he lives.* Mia scanned down the page. The words *By the time you get this, it will all be over* and *won't get his hands on my baby's money* jumped out.

She might have been in a rush to get it mailed, but Mia could bet she hadn't planned to get such quick delivery service.

"Nick," she said. "I have to go. I think Betty Crocker Morlen is planning to kill somebody."

# XLV

*It was as if she rejoiced that she'd thrown away
her life for her child. When he joined the
angels he would remember that a mother on
earth had loved him.*

*Way-jing* something. *Way-jing-gish.* Or something close to that.
McIntire opened Frederic Baraga's dictionary of the Ojibwa
language to the Ws. Twyla Wall had heard McIntire's mention
of Esko Thomson and his mining partners. It had triggered
something. What was it she had said? McIntire could most
always trust his ear for language, but hearing Twyla speak was
enough of a shock to obliterate her words. Or word. If she
hadn't repeated it, he'd never have gotten it at all. And the
chance of it being entered in the bishop's nineteenth-century
reference might be slim. Way-jing? He scanned down the
page. *Wegwagi, wegwissmind, Weiejingeshkid.* That could be
it. Definition: *He that is cheating habitually, cheater, swindler,
embezzler, deceiver, imposter, seducer.* Well, that was Esko to a
T, no doubt about it. Except maybe for the seducer part. It
didn't take some ancient crone to tell him that Esko Thomson
was not the soul of integrity. But Twyla Wall hadn't seen the
man in close to fifty years, maybe more. Never seen the man,
for that matter. Twyla knew only the boy. What could he have
done that long ago that the woman would still remember and,

more to the point, that would move her to break her silence? Well, time doesn't mean much to a lot of old people. It probably never had to Twyla. Fifty years or five minutes, it might be all the same. McIntire felt a shiver when he remembered that hollow laugh.

He hadn't yet said anything to the sheriff about Bonnie's rendezvous with Greg Carlson. It had slipped his mind when he'd made that twenty-mile trip to town with the surveyor's arrow. It could wait until later. Maybe until the sheriff had seen the light and got the warrant to search Esko Thomson's so-called home. McIntire could bet dollars to doughnuts that's where they'd find Bambi Morlen's camera. Maybe Leonie could use it when she did her photographic essay for *Picture Post*. Now there was romantic for you.

But right now he had Gösta to occupy his time, if not all of his mind. It was aggravating. He found it impossible to devote his brain to his work, but when he put it aside, the tale of guilt and atonement pushed its way into his every thought. With Leonie and Siobhan off in the Lincoln to purchase a wedding trousseau, he had the house to himself. Now was the time. He could even have the freedom to work in the kitchen.

The next five minutes he spent in furious concentration over the beautiful Marianne and her affliction with introspection. *While she lay and looked at herself with those icy staring eyes, all natural feeling died within her.* Is that what had happened with Bonnie Morlen? Had she lived so much of her life as a fraud, pretending to be what others expected, that she had completely lost the real Bonnie and could now only sit back and observe? Had her life, like the detached Marianne's, *become a drama where she was the only spectator?*

Kelpie lifted her head from the rug and gave a half-hearted woof. McIntire glanced up to see a determined-looking Fratelli tramping through the few inches of new snow to his door. The detective was dressed in his prospecting ensemble, minus the Geiger counter.

"I'm going after it," he told McIntire. "I'm through letting that scrawny old geezer buffalo me."

"That twelve gauge didn't look too scrawny."

"I got a gun, too."

"I know," McIntire said. "Passing them out like candy, I hear. Take my word for it, that scrawny old geezer might be a good one to stay away from."

"I ain't asking for your advice," Fratelli stated. "I've just come for directions. The track we walked out of his place on was a lot closer to the mine than the way we went in. How do I get to that trail from this end?"

The trail they had come out on would have taken them to a fairly passable logging track and eventually to a township road, if they hadn't branched off to get to Carlson's camp and their vehicles. But McIntire wasn't eager to give the P.I. directions that would put him in Esko Thomson's sights. He hedged. "I don't know that I remember myself. If you go south from town, there's a road to the left somewhere, about a mile after you cross the river. But, what with the snow, it's liable to be a swamp. I doubt the Morgan could get through. And there are roads and trails turning off all the way along. You could get lost."

Fratelli wasn't that easy to discourage. "Let me see that map."

"I've turned it over to Koski."

"Draw one for me."

McIntire tried to look apologetic. "I haven't been in that neck of the woods since I was a kid. I used to go with my dad to Thomson's to pick up his weekly supply of what he called cider. That was thirty-five years ago. Even if I could remember the lay of the land then, it's probably completely different now."

Fratelli's face said he didn't believe a word of it. McIntire gave up beating around the bush. "Look here, Melvin, you don't have a ghost of a chance of slipping past Esko to get up to that mine. He'll spot you before you get anywhere near your precious Geiger counter, if he hasn't already taken it to town and sold it. If you're insisting on going, you'll have to take the path in through Carlson's camp. And watch your step. Maybe you can get Greg to go with you."

Fratelli answered with a "humph" and slammed out the door. A sharp crease graced the freshly laundered denim dungarees.

◇◇◇

Father Berling was once again to be left in the lurch. McIntire had brewed fresh coffee and renewed his attack when a quick succession of raps sounded at the storm door. McIntire heard its hinges creak and rapid steps cross the back porch. The kitchen door burst open. Mia Thorsen stood red-faced and panting.

"John, it's…" She paused for breath. When she began again, her words were calm and deliberate. "I think somebody'd better check on Bonnie Morlen. She's finally done it. Gone over the edge. She's going to kill her husband. And maybe herself, too." She stood in the porch in her snowy overshoes and handed him the letter.

McIntire read quickly. "Did you call Koski?"

"My phone is…out. That's why I came here. Don't you think we should get somebody over there? She must be planning to do it today. She mailed the letter this morning. She wouldn't have expected me to get it until tomorrow or the next day, but Nick brought it straight home."

In answer to McIntire's look, she added, "He's sick."

McIntire cranked the phone and asked for the mansion. There was no answer, which meant absolutely nothing with respect to whether either of the Morlens were at home.

"Oh God! Maybe she's already done it. Maybe they're both dead!"

"Mia," McIntire told her, "I don't think it's Wendell she's after."

"Oh?"

"She's out to get her son's killer, Greg Carlson."

Mia only stared and gripped her pigtail.

"When Bonnie identified Bambi's body, the sheriff also asked her to look at the articles he had with him when he died," McIntire told her. "One of the things was the jacket he was wearing. Bonnie had seen that jacket on the evening that her son died—in Greg Carlson's panel truck. So she concluded that Carlson and Bambi were together later that night. She didn't know that Carlson had to park the truck about a quarter mile from his camp, so Bambi and Ross often left stuff in it to save the bother of walking up the trail. Bambi did fetch his jacket from the car, but he didn't have to go anywhere near Carlson to do it."

"What the devil was Bonnie doing in Greg Carlson's car?" The wrench on the braid seemed close to yanking it from her head. "Oh, brother, you're kidding! Bonnie and Greg were...? The night Bambi died?"

McIntire nodded.

"How could I have been so stupid? The first time I went to see Bonnie, he showed up, nervous as a cat. And she had already set two cups out. I should have realized she was expecting somebody that wasn't me. When she went to the door, she made this big to-do about her husband not being home, but he should come in anyway." She looked down at her dripping overshoes, and stepped hastily back onto the mat. "I'm sorry, I should have told you. I just didn't think."

"There was no reason you should have been suspicious." McIntire tried to reassure her. "It might have seemed odder if Greg Carlson hadn't paid a call on Bambi's parents."

"Maybe so." She didn't sound convinced. McIntire wasn't either. "But," she went on, "if Bonnie knew Greg had killed her son, why would she have continued an affair with him? Or even fed him cocoa?" Her eyes opened wide. "Egads! John, she might have been trying to do away with him then. There was a plate of tart things on the table. When I sat down, she said they were stale and fetched in a fresh supply."

"Carlson was, not to put too fine a point on it, puking his guts out all that night."

"Well," Mia said, "they were thimbleberry. They'd make me gag, too. She didn't have to worry about getting the wrong person. I didn't touch them." She shuddered and shook her head. "She was trying to *kill* that man. Right there in her tidy little kitchen, mixing up poisoned tarts."

"She was avenging the death of her only son."

Mia sagged against the coats that hung on the wall. "I guess I can understand that. But why the homemade execution? Why not go to the police?"

"Michigan doesn't have executions. She didn't want the police to get to him first."

"Oh, lord." She looked as she might if she'd consumed a bucketful of thimbleberries. "I've done it again!"

"You put the poison in the tarts?"

She didn't smile. "Koski asked me to tell Bonnie that he's close to arresting somebody. He didn't say who."

"He didn't say who, because there wasn't a who." The sheriff's plan to smoke out Bonnie and Wendell Morlen. It had worked admirably.

Mia took the letter and scanned it again. "Bonnie must have told Greg about Bambi not being Wendell's son. If he got the idea that Bonnie only stayed with her husband because of her child, he could have figured with Bambi out of the way, Bonnie would leave Wendell and marry him, and he'd reap the rewards. In getting rid of Bambi he'd kill two birds with one stone. See to it that Bonnie would be filthy rich and get the husband out of the picture in the bargain."

"And move right in to provide support and sympathy."

"The poor woman must have been eaten alive by guilt," Mia said. "And imagine the humiliation—and the rage. How did she ever manage to behave even as close to normal as she did?"

McIntire took his coat from the hook.

"I'd better come with," Mia offered. "If Bonnie Morlen would listen to anybody, it'd be me."

"What the hell are you talking about? She's a raving lunatic, and she's got a gun! I'm not going anywhere near that maniac, and neither are you! Koski can handle her." McIntire took the telephone receiver off the hook. "I'm just hoping to get to Greg Carlson before she does."

"Ah, so you're not going after a demented woman with pitiful aim. You're on the trail of a cold-blooded murderer."

"No," McIntire said. "I'm not convinced that Greg Carlson is a murderer of any sort. Anyway, Fratelli's probably with him. I don't think we need to worry." McIntire gave a few cranks on the phone and asked for the sheriff.

# XLVI

*Must not the outcast go the way of outcasts?*

The layer of wet snow, combined with the recent unaccustomed traffic to Greg Carlson's camp, hadn't rendered the road any more easily traversed. The ruts were deeper, the sand looser, and the low stretches had degenerated to hog-wallows. McIntire kept in second gear and winced at the occasional ominous scraping of the Studebaker's muffler.

"Why did you want to come?" he asked.

"It's time I started developing a backbone."

McIntire resisted mentioning that Mia was about the boniest person he'd ever met, an observation he would have made without a second thought prior to the episode of the skirt and the tears. "I hadn't noticed you lacked a spine."

"What? I can't believe you say that! I've never done a thing in my whole life. Have never left the house I was born in. First my parents took care of me, then my husband. That's it, the story of my life—Ma, Pa, Nick, beginning, middle, end."

"You could put it that way, or could say that first you took care of your mother, then your father for awhile, then your husband."

"John," she sighed, "everything I've ever needed has always been provided for me."

That was definitely debatable, but not a subject McIntire wanted to get into. "I have a feeling this doesn't have much to do with chasing down murderers."

"Nick is sick."

"So you said." Nick would likely perk up by the cocktail hour.

"I mean he's really sick. He's not going to get better." She hunched down into her heavy jacket. "He's got Parkinson's."

The car skidded and McIntire yanked the wheel. "Oh, Lord. Mia, are you sure?"

"He'll just go on getting worse until he's a complete invalid and…."

"I can't believe it." He couldn't. Nick Thorsen incapacitated. Frail. It was beyond comprehension. "I'm so sorry, Mia. You know if there's anything I can do you only have to ask."

"From Mama, to Nick, to the neighbors. Thanks, but I have to take care of myself now."

"And Nick." McIntire had to admit that, to him, that was where the real tragedy lay.

"Yes, Nick, too. For as long as necessary."

"I'm so sorry, Mia." There should be something more he could say.

"I thought it was just the drink," she said. "I didn't even consider that it might be some disease. I was too selfish, too caught up in thinking about myself to see it, and all this time he's had to live with knowing he's going to die."

"Nick was the selfish one not to tell you. He's got no one to blame but himself if you thought it was the effects of alcohol. He *is* a drinker."

She looked at him with what might have been gratitude. "When he's gone there'll only be me, and when I'm dead that's it. Both our families will have died out." She sat up straighter. "Well, there's always Annie Godwin. I have one last shirt-tail cousin left. I'm a step ahead of Nick there, anyway."

Apparently she was still not aware that Annie Godwin had a big half brother or sister somewhere that was a whole lot more closely related to Nick than Annie was to Mia. McIntire wondered if Nick would ever tell her. Probably not. He wondered if he, himself, would ever tell her. Absolutely not.

The muddy road that dead-ended at the trail to Carlson's camp had become a parking lot. Three cars sat nose to tail: Carlson's truck, the Morgan, and Wendell Morlen's Cadillac. McIntire drew the Studebaker to the end of the parade. Mia stayed hunched in her seat.

"Looks like they all made it this far," she said. "How do you suppose Bonnie knew how to find the place?"

"Greg told her I suppose. Maybe she's even been here before."

"Oh. That's right."

"Stay put. I'm going to look around the cars." McIntire stepped out into the soggy snow and peered in and under each vehicle before returning to the passenger side of the Studebaker. He opened the door and motioned for Mia to get out. "Come on. Stay close to the trees."

They crossed the creek, which now carried a narrow trickle of water. Two sets of footprints showed in the melting snow. One was large and lug-soled. The other smaller, the smooth imprint of a rubber overshoe.

The silence was suffocating. When Mia opened her mouth to speak, McIntire touched his forefinger to her lips. She grasped the hand in both hers and held it. "Why?" she asked. "If they're up there, and they're this quiet, they're dead."

Mia's fingers were cold as death, and instantly the old protective instinct, the compassion that had eluded him when she told of her husband's illness, became overpowering. He opened his coat and pressed her hands against his chest.

The pale blue eyes locked on his. She bit her lower lip, but didn't pull away. McIntire bent, hesitating with his mouth almost touching hers.

When she spoke he could feel the warmth of her breath on his lips. "Are you waiting for me to stop you? Waiting for 'Oh, John! No, we mustn't!'? Well, don't expect me to do it for you. I've got no reason. I'm cold, I'm scared, I've spent thirty years married to a man who chases after anything in a skirt and I've…I've ached for you every day of those thirty-two years. So you can just take care of your own conscience!"

"Mia, I—" A sudden shriek sent them scrambling apart. A bluejay swooped across the path.

She stared at him for a second, then shrugged, thrust her hands into her pockets and stalked up the trail.

The area in front of the cabin was deserted, but the smell of wood smoke hung in the air. McIntire left Mia concealed behind a fallen beech and skirted the clearing to approach the cabin from the rear. One look through the smudgy window told him that the cabin was without occupants, living or dead. He rejoined Mia, who had already left her hiding place and was staring down the trail that led deeper into the woods, the one that McIntire and Melvin Fratelli had first taken to Bambi's gold mine.

More tracks showed here in the soft snow. Three sets this time.

Mia frowned. "So they all trooped off together?"

McIntire studied the tracks. "I don't think so. It looks to me like Bonnie followed them. You can see her tracks over the larger sets. I hardly think that two gentlemen like Greg Carlson and Melvin Fratelli would leave a lady trailing along behind."

"Well, aren't you the regular Tonto? I imagine you can put your ear to the ground and tell me where they're going, too?"

"Oh, no need to stick my head in the snow. I know exactly where they're headed," he responded. "There is a quicker way to get there."

"So should we take it? Head 'em off at the pass?"

"The other way goes precariously close to Esko Thomson. Maybe we better go this way, after all. We should be able to catch up with Bonnie. I can't imagine her making it through here on her own."

"She's a woman on a mission."

The route did not follow the way that McIntire had taken with Fratelli, but took almost a straight path to the mine. Carlson must know his way around better than Bambi and Ross had.

As they progressed to higher ground, the light snow cover shrank, and on the open hillsides disappeared, swept away by the wind or melted by the more direct rays of the sun. By the time the tracks they followed gave out completely, they were near enough to the mine that McIntire had no trouble finding his way. They had traveled the distance in a little more than an hour without encountering Bonnie Morlen.

Mia gave a tiny gasp when the black hole gaped before them. McIntire once again signaled to her to stay where she was and went forward. No sound issued from the cave. The grass and fern before the entrance was trampled into the wet earth, but it was impossible to tell how many, if any, people had gone inside, or if any of them remained there. If there was anyone inside, McIntire could come to no conclusion other than that they were dead. Mrs. Morlen and the two men would have no reason to be whiling away the afternoon in a damp hole in the ground.

A rustle of leaves and a snapping of twigs behind them brought McIntire to a halt and Mia to his side. They listened. McIntire could hear little but the blood pounding in his ears. Finally Mia put her hands, fingers extended, to the sides of her head—antlers. McIntire nodded, inhaled, and called out, "Carlson, you in there?"

His voice boomed in the stillness, making the silence that followed even more profound. "Is anybody in there?" He called again. No answer came.

He took Mia's arm and together they ducked through the narrow opening. Inside it was even blacker than he remembered. He hadn't thought to bring a flashlight, but even in the darkness, McIntire could feel that they weren't alone. He stepped to the side of the door to let in the meager light, pulling Mia with him. The stark white features of Bonnie Morlen materialized near the cave's left side. She was flanked by Greg Carlson and Melvin Fratelli, all with legs straight out in front of them, backs pressed into the earthen wall. They stared at the newcomers. Carlson and Fratelli showed a mixture of fear and embarrassment. Bonnie Morlen might have been comatose. None of the three spoke.

McIntire stepped forward. "What the hell is this? You look like a bunch of—"

"This here's a private shindig, Mr. McIntire, but you and your lady friend are welcome to horn in." The raspy voice came from behind, and McIntire felt the familiar prod of Esko Thomson's trusty shotgun between his shoulder blades.

"Esko, you jackass. Put that thing down before you hurt somebody." Mia spoke with the confidence of anger.

"Shut up, Missy! Both of you get over there and join the group."

"It's Mia, you idiot, got that? Mia, not Missy." Thomson swung the shotgun toward her. Mia moved to seat herself between Fratelli and McIntire.

"See if you ever get extra beans out of me again!" She dropped onto the earthen floor.

McIntire muttered, "Beans?"

"At the dance. The old fool," she raised her voice, "sweet-talked me into more beans."

"I said, shut yer trap!"

McIntire whispered, "Esko was at the dance?"

Mia's reply was taunting. "Oh, Esko always manages to hitch a ride to the dance. It's his big night out. He's a regular social butterfly, didn't you know?"

Thomson kept the gun trained on Mia's chest. Its barrel shook, as did the high-pitched voice. McIntire could see the glint in the black eyes, and clearly hear the rapid in and out of his breath. "Now, it ain't that I'm not just thrilled with the unaccustomed pleasure of your company, but why the hell are you all snooping around here? I want some answers and they'd better be good or—"

"Or what? You gonna shoot us, Esko?" Mia broke in. She gave a grunt at McIntire's jab to her ribs.

Bonnie Morlen jerked out of her stupor. Her voice, clear and strong, reverberated in the cavern. "Go ahead. Kill me. It'll save me the bother of doing it myself. But may I please request that you do me the favor of shooting this son of a bitch first so that I might have the extreme pleasure of watching him die."

The son of a bitch her gesture indicated, Greg Carlson, sputtered, "Bonnie! What—"

"Save your breath, Greg. I know it was you. You who fed my son poison and stabbed him in the back. I wish you could die that way, too. Suffering and slowly bleeding to death."

Carlson ignored the gun leveled at his head and swung around. "How could you ever get such an idea? Why would I want to hurt Bambi?"

"Hurt him? *Hurt?* You wanted to kill him, and that's what you did. To get to his money by getting to me. But why did you have to turn him against me first? Why did you tell him about Anatole?"

Carlson merely gaped.

"Oh you were so precious, pretending to be so in love, pretending to be so sorry. Well, I'll tell you something. You're not the only one that can put on an act. I've always known it was you. I've known since I saw my son's body that it was you who killed him."

"Bonnie, what are you talking about?"

"I'm talking about his jacket, you moron! His high school letter jacket. He had it on when he died. It was there when I looked at his body…on that table…he was so cold. The doctor had taken his jacket then…." Her voice faded, then rang out again with the tones of a trained soprano, "But when I left you at midnight, it was in your car!"

The hands that gripped the shotgun stopped shaking.

"The law will take care of your son's murderer, Mrs. Morlen." McIntire frantically searched for words. "We don't want to let his evil spread by making Mr. Thomson a killer, too."

Carlson jaw dropped again. Thomson's breathing slowed.

"And," McIntire continued, "if Mr. Thomson will lend me that shotgun, I'll take the killer in right now."

It was going too far. He knew it the minute the words escaped his lips.

"Like shit!"

"*Weiejingeshkid.*"

A scrape sounded at the adit and it was filled with Adam Wall. He wore the brown uniform of the Flambeau County Sheriff's Department and carried a flashlight and a serious-looking handgun. He leveled both at Esko Thomson and spoke the word again.

"*Weiejingeshkid.* Have you heard that before, Esko? From my grandmother? Remember her? She cooked your meals, washed your clothes, emptied your piss-pot, back when you first came here...you know, way back in the old days when you were only a girl."

The shotgun barrel shook, then dropped, and Esko turned to Adam Wall. The light from the torch showed a face small and pale under the thicket of hair. It was a face bereft of all hope. The glitter was gone, and the eyes were empty pools.

"Did Bambi find out?"

"I don't know his name." Thomson's voice was a whisper.

"His name was Bambi Morlen. That woman over there is his mother."

The shot, in the small space, was like an exploding bomb. Esko Thomson dropped to the earth. Bonnie Morlen swung the pistol toward her own chest.

Fratelli made a grab for the gun.

For a time there was no sound but Mrs. Morlen's soft sobbing.

"Hey, this is mine!" Fratelli sounded truly hurt. "You stole my thirty-eight!"

"He's a woman? Oh, come on!" Mia rose to her knees and slowly crawled to Esko as if approaching some new and fascinating species.

Thomson clutched the toes of his left foot in both hands. Blood welled between the dirt-caked fingers.

"You were the ma'am Bambi was talking to?"

"Shut up."

"But you've got a beard."

"Shut up, Missy!"

"Mia! I said it's *Mia*. Get that, and get that straight, M-I-A, *Mia!*"

McIntire moved forward and faced Thomson. "Estella?"

Thomson sucked in his breath. "My sister. She died."

Mia turned to McIntire. "How did Bambi know?"

A good drenching by a skunk could lead most anyone to shed her trousers on the spot. Bambi's penchant for surprising people with small animals in unexpected places and hanging around to observe the results seemed to have been his undoing.

"Later," McIntire said. He turned back to the man—could this ragged and pathetic human really be a woman?—on the ground. "What happened to Estella?"

Esko Thomson released her grip on the injured foot and began undoing the buttons on her patched and faded plaid mackinaw. "Estella is dead," she said. She struggled to her feet and let the jacket fall to the ground. The heavy cotton shirt underneath was clean, pressed, and showed no sign of wear. A whimper escaped Bonnie Morlen.

"Estella, is dead," Esko said again. With jerky, prolonged motions, she slipped suspenders, strips cut from an inner tube, from her shoulders to dangle from her waist, removed the shirt and placed it carefully on the coat. She stood, shrunken and shivering, the blood from her hands smearing the grayed fabric of her wool union suit. "*Estella*," she loosed a button from its hole, "*is*," a safety pin thrown aside, "*dead*," a button flew. "*Estella…is…dead*," she continued the litany as, with agonizing slowness, she twisted open the buttons in a macabre strip tease.

McIntire felt a clutch at his throat and reached for Mia's hand. The underwear fell away, exposing the sunken and mutilated chest. With a bloodied finger, Esko traced a cross-shaped scar on the single small slack breast.

"Estella is dead," she repeated. "No girl could live after what they did to her."

# XLVII

*The side of her being which was turned*
*toward the outside world would never do her*
*inner person justice.*

Myrtle Van Opelt's office was no bigger than a roomy closet. In fact, McIntire knew, it had been a closet in the days when this building was a hotel. The shelves for holding sheets and blankets were now stacked with a neat collection of books and brown file folders. It was also noisy, being located on the floor above Karvonens' store and wedged between the room that housed the telephone switchboard and Miss Van Opelt's courtroom. Unfortunately the courtroom was in use at the moment. Elsie Karvonen gave her piano lessons there on weekends. The strains of *Claire de Lune* floated through the thin walls. Not one of Elsie's more promising students, McIntire hoped.

Siobhan wore pale green and carried a bouquet of russet-colored chrysanthemums and autumn leaves. She fiddled with its ribbon, edgy, as if she hadn't had prior experience in the role. Her groom posed with one leg casually draped over the edge of the old teacher's desk, radiating his usual charm. Once again decked out in his brown serge suit, Melvin Fratelli seemed to accept his status as best man with good grace, although his congratulatory arm around Siobhan's shoulders had lingered a bit and been embellished by an extra squeeze.

"I've nothing borrowed and nothing blue, but thanks to Leonie, I have a genuine sixpence for my shoe, and it's giving me a blister." Siobhan tapped her toe. "Where is that woman?"

"She's helping out down at the store," McIntire said. "She'll be up in a minute."

A creak sounded from the stairwell, followed by a thunk, a huff, and dead silence. The assembled party exchanged glances. Another creaking footfall, another landing of a cane, another gasp for breath, another pause. Like the interminable approach of an executioner, Justice Myrtle Van Opelt made her laborious way up the stairs.

Siobhan was turned away from the group, facing the darkening window. The nervous anticipation had faded and her reflection showed a mixture of sadness and resignation with a smattering of fear. McIntire suddenly felt the force of her loneliness. What else could be pushing her into this alliance with a man she hardly knew? Well, hadn't he done the same with Leonie? And he'd never had cause to regret it.

Justice Van Opelt's finger-waved head poked around the corner. "All ready then?" She aimed a menacing look in Jantzen's direction and waved the walking stick. He wisely leapt off the desk. Miss Van Opelt moved to stand before it.

"Bride!" The stick hit the floor. Siobhan leapt to attention. "Groom!" Another whack, and Jantzen obligingly took his place. "Witnesses!" Two lighter taps. Leonie and Fratelli stepped forward.

Miss Van Opelt glared them all into *nobody move a hair* and hobbled behind the desk. A few seconds of rummaging in a drawer produced a bible and a faded blue book, *Township Officers Guide* of the state of Michigan…1938 version. She consulted the index in the back and turned to the appropriate page.

"License, please!"

Rudy Jantzen produced the folded paper. Miss Van Opelt put it to her nose, moving her head from left to right as she scanned down the page. She acknowledged defeat with a grunt.

"Mr. Jantzen," she said, "place your hand on the bible. Do you solemnly swear that you know of no legal impediment to your marriage to Miss," the justice gave a sniff, "Mrs. Henry?"

Jantzen so swore.

"All right then." Miss Van Opelt lifted the book to her face. "Marriage is a civil contract." The ceremony was underway. "Mr. Jantzen, do you wish to be united in marriage to," a cough, "Mrs. Henry?" He did. Mrs. Henry reciprocated, and within two minutes, by virtue of the laws of the state of Michigan, Justice Van Opelt pronounced the happy pair husband and wife.

Jantzen planted a kiss on his bride's lips, a bit too long to be seemly. Siobhan kept her eyes on her former teacher throughout the operation. McIntire stepped up to confer his congratulations.

"Hold your horses. We need to make this legal." The justice looked from McIntire to her curved-back chair. He sprang forward to pull it out and accepted custody of the cane as she seated herself. Once more she bent to the desk drawer, this time coming forth with a fountain pen and a bottle of black ink. She spread the marriage certificate before her, scratched in some pertinent information, and beckoned to the witnesses. The shift in places necessary to bring Leonie and Fratelli to the fore separated Siobhan from her new husband, leaving him stranded by the window while she was backed against the closed door. Her case of nerves seemed to have vanished completely. She smiled and watched as Leonie signed her name with a flourish and passed the pen to Melvin Fratelli.

The detective bent over the paper, "Siobhan and Rudy," he mused. "I don't know. Somehow that doesn't sound quite… Mr. and Mrs. Rudy Jantzen…Siobhan Jantzen…."

What the hell was he up to?

Fratelli turned to the groom. "It doesn't have quite the right ring to it. Maybe you should have gone by 'Rudolph Stevens,' or how about 'James Rudolph'?"

Jantzen edged toward his new wife. Siobhan's smile froze and she pressed her back into the door.

Fratelli stepped into Jantzen's path and pulled a folded card from his breast pocket. "Rudolph Jantzen, Rudolph Stevens, James Rudolph, James Stevens, James Edwards, Elwyn Peake…." He looked up. *"Elwyn Peake?"*

Jantzen shrugged.

"…Elwyn Peake, and, last but hardly least, Stephen Jones, as an officer of the government of the United States, I'm placing you under arrest."

Siobhan placed her bridal bouquet on the desk. She opened her shoulder bag and drew out a set of handcuffs. "Good work, Agent Fratelli."

"You did okay yourself, Agent Henry."

The groom obediently extended his hands. Siobhan shook her head. "Over here." She secured him neatly to a mangle left from linen closet days.

Fratelli turned to a scowling Justice of the Peace. "Miss Van Opelt, if I may use your telephone, there's a U.S. Marshal in Marquette waiting to give this man a ride to Detroit. Maybe the county can put him up tonight in their honeymoon suite."

"Don't have a phone. You'll have to go down to the store."

Fratelli went out.

McIntire looked at the disappearing back. "He's FBI?"

"Spooky, ain't it?" Siobhan shook her head.

"You, too?"

Siobhan touched his arm. "I'm sorry, John, and you, Leonie. I'd have told you if I could. We've been after this guy for three years. He's married seven women, and believe me, none of them lived happy ever after. Two of them didn't live at all."

"My fee is fifteen dollars." Miss Van Opelt picked up her cane. "For a marriage, fifteen dollars."

Siobhan picked up the certificate and ripped it into minuscule pieces. She made as if to toss the shreds into the air confetti style, glanced at the justice and deposited them in the waste basket.

"It's still fifteen dollars."

McIntire handed over a pair of bills. "Call it a wedding gift."

Justice Van Opelt inspected the bills, folded them, and slipped them into her apron pocket. "Take your criminal," she said, "and leave my office."

Leonie sidled up next to her husband and spoke low. "I've a little wedding gift for you, too."

"Right here?"

"Shut your eyes, and open your hand."

"Right here?"

McIntire held out his hand, but under the circumstances decided to keep his eyes wide open. Into his palm, Leonie placed a fifteen-amp fuse.

"There's more where that came from."

"Better hang on to it, Leonie," he said. "Siobhan probably has to give that car back. She may not be leaving quite so soon after all."

Melvin Fratelli returned, looking as exasperated as any man who'd tried to make a telephone call of a sensitive nature on Flambeau County lines. The sight of the tethered Jantzen restored his composure. He unlatched the cuff from the mangle and snapped it onto his own wrist.

He offered his other hand, but no apology, to McIntire. He asked, "You've done government work?"

"Translating," McIntire told him.

"How'd you like to do some more?"

"More translating?"

"No."

"Spying on my Finn neighbors for Joe McCarthy?"

Fratelli smiled. "You make it sound so sleazy."

McIntire had no opportunity to respond. Myrtle Van Opelt unceremoniously herded them to the door. As they obediently trooped out, she brought her stick up to McIntire's chest.

"Johnny," she demanded, "what's going to happen to that woman now?" In anyone else, McIntire would have read the look in her eyes as concern, maybe even compassion.

"The marriage wasn't legal, Miss Van Opelt," he told her. "Siobhan's a government agent. I suppose she'll go to work on another case." He couldn't help adding, "Not around here, I'm sure."

The look Myrtle Van Opelt aimed at Siobhan's retreating back was neither concern nor compassion. "Esko Thomson," she stated.

"Oh," McIntire said. "I imagine he—excuse me, *she*—will spend the rest of her life in prison. That alleged woman trailed an eighteen-year-old boy like he was an animal, waited in the weeds and threw a spear into his back. She committed cold-blooded, premeditated murder, and walked around wearing her victim's clothing."

Justice Van Opelt tapped the cane lightly on her former student's chest. "A woman's not always an easy thing to be," she said. "It would have been impossible for Esko. Tortured and mutilated and thrown on her own when she was still a child. She had nothing. Except a tough and creative mind. As a man she managed to survive. She had a lonely and isolated life, but she had a life. And your precious eighteen-year-old boy would have destroyed it." The next tap was not so light. "I call it self-defense."